RAPIER

Rey-pee-er
noun

1. a longer, heavier sword, especially of the 16th and 17th centuries, having a double-edged blade and used for slashing and thrusting.

2. a 24th century starship operating as a privateer raiding the merchant ships traveling between the colonies of mankind.

R. A. "Doc" Correa

Paige;

I hope you enjoy the story.

R. A. "Doc" Correa

PAGE PUBLISHING, INC.
New York, NY

First originally published by Page Publishing, Inc. 2017

ISBN 978-1-68409-574-2 (Paperback)
ISBN 978-1-68409-575-9 (Digital)

Printed in the United States of America

PROLOGUE

"Shit, I'm going to be late!"

Kathy hops out of the bathroom of her tiny flat, pulling up her pantyhose. She looks at them as she does. "Damn, I've got a run in them," she growls at the streak on her right thigh. Maybe no one will notice. *You'd think that with all this new technology, being able to travel among the stars, that someone could invent pantyhose that don't run.* She frowns at the thought. Kathy adjusts her skirt so the patch she sewed will be covered by her coat.

Kathy looks in the mirror. Her dark-brown hair has a graying streak by her right temple, but her deep brown eyes are still bright and full of life despite everything. *Everything—space battles, raids, sword fights—and all this time trying to raise a young girl among battle-hardened raiders. It's amazing that all my hair isn't gray.*

Her white blouse is fraying in places, so to keep it covered, Kathy puts on the leather bustier he gave her. It still fits like the first time she wore it. Her figure hasn't changed much at all, even after having a baby.

For a moment she thinks of him, a tear forms in her eye. Kathy rubs his wedding ring, which she wears on her ring finger. "No time for this!" she admonishes herself. Still, she can't help see the dark-brown eyes, salt-and-pepper mustache, graying hair, and devilish smile—a smile Kathy sees every night in her dreams.

Kathy looks around her flat. It's small and sparsely furnished, barely enough room for the three of them, and she can't even afford this. Still, it's better than the cells the Americans kept her and the others in. The bastards, how dare they. There was a deal, a deal that

3

has given them the edge in the current war, and they didn't even try to keep their end of it.

Since her "rescue" (that's how the Americans touted it in the media when they released her, Cindy, and little James—the Americans rescued them from pirates), she's been trying to get by. The brothers gifted her almost all their loot. It was washed very clean by it being passed through numerous corporations, off-planet banks, and other entities. But the Earth government, particularly the Americans, has kept it from being released to her, claiming it was the ill-gotten gain from piracy. Piracy, that's almost funny; it didn't seem like piracy at the time. Somehow it seemed like justice. Justice for those that were abandoned, justice for those who were senselessly slaughtered, justice for those enslaved.

The truth is, the Americans don't want it known what happened to the people they wouldn't fight for and the Chinese definitely don't want the truth of what they've done to come out. They know more colonies will join the war against them.

Oscar looks lazily at her from the table.

"If you don't have anything helpful to say, don't say anything," she says to the cat. He just rolls over, keeping his eyes on her and answers, *Meow*.

"Thanks," she replies mockingly. Oscar responds with his usual indifference. Kathy hears the cab honk for her and rushes out the door with her bag and coat. She waves bye to little James and shouts, "Thanks, Mrs. Fuji. I love you, James."

"Good luck, Kathy!" Mrs. Fuji shouts in reply. Little James waves and says, "Bye, Mommy."

"The Galactic Geographic building," she tells the driver as she enters the cab. "Yes, ma'am," the cabby replies as he swiftly cuts into traffic.

The cab drops Kathy Masters off in front of the Galactic Geographic building. It's been over eleven years since the last time she was here. It looks the same as it did the first time she saw it. But she is definitely not the same as when she first was here.

She enters the lobby, walks to the lift, and pushes the call button.

The last time Kathy was here, it was just her. A twenty-year-old gifted photographer being offered the chance of a lifetime, to photograph the creatures of a newly discovered planet before full colonization begins. Now it's Kathy, her son James, and Cindy.

The lift doors open. She enters and punches the button for the thirteenth floor. Her thoughts continue.

Cindy, her adopted daughter, a very brash and creative sixteen-year-old. The two of them have been together since she was five, but she's definitely not five now. They've been back on Earth for just over two years, and she's proven to be quite a handful. Five times now, Kathy's been called to school because she's been fighting. Not the silly girl fights most high school girls have, no. She's been kicking the butts of the boys in school, specifically the jocks. She likes fighting wrestlers and football players the most. One time, Kathy entered the principal's office to find she had beaten and tied up three eighty-kilo linemen.

And the capers she's pulled off—a floating gambling ring at school, the fake-diamond scam, and her favorite, the Gibb switch. That one nearly got her arrested by the Feds. Yet whenever Kathy looks at her, she still sees the frightened five-year-old she shared a cell in the brig of the *Rapier* with—the young girl she raised among a crew of the roughest raiders in human space. Their princess, their daughter, their lovely child that they entrusted to Kathy to teach how to be a woman.

The lift door opens, and Kathy steps out into the hallway.

Kathy has tried to work as a photographer since she returned, but no one will hire her. They all look at her with the same expression, but it's their eyes that tell the truth of what they are thinking. She's a pirate, a thief, and a cutthroat. They all fear her. *Good, she likes it that way. Who needs them anyway?*

But her heart hasn't been in it. Still with the Feds holding her money, she's broke. She can't take care of little James, Cindy, and herself this way. So she's decided to play her last card. The pics. *I sure hope this is the time the gods spoke of, please let it be.*

Kathy walks into the Galactic Geographic offices, walks up to the receptionist, and announces, "Kathy Masters for Mr. Baker."

"One moment, Miss Masters," the receptionist says coldly. Kathy can hear it in her voice, pirate. *She can go to hell!*

The pictures, they're all Kathy has left from those nine years. As difficult as they were, Kathy and Cindy think of them as the best of their lives, and she misses them. She misses all of them—especially him, Commodore Black.

The receptionist says, "He's ready for you, Miss Masters." She points down the hall. It's there again in her voice, *pirate*. But she's not just any pirate—no, indeed. She's the pirate that caused the war. She survived to tell part of the story—that and what was recovered with her was all it took. And now the colonies of seventeen nations are at war with the Chinese, and it's been the most bloody of conflicts.

Kathy knocks on the door. A man opens it. "Come in, Kathy. Please have a seat. How long has it been?"

"Eleven years," she replies.

"Yes, I remember. I gave you the assignment for Beta 3 Epsilon. That was the beginning of your adventures."

"Yes, yes, it was," Kathy says.

"Well, what can I do for you?" She looks at him and can tell he plans to blow her off, just like the others. But she hasn't shown him the pictures yet. Pictures and vids of life as a privateer, a life she never expected, a life unknown here on Earth.

"I know it's not your usual fare, Steve, but I have an exclusive for you. One I know your readers will eat up."

"Really, and what would that be?"

"The exclusive story of my nine years on the *Rapier*. Logs, journals, and pics, plus vids."

"Pics of everyone?" he asks.

"Yes, everyone."

"Even him?"

"Him who?"

"You know, him."

"Why can't you people say his name?"

"I don't think that's important."

"His name is Black. Commodore James Ulysses Black!" She is nearly shouting. "And he was the most decent man I ever knew!"

"Yes, of course he was. But he was a pirate, the most infamous pirate captain since the Spanish Main."

"He was a husband, a father, and a good, decent man," she snaps back.

Steve Baker says nothing. Silence hangs between him and her for several moments. Then he says, "I really don't think I can help you."

"You haven't seen the pictures."

He looks at her a moment. "Okay, let's see them."

Her holographic display projects a screen between her and Steve. She starts going through the pictures of life on the *Rapier*. Tears build up in her eyes. Kathy never realized how many pictures had Cindy in them—Cindy in the pilot's seat of the *Rapier* with Captain Gibb at her side, Cindy in engineering learning about antimatter reactors, Cindy flying the shuttle under the instruction of Captain Rawls and Commodore Black teaching her the art of the sword.

"That's him?" Steve asks.

"Yes," she replies sadly.

"He doesn't look all that dangerous. Flamboyant to be sure. Stern certainly and yet grandfatherly, but not dangerous."

Kathy whispers, "Looks can be deceiving."

The next pic is Cindy and Kathy looking out the observation dome, watching the great whales near Pi Delta Epsilon. They look like the great whales of Earth, "swimming" in the gas clouds like it were water. The look of awe was on their faces. Steve stops. "You actually saw these?"

"Yes, yes, we did. As a matter of fact, we swam with them, Steve."

"Swam with them?" Steve asks.

Kathy brings up the next pic. Cindy sits atop the "whale" as Commodore Black swims beside them. "Yes, Steve, we swam with them."

Then the elusive "Dire Wolves" of Pi Beta 2. Cindy, in this pic a precocious twelve, sits atop one of the great predators with Commodore Black and Captain Gibb standing beside them. Steve whistles, "Your daughter really rode one of these?"

"Yes," she replies. "Actually, we all did." Kathy brings up the next pic. Cindy, Captain Gibb, and Commodore Black race across the plain on the backs of wolves with the whole pack running around them.

"People don't believe they exist."

"They do."

"We'll have to verify these aren't manipulated."

"Of course," she says.

Then the next pic. "What are those?" he says truly surprised.

"Those are gods," she says to him.

"Gods?" he asks.

"Yes, the gods of the aquatic natives of Safe Port."

"We've been on Safe Port for eighty years now. No one has seen anything like this."

Kathy looks at the picture—she, Cindy, and Captain Gibb are in their deep suits, floating before the massive god of the nanchiks, the squidheads of Safe Port. The next pic shows the god sitting on its dais, with Cindy, Captain Gibb, and Commodore Black standing before it. The one after that shows the city of the gods as they approach it. She softly says, "No one has dived in the right place or deep enough to see them."

He thinks hard.

"There's more, you know," Kathy tells him.

"Okay, okay. I'll pay you two hundred thousand plus half a percent of net sales, but that's for the whole story."

"Of course," she replies.

Steve turns on his transcription bot then asks "So how did it begin?"

"Begin?" she mumbles. Kathy looks at him and says, "It began right here. It began when you offered me the job, gave me the tickets, and drove me to the shuttle port."

CHAPTER 1

THE SS AMERICA

Kathy Erin Masters had never been off Earth before. Having lived in a rural area in Australia for all her life, she never expected to get off-planet. But then she did some photography in the outback and made a name for herself. So the Galactic Geographic Society hired her to get pics of the flora and fauna of a newly discovered class-M planet all expenses paid. She'd have a year to finish the project before colonization begins. Steve Baker, then senior VP of the Galactic Geographic Society, drove her to the Sydney shuttle port. Kathy remembers that they talked but doesn't remember what was discussed. She was too blown away with her new job to be able to focus on talk.

Kathy took the shuttle from Sydney to the Congo, then rode the "beanstalk" to the orbital platform. Being on the orbital platform was breathtaking. The view of the Earth was indescribable, and the view of the moon, *Nowhere on Earth can you see such a view.* She filled a memory card with pics.

Plus there were so many ships from all of human space. The great passenger liners, the boxy freighters, and the sleek deep-exploration ships, they were all there.

She boarded the SS *America* to travel to the newly discovered planet, Beta 3 Epsilon. Not its usual route, the *America* would drop off Kathy and some scientist explorers and their families, after which it would carry Chinese dignitaries to their Imperial Capitol.

The trip is a three-week journey, and the three weeks are the most fun of her life—first-class shows, gourmet meals, dancing, a casino, and the mysterious Jim.

Kathy was playing blackjack for the first time in her life when the tall redheaded man sat beside her. She chanced a glance at his face and saw the most incredible green eyes and that devilish smile.

The third hand she played gave her a pair of queens. That's when the stranger leaned over and said, "You know you can split those and play two hands."

Kathy blushed but said nothing. She didn't take the strangers advice, played the hand, and won because the dealer only drew a nineteen. The stranger nodded his approval and focused on his hand. Four hands later, Kathy draws two nines. She asks the stranger, "How do you do a split?"

He faces her and says, "Tell the dealer you want to split your hand."

So Kathy flips up both cards and tells the dealer, "I'm splitting my hand."

"Now bet on the card on the left."

Kathy puts down fifty dollars on the left card.

"Tell the dealer to hit the left card."

Kathy says, "Please hit me." She is indicating the left card. The dealer turns up a ten of hearts for her.

The stranger says, "You're most likely to go bust here if you take another card so hold on the left. Now bet on the right card."

Kathy puts down another fifty dollars on the right card. "Hit me."

The dealer turns up a four of clubs.

"Excellent," says the stranger. "You've got a good chance of winning on that one. Increase your bet and take another card."

Kathy adds another fifty dollars and says, "Hit me."

The dealer turns up an eight of spades. "Twenty one, the lady wins," the dealer says.

Kathy squeals in delight.

"Great," says the stranger. Most of the rest of the table fold, but the stranger, that has a seven of diamonds and a two of clubs, takes another card. The dealer turns up a ten of clubs for him.

"I'll hold," he says to the dealer.

The dealer turns up his cards. "Seven of hearts, six of spades, five of clubs." Then the dealer turns another card. "Four of hearts, dealer is busted." He nods to Kathy and the stranger. "Winners," he says.

Kathy squeals loudly and hugs the stranger. "Thank you, thank you."

He smiles. "You're welcome."

"I'm Kathy," she says after a moment. She's surprised at her being so forward. She's normally standoffish around men.

"Hi, Kathy, I'm Jim." He flashes that smile, and she feels warm inside.

"I'm pleased to meet you, Jim," she says blushing.

Jim gathers up his winnings and puts them in his pockets. Then he gathers Kathy's and hands them to her. "Let's dance," he says. Before she can react, he takes her hand and leads her to the dance floor. Though Kathy never danced much, she finds that Jim is such a good dancer she feels she's floating around the dance floor. "You dance well, Kathy," Jim says.

She blushes. "No Jim, it's you that dances well. I'm just following your lead."

They spend the night on the dance floor. Soon it's very late, so Jim walks Kathy to her cabin. "It's been a pleasure Kathy. May I meet you for dinner tomorrow night?"

"Yes, I'd love that, Jim."

* * *

Jim Gibb enters his cabin. He sits on his bed and opens his briefcase. He moves the files out of the way to reveal his comm unit. Jim checks the message log, nothing but the "keep alive" signal. He presses a button and sends a prerecorded message out. Once the transmission verified light comes on, he secures it and places it under the bed.

Jim lies back on his bed. He smiles as he thinks about Kathy. She's a delight. If his life were different, perhaps she could be part of it. Attractive, talented, smart, and in many ways innocent, she very much reminds him of his aunt. But his life is what it is, and he has no interest in romantic entanglements. Nonetheless, it will be nice to have some company for the trip. *I hope she'll be okay when it's time.*

* * *

For the rest of the voyage, Jim picks her up for dinner every evening, then a little gambling, a couple of drinks, and dancing late into the night. The two of them spend every free moment together. The whole time, Jim is a perfect gentleman. He's always interested in what she thinks. He asks about where she's from, if she has a boyfriend, whether she goes to college, and why she is on this trip. When Kathy tells him she's working for the Galactic Geographic Society to photograph the life on Beta 3 Epsilon, Jim replies, "How wonderful. Do you have any of your previous work?"

Kathy pulls out her holographic projector and shows him her work from Australia.

"Those are awesome!" Jim exclaims. "I bet you'd like these." He pulls out his projector and displays pictures from various worlds he's visited. Kathy is totally fascinated.

"Though my work is not as good as yours, I thought you'd like to see these. I've visited twelve different worlds and had a chance to take pics of all sorts of animals most don't get to see."

Kathy is fascinated, especially by the pics of the elusive Dire Wolves of Pi Beta 2. "Wow, they look dangerous," she says.

"They are vicious predators, but amazingly, they are very docile with humans," Jim replies. "Most people don't believe they exist, because they are very elusive. My uncle and I spent several weeks looking for them. When we did find them, we spent several days among the pack. It was fascinating."

Kathy is impressed by his passion for these creatures. "I'd love to be able to do that, Jim, spend all that time among such creatures."

"Perhaps you'll get your chance on Beta 3 Epsilon. The one thing we didn't find on Pi Beta 2 was the rumored native tribes.

Though humans have been there for over a hundred years, no one has seen them. That would be truly exciting."

Kathy hears the passion in his words. *He must be a great explorer.* The two of them spend hours comparing pics. To Kathy, he's the most interesting man she's ever met. Kathy is fascinated with Jim and wants to know more about him. At first, she's too shy to ask him any questions. But after two weeks, she feels so comfortable with him she decides she's going to ask him about where he's from and what he does. At dinner, she says, "Jim, it's obvious you're not from Earth. What colony did you grow up on, and what is it like?"

"Oh, it's no place you've ever heard of. Way out of the way, and nothing interesting ever happens there."

"No, really, I'd like to know."

"Seriously, Kathy, it's an out-of-the-way place, and nothing goes on there. I'd just bore you to death talking about it."

"Well, what do you do for a living?"

"I'm just a space bum, Kathy. I take odd jobs where I find them, and that's pretty much it."

"They must be good-paying odd jobs. I mean, traveling on the *America* isn't cheap."

"That's true," Jim says. "But odd jobs can be very profitable."

"How?" Kathy asks.

"Well, take this job. My employer pays all my expenses, gives me a stipend for meals and gambling, and all I have to do is take a trip on this ship."

"That seems strange. I mean that much money to essentially take a vacation."

"Well, it's a dirty job, but someone has to do it," Jim says with a grin. "Besides, what you're doing is far more interesting than anything I do."

"I don't think so. All I do is take pictures."

"And what pictures, Kathy! You have an amazing eye that catches aspects of what you're photographing that others simply do not see."

Kathy blushes and says, "They're not that good."

"Oh yes, they are. Few people have such talent."

Over the next few days, Kathy tries again to ask him about his childhood and where he's from, but he always changes the subject and dodges the questions. He never tells her much at all. Still, he's so fun to be with she lets it go as a strange quirk.

* * *

Jim lies on his bunk. He's worried. *Did we miss contact? The America arrives at its destination in just two days, we are out of time.*

Kathy is too curious. It's hard to hold back telling her about his home. Perhaps that's because he feels so comfortable with her; she is so much like Aunt Jenny. Perhaps too much.

The signal alarm sounds from his comm unit. He pulls the case from under his bed and opens it, then checks the unit. There's the message: "In position, signal when ready."

Jim gets his bag out from under the bed. He removes the pistol from inside and checks the magazine. Then he checks the charges, all ready. He stands and exits his cabin.

Quickly he moves down the passageway to engineering. Jim carefully opens the hatch. Looking inside, he sees the night crew; they are playing cards. *Good.* Jim slips inside unnoticed. First, he finds the main power coupling. Jim sets a charge on the line and sets the timer for three minutes. Next is the ship's gravity generator. He links it to the first charge so they'll detonate simultaneously. He moves to a safe location and signals the *Rapier. Now it starts. Good.*

* * *

"Captain, I'm receiving Mr. Gibb's signal."

"Excellent, Mr. Garrett, all ahead flank."

"Aye, Captain." The *Rapier* moves away from the comet it was hiding behind and speeds toward the *America.*

* * *

14

On the bridge of the *America*, the sensor alarms sound. "Captain, there's a ship closing fast on us." The captain looks at the sensor readout, then at the view screen. "Pirates! Sound the alarm, get the security teams ready."

*　*　*

Two days out from Beta 3 Epsilon, the ship's alarms start sounding. The captain says over the intercom, "All passengers to the lifeboats. Crew, prepare to repel boarders!" But Kathy decides to look for Jim first. She goes to his cabin, and it's empty. "Jim, are you in here?" she shouts. There's no reply, so Kathy heads to the lifeboats. *Where can he be?*

*　*　*

Cindy looks about as Mommy and Daddy rush down the passageway. There is an alarm sounding in the ship. It's so loud.

"Mommy, what's wrong?"

"I don't know, baby. But we'll be okay."

Daddy trips and falls down, hurting his ankle. Mommy sets Cindy on the deck. "Run, baby. We'll catch up."

"Mommy, I don't want to."

"Run, baby, now!"

Cindy starts running down the passageway as Mommy goes to help Daddy. While Mommy helps Daddy up, there's an explosion. Cindy starts to float down the passageway, her golden tresses drift about her head. Suddenly, there's a loud explosion next to Mommy and Daddy. Cindy watches her parents fly across the passageway, smashing against the bulkhead. Then blood, so much blood. Cindy screams, "Mommy!"

There's a hole in the side of the ship now. Men start moving through it into the *America*. They spread out and rush down the passageway, several running past Cindy. Cindy thinks, *Why can they run while I'm floating?*

One of the men wears a big floppy hat. He's holding a sword in his right hand and a pistol in his left. He's telling the other men what to do. He says to a fierce looking black man, "Mr. Rawls, they'll be in the first lifeboat down this passageway. You know which ones we want. Don't let them get away."

"Aye, Captain," then the big man runs past Cindy followed by several more.

Cindy screams again, "Mommy!" The man in the hat looks around. He sees Mommy and Daddy floating by the bulkhead. He goes and looks at them and shakes his head. Then he looks at Cindy. The man in the hat says, "Mr. Hansen, take the child to Doc Smith." Another man looks at him for a moment. "Now, Mr. Hansen!"

The other man walks over to her. "It's okay, sweetie," he says. "I'll take care of you." Cindy tries to get away from him, twisting and wiggling to escape his grasp, but he grips her tightly. The man puts a smelly cloth over Cindy's face, and she goes to sleep.

* * *

Mr. Rawls and his team arrive at the lifeboat. There is a short firefight, and half a dozen Chinese guards are gunned down, as well as two of his team. Quickly Mr. Rawls takes several Chinese into custody. He then says to the other passengers, "You'll be fine. The damage to the ship can easily be repaired. Stay here until we're gone." Then Mr. Rawls and his team hurry back down the passageway the direction they came from with their captives and the bodies of their fallen comrades.

* * *

As she runs down the passageway, Kathy hears an explosion. The ship heaves and shakes, the engines shut down, the gravity goes off, and Kathy finds herself drifting near engineering. Another explosion and then the sound of small arms fire. Most of it seems distant. The voice over the intercom directs the ship's security, "Repel boarders port side, repel boarders port side." The alarm continues.

Kathy hears shots being fired in the engineering compartment. One of the crew drifts out of the hatch to engineering, blood floating around him. Another crew member tries to run out of the compartment only to be hit in the back. He tumbles down the passageway.

Kathy is stunned to see Jim step out of engineering. He's carrying a bag and a pistol. Jim shoots both crewmen a second time. Kathy shouts, "Jim!" He turns and sees Kathy.

At first, Jim doesn't recognize her. He raises his pistol and takes aim, then recognition crosses his face. He smiles and starts to lower his pistol.

A deep voice from behind her commands, "Belay that, Mr. Gibb."

Jim finishes lowering his weapon and says, "Aye, Captain."

"Secure her, Mr. Hahn!"

"Aye, Captain."

Kathy tries to turn to see who spoke, but someone gives her a shot of sedative, and she passes out. Hearing a deep voice giving commands, she dives into darkness, swimming through swirling blackness.

CHAPTER 2

CAPTIVE

When Kathy wakes, the gravity has been restored—at least it seems so, but she can't move. Soon she realizes she's chained to a bulkhead, when Kathy moves, the chains rattle.

It's dark near the bulkhead, the lights are dim, but Kathy makes out two figures in front of her. Eventually, she recognizes that the taller man is Jim. He's talking to a man just a few centimeters shorter than him.

"Why'd we take her onboard, Captain?"

"Because I said so," the other man says.

"Aye, Captain," Jim replies.

"Mr. Gibb, please see to the other captives. Make sure the little girl is treated properly."

"Aye, Captain."

The captain moves closer until he's just a meter away. He's still shrouded in shadow, and Kathy can't make out his face. He's looking her over. The man is roughly eighty kilos, Kathy judges from his build. He was once athletic but now shows some weight gain. He has a pistol on his right side, slung low on his thigh, another near his belt buckle, holstered for a left handed draw, and a sword—he actually has a sword —on his left side. He wears a blue coat that looks like it came straight from the 1500s—thigh-high leather boots and a wide-brimmed leather hat with a large ostrich feather on the right side. His arms are crossed over his chest as he looks Kathy over. "How do you like our brig, miss?" he asks. Kathy looks about and can now see the bars of a cell. "If you promise to behave, I'll unchain you."

Her head is still foggy. She tries to answer, but her words are garbled. The man says, "Just nod your head if you'll behave." Kathy nods. He moves closer, now she can make out some of his features. He's older; his hair is graying and thinning. A mustache with some gray in it. His skin shows the signs of aging. As he unlocks the chains, he says, "Now, Miss Masters, you will behave, won't you?"

Kathy tries to struggle when he releases her, but he's too strong for her. "I told you to behave," he says. He moves over to the cot, pulls her over his lap, and paddles her bottom. Then he sets Kathy on the cot. "Such a nice bottom," he says. "I believe you will fetch a pretty penny, a pretty penny indeed. Then maybe..." He leaves the sentence hanging, stands, and walks out of the cell, locking the door behind him. "Then maybe..." he says as he walks away.

Kathy sits in the cell, looking about. "Then maybe what?" she asks herself.

* * *

Captain Black walks down the passageway to the bridge. *Mr. Gibb was right, she looks just like my Jenny.* For a moment a memory he's been keeping locked up sneaks out. Jenny sits on a chair painting while he follows little Mary as she chases butterflies. The Captain forces the memory back into its cubbyhole. Then he asks himself, *Why did I bring her onboard? And the child, what am I going to do with her?* The captain finds himself wrestling with these thoughts the rest of his watch.

* * *

She's lost track of time. Kathy knows she's been fed several times, but it's impossible to keep track of how long she's been there. Has it been hours? Has it been days? Has it been weeks? She just doesn't know. She does know she's seen the captain at least twice. Kathy woke to see him standing by the cell door, looking at her. When he noticed she was awake he left.

Kathy watched him walk away; that's when she noticed it. Sometimes for the first few steps, he limped. Sometimes he would drag his left leg. Then he'd walk purposefully down the corridor, and the limp would go away.

One time Kathy could see his face and arms in the low light. His face was set and stern, but she couldn't see his eyes, they were hidden in the shadows. He has several scars on his arms and a plain gold band on the ring finger of his left hand.

* * *

After awhile, Kathy notices voices, but she can't see anyone. She decides they are coming from other cells. One of them catches her ear, a young girl crying. She decides the child is near her and calls out to her, "Little girl, it's going to be okay. Everything will be okay."

"No, it won't!" the young girl replies. "My mom and dad are gone, and we can't get out."

"I'm sure we'll be okay. This has to be some kind of mistake. They'll let us go home soon."

"I don't have a home to go to now," the little girl says. "We were moving to a new planet, my mom and dad and me. Now they're dead, and I have nowhere to go."

Kathy's heart is breaking as she talks to her. "What's your name?"

"Cindy."

"Hi, Cindy, I'm Kathy. I think we're going to be great friends." They talk for hours about anything just to keep their minds off things. Later, a crewman comes to serve Kathy food. "I want to see the captain!" she shouts at him. "I want to see him now." He doesn't say anything. "I demand to the see the captain!" she shouts.

"You will, Miss Masters," he says. "You will."

"What did we do? Why are we in jail? I didn't even know the *America* had a jail."

"Brig, miss," the crewman replies. "Onboard a ship it's the brig, and this isn't the *America* miss. Oh no, it's definitely not. This is the privateer *Rapier*, and you, miss, are part of the loot we liberated from the *America*, and a pretty penny you'll fetch." He leaves as she sits stunned on the cot. Then she smells the food again, and it smells so very good. She feels her stomach growl; she's famished. Kathy finishes her meal. As she does, she thinks, *Pirates, I'm in the hands of pirates in this day and age.* Kathy starts eating the last piece of bread. She hears Cindy crying.

"What are they going to do to us, Kathy?"

"I don't know." Kathy starts crying and breaks down a little. "I just want to go home," she cries. The two of them sit in their cells fearfully waiting for what happens next.

* * *

Captain Black sits in his chair on the bridge of the *Rapier*, sipping hot cocoa. It's time to decide what to do with his prisoners. *Where shall he take them?* In his brig are Colonel Chen and several members of his household. It's all he can do to not kick the bastard out the airlock. Him and everyone with him. But doing that will not compensate the brothers, and they've earned their compensation.

And what about the woman and the little girl? They were not part of his plan at all. He could sell them—that's what the crew expects. But that really doesn't sit right with him. *What to do? What to do?*

Well, for the Chinese, I think Ahmed would do. Yes, that perverted bastard would serve them right. Mr. Garrett breaks his chain of thought by saying, "Captain, we have a jump point forming."

"Where at, Mr. Garrett?"

"Bearing 135, twenty kilometers."

Mr. Gibb cuts in. "Captain, I'm getting readings for a Farragut class destroyer."

"Shit! Helm, bring us to 235 plus 35. Flank speed, spin up the hyperspace engines, all hands action stations."

* * *

Tired from crying, they fall asleep only to be woken by a shudder that shakes the entire ship. Kathy screams. The klaxon sounds, *Oooga, oooga.* "All hands to action stations!" shouts the intercom. Another violent shudder shakes the ship.

Cindy is crying loudly. "Kathy, Kathy, what's happening?"

"I don't know, Cindy!" she shouts. Kathy can hear others in the brig cry out in fear.

The gravity cuts off, and she starts to float. Kathy can tell the ship is making a hard change in course because she was floating toward the wall, but now she bumps into the ceiling. Then Kathy feels the ship make the sudden translation from normal space into hyper-space. The violent maneuvers stop. A little while later, the gravity is restored, and she slams onto the deck, striking her head on it. Kathy feels the hum of the engines through the deck plates. She scurries under the cot.

"Damage report." Booms out of the intercom.

"Port Nacelle took a direct hit. Engineering is at 40 percent power. We'll have to make repairs soon, Captain."

"Get on it, Mr. Simms."

Kathy crawls further under the cot, fearing the sounds. Two crewmen start checking the captives. One finds Kathy dizzy and bleeding.

"Get the doc!" he shouts to the other. "Now, missy," he says to her. "Come to me, and I'll have the doctor care for you. You're no good to us if you're hurt, lassie."

Kathy tries to get further under the cot, putting herself right into the corner of the cell. He leaves for a moment, then comes back with a little girl. Kathy can tell from her voice it's Cindy.

"Now, come on out, missy. You don't want me to hurt the tyke now, do ya?" Cindy has long blond hair and crystal blue eyes. She's roughly 108 centimeters tall and perhaps weighs 18 kilos. There are a few cuts on her arms, and some bruises. He moves closer. "I've not hurt the lass," he says, "but I will if I have to."

By that time Kathy's head is spinning and she's having trouble talking. The crewman reaches in and takes her arm and pulls firmly on it. She's too weak to resist and he pulls her out from under the cot. Blood runs down her head and she's seeing double. She collapses.

Kathy feels like she's in a fog, and she's drifting through metal corridors filled with bright lights. A gentle voice keeps saying, "You'll be okay, miss." She drifts in and out of consciousness. Unfamiliar faces stare at her. She knows she is being touched all over. Kathy catches snippets of conversation and a strong admonition. "Don't touch her like that, damn you! The captain will keel haul you for that. Now clean up that cut!"

She blacks out again, and when she comes to, she's in a hospital bed. There are monitors attached to her; an IV is running into her arm. There are curtains pulled around her, and in the bed next to her is little Cindy. After a bit, a man in a white coat comes to Kathy's bed. He shines a light in her eyes and takes her pulse. His hands are gentle. "I'm Doc Smith. My miss, you took quite a spill. The nanites are repairing all the deep injuries." Kathy's head still spins, and all she manages to do is mumble. "Don't try to talk yet. You'll be right as rain in a few hours, but you need to rest now."

Kathy tries to move her head, but she can't even hold it up and gets dizzy from the effort. In her head, she says, "Let us go," but all that comes out is "Wvjvbnhiggxffbj."

"Just relax, miss," Doc Smith says. "Zero-g maneuvers can do some damage."

Suddenly, Kathy can feel someone else is present. She didn't hear anyone come in, but he's there now. She looks, and it's the captain. He's looking at her with dark-brown eyes. The captain is wearing a coat that could come right out of a book of the old pirates and a hat that would match it—dark blue, old, and worn in places.

The blanket slips down Kathy's chest as she tries to move her arms. She can't move them far because they are chained to the bed rails.

"How is she, Doc?" His voice is low and cold.

"She'll be fine in a day or so, Captain. She really took a hit in those escape maneuvers of yours."

"Better that than we all die," the captain replies coldly. The cut on her head starts to bleed again as she moves more. "Cover her up. I don't want any of these scurvy dogs getting ideas."

The doctor pulls the blankets up over her and tends to the bleeding. Kathy sees the captain is holding a teddy bear. He tips his hat to her and moves over to Cindy's bed, she's obviously sleeping. He looks at her for a moment, not showing any emotion. The Captain gently tucks the teddy bear in next to Cindy, turns, and looks at Kathy one more time, then leaves. "You need to sleep, miss," the doctor says. He puts some medicine in through the IV tube, and she drifts off.

* * *

Sometime later, Kathy wakes up. She feels much better. No aches, not dizzy, and her thoughts are clearer. Kathy sees Cindy is sitting on the edge of her bed, holding a fluffy teddy bear. Kathy tries to move her arms, but she can't move far. They're still chained to the bed rails. Still, she feels she has full control of her body now.

"Are you okay, Kathy?" Cindy asks.

"I feel okay."

"Good. I'm scared," she says.

"Me too, sweetie." Kathy tries to sit up and notices the IV is still in her arm. She goes to rip it out, but there's not enough slack in the chains. The curtains are pulled back; a different man in a white coat is standing there.

"Don't try to sit up," he says. "The chains won't let you." He hands Kathy a control pad. "This will lift up the top of the bed so you can be sitting," he says. "Smiley, go get Doc. He wants to check her out when she wakes."

Kathy starts thrashing and crashing about. "Let me go!" she shouts and knocks the pad off the bed; it crashes onto the deck.

When she starts shouting, the man in the white coat sternly says, "Be quiet, or I'll gag you! There are good brothers before the mast in here. They need rest to heal, so knock it off."

She hears Doc Smith shout, "Leave her alone, Crabeye."

Kathy yells, "Let us go!"

Doc Smith comes up to her as the other man leaves. "Calm down, miss," he says. "There's no place to go anyway."

"Take me home!" she yells.

"If you promise to calm down, I'll give you more slack in the chains. As far as going home goes, well, that's up to the captain."

Kathy yells, "Let me go home!"

"Miss, I've got wounded men in here, if you don't stop I'll have to give you a sedative, now just calm down."

Then Kathy breaks down in tears, crying loudly, "I miss home."

Cindy says, "Please, Kathy, don't yell anymore." She gets into bed with her and snuggles close. Kathy keeps crying; Cindy starts to cry too. "It'll be okay," she whimpers. "I'll protect you."

The doctor wipes away Kathy's tears. "I expect the captain is holding you for ransom," the doctor says. "As soon as it's paid, he'll let you go." Kathy cries more, but it's much softer now. She knows there's no one that would pay her ransom. Her parents didn't even attend when she got the award for her photography. "And don't worry, he's already told the crew not to touch you. He's made it very clear that he'll space anyone that does. Now quit struggling, and I'll give you some more slack." The doctor gives Kathy more length on each chain. "There," he says, "now you can feed yourself."

Food arrives. A steward places a tray on the hospital tray table of Kathy's bed. The doctor breathes in the smell of the food, and he grins. "This may be a privateer, but we have the best cook in the galaxy." She pushes the food off the hospital tray table. It spills everywhere. The steward cleans it up.

"You need to eat, miss," Doctor Smith says. "You need your strength." He sits Cindy on her bed and sets up her tray. Then he comes back to Kathy. Kathy just lies there and ignores the food. "Perhaps some more rest," the doctor says. He gives Kathy a shot, and she goes back to sleep.

When she wakes, Cindy is tugging on her arm. "Wake up, Kathy. We've stopped moving," she says. She wakes real hazy. Then she pulls Cindy close. Kathy listens and hears the sound of the engines has changed. Instead of the hard thrum of propulsion, she hears the soft hum of low power. Kathy tries to move. She has more room to move but is still chained to the bed. The top of the bed is raised a bit; she's not quite sitting. The control pad is pinned to the sheet near her hand, and someone has brushed her hair.

Kathy tries to pull at the chains but only manages to tangle them around her head and neck in the process. The chains leave bright-red marks across her neck, but the marks fade quickly. Some of the nanites are still active. Cindy helps her get untangled, then she whispers, "The captain brushed your hair. He washed your face too." Cindy points at the neck of her hospital gown. "Look," she says. Kathy looks. There's a white Lilly pinned to her hospital gown.

More food is brought in. Kathy tries to ignore it, but she is really hungry, and it smells fantastic. The steward says, "Now don't be throwing Cookie's food on the deck, miss. It hurts his feelings. Cookie made this special for you. It won't do to waste it."

Doc Smith feeds her by hand. "You have to eat, miss," he says, and her hunger is quickly overcoming any resistance. Kathy realizes she's being fed the best roast lamb she has ever tasted. "The captain wants you fed and cleaned up. Once you've eaten, Cindy is going to help me give you a shower."

When Kathy finishes, the doctor chains her wrists together, unhooks the chains holding her to the bed, and helps her to a shower stall. An orderly changes her bed while the doctor and Cindy help her shower. The doctor dries Kathy off and puts her in a clean hospital gown. Cindy brushes her hair. Then they get Kathy back into bed, and the doctor chains her arms to the rails. He looks a little embarrassed as he does. "Sorry, miss," he says. "Captain's orders."

CHAPTER 3

NOT FOR SALE

The *Rapier* is docked on Muhammad's world. Captain Black stands on the pier not far from his ship. Jim Gibb stands next to him as they wait for their customer. "I hate this run, Mr. Gibb," Captain Black says. "It's like going back in time three thousand years."

"Aye, Captain," Mr. Gibb replies.

As its name implies, Muhammad's world is a fundamentalist Islamic colony. It is ruled by the mullahs and governed by sharia. This is no place to make a mistake, and penalties for mistakes are severe. Captain Black never allows shore leave when on this world, and it seems the crew has no argument with this policy. The only reason the *Rapier* ever comes here is to sell the Chinese captives it captures that have a well-deserved reputation, particularly when they earned it in the last war. Though it sickens him, the contract requires this of Captain Black, and he is a man of his word.

Though thousands of people are working in this port, few are women, and the few women seen are totally covered and escorted by men. On this world, no woman wears anything but a burka in public, and they go nowhere without a male family member as an escort.

A limo and a truck approaches the pier. They stop nearby, and a well-dressed man gets out, he's lean with a dark complexion. Ahmed Mustafa bin Abdullah is of Arab descent, his features clearly show his Middle Eastern ancestry. He walks proudly toward the

27

ship. Considered one of the richest men in the galaxy, he is clearly impressed with himself. His wealth and political power are far-reaching and insulate him from being held responsible for his well-known debauchery and cruelty.

"Black, you old space dog, how are you?" Ahmed asks as he shakes the captain's hand.

"I'm well, Ahmed. I hope the same can be said of you."

"Ah, Allah has blessed me with good health. So what prizes do you bring me this day?"

"Come and let me show you."

They enter the ship and go to the brig. En route, they pass a number of crewmen going about their duties. As crewmen often do, they speculate on how much they'll make on the sale of the captives. Kathy and Cindy come up in the conversations as the men debate how much they might bring. Though trying to not be overheard by the captain's guest, Ahmed has very sharp ears and picks up on the discussions.

"We grabbed these captives off an American ship, one of the big luxury liners. They were bound for the Chinese imperial capitol, but I was thinking they'd prefer to stay with you, Ahmed."

"And I am certain you're right about that, old friend. I have so many amusements that I'm sure they will enjoy," Ahmed replies with an evil grin.

The *Rapier* holds eleven captives in its brig: four men and seven women. All are Chinese. The women are in their twenties and are distant members of the Chinese imperial family. Three of the men are also in their twenties and related to the emperor, but one is over forty. Though not in uniform, he has the bearing of a military man. Unlike the fearful countenance displayed by the other captives, he stands ramrod straight and exudes the presence of one that is in command. Ahmed looks him over carefully, and soon he recognizes him.

"Colonel Chen, your reputation precedes you. I would be so pleased to have you as a guest." Then he bows to his new "guest."

The Chinese captive glares at him. "I was hoping you would have something special for this one," Captain Black says as he points to Chen.

"Oh, my friend, I'm certain I can find something appropriate for so distinguished a visitor."

The Captain leans in and whispers into Colonel Chen's ear, Ahmed overhears him say, "This is for Jenny, Mary and Lan you bastard." The colonel glares at Captain Black with hate filled eyes. "Then I'll give you a special discount for him," the Captain replies to Ahmed

"And the rest?"

"A group rate would be appropriate, I think."

"Thank you, my friend. I'll take them all. Now I overheard your crew saying you have two more female captives. I'd like to see them."

"Yes, but they were injured during battle and are in sickbay. I'm sure they'd not interest you."

"Perhaps, but I'd like to see them anyway."

Captain Black thinks on it a moment. He doesn't really want them exposed to Ahmed but a certain diplomacy is required here. "Certainly, old friend," the captain finally says.

Captain Black leaves Mr. Gibb to oversee the transfer of the captives, and leads Ahmed to sickbay.

* * *

Steve cuts in. "He sold people?"

"Yes."

"He sold people. He actually sold people to this Ahmed character."

"Yes."

"And one of those people was actually Colonel Chen, commander of the most successful unit of the Imperial Chinese army and hero of the Chinese people from the Genetics War?"

"Yes, though I know little of who the man was."

"And you love this man?"

She looks at his wedding ring on her finger; she rubs it, feeling the tape she wrapped around it so it doesn't fall off. "Yes."

"How can you?"

"You don't know the whole story, Steve."

"Really, nothing excuses that. Nothing!"

"True, nothing does. But you don't know the whole story."

"Well, enlighten me."

"They were walking…"

* * *

Kathy hears a voice coming down the passageway. "I want to see this other woman your crew was speaking about. I've heard them say that she's quite lovely."

She desperately seeks a means of escape. Kathy tries to pull herself out of the chains; she tugs furiously. The wrist cuffs are padded, so she doesn't injure herself, but she can't get free.

The captain and another man enter sickbay and walk over to her bed. The stranger is obviously important and very rich; he's dressed in the most expensive suit she's ever seen. He looks Kathy over appreciatively and then Cindy. She can see he is of Arab descent, and he has what on old Earth would have been called a Middle Eastern accent when he speaks. "By Allah, I will take these two," he says to the captain.

Kathy yanks at her chains, yelling, "Let us go!"

"I'm holding them for ransom," the captain replies coldly.

"I'll pay you much more than any ransom you might get." Cindy is crying now; she holds onto Kathy tightly, as Kathy thrashes about in the bed.

"I'm holding them for ransom," the captain says again. "Doc, calm her down." The doctor gives Kathy a light sedative, not enough to knock her out, but it takes the fight out of her.

"Now hear me, Captain. You need my good will. I want them now, and I'll pay well for them." Ahmed states.

The captain looks at the man. "Ahmed, we've had a very profitable relationship for years now, and I'd like to continue that, but don't threaten me, and don't try to push your weight around on my ship. It would be a real shame if the federation government found out about all our 'transactions.' I think they'd get really upset. For now, I'm holding these two for ransom. They are not for sale. You've already seen the women I have for sale, and they are yours, so by all means, take them, but these two I'm holding for ransom and that is that."

Kathy says, "I'm a fish."

Ahmed mutters, "I hate what those drugs do." He looks at her with distaste.

"Me too," says the captain. "Come, Ahmed, let's conclude our business. I have repairs to make and must visit the widows of two of my crew."

"Perhaps you're right, Captain." Ahmed looks at Kathy with a mixed expression, distaste for the effect of the drugs and lust for what he could do to her in his 'playroom.'

Kathy yells, "Stop!" Ahmed and the captain stop and turn toward her. The captain looks at her and says, "Yes, Miss Masters."

Kathy starts quacking like a duck and trying to flap her arms. Captain Black shakes his head. "Doc, we need to find better sedatives. I really don't like the effect they have."

Doctor Smith says, "Well, Captain, unless we raid a hospital ship, this is the best we can get here, and those are all protected by military units."

"Hmm," the captain mutters. He and his guest leave sickbay.

The doctor whispers in Kathy's ear, "You can stop now. We both know the sedative isn't making you do that."

"Well, he left, didn't he?" Kathy says. "Muslims don't like crazy people." Then she goes silent.

* * *

Captain Black walks Ahmed back to the dock. "Ahmed, I hope you enjoy your new acquisitions."

"I'm sure I will," Ahmed replies. The captives have been loaded into the truck that waits next to Ahmed's limo. They shake hands, and Ahmed walks to his waiting vehicle. Captain Black watches him leave. He calls Mr. Gibb over. "Make ready to depart, Mr. Gibb."

"Aye, Captain. Shall we be at action stations as well?"

"Perhaps that would be wise."

"Aye, Captain."

Captain Black considers his situation. On this world, antagonizing someone like Ahmed can have fatal consequences. He could have them ambushed. He could sell them out to the Chinese. He could hire assassins. So many options for someone like him. One thing's for certain—he's not happy about not getting what he wanted.

Captain Black walks into the *Rapier* and heads to the bridge. *This could be dicey.* The crew has everything ready by time he gets there. Mr. Gibb has the ship set for departure. All the stations are manned. Systems are all powered up, as are the weapons. He sits in his chair and commands, "Take her out, Mr. Gibb."

"Clear all moorings, helm maneuvering speed, make course 001 plus 77." The *Rapier* begins to rise.

"Muhammad Control, this is the *Rapier* departing on vector 001. Please advise on traffic," Captain Black tells them.

"*Rapier* all clear for full ascension. Do not exceed standard maneuvering velocity."

"Roger, Muhammad Control, accelerating on vector now."

The *Rapier* picks up speed. For several minutes, everything goes normally. As the *Rapier* reaches orbit, Muhammad Control calls them, "*Rapier*, you are directed to move into the customs queue for inspection."

"Roger, Muhammad Control, enter customs queue." Captain Black switches off the comms. "Mr. Gibb, prepare to jump to hyperspace."

"Aye, Captain."

"Tactical, what ships are near us?"

"There's a cutter moving to cut us off, Captain."

"Stand by, Mr. Andjek, it'll be a blind shot. I don't want to give away we're targeting him, so no weapons lock."

"Aye, Captain."

"Use a full spread of missiles and stand by on particle beams."

"Aye, Captain."

"Captain, jump to hyperspace plotted," Mr. Gibb calls out.

"Thank you, Mr. Gibb, stand by."

The *Rapier* is near the point where it must turn to enter the queue. The cutter is blocking its path. "Fire, Mr. Andjek." The ship shakes as the missile batteries fire. Eight missiles streak toward the cutter. "Punch it, Helm." The *Rapier* leaps forward. The cutter maneuvers away from the missiles. One locks on, but the others wander away. As the *Rapier* accelerates, Captain Black commands, "Make the jump now, Mr. Gibb."

"Aye, Captain." The ship makes the translation to hyperspace. It speeds rapidly away from Muhammad's world.

"What course, Captain?" the helmsman asks.

Captain Black ponders the question. *Where to next?* He runs through his options, then the nearest option pops into mind, and that's where the families of the crewmen he lost boarding the *America* live. "Set course for Freeman's Colony, Helm."

"Well, Captain, I'm guessing we won't be going back there again," Mr. Gibb comments.

"Yes, Mr. Gibb. In a way, that's a relief. I really don't like that run anyway."

"Yes, Captain, and I don't think I'll miss Ahmed at all." The two of them chuckle.

* * *

Kathy and Cindy hold each other tight as all the maneuvering takes place. It's so scary not knowing what's happening but hearing all the action over the intercom. It was even scarier watching Doc Smith and his crew prepare for possible casualties. Then the emergency jump to hyperspace, and it was all over. The crew stand down, and everybody relaxes.

Both Cindy and Kathy are emotionally drained. The exhaustion sets in. First, Cindy drops off into a fitful sleep. Kathy cradles her, watching as she snoozes. *How innocent.* Soon Kathy drifts off herself.

Much later, Kathy wakes. It's late at "night," and her head is a bit foggy from the sedatives. She can hear Cindy sleeping; she's lying in Kathy's bed.

In the shadows, sitting in a chair, she can see the outline of the captain. He's still in his pirate coat, hat and his long leather boots. She can feel him looking at her. He mumbles, "Then maybe." The captain stands up and walks out of sickbay.

CHAPTER 4

SLAVE TO SISTER

When Kathy is feeling better, she and Cindy are moved back to the brig. There are no other people in the brig now. The girls are put in the same cell. There are now two cots, and the crew put up walls so Kathy and Cindy can dress or use the toilet in privacy. The crewmen are now more polite to Kathy and Cindy, but they are still a rough bunch.

* * *

Captain Black stands on the bridge of the *Rapier*. He considers his next move. The ship needs repairs, and the crew can use some rest. Finally, he decides. "We'll be staying on Freeman's Colony for a while, Mr. Gibb."

"Aye, Captain. Helm, steady as she goes. All stations, check for damage. Make a security check for trackers. Engineering, keep power at 80 percent."

Captain Black watches with pride as Mr. Gibb efficiently guides the *Rapier* on her course and checks for any surprises Ahmed may have left. *He should have his own ship*, Captain Black thinks to himself.

* * *

The ship moves on for awhile. During this time, Kathy and Cindy grow closer. Kathy tells Cindy all about Australia, except for the dead lands and the nomads. Cindy particularly loves stories about the koala.

A few times, the captain takes them to the observation dome. He teaches Cindy about the stars they are using to navigate by, and the captain has the ships cook, Cookie, bring cookies and hot cocoa to the observation dome for them. Kathy is surprised by how gentle the captain is with Cindy, it's like he's a totally different man.

After about a week, the ship stops again.

* * *

Captain Black has Mr. Gibb bring the *Rapier* into port at Freeman's Colony. The whole process is flawless.

"Approach speed, Mr. Rawls."

"Aye, sir," Mr. Rawls replies. "Steady in the approach circle."

"Slow to maneuvering, Mr. Rawls."

"Aye, sir."

"Mr. Hansen, get your dock crew in position."

"Aye, sir." The *Rapier* gently bumps the pier.

"Secure the ship, Mr. Hansen."

"Aye, sir."

"Ship secure, set your ground crew, Mr. Hahn."

"Aye, sir." The captain smiles with pride. *Yes, he should have his own ship.*

Once all is secure, Mr. Gibb approaches the captain. "Sir, may I have a moment?"

"Yes, of course."

"Sir, I was thinking perhaps I should talk to Munson's parents and Jackson's wife."

"That's my responsibility, Mr. Gibb."

"Yes, sir, but I was thinking I could take this one, and perhaps you could take the ladies ashore. It would be good for them to stretch their legs, and you could use the break. Besides, someday I may be a captain, and I should know how to do this, sir."

Captain Black thinks a moment, then says, "Perhaps you're right, Mr. Gibb. The quartermaster and the purser have everything ready. Please be gentle with the relatives. This is a very hard thing for them."

"Aye, Captain. Uh, sir, enjoy the time. They're good ladies."

"Thanks, Mr. Gibb. I'll take that under advisement."

"Uh, Captain, what are we going to do with the ladies?"

"What do you mean, Mr. Gibb?"

"It's obvious we're not treating them as loot, which I'm onboard with. But then, why are they here?"

"I believe we owe a debt to young Miss Cindy," Captain Black replies.

"How so sir?"

"We killed her parents when we boarded the *America*, Mr. Gibb. It was an accident, but they're still dead. And they weren't our enemies, which makes it a greater offense."

"Okay, sir, I can see that. But what of Miss Masters?"

"I'm not sure, Mr. Gibb. On that, I'm not sure."

* * *

After a bit, the Captain and a couple of crewmen come into the brig. He has one of them hand two dresses to Kathy, then the two crewmen leave. "Put them on," the Captain says, then he leaves their cell.

There's a dress for Cindy and one for Kathy. Both are based on sixteenth-century fashion. The dress for Cindy is satin cut in a young royalty style. The dress for Kathy is just like a sixteenth-century bar wench. Kathy helps Cindy dress, then tries on hers. It exposes a lot of her breasts and clings tight at the waist. There's a leather bustier that fits over her blouse, which she puts on.

* * *

While the girls change Captain Black waits outside the door. As he does the Captain asks himself, *What am I doing? Little Cindy is adorable, but is this the right place for her to be? And the woman, Miss Masters, why am I keeping her here. Is it because she looks so much like Jenny? My God what am I doing?*

* * *

Once they have changed, the Captain appears again. He opens the cell and steps in. Then he puts a leather and lace collar on Kathy's neck and attaches a chain and leather leash, which is just over two meters long. He points to Cindy. "She's in your charge," he commands. "Don't misplace her." The Captain has Kathy pick up Cindy and carry her as he leads her out of the cell, holding the leash.

Captain Black takes Kathy off the ship onto the docks. She looks back at the *Rapier*. It's long and sleek, like a barracuda. If it were a navy ship, it would be described as a corvette, about the size of a destroyer escort but classified as a scout. There's some repaired damage on the hull. Two hyperspace generator nacelles on foils are on either side of the ship. A large high-thrust impulse engine is visible, protruding from the stern. Jack turrets for particle beams and rail guns run along the top and bottom of the ship's hull. A ship that size would be manned by a crew of about two hundred. The ship is certainly larger than Kathy thought.

They walk down the docks to where the streets start. There's a large sign that reads, "Welcome to Freeman's Colony." Kathy looks at the first off-Earth city she's ever seen. Thousands of people hurry about. Neon signs flash their messages. Prostitutes walk about openly. It's bizarre; nothing she ever expected.

"Keep tight hold of her, Miss Masters," the captain says. "They'll steal her in a blink." He heads down the street, leading Kathy along by the leash. When they come across some fresh produce, the captain calls the ship. "Cookie, there are fresh vegetables and meats in the market. Have the steward get down here and purchase some."

They move on. Everywhere there are rare commodities for sale. Exotic creatures, fine clothes, casks of wine, just about everything someone can think of. The captain leads the girls further down the street. Eventually, they enter a tavern. The captain leads Kathy and Cindy to a table in back. A tavern wench brings ale for Kathy and the captain and a Coke for Cindy. The captain orders roast and potatoes for everybody to eat. The food is good, and there's plenty of it. The captain looks at them and says, "I thought you ladies could use a little time off the ship."

The captain talks about shipping, pirate raids, deep space travel, crew stuff, mostly small talk. Then he talks about children. Of all the things she would expect from him, talking about children is totally from left field. Kathy looks closer at him. He's obviously in his sixties, weathered skin and sad eyes. Very sad eyes.

The captain talks a little about how children need schedules and security. They need to know they are safe and being cared for. It's almost unbelievable. This man sitting there, wearing a sixteenth-century pirate coat, hat, and boots, carrying modern pistols and an ancient sword, talking about what children need. Still, he seems cold and factual. The only sign of human emotion is the sadness in his eyes as he talks.

Kathy can't help it; she speaks out, "What does a monster like you know about what a child needs?"

He looks at her for a moment. His eyes are now almost lifeless. "Miss Masters, I wasn't always a privateer."

The three of them finish their lunch in silence. He pays for the meal, takes hold of Kathy's leash, tells Cindy to hold her hand, and they leave the tavern. As they walk down the street, Kathy notices that no one seems to care that she is on a leash. As a matter of fact, there are several people leashed or chained. To the denizens of this city, it is normal; they don't notice it at all. It strikes Kathy as weird. That someone would own another person is totally alien to her. Though it happened on Earth in ancient times, the very thought of it today is repulsive, yet here, it is obviously the norm.

A few other men that are obviously pirates also walk the streets. The townspeople often make way for them. But even the pirates seem to show Captain Black courtesy and respect. Many tip their hats and say, "Good day, Captain." Kathy holds Cindy's hand tightly; Cindy holds tight to her as well. As they move, the captain places himself so that others must go through him to reach them.

After a few minutes, they enter a store, a toy store. The owner is quite surprised to see the three of them.

Kathy's collar is getting sweaty underneath, and she starts fiddling around with it. It loosens. The captain takes out an old-fashioned linen handkerchief when he sees her fiddle with the collar. "Here," he says, "don't move." Kathy stands still. He loosens the collar and carefully wraps the kerchief around the leather. "That should help a bit," he says "We'll get you something nicer shortly."

She stays silent, holding Cindy against her. Captain Black kneels down to Cindy. "One toy, whatever you want, little princess." He stands back up and says to Kathy "Go ahead and look around." Then Captain Black unhooks the leash, and stands by the door.

Kathy walks around with Cindy. Every kind of toy imaginable is in the store. Cindy carefully takes each toy to look at, then gently puts it back. Cindy's eyes light up when she sees a lifelike doll, it's wearing a dress much like the one she's wearing. It's the latest in robotic dolls and very expensive. Cindy comes and takes Kathy by the hand, pulling her to the doll.

"Kathy, look. She's so beautiful."

"She is."

She smiles at Kathy. "Can I have her?" she asks.

Out of nowhere, a shop attendant appears, scaring the girls, and they both scream. Kathy grabs Cindy, falling down on her bottom. The captain moves forward with sword drawn, but the shop attendant isn't dangerous. The captain stands between the attendant and the girls. While the attendant cowers, the captain turns and picks Kathy up as she holds Cindy like a baby.

The shopkeeper says, "Please don't hurt him," to the captain. The attendant is a young man, but it appears he had been injured while growing up. "It was the Chinese sir," the shopkeeper tells Captain Black. "They came when he was a young boy. One of their soldiers thought he didn't show the proper respect and kicked him in the head, now he's 'simple' and has trouble walking and talking. He means no harm sir."

Cindy points to the doll and the young man gets it then brings it to her. "Prettttyyyyy," he mumbles.

"Yes, she is," Cindy says. Then she hugs the attendant. "Thank you for bringing her to me." The young man turns red.

The captain is holding Kathy after helping her up from the floor. She notices the captain has a firm hold of her arm, and she starts to squirm a bit. He lets go and takes a step back from her.

Cindy looks at him and asks, "Sir, can I have the doll?"

The captain nods yes to her and says, "Of course, princess." He moves them over to the store's counter and pays the shopkeeper. Then the captain gives the shopkeeper an extra tip. "Here, sir. I hope this will help in caring for your boy. My quartermaster will contact you today. He has some goods for your store." Then the captain hooks the leash back onto Kathy, and they leave the store.

Captain Black guides them to another store, one that sells women's clothing. When the clerk comes up, the captain points to Kathy's collar, a rash is starting to break out by the time they walk in. "We need something nicer and more comfortable for her. Please make sure it's hypoallergenic."

"Yes, sir, I have just what you need," he says. He comes back with a satin black collar, which has a small cameo on the front.

The captain says, "Yes, that will do fine." He unfastens the collar Kathy's wearing. She starts to take a step away. The captain steps forward so she doesn't go far. "Let's not make a scene, Miss Masters," he says softly. He starts to put the new one on, then stops. By this time, her neck is red. The captain asks the clerk, "Do you have something that will help the redness and chafing?"

"Yes, sir, I do," the clerk replies. He gets a jar of balm. "Try this, sir."

Kathy holds Cindy close against her legs. She's focused on her new doll and misses most of what's going on. The captain gently rubs the balm over the red area of Kathy's neck. It's cool and soothing. Then he secures her new collar.

She looks at the captain. He seems a very cold man—not cruel, just uncaring—yet over the past couple of hours, she's seen something different about him, like somewhere buried deep inside is a gentle, caring person.

After paying the clerk, he says, "Time to check on the repairs."

They walk back down the street to the docks. Kathy notices men looking at her, but when they recognize Captain Black, they all turn away.

When they get back to the ship it looks like work repairing the damage had started, but no one is working now. Upon entering they find the passageways are empty.

"Damn!" the captain says under his breath. Kathy yawns, and she moves closer to the captain. He leads the girls down the passageway to the main mess. All the crewmen are gathered there; they are arguing loudly. Everyone gets quiet when the captain walks in. Kathy stays behind the captain as he moves to the head of the table taking Kathy and Cindy with him. Then he sits, the crew keep silent. "Mr. Gibb, I expected work repairing my ship to be going on. Why are we having a brotherhood meeting?"

Kathy looks questioningly at the captain. *What's a brotherhood meeting?*

Mr. Gibb stands and says, "The men feel that you've claimed these two, Captain. They know that Abdullah was offering to pay big for them, and you didn't accept. They feel they should be compensated. They feel you owe them their cut."

"Do they?" Captain Black says. "Well now"—he starts to speak in a calm, clear voice—"all you men know what Ahmed Abdullah is like. All of you know what he would have done to both of them, what he would have done to the young girl. We be honest privateers. We're cutthroats, and there's no doubt of that, but would any of you be able to sleep knowing what he'd do to the young lass?" His voice grows in strength. "We're privateers, not animals! In our profession, we must deal with unsavory, evil men, but there are some lines none of us have crossed, none of us!" Captain Black points at Mr. Hansen. In a stern voice, he demands, "Mr. Hansen, you brought the lass on board. You carried her to Doc Smith. You've held her in your arms. After that, will you take money, line your pockets, and give over the lass to Ahmed?"

Mr. Hansen looks uncomfortable. "No, sir, I could do no such thing."

The captain points at the cook. "And you, Cookie, you've made special meals for her. Now can you turn her over to a monster like Ahmed just to put some silver in your pocket?"

The cook turns red. "No, sir, never."

Next the captain calls on the doctor. "Doctor, after caring for the little one, is there any amount of money you'd accept to leave her with Ahmed Abdullah?"

"Not a chance, sir!"

Mr. Rawls stands and says, "Okay, Captain, but what shall we do with the child? And there's still the matter of the woman."

"Our savior Jesus said what we're to do, Mr. Rawls."

Kathy looks surprised. *Jesus? This pirate speaks of Jesus?* One of the mates sees the look on her face. He leans in and says, "The captain holds services every Sunday. We be privateers, but we know who Jesus is."

Captain Black continues, "Jesus said suffer the little children to come to me. If that's good enough for our Lord, that's good enough for us."

"What are you proposing, Captain?" Mr. Gibb asks.

In a strong stern voice, Captain Black states, "She be an orphan, Mr. Gibb, an orphan because of our actions. We didn't mean to, but we killed her parents boarding the *America*. It only be right that we make recompense. We shall adopt her. She shall be our daughter, every one of us a father to her. We will teach her all we know. But though privateering be an honest profession, it's not enough for a young girl. A girl needs to learn how to be a lady, how to be among decent folk."

"How do we teach her that, Captain?" Mr. Hahn asks

"Miss Masters is how, Mr. Hahn. I be compensating the crew for what she was worth to Abdullah. That's fair, and we brothers are fair to each other, but now we take her on as crew to teach young Cindy how to be a proper lady, teach her makeup and style, all the things we can't. She will be a paid part of the crew, though on probation until she proves herself true."

Kathy looks at the faces of the crew. They're all looking at Cindy. Some even have tears in their eyes. Here she sits among some of the most-feared raiders in the known galaxy, and they're looking at this little girl they all feel they've wronged, some openly weeping. Captain Black stands up from his chair. "What say you, brothers?"

To a man, they all shout, "Aye!"

"And to Miss Masters being one of us?"

"Aye, Captain!"

"Then it's settled. Mr. Rawls as you are purser, transfer the appropriate sum from the captain's share in equal shares among the crew as recompense for Miss Masters. Assign her a pay code. Assign them the largest cabin available near mine. Give them access to the clothing stores. Be sure they have the needed ship's uniforms and all the ladies' clothing they need. Each man will start to teach young Cindy their job, make her a first-class mate."

"Aye, Captain!" they all shout.

"Now introduce yourselves to our new daughter and then get back to work. We weigh anchor in three days."

"Hurrah!" shouts the crew. They come by one at a time to hug Cindy, tell her their name and what they're assigned duties are. They each shake Kathy's hand and say, "Welcome aboard, Miss Masters. Welcome to the brotherhood." Lastly come Mr. Hahn, Mr. Gibb, Mr. Rawls (the purser), and the ship's supply chief.

Mr. Rawls says, "Come with me, Miss Masters. I'll set you and the lass up with your quarters."

The supply chief says, "Then I'll get you ladies outfitted proper."

The rest of the crew go back to repairing the ship. The captain walks down the passageway a few steps behind the girls. He stops before his cabin door. "I'll be teaching you ladies the art of the blade. Mr. Gibb will teach you pistol. If you learn that proper, Mr. Hahn will teach you rifle. We'll see where we go from there. School starts in the morning." He tips his hat to Kathy and Cindy and then enters his quarters.

The cabin they're assigned is right next to the captain's. It has two bunk rooms, a sitting area, and a kitchenette. The supply chief gets both of them four sets of crew dungarees and linen, towels, pillows, etc. Then he takes them to a compartment that's filled with women's clothes, every type imaginable.

"We have much here to sell, but as crew, you get your pick before we do." He leaves Kathy and Cindy to pick whatever they wish.

CHAPTER 5

BLUE STAR

Four weeks go by rapidly. The captain teaches Kathy and Cindy how to use a sword, very elementary at this point. The captain has a special sword made for Cindy. It's barely a long, skinny knife, but for her it's a rapier. Mr. Gibb spends an hour a day teaching Kathy and Cindy how to handle a pistol, how to tell a slug thrower from a plasma pistol or a laser and how they work.

It took a week for the repairs to be completed, which was a few days longer than the captain wanted. As soon as they are finished, the *Rapier* sets out on the hunt. Captain Black tries to avoid US-flagged ships for now, but he's not as discriminating about German, French, and British ships, and for some reason, he'll go out of his way to run down a Chinese ship.

It's after dinner on a Sunday. It still surprises Kathy to see Captain Black being a preacher on Sunday mornings. Amazingly, he's actually good at it, preaching old-time fire and brimstone. But now she and Cindy have the observation dome all to themselves. The two of them sit in the observation dome on a nice big cushiony reclining chair. Cindy sits on Kathy's lap, the two of them wrapped in a blanket. The cook brought them both cookies and hot cocoa.

Cindy's adapting to her new status as ship's daughter quite well. It's a little harder for Kathy. As she dips her cookie in her cocoa and nibbles on it, she ponders on what it is she's doing, how can she stay on this ship.

"He makes excellent cookies doesn't he?" The captain's voice surprises them.

"Yes, he does," Kathy replies.

Cindy says in a sad voice, "Is it time for lessons, is it?"

"No, princess. It's time for stargazing and cookies."

Kathy and Cindy look about, and the captain is standing behind them, looking at the stars. He points to a bright-blue star that's "close."

"That's where we're heading."

"Why?" Kathy asks.

"Lots of fat Chinese merchantmen pass by there," the captain replies. It sounds like he's leaving something unsaid. "The blue star will go nova someday," he continues. "It has a black hole companion that causes it to have an equatorial disk. You'll see it when we get close."

"Oh," Kathy replies.

"Nearby is a small blue planet. It's very much like Earth used to be. People live near the sea there."

"Really?" Cindy says.

"Yes, princess. A tiny little sea and spaceport used to be there, and intelligent sea creatures live nearby. They talk and trade with the people in the village."

"Wow!" she says with excitement.

"They look like big fish-eyed squids, and they can talk like men do. They make living toys, and I'm going to get you a puppy or a living doll when we get there, or maybe a ship's cat."

Kathy lies back into the chair, and her head brushes the captain's hand. He doesn't move, then he touches her hair. His touch is light, his hand strong. She looks up at him. He grins at Kathy and asks, "What would you like, Miss Masters?"

"Nothing," she says softly.

"Well, think about it, miss. You might decide on something when we get there." He looks back up at the star. Kathy notices a single tear run down his cheek. "Cindy, it's a beautiful planet to live on, and you'll love the squid people. They'll make a living pet just for you."

"What's wrong?" Kathy asks.

He looks at her. "Nothing, miss, just something from another life—a life long gone. Have a good evening, ladies."

Suddenly, Kathy pulls the captain down onto the chair and just hugs him. At first, he's stiff, but after a few minutes, he hugs her back. Cindy manages to squeeze into the hug.

"Thanks, my ladies," the captain says with a slight smile.

"Why are we going to this planet?" Kathy inquires.

The captain stands slowly. "Good hunting, miss, good hunting. And perhaps something special for the two of you."

"Oh."

He tips his hat and leaves the observation dome.

* * *

Over the next two weeks, the star grows larger. Soon they can see the disk about the blue star.

Cindy loves being a privateer. She starts swinging her wooden practice sword around every opportunity she gets. She even wears thigh-high boots and a broad-brimmed hat like the captain's. She has mini sword fights with any of the crew that walk past. All the crew give her a short fight, then let her take them when she challenges them. It often disrupts getting work done, but they all make allowances for that.

Kathy watches her with a strange feeling of pride. She always wanted a daughter of her own, but she never imagined raising a daughter like this. And Cindy has bonded with Kathy as if she were her natural daughter.

Cindy crawls along the passageways and chases a crewman down. When she returns, she says, "Hey, where is my button?" She checks her pockets and pulls it out, then she runs into Kathy's arms and says, "I found a button."

"I've been meaning to ask"—the captain is standing behind them—"Miss Masters, what was it you did before we brought you aboard?"

Kathy turns, surprised. Sometimes it gets unnerving never hearing him approach. Cindy hides the button quickly. "I was a photographer, I was supposed to take photographs on a new planet," she replies.

"A photographer, well now…" He thinks for a moment then asks, "Would you consider taking pictures of the ship and crew? You'd be the first person to ever document what happens on a ship of the brotherhood."

"I could, but my camera was destroyed in the attack on the *America*."

He grins. "There are plenty of cameras in stores. Take your pick of whatever you need."

Kathy smiles and says to Cindy, "Let's go to the shop."

"Oh boy!" she shouts. She pulls out the tiny silver button and says, "I found a button."

The captain smiles. "That looks familiar," he says.

"No," she says with a grin as she grips it tightly.

The captain pulls a button off his shirt sleeve. "Here, I think your button needs a friend," he says, and he hands it to her.

She looks surprised, and she giggles and wiggles in Kathy's arms as she puts the two buttons in her pocket. The captain tips his hat to them and heads down the passageway.

Kathy and Cindy go to the ship's store, holding hands. When they get to the store, the chief grins and asks, "What can I do for you, ladies?"

"A camera," Kathy says.

"A camera, this way, miss." The chief heads to a cabinet as Kathy walks after him with Cindy. He opens it. There are over fifty cameras inside, all types, including the new holographic ones. Kathy points to one in the corner. The chief pulls it out. "Good eye, miss." He hands her the camera and some more equipment to go with it. As Kathy takes hold of it, Cindy runs off to a gun stand. Kathy asks the stores chief, "Are those loaded?"

"No, ma'am. I keep them deactivated."

"Good."

There are over seventy sidearms on display, all chained to the shelf top.

Cindy says, "Mommy, I want that one." She's pointing to a small laser pistol.

Kathy smiles and says, "Not yet, sweetheart."

The chief says, "It's a good training pistol if you keep it set to low power." The chief whispers to Kathy, "I can have Mr. Gibb use that for training and keep it in his locker when she's not using it."

"It may be best. I don't want her using anything more powerful," Kathy says. "I might come back later for it."

"Sounds good, miss," the chief replies.

Kathy hands him the money for the camera, but the chief says, "The captain has already taken care of it, miss."

"Oh," Kathy says. She then gives the chief a small amount to keep the pistol.

He hands her a gumball. "For the little one later," he says softly. "Have a good day, ladies." He hugs Cindy. "Be good now, matey."

Kathy says "Thank you" and picks Cindy up. Then Cindy pops her head up and shows him a familiar button.

For the next week, whenever Kathy is not training, she's taking pics. Cindy becomes fascinated with her photography, so Kathy lets her take a photo everywhere she takes one. The crew hams it up a bit whenever she's taking pics which makes Kathy and Cindy grin. Taking pics, Kathy gets to see more of how the ship works, and the crew always takes time to show Cindy what they are doing. Though Cindy is only five, she's smart as a whip and catches on fast when the crewmen take the time to show her how things work.

Later, Kathy takes a photo out of the observation dome. It seems idyllic; the stars are beautiful. The big blue star is much closer now; Kathy can see matter being pulled from the star into the disk, swirl around the star, and then flow off to a point and disappear into the black hole.

Kathy gives the camera to Cindy. She takes a photo through the dome of what seems blank space. Cindy shows the picture to Kathy. "Mom, do you see the ship in my picture?"

"No, sweetie. Let's take the photo to one of the crew and show him."

Cindy spots Mr. Gibb and takes the photo to him. "Mr. Gibb, look at my pic." He grins at her and looks at it. She says, "I see a ship."

"That's really good, sweetie," he says to Cindy.

At that moment, the klaxon sounds, then the captain's voice comes over the intercom, "Action stations, stand ready to pursue." Kathy stands up and looks at Cindy. She's scared; the sound the klaxon makes is unnerving.

Mr. Gibb says, "I need to get to my station. You two should come to the bridge with me."

Kathy picks her up and hands Cindy to Mr. Gibb, she clings to him. Mr. Gibb leads Kathy to the bridge. The captain stands in front of his chair. "Mr. Bonds, bring her to 137 minus 23."

"Aye, Captain."

"Give me holographics, Mr. Garrett."

"Aye, Captain." He adjusts some controls, and a holographic sphere appears. Kathy walks in with Cindy and Mr. Gibb. Cindy sobs in Mr. Gibb's shoulder as the klaxon is still sounding.

The captain looks over. "Have them stand by the bosun's station, Mr. Gibb."

Mr. Gibb leads them to a chair and sets Cindy in it. Kathy looks over at the captain as he gives orders. "Ready main batteries, Mr. Andjek. Turn off the klaxon, Mr. Garrett."

"Aye, Captain."

Cindy gets up and says, "Mommy, up. Mommy, up." Kathy picks her up and sits in the chair putting Cindy on her lap.

"Bring secondaries online, Mr. Andjek."

"Aye, Captain."

"Mr. Gibb, report ships status," commands Captain Black.

Mr. Gibb gets on the comm net, after a minute, he reports, "All ship's systems are manned, Captain. Power at 105 percent. Boarding party is in the armory."

"Very good, Mr. Gibb. Keep me in her blind spot, helmsman."

"Aye, sir."

Kathy takes pics of the bridge crew doing their jobs. Cindy wanders over to the captain and says in a sweet but sobbing voice, "What are we doing, Daddy?"

Kathy is surprised at Cindy calling the captain Daddy. "It's okay, my princess. We're being privateers. We're about to take a fat Chinese merchantman." Kathy detects actual hatred in his words.

It takes twenty minutes to maneuver the ship into position. Kathy gives Cindy the camera, and she takes a photo of the tactical holographic display. She watches as the blue dot, the *Rapier*, and the red dot, its prey, move closer to each other.

"Keep those asteroids between us and those people, helmsman."

"Aye, Captain," Mr. Bonds replies.

Cindy climbs into a spare chair next to the captain.

"The sensor station reports forty kilometers, Captain," Mr. Gibb says.

"Weapons stand by, all ahead flank," the captain commands. The ship lurches forward, gaining speed, closing rapidly on the Chinese ship. Kathy takes the camera from Cindy and takes a photo of her in the chair.

"Stand ready." The captain is totally focused now.

"They've seen us, Captain!" Mr. Gibb shouts. Kathy can now see the ship on the view screen; it is obviously turning to bring its weapons to bear.

"Fire main batteries!" commands the captain. The ship lurches again. The particle beams from the main batteries cut through the void.

Cindy says in her pirate voice, "Make ship go boom." To her, this is no different than the video games she's been playing. At that moment, both beams hit the freighter amidship; bits of the ship's hull are torn off its flank, and a hole opens up in its side. Cindy giggles, "Ship go boom, ship go boom."

The Chinese ship fires back and misses wide.

"Missile battery give them a salvo," the captain orders. Four missiles tear through the dark. The Chinese ship attempts to turn away. Three missiles miss; the fourth rips into the ship's engines. Large pieces of the ship are tossed into space, and its engines go offline. Cindy jumps up and yells, "Yayyyyyy! We killed the ship!"

"Yes, princess, we killed the ship," the captain says.

Kathy can hear satisfaction in his voice. She looks at the captain and says to Cindy, "We must be on our best behavior."

"Prepare to grapple," the captain commands. "Mr. Gibb, you have the con." The captain leaves the bridge.

Mr. Gibb gives the command, "All parties prepare to board."

Cindy is watching everything the view screen shows her. Her inquisitive mind takes in everything, but she is still relating all this to a video game.

Mr. Gibb commands, "Bring us up on the port side, helmsman."

"Aye!" Mr. Bonds responds.

Kathy leans in and whispers to Mr. Gibb, "I don't want Cindy to see violence yet. Should I take her to our room?"

"She won't, Miss Masters. The captain will keep it on their ship."

"Good," Kathy replies. Her insides feel twisted. *People are being killed, and my little girl is going to be exposed to this, if not today soon. How do I protect her from the inevitable? And how do I feel about this, people are being killed? Am I part of this? Am I responsible for this too?*

Cindy climbs into the captain's chair. She's watching everything closely.

Both ships are side by side. The boarding tubes with the breaching charges extend from the side of the *Rapier*. The grapples fire, pulling the ships together. The tubes bang against the Chinese ship's hull. The captain's voice comes over the intercom, "Now, Mr. Gibb."

Mr. Gibb pushes a button on the captain's panel. An explosion shakes both ships, punching two large round holes in the Chinese freighter's side. Mr. Gibb commands, "Boarders away."

Cindy sits up in the captain's chair, looking like a big tough pirate.

Kathy fell on the deck when the breaching charges fired. She gets up and dusts herself off, then notices a rip in her dress along her thigh. Some of the bridge crew make wolf whistles. Mr. Gibb shouts, "Stow it, mates, she's part of our crew!"

They give out a collective "Awwwww!"

"We're in a battle, lads. Keep your eyes and minds on your jobs!" Mr. Gibb commands. They turn back to their stations.

They can hear all the action over the intercom. Mr. Gibb turns off the crew video so Cindy can't see the close battle and pipes it all to a monitor at his station.

The holographic display changes to the diagram of the enemy ship—red dots for the Chinese crew. Blue dots, the *Rapier's* crew, rush through openings in the side of the Chinese ship. Blue dots rush up to red dots; the red dots turn yellow and stop moving; the blue dots rush on. One of the blue dots has a special character over it. It's then Kathy realizes the captain is leading the boarding party. *The captain is leading the fight* is all Kathy can think about.

Kathy picks Cindy up, sits in the captain's chair, and cuddles her. They watch as the dots move about. Some dots stay red. They are herded away by blue dots, but most of the red turn yellow and stop moving. Soon the only red dots left are the Chinese that were taken prisoner.

Cindy asks, "Why aren't those red ones yellow?"

Mr. Gibb says, "They're captives Cindy. They surrendered instead of fighting."

Cindy asks, "Are they being interrogated?"

Kathy says to Mr. Gibb, "Interrogation has been her word of the week. She can't stop saying it."

He smiles. "Yes, sweetie, they're being interrogated."

The captain's voice comes over the intercom. "Send over the store's chief and his team. Tell Doc Smith we've got five for sickbay. We've lost Mr. Reed though. Check his records so we can settle with his next of kin."

It takes three hours to remove the loot. Four of the Chinese are brought on board. Then the captain does something Kathy wasn't expecting; he executes the remaining captives. It's all on the display—red dots turn yellow. Mr. Gibb turns it off before Cindy notices.

"Oh my," Kathy says to herself, "how could he?" Kathy gives Cindy a gumball to keep her mind off the display. All everyone on the bridge can hear is the pop of Cindy's bubblegum.

Finally, the captain's voice comes over the intercom, "All hostages and crew have returned, Mr. Gibb. Cut her free." Mr. Gibb hits the grapple release, and the Chinese ship drifts away. Shortly, the captain returns to the bridge. "Ready secondary batteries," he commands.

"Ready, Captain."

"Three salvos, fire." The ship shakes three times; the rail guns fire their payloads. The solid shots smash into the Chinese ship; it breaks up into small pieces. "Make course for Safe Port," Captain Black commands. The *Rapier* pulls away, picks up speed, and heads toward the blue star.

By this time Cindy is a little sleepy, and Kathy takes the gum out of her mouth. The captain sees she is starting to get heavy for Kathy and walks up to her, picks Cindy up, and says, "Let's tuck her in, Miss Masters."

"Thank you," Kathy says softly. She walks with the captain as he carries Cindy to their quarters.

As Kathy opens the door, he asks, "May I come in?"

"Yes, of course. You're always welcome." Then Kathy asks him, "Why did you kill the other hostages?"

He walks over to Cindy's bunkroom and lays her on the bunk. He smiles at her, gives her a little kiss, then stands, and turns to Kathy. "To answer your question, Miss Masters, it's a debt owed."

"Okay." The answer confuses her, but for now, she'll let it go. *No, I can't let it go.* "Captain, they had surrendered. They stopped fighting. How could you just kill them? I thought you were a better man than that."

The captain actually looks hurt. "I know you don't understand, that you're new to all of this. These people have murdered my family, my friends, everyone I used to know. They still murder us. It's war, Miss Masters, the worst kind of war."

Kathy's not sure what to say or think so, for now, she's going to let it wait. She says to the Captain, "I have a cup of cocoa, if you would like it?" As she says it, Kathy notices a long cut in his coat. She gets up to look, then she sees the bandage over his abdomen, it was hidden by his coat. "You're hurt!" Kathy shouts as she rushes to him.

He catches her as she does. "Yes," he says, "I'll be going to see Doc Smith now."

"I'll come with you."

"Thank you," he says to her. Kathy helps him walk down the passageway to sickbay. Once there, the captain says, "Doc, how are my men?"

"They'll be okay in a couple of days," he says. "Seems they're more worried about you. What happened?"

"Can you look at his side?" Kathy says. "Please help him," she pleads.

The captain removes his coat; blood is seeping through the bandage. The doctor removes the bandage, which reveals the captain has a cut from a sword. It's through the skin and halfway through the muscle. Kathy gasps when she sees it.

"That's a nice one, Captain," Doc Smith says.

"Please help him." Kathy is near tears now.

"I've got him miss," the doc says. "Lie down Skipper."

The captain starts to lie back on the table, but halfway down, he collapses. At that point, they can hear Cindy yelling, "Mommy, Mommy, where are you Mommy?"

"Go take care of her," Doc Smith says. He starts to clean the captain's wound.

"Please save him," she says.

"He'll be fine, miss. He's had worse."

Cindy starts to walk through the door. Kathy rushes to her and says, "Mommy's bought you a surprise." She scoops Cindy up and takes her down the passageway to the ship's store. "Mommy got you something special."

"What, Mommy?"

The chief is there doing inventory of the recently captured loot. Kathy says to the chief, "Somebody is here to get her surprise."

He pulls out the laser and hands it to Kathy, along with five power packs. She gives the chief the rest of the payment. "Thanks, miss," the chief says.

"Look what Mommy got you," Kathy says.

She jumps up and down. "Oh my, Mommy!"

Kathy says, "You can't use it without Mr. Gibb around, okay?"

"Yes, yes!" At that point, Mr. Gibb walks past. Cindy runs to him, so Mr. Gibb stops. "Look what I have!" she says with excitement.

"My Cindy, that's a fine pistol." He checks to be sure it doesn't have a power pack.

"Mommy says I can't use it without you."

"Well, we'll use it tomorrow."

Kathy walks over and gives Mr. Gibb the power packs. "Just to be sure the little pirate doesn't get them."

He nods at that, and he puts them in his coat pocket. "How's the captain?" he asks softly.

"Collapsed the last time I saw him in sickbay."

He nods to Kathy. "Take the little one to bed. I'll make sure he's okay." Mr. Gibb heads to sickbay.

"I will. Thank you," Kathy says as she picks Cindy up and says, "Let's go to bed."

It's very late when Kathy hears a knock at the door. She gets up quietly to answer it, sneaking across the deck, avoiding the noisy spots. She opens the door, and Mr. Gibb is standing there. "What's up?" Kathy asks.

"The captain is sleeping, miss," he replies.

"Good."

"I don't think there will be sword practice for a few days."

"Is he stable?"

"Yes, quite stable." He starts to leave then stops. "You should know this," he says. "The captain lived near Safe Port. He had a wife and a little girl. Then the Chinese came. It was during the Genetics War. They killed his family while he was out with the squid people— we both were. That's why he takes down every Chinese ship he sees. He's been privateering ever since."

"Oh my," Kathy's time with the Nomads in the Dead Lands of Australia flashes through her mind "I don't have a family, you know. My parents disowned me as a child. I had to find my own way."

"You do now, Miss Masters. You have 170 brothers now."

"Cindy and I have a great family now."

He smiles. "And we have you now." He hugs Kathy, then heads down the passageway.

Kathy calls to Mr. Gibb as he moves down the passageway. "What time for her training?"

"Right after breakfast, Miss Masters." He smiles and heads on toward his quarters.

"Okay," Kathy says as she goes back into hers.

CHAPTER 6

SAFE PORT

The *Rapier* is much closer to the large blue star now, and Kathy can see another smaller yellow star nearby. It's a failed trinary star system. Had the yellow star been a little closer, it would have been a true trinary system, and the yellow star would be collapsing like its blue neighbor. It's just far enough away where the gravity affects it but not close enough to be consumed by the black hole.

Kathy walks to breakfast with a sleeping Cindy in her arms. The crewmen have a spot for the two of them near the captain's table, and the cook has made Cindy's favorite breakfast—Koala-shaped pancakes with blueberries for eyes and nose. Cindy slowly wakes up, and Kathy puts her in her chair.

The captain has finished his breakfast; he sits in his chair, sipping cocoa. It's been four days since he was wounded. The nanites Doc Smith uses have worked their "magic," no one would know how injured he was from his appearance. Kathy goes to the captain and asks, "Are you okay?"

"Good morning, Miss Masters," he says. "Thank you, but it'll take more than a Chinese cutlass to slow me down. We'll be at Safe Port soon. Would you and Cindy like to go ashore with me?"

Kathy hugs him. He hugs back, though he tries to keep it "formal."

"I'm glad you're okay. Yes, we will."

"Excellent," he says. "I'll take you to meet some of the locals."

"Okay," she replies.

He stands and says, "I need to be on the bridge. The watch is about to change."

"Okay, Cindy may want to come up."

He gives Cindy a hug. "That'd be fine," he says over his shoulder as he goes.

Kathy eats her breakfast. The crewmen try hard not to look her over in her pajamas, but they are guys, and though they behave, they still can't help looking.

Cindy eats all her pancakes and asks for more. This makes Cookie very happy; he loves having a little girl to cook for. He whips up another order of pancakes for her, and she wolfs them down.

When they're done with breakfast and dressed, they go to the bridge. Cindy runs in straight to the captain. He picks her up and sets her on his lap as he gives commands to the bridge crew. The *Rapier* is now on approach to "dock." There are several small asteroids that orbit near Safe Port. Because the *Rapier* is a privateer and this is now Chinese-controlled space, the *Rapier* will "anchor" close to a little used asteroid.

Cindy says, "Why didn't you give me good-night cuddles last night?"

"I'm sorry, princess, I'll not forget again." Then the captain asks Cindy, "Princess, would you like to dock the ship?"

Her eyes light up. "Yes!" she says excited. The crew look up at the captain when he says that, concern on their faces.

"Okay, I'll tell you what to say and when to say it this time. Next time, you'll have to remember though."

She smiles and bounces in his arms, then stands in front of the captain's chair. He kneels down and whispers in her ear, and she gives the commands, "Reduce speed to one quarter impulse, Mr. Gibb."

"One quarter impulse. Aye, Captain."

Next she says, "Two points to starboard, helmsman."

"Two points starboard, aye, Captain." She's really excited that the crew are calling her captain.

Mr. Gibb smiles at Kathy. "She'll be a fine sailor, Miss Masters."

Kathy replies, "I hope so."

Next, Cindy orders, "Reduce speed to maneuvering, Mr. Gibb."

He replies, "Maneuvering speed, aye, Captain," and grins at her. After fifteen minutes and one minor oops, the *Rapier* is tied to the asteroid pier.

"That was good sailoring," the captain says to her.

Kathy feels a little dizzy. "I feel a little funny," she says.

Mr. Gibb notices and steadies her. "It's the gravity here. The big star and the black hole can make you feel funny until you get used to it."

Cindy runs up to her. "Kathy, I docked the ship!" She hugs her leg, smiling.

Kathy goes to pick her up saying, "That's excellent," and collapses. Mr. Gibb catches her and holds her steady.

The captain says, "Mr. Hansen, you have the con. Mr. Gibb, Miss Masters, and Cindy, you're with me and the shore party."

"Yes," Kathy says.

"Aye, Captain," Mr. Gibb replies.

They go to the shuttle bay. The crew have loaded the shuttle with booty taken from the Chinese merchantman. The captain has Kathy strap Cindy into the copilot seat. He leans over her seat close to Kathy. "Cindy, Mr. Rawls is going to show you how to fly the shuttle."

"Oh my," Kathy murmurs.

Mr. Rawls is a big black man from a South African colony; his ancestors were probably Zulu. He stands about 185 centimeters tall, and looks like he weighs 90 kilos, which seems to be all muscle. His hair is long and braided in dreads. Though fierce in appearance, Mr. Rawls is the jolliest person Kathy has ever met.

"Miss Masters, if you'll sit next to me," the captain says; he points to the seat behind Cindy and sits in the one behind the pilot. Kathy sits in the seat next to the captain. Mr. Rawls explains the controls to Cindy, goes through the checklist with her, and has her start the engines. The shuttle comes to life. Kathy straps in tightly to the seat.

The shuttle bay doors open, and Mr. Rawls steers the shuttle out. When it's clear of obstacles, he lets Cindy steer for a bit. He shows her how to compensate for drift, and the two of them take the shuttle to the planet's orbit.

Kathy grips the seat; her breathing is a bit excited. Between the weird gravity and the fact a five-year-old is flying her through space, it's all a little much to take in. The captain reaches over and holds her hand. "It'll be fine, Miss Masters," he says softly. She gives an unconvinced smile.

Mr. Rawls takes over the controls, and the shuttle heads down to the planet. Kathy grips the captain's hand tighter. The shuttle gingerly slips through the planet's atmosphere. Dropping below the clouds reveals the surface of this world. It's a beautiful world—blue skies, grass, and trees very similar to Earth. Most of the signs of the Chinese invasion are overgrown now. But occasionally, they see the ruins of a building or a small town and sometimes an impact crater.

"How awful," Kathy says at the sight of the ruins.

The captain says with some anger, "The bastards used mass drivers when they invaded."

"Oh, please don't swear in front of Cindy," Kathy says quietly.

The captain looks at her a moment, then replies, "Yes, Miss Masters. I'll be watching my words more closely."

The shuttle lands by the edge of a small city in a little valley. It's fairly primitive in construction. No concrete or steel, almost everything is made of wood. There are people waiting; none are Chinese.

Kathy gets off the shuttle, carrying Cindy, wrapping a blanket around them to keep her safe. The crew open the cargo doors, and people start off-loading the shuttle.

The captain says, "The Chinese take everything from them—clothes, food, medicine. They leave barely enough for them to survive. So when I can, I bring some back, and I compensate the crew from my share so they get their booty."

Kathy looks at him with an expression of understanding. She had never heard of such things back on Earth. Here she is confronted with the reality of life in the colonies, and it's nothing like what she's been told. No wonder he hates the Chinese so virulently.

Mr. Gibb greets a local. "Miss Masters, I'd like you to meet my brother John," he says.

"Yes," she replies. Kathy notices that John wears a pastor's collar.

"Good to meet you, Miss Masters," he says.

Kathy smiles at John and shakes his hand while she snuggles Cindy.

Mr. Gibb continues, "Mr. Reed has no family, so we're going to bury him here. My brother will conduct the services."

The people seem very friendly toward Mr. Gibb, but they are standoffish toward Captain Black. They all attend a short service for Mr. Reed with the captain standing in for his family. Once it's over, they all go back to the shuttle. As the townspeople unload the shuttle, the captain says, "Let's go, Mr. Gibb."

"Aye, Captain," he replies. He says goodbye to his brother, and they all head to a ground skimmer. Mr. Gibb takes the driver's seat of the skimmer.

"You have the detail, Mr. Rawls," the captain says.

"Aye, Captain," he replies.

Kathy pops a hood around Cindy's head; she struggles a little. "This should keep your head and neck warm," she tells Cindy.

"Mom, I'll be okay."

The captain gives Kathy a knowing grin, then helps her and Cindy into the skimmer.

Mr. Gibb drives the skimmer like he was born to it. It stays a meter above the ground, racing through the countryside. Kathy cuddles with the captain, keeping Cindy covered. Captain Black puts his arm around Kathy.

The whole time, Cindy pushes and struggles to wiggle out from under the covers, and Kathy keeps covering her up. Finally, she squirms away from Kathy and hops onto Mr. Gibb's lap. Mr. Gibb shows Cindy how to use the controls. He even lets her drive for a bit.

Soon the skimmer approaches the ocean. It's a beautiful blue green. Light breakers are rushing to the shore and crashing into the rocks.

Kathy cuddles into the captain's shoulder. Captain Black holds her close, for this short time he seems at peace.

Mr. Gibb brings the skimmer to a halt near a churchyard. The church is in ruins, and most of the yard is overgrown. One small section, the graveyard, is well maintained though.

"Five minutes, Mr. Gibb," Captain Black says softly. "I'll be right back," he says to Kathy and Cindy, "You two wait here with Mr. Gibb." He gets out of the skimmer, walks into the churchyard, and goes to the graveyard.

Mr. Gibb watches him walk over to a plot with several head-stones. He turns to Kathy and says, "You and Cindy are the first thing that has made him smile since the Chinese came."

Kathy asks, "Are they in there?"

"No, there was nothing left to bury. Just a marker with their names. The Chinese hit most of the farms first for some reason. They hit us at night and used mass drivers. Asteroid-sized rocks crashing into the ground, just like atom bombs." He shakes his head.

Kathy doesn't know why, but she asks, "Was his whole family killed in the attack?"

"Oh no, Miss Masters, some of us survived."

"Us?" she says.

"Yes, us. The captain is my uncle."

"Your uncle?"

"Yes, my mother was his wife's younger sister."

"Oh, are you going to see your mother?"

"No, miss. She was killed the same night. The captain and I were at sea, submerged. When we surfaced, everything and every-body was gone. We were an American colony then. We called for help, but none came. The only thing that came was Chinese troops, thousands of Chinese. They herded all us white devils here at Safe Port, leaving us to the elements. Not one building still stood, the farms were all burning, no food. They left us here to die, and the Americans never came. They left us to be killed by the Chinese."

"Is that why you attacked the *America*?" Kathy asks.

"Yes, miss. We don't attack as many American ships as Chinese, but that's why we attack them."

"Does the captain have other relatives on the *Rapier*?"

"A few, Miss Masters, but all of us lost family in the attack."

"Is that why you're on the *Rapier*?"

"No, miss. I'm on the *Rapier* because he is."

Captain Black gets back into the skimmer. "Let's go Mr. Gibb," the captain says.

"Aye, Captain." The skimmer scoots off. Mr. Gibb drives down the seashore to a rocky cove. There's a cave among the rocks. The water forms a natural lagoon inside it, and in there is a small submarine. It can easily carry up to twelve people. The captain points to it and asks Cindy, "Princess, would you like to sail a submarine?"

"Oh yes!" she says excitedly. Kathy looks at it and feels a little claustrophobic. It's actually smaller than the shuttle, and the inside is smaller still. And the thought of it going underwater gives her chills. Everyone gets inside. Mr. Gibb takes Cindy through the pre-operation checklist, then has her start the engines. She giggles as they start up. Kathy's stomach sinks. The captain dogs the hatch closed, and the little sub slips out to sea.

"Where are we going?" Cindy asks.

"To find a friend," Mr. Gibb replies.

The sub slips silently under the water. The front of the sub is a clear canopy, much like the B29 of WWII. Cindy sits beside Mr. Gibb and steers the sub as he gives her instructions. Soon Mr. Gibb has Cindy surface the sub. It rises up near a small island.

Kathy climbs out of the hatch after Captain Black. He makes a strange call, a sound she's not heard before. Something starts moving on the little island. It walks out of the bushes near the shore, and for the first time ever, Kathy sees a nanchik. It's almost two meters tall, with flipper feet, four dark eyes, and tentacles hanging from its head. It responds to the captain's call, making a similar sound, then it swims out to the sub.

"That's Porge," the captain says. "Well, technically, it's Porge number 12."

"Number 12?" Kathy asks.

"Yes. They only live twenty years, but somehow, their gods bring them back with all their memories. My grandfather and father had dealings with Porge, and he remembers them perfectly."

"Really?" she says.

The nanchik climbs onto the sub. "Heblo, Cptin Blck."

"Hello, Porge. How have you been?"

"Gbbd, bt mss fends."

"We miss you too, Porge."

"Is Porge really his name?" Kathy asks.

"No, Miss Masters, but we can't pronounce it. Let's go, Porge," the captain says.

"Gbo wrrr?"

"To see the gods, Porge."

"Wby?"

"The ladies need some things, Porge—things only your gods can provide."

"Obk," Porge replies. He dives into the water.

"Back inside, Miss Masters. We have to follow him."

Kathy goes back to her seat. Cindy points at Porge floating outside the sub's nose. "Look, Mommy, it's a nanchik!"

"Yes, sweetie, I see."

The captain dogs the hatch, and Cindy dives the sub under Mr. Gibb's instruction. The sub dives deep, very deep. The hull starts to creak from the pressure.

Finally, Mr. Gibb says, "Level off, Cindy. We can't go deeper in the sub. Follow Porge."

Cindy and Mr. Gibb steer the sub following the aquatic. It leads the sub to an underwater cavern in the side of a submerged mountain. Kathy realizes she's been taking pictures the whole time, ever since she first saw the nanchik. The pictures are incredible, especially the ones of Porge leading the sub. Now she's shooting them entering the cavern. Mr. Gibb takes the controls and carefully guides the sub into the cavern, then surfaces in an air chamber inside.

Captain Black says, "Ladies, we're here so Porge's gods can give you a special gift. They are consummate bioengineers. They've made all the nanchiks and the living dolls that are sold all over civilized space. But for you, they are going to make special eye and ear enhancements, contacts if you will—very useful. Thermal vision with digital readouts and ranging. Enhanced hearing and nerve implants that will speed up your reflexes."

"And a puppy or a kitten!" Cindy cuts in.

"Yes, princess, a puppy or kitten. But we have to go deeper, and the sub can't take it. So we have to use special diving suits. The thing is, we'll have to breathe liquid, and that will take getting used to."

Kathy looks at him. "Liquid?"

"Yes it's a special fluid, heavily oxygenated, but it can feel like drowning, so you'll have to trust me and be strong my ladies."

Cindy is excited to try it, but Kathy is a little nervous at first. Actually, she's terrified but is trying to put on a brave face for Cindy.

They exit the sub and get on a little beach. There's a vault door built into the rock. Captain Black opens it. "This is what we were building when the attack came," Mr. Gibb tells Kathy. The vault door swings open. Inside is a row of extreme-pressure deep-diving suits. They are hooked up to continuous charge systems. Mr. Gibb starts the system checks on the suits. Cindy follows him about as he does all the checks. He shows her how to start the checks and read the system reports. The captain goes to a locker. He draws up four injections.

"You didn't say anything about shots," Kathy says to him.

He stops for a moment. "They're a special mild hypnotic used by deep divers. You won't feel anything, I promise, but they make it easier to breathe the liquid." Kathy's a little dubious.

Mr. Gibb starts to suit up Cindy. It takes some doing to put together a suit small enough for her. She looks like a little yellow Michelin Man when he gets done. Then Mr. Gibb gets Kathy suited up. Once he's done, she looks in a reflective sheet of metal. The thought hits her, *definitely not high fashion.*

Mr. Gibb rigs up the captain, then the captain gets him rigged. Porge floats in the "lagoon," watching what's going on with mild indifference. The captain gives Mr. Gibb a shot, then he kneels down and gives Cindy her shot. He comes over to Kathy. She takes a step back.

"It's okay, Miss Masters." He reaches over and gently places the injector next to her neck. "There, done," he says. She didn't feel it at all, but she does feel very calm, even when Mr. Gibb puts her helmet on. Then he gives himself a shot.

The liquid starts to fill Kathy's suit, then the helmet. At first, she feels a little panic. The system is programmed to stop filling just below the eyes to allow them to fill their lungs. The liquid fills her mouth and nose. She calms a little, then the liquid starts to fill her lungs. It's weird. Actually beyond weird. She breathes in and out; the fluid flows in and out. Part of her mind says I'm drowning, but it passes quickly. When her breathing normalizes, the liquid continues to fill her helmet until there's no air left in the suit. The captain connects a cable from him to Kathy. Mr. Gibb connects a cable from her to Cindy, then he hooks up to Cindy.

"Follow me," the captain says. Even though the earbuds of the comm link are set firmly in her ears, it still sounds a little like he's talking to her through water. They follow the captain to the edge of the lagoon, then all of them jump into the water. They slip slowly below the surface. "Turn on your lights, everybody," the captain says. The lights illuminate this unusual aquatic world.

The captain made sure Kathy had an underwater camera. "Take as many pics as you like," he says. "But ask before taking pics of the gods."

Porge holds onto the captain's harness and pulls all of them through the water. They go down deep, far deeper than the sub could ever go. Kathy sees the most amazing sea creatures. She just can't take pictures fast enough to capture it all—whale-like creatures diving or breaching the surface, playing tag. Large sharklike denizens hunt schools of smaller fish. Jellyfishlike floaters, mollusks. It's breathtaking.

After an hour, they all touch bottom. Porge leads them across the bottom for half an hour. And then they see it. It's actually a city, and the buildings are gargantuan.

"No pictures yet, Miss Masters," the captain admonishes. She lowers her camera.

After another fifteen minutes, they walk through a doorway that's literally big enough for a liner the size of the *America* to pass through. They enter a massive main hall. Huge columns hold up the building. Lights line the hall. It takes ten minutes to walk to the next doorway. As they pass through it, Porge moves to the side and bows down. Seated on a massive dais is a creature Kathy has no words to describe. She is now facing one of the nanchik gods.

It sweeps the four of them with its four giant eyes. As the eyes cross her alien thoughts run through her mind. They're not hostile thoughts; instead, they're inquiring, probing thoughts. It seems they look all over her mind, drawing out her memories, taking them all in, and then placing the memories safely back where they were before the probe. The last memory is her photography, how it defines her, how much she wants to record all of this, and an answer, *Yes, but.*

"But what?" she says in reaction.

But you may not show anyone your pictures and vids until it's time.

"How will I know when it's time?" flashes through her mind.

You'll know. she hears/feels in reply.

The hours they're in the city of the nanchik gods flash by like a waking dream. So many things happen. So much is unsaid but known. Kathy would easily believe it's all an illusion. She blacks out for a few moments. When she wakes, she hears/feels, *Try them.* Kathy blinks, and her eyes now see like a thermal imager. She blinks her right eye, and a reticle with data readouts appear. As she turns her head, she sees different objects she hadn't noticed before. The size and range information appear in the lower right-hand corner of her eye. She blinks again, and her eyes see normally.

Hearing forms in her mind. Then she listens. All kinds of sounds crash through her head. *Focus.* She listens in on one sound, focusing her hearing on it. Suddenly, it's clear; she's listening to the call of a deep-sea crustacean. After turning her new hearing off, she hears/feels, *Visual and hearing tests completed.* She falls asleep again. When she wakes she hears/feels, *Physical enhancement tests completed.*

"It's time to go now," the captain says. Kathy turns and leaves. Porge rejoins them and guides everyone out. The captain directs everyone to start the surfacing protocol for the suit, and they begin to rise. On the way up, Kathy notices Cindy is carrying a small egg-like thing.

It's all too much, sensory overload. Kathy remembers little of the journey up to the cavern—strange images and sounds. Next thing she knows, Kathy is lying on a cot. She looks around. She's in the vault in the cavern.

"Ah, I see you're back, Miss Masters," the captain sits in a folding chair beside her. Cindy is sleeping on the cot next to her, holding a tiny furry fluff ball. "It's time to return to the ship," the captain says.

The journey home seems to rush by—the sub, the skimmer, then the shuttle. As they approach the *Rapier*, it comes to Kathy, it's been four days since they went to the surface of Safe Port. Four days. Cindy keeps playing with her new implants and her kitten.

"Kathy, this is great," she says with a giggle. She sits in Kathy's lap and snuggles close. "I love you, Mommy," she says.

Kathy looks closely at the kitten. Most of the species of cat had been wiped out during the last war on Earth. She'd only known of cats from pics and vids. But now she holds an actual kitten in her hand. "The god told me it was a Maine Coon, a special one. It's going to get as big as a large dog. It'll weigh almost forty kilos. I think I'm going to call him Oscar," Cindy says with a big grin.

Mr. Rawls deftly guides the shuttle into the *Rapier's* shuttle bay. A feeling of peace flows over Kathy. *I'm home*, she thinks. A deep alien thought appears in her mind, *Yes*. She closes her eyes and lets the thought form again, *I'm home*.

* * *

Steve interrupts her. "Hold on, Kathy. Transcription bot, pause." The bot stops recording. "Are you telling me that you have bio implants that let you see in the dark and hear things others can't?"

"Yes," she says softly.

"That's impossible. I mean we have microtechnology that lets us do these things, but a biological implant, no such thing is known in the galaxy, nowhere in the known galaxy."

Kathy thinks back on something Commodore Black once told her. Before she knows it, the words are coming out of her mouth, "Mr. Baker, of all the known universe, we know so very little." She blinks and activates the thermal imaging and ranging, then Kathy looks through the wall to the reception area. The snooty reception-ist is getting coffee. Kathy watches her walk to her desk. She picks up the phone and starts talking. Kathy listens for a minute. Steve watches her intently. "Your receptionist just got some coffee. Her desk is exactly five meters and seven centimeters from where I'm sit-ting. She's talking to her friend Jean about some guy they met last night. They're planning to go to the same club tonight, hoping he and his friend will be there."

Steve picks up his phone and cuts into her line. He listens for a moment, then says, "Miss Williams, please get me a coffee and a..."

"Cocoa," Kathy says.

"And a cocoa for Miss Masters. Tell your friend goodbye and understand that I'm paying you to work, not gossip with your friends. If it happens again, you're fired."

"Yes, sir," she replies.

Kathy blinks the implants off.

"And you have a cat from an extinct species that these creatures created based on your and Cindy's memories?" he asks.

"Yes, Oscar, and he is definitely a cat," Kathy replies.

"And those rare dolls are actually alive? And these creatures cre-ated them?"

"Yes, Steve," she answers.

Steve looks at her. "Do you know what this means?" he asks.

"What it means is *America* will finally fight for Safe Port but not for the right reasons."

"Does the government know about your implants?"

"Yes, that's why they kept Cindy and me for so long. They interrogated us. Tried to find a way to remove the implants. Tried to reverse engineer the implants, tried everything, but now they know they have to work with the nanchik gods to get them, so *America* will fight to regain Safe Port."

He looks deeply into Kathy's eyes. She sees fear in his, and she knows that now he truly believes her. "Continue transcription," he says, and the bot starts recording again.

CHAPTER 7

CHANGES

Kathy starts speaking, "For the next seven months, the *Rapier* raided throughout Chinese space. In that time, we took eleven Chinese merchantmen and four auxiliaries, including a patrol boat."

"Kathy you just said *we*," Steve cuts in. "You meant *they*, didn't you?"

Kathy stops and thinks for a minute and pulls up a picture. It's of Cindy sitting at the weapons station. She's eleven. Captain Gibb stands next to her, and just beyond at the navigator's station, she sits working the controls with Mr. Reynolds guiding her.

"No, Steve, I meant *we*. Two things of import happened at the end of the seventh month." She continues, "First was Cindy's sixth birthday..."

* * *

Cindy wakes up early and runs from her bunk to Kathy's. "Kathy, wake up, wake up." She jumps up and down on the bunk. "I'm six today!" She twirls, saying, "Six, six, six."

Kathy wakes. "It's too early," she squeaks.

"I'm six!" Her jumping on the bunk makes Kathy realize she has a full bladder. What really drives it home though is Oscar jumping onto her belly—that almost makes her pee. She hops out of the bunk and goes to the "head." While Kathy's in there, she wonders, *Why do they call it a head? It's a bathroom anywhere else but on a ship. On a ship, it's a head.* Kathy looks in the mirror, then frowns. Her hair is a mess, and she needs mascara and lipstick. She starts cleaning up while Cindy keeps jumping on Kathy's bunk. Oscar meows in protest.

"Kathy, do you think I'll get presents?" she asks.

"Not if you break my bunk," Kathy replies. "Now go get ready for breakfast. Cookie will keelhaul both of us if we're late again, and we have small arms training with Mr. Gibb this morning."

"Yes, Mommy," Cindy replies and rushes off to her room to get ready.

Kathy thinks, *It's funny that she usually calls me Mommy when I make her do things.*

They barely make it in time for breakfast. Cookie playfully scolds Cindy for being late, but he makes his special pancakes for her. The morning rushes by, then lunch. In the afternoon, the captain only trains the two of them for an hour. "Now go get ready," he says to Cindy. "I think the crew are going to have cake and ice cream for you, and I want you to look like a princess today because you are our princess." He gives Cindy a hug then shoos her off. He walks up to Kathy. "Miss Masters, I've asked the chief to get a special dress for Cindy and one for you too. He picked them up on our last supply run. He says they're truly lovely. I hope you don't mind."

She grins and says, "Thank you, Captain."

"My pleasure, miss," he replies. "I best get cleaned up myself." He touches Kathy's hand for a moment, tips his hat, then leaves the training room. Kathy stays a moment, enjoying the warm feeling from his touch, then she heads to the ship's store. The chief greets her.

"Ah, Miss Masters, I bet you're here for these."

"Thanks, Chief," she says. She goes to pay him.

"The captain's already taken care of it, miss."

"Oh," she replies. Kathy heads back to her quarters, showers, gets Cindy dressed, and does her hair. She really does look like a princess. Then she gets herself ready. The dress is unbelievable, and it's a perfect fit. Kathy stares into the mirror. *I look like a princess.* Then she frowns. *Except for my hair and makeup.* She frowns again and starts to do her hair. She's not satisfied with her hair and makeup, but it's time for the party.

When Kathy and Cindy get to the mess, all the off-duty crew are there. Mr. Gibb puts a tiara on Cindy's head. He stands up and says, "I declare Cindy a princess of the brotherhood."

The crew all sound off with "Aye, Mr. Gibb."

He says to Cindy, "That makes it official then. You are now Princess Cindy de *Rapier* Rex!"

All the crew shouts, "Long may she reign!"

Cindy looks at Mr. Gibb and asks, "Does that mean I can give the captain orders now?"

Everybody starts laughing. Finally Mr. Gibb says, "Yes, princess, but don't tell him that. He won't understand."

"Okay," she replies. "It's our secret then."

The crew all laugh and agree to the secret. Kathy looks about and then leans in. "Mr. Gibb, where's the captain?"

"Standing watch, miss, so the crew can come to the party. He'll be along when the watch relief comes on."

The party starts in full. There is singing, dancing, and games, including pin the tail on the donkey and blind man's bluff. And presents, lots of presents—mostly small things, little toys and dolls, jewelry and games, clothes and some daggers. And from the captain, a new sword.

There's also a small box for Kathy. It's from the captain. She opens it and finds a very delicate diamond broach. It's shaped like a flower, a lily, with the diamonds as the stamen. Kathy holds it against her chest, then rushes to the bridge. The captain is sitting in his seat, sipping cocoa. There are two other crew on the bridge, but she doesn't notice them. Kathy jumps onto the captain's lap. "Thank you, thank you," she says and hugs him tight.

"Miss Masters, please," he says, "I'm on duty."

Kathy calms a little and notices all eyes are on the two of them. She blushes, kisses the captain on the cheek, and stands up.

"I take it you got the gift," he says.

"Yes." She says grinning.

"I take it you like it?"

"Oh yes."

The captain smiles. "I'm glad you like it. And does Cindy like her gifts?"

"Yes, very much."

* * *

Kathy is interrupted in the telling of the story by her phone ringing. When she answers it, it's the principal of Cindy's school. She speaks quickly to him, then hangs up.

"Steve we'll have to continue this tomorrow. I have to go get Cindy."

"One second, Kathy." Steve buzzes his receptionist. "Clear my schedule for tomorrow. Reschedule the meetings I have to have."

"Yes, Mr. Baker." The receptionist replies.

He looks up at Kathy. "I'll be here by 8:00. Please come in as soon as you can."

"I'll try to be here at eight," she replies. Then she asks hesitantly, "Could you advance me some of that money? I need it." Kathy is more embarrassed than she's ever been.

"Of course," he says. He hands her $500 cash and writes her a check for $10,000. Kathy takes them and puts them in her worn purse.

"Thank you," she says without looking him in the eye.

"It's okay, Kathy," he says. "I know it's been tough since you were rescued."

"Yes, rescued," she says softly.

When Kathy gets to the street, she hails a cab. After giving the driver directions to Cindy's school, she sits back, relieved. Now she can pay the back rent and get something other than ramen to eat. When Kathy gets to the school, she heads to the principal's office. Cindy is sitting in a chair by his door. She looks up at Kathy.

"Hi, Mom," she says. And for a moment, she looks much like she did on the *Rapier*. Kathy rubs his wedding ring then knocks on the door.

"Come in, Miss Masters," the principal says.

She looks at Cindy. "Let's go," she says to her.

It only takes five minutes; she's been expelled. Kathy calls a cab. The two of them wait in front of the school; neither says anything. A couple of the kids wave at Cindy. They look like kids that would be outcasts among the students. Most of the kids give Cindy either looks of hatred or fear. The two of them get in the cab. Finally, Kathy can't hold back.

"Did you really have to tie the captain of the football team and his cheerleader girlfriend to the gym wall?"

"Uh, Mom…"

"In their underwear?"

"They're both scurvy assholes."

Kathy snaps, "You're not a damn pirate, young lady. You don't use that language. And this is the second school you've been expelled from this year. Sixth since we were released."

She gives Kathy that familiar look. "Mommy, I'm sorry," she says, but Kathy knows she's not. Being back has been hard on both of them, but it's like it's killing Cindy inside. She hasn't smiled since that day, and Kathy wonders if she ever will again.

"I've sold our story," Kathy says to her. "It's good money. Now we can get a small house and live like normal people."

"I'm not normal, Kathy," she snaps, "and neither are you. And I don't want a house. I want to go home. I want to go where we both belong, Mom." Her words cut deep, and tears run out of Kathy's eyes.

"We can't go home, sweetie. It's gone. The *Rapier* is gone."

"Then let's get a home of our own. We can get Thom and Mike released. Doc and Cookie would go with us. And Lien, she'll go with us to help with little James. I'm sure of that. That's a crew, Mom. The seven of us can make a home of our own. And maybe Captain Gibb and the commodore got away. Maybe they'll find us if we go back out there." Kathy looks at her through her tears and doesn't have to say a word. She knows what Kathy would say. She bursts into tears and holds Kathy tight; it's a very tearful ride to their flat.

In the morning, Cindy goes with Kathy to see Steve. He grins when he sees her, "I've very much wanted to meet you," he says to Cindy. She just nods. "Please sit," Steve says as he points to the chairs before his desk.

While they sit down Steve looks them over. Kathy is wearing the same dress suit she wore the day before, but has her coat off. Cindy is wearing shorts and a tank top. He notices she is quite pretty, long blond hair in a braid that goes down her back to her waist. Her eyes are crystal blue. She's about the same height as Kathy, roughly 155 centimeters. Like Kathy, Cindy is lithe, maybe weighing 50 kilograms. But what really catches his eye are the tattoos on Cindy's left arm. They're located on the inner aspect of her arm and are quite detailed. Steve looks over at Kathy and notices 'ink' showing through the thin material of her left sleeve.

He has his receptionist bring him coffee and cocoa for Kathy and Cindy. When everyone has their drinks, Steve says, "What was the second thing?"

"Excuse me," Kathy replies.

"The second thing, yesterday you said two things happened at the end of those seven months?"

"Oh yes, well, the second thing was…"

* * *

It's been a week since Cindy's birthday. Except for training, the captain has been busy. They've hardly seen him. It's "evening," and Kathy sits with Cindy in the observation dome. The stars seem more beautiful tonight, and she uses the computer to teach Cindy about the stars in this sector. Suddenly, Kathy feels someone standing near her. She turns around, and Captain Black is standing behind her.

"Good evening, Miss Masters." He nods his head to her then picks up Cindy and gives her a big hug.

"Good evening Captain," Kathy says. For some reason, she can't help but smile.

"I thought I might find you two up here." He points to a cluster of dust. "We're headed there for gunnery practice."

Cindy squeals. "Can I fire the big guns?"

The captain replies, "Well, that's why we're headed there. It's time you learn the weapon systems."

Kathy asks, "Is that a good idea? She's still a little girl."

"She'll do fine, Miss Masters," the captain says, grinning. "We'll be there tomorrow." He puts Cindy down. "I've got to get back to the bridge. We're upgrading our maneuvering engines, so I'll be at it most of the night." He starts to leave then stops. "I'm going to take dinner in my quarters tomorrow night. I was wondering if you ladies would join me?"

Kathy blushes a little, then before she can answer, Cindy jumps up and says, "Oh yes, we will be there."

"Excellent," the captain replies. "I'm looking forward to it." He returns to the bridge.

It takes Kathy awhile to get to sleep that night, and morning comes too soon. All she can think of is dinner tonight. Cindy wakes her. "Get up. We can't be late," she chirps. "Up, sleepy head." She's already dressed and she's brushed her teeth too. Kathy climbs out of her bunk, washes up, and gets dressed for the day. After breakfast they head to the bridge. Mr. Gibb meets them on the way.

"Good morning," he says.

"I'm going to fire the big guns," Cindy almost sings.

"I know," says Mr. Gibb. "And I'm going to teach you how. And guess what."

"What?" Cindy nearly screams with excitement.

"You're going to get to fire the particle beams and the rail guns."

"Really!" she squeals.

"Yes, ma'am," Mr. Gibb replies.

Cindy jumps up and hugs him. Though Kathy is smiling, she can't help being a little concerned. "Those are very powerful weapons," she says.

"Don't worry, Miss Masters. I'll be right with her, and the captain plans on teaching you the tactical station."

Her heart skips a beat. He's going to be teaching me himself, and tactical is kind of closed in. We're going to be very close.

The day rushes by way to quick. Cindy blasts asteroid after asteroid into dust. The beams are flashy, but it's the rail guns she really loves to shoot.

Kathy and the captain spend the whole day in tactical. She didn't realize how much there was to learn—sensor arrays, 3-D holographic projections, relative velocity course plotting, just so much. But the captain is a really good teacher, and she picks it up quickly. Several times, he touches her hand, and the warmth of the touch lingers. Kathy can see the captain feels it too, but he doesn't pursue it. Still she can't miss the gentleness in his voice.

Dinner is magical. Kathy decides to wear a very fashionable dress. It's not cut too revealing, but it does enhance her figure. And she dresses Cindy in a beautiful dress as well. When they enter his quarters, the captain pins a corsage on Kathy and then Cindy. To her surprise, the captain wears a suit and has two stewards in his quarters to serve everything. He sits across from Kathy, and most of the evening she catches him looking at her. At the end of the evening he gives Cindy a small gift, a gilded music box. Then he gives Kathy a small pair of diamond earrings. He says as he puts them on her ears, "The night before the attack, I bought these for my wife. Then Mr. Gibb and I went to the underwater mountain to work on the diving suit vault, so I never got to give them to her. But I kept them all this time." He lightly kisses Kathy's forehead "Now, I know I was supposed to give them to you."

He walks them to their quarters. "It's been a lovely evening, my ladies." He kisses Cindy on the top of her head. "Good night, my little princess," he says. Then he kisses Kathy lightly on the cheek. "Good night, Miss Masters." He steps back and gives them both a slight bow and returns to his quarters.

* * *

Captain Black removes his coat and tie, as he hangs them in his locker he finds himself thinking about the girls. While he takes off his trousers thoughts of his wife and daughter mix together with his musings about Kathy and Cindy. Soon they coalesce into a whole.

Would Mary have turned out as energetic and precocious as Cindy? If she were here today would they become friends? Would I bring Mary onto this ship?

And Kathy, what about her? It's uncanny how much she looks like Jenny? If they were the same age people would mistake them for twins. As he puts on his pajama bottoms an even more disturbing thought crosses his mind. *Is my attraction to her genuine or because she is so much like Jenny? God I miss her so, is that why I want to be around Kathy so much? I'm an old fool, I'm forty years older than her, there could never be anything between us.*

Captain James Ulysses Black slips into a deep but troubled sleep as these thoughts dog his dreams.

* * *

The next morning, more gunnery training. Cindy has a knack for gunnery. The captain is watching Kathy run tactical. She feels his gaze on her, and it makes her feel warm inside.

The *Rapier* is moving slowly out of the asteroid cloud. Careful navigation is required to avoid all the flying rocks. Where a rock could be a hazard, Cindy blasts it with the particle beams. Late in the morning, Kathy notices a red dot appear on the tactical holographic projection. Before she can say anything, the sensor operator speaks up. "Captain, I've got a ship moving into range."

"What do you have, Mr. Reins?"

"Looks like a Beijing class merchantman, bearing 56 minus 23."

"Put it on the screen." The captain moves toward his chair.

"There it is, Captain," Mr. Reins says.

"Magnify." Displayed on the view screen is a large Chinese merchant ship.

"Time to intercept tactical?"

Kathy checks the relative movement of both ships. "About twenty minutes at current speed, Captain," she replies.

"What's our weapons status, Mr. Gibb?"

"All weapons fully charged and ready, Captain."

"Helm, plot an intercept."

"Aye, Captain," Mr. Rawls replies.

"Mr. Gibb, action stations, silent running."

"Aye, Captain." Mr. Gibb goes to the XO station and sets the crew on alert. "Action stations, silent running."

"Mr. Jamison, charge the neutron armor."

"Aye, Captain."

Kathy looks about and notes the Captain isn't having crew take hers and Cindy's stations. She speaks up, "Captain, she's just a little girl. I don't think she should be manning the main batteries."

The captain looks around, then remembers he set the gunner to other duties. It'll be several minutes until he could get to the bridge if called. "Mr. Gibb, man weapons, please."

"No!" Cindy protests. "I can do it."

Before Kathy can say anything the captain speaks up, "I know you can, princess, but Mr. Gibb needs the practice."

Sullenly she slips out of the gunner's seat. Mr. Gibb slips in and pulls her onto his lap. She sits there, grinning. The captain commands, "Belt in, everyone."

The *Rapier* creeps closer to the fat Chinese merchantman. The captain uses the asteroid cloud as cover, carefully slipping nearer to the Chinese ship. Soon the ship is in weapons' range. Suddenly the fat merchantman tries to turn away and moves in a downward direction, exposing an armed sloop that was hiding behind the cargo ship.

"Damn," the captain swears. "An auxiliary, Mr. Gibb, what do you think?"

"He's faster than we are, Captain, and we're too close to run."

"Aye, Mr. Gibb. Engineering, give me all the speed you can. Helm, three points off the starboard bow minus 180. Now!"

The helmsman turns toward the sloop, then dives fast. The ship plunges down. The sloop has turned toward the *Rapier*. It starts to pick up speed. Kathy looks at the dots on the tactical display and hears herself call out, "The sloop is closing, Captain, picking up speed." All the time she's thinking, *Is this really happening?*

"Hold steady, helm. It'll be a snapshot, Mr. Gibb. Be ready." The sloop is closing fast now, but it hasn't dived after the *Rapier* yet. "Range to target, Miss Masters?"

"Fifteen kilometers, Captain." She marvels at her voice. She's scared silly, but her voice sounds calm and professional.

"Helm, plus 165, give me full speed, use our new boost system." The ship pulls nose up. Additional power goes to the maneuvering engines. The ship leaps forward. The tactical system is screeching; *the target is in range, the target is in range.* "Fire!" shouts the captain.

Mr. Gibb hits the particle beam fire button. But before he can react, Cindy hits the rail guns and pumps the fire button four times. The ship shudders with each salvo.

The beams hit the sloop on its neutron armor. The armor bleeds most of the power out of the beams but enough gets through to punch a hole in the sloops hull, followed by the impact of eight solid slugs from the rail guns. With the neutron armor drained by the beams, the rail gun slugs rip right through it.

Sloops are small and have to be so fast they have no physical armor; it's too much weight. With no resistance from the neutron armor, the slugs blast through both sides of the sloop. It buckles and snaps in half.

The magnification is still on high, and Cindy sees bodies rush out of the now-dead sloop as the ship decompresses. Some are still alive as they are dumped into the vacuum of space. She can clearly see them struggle as the vacuum sucks the breath of life out of them. They start to swell up as their blood boils, and parts of their bodies burst from their internal pressure. The captain changes the magnification, but it's too late. Cindy has seen everything. She's horrified by what she just did and runs to her quarters, crying.

"Mr. Reins, relieve Miss Masters."

Kathy has already vacated the seat, heading after Cindy. She runs down the passageway after her, listening to commands from the captain as he engages the merchantman.

Cindy is under her covers, crying, holding Oscar tightly against her chest. Kathy runs in and takes her in her arms. She's screaming, "I killed them, I killed them!"

"It's okay, darling," Kathy says. "They'd have killed us if you didn't." Kathy knows Cindy doesn't believe that. She's not sure she believes it either.

"They were still alive, Mommy, still alive." She shakes violently.

Kathy vaguely hears the command, "Boarding teams to stations." The ship shudders as the grappling lines are fired, then another shudder from the breaching charges. "Boarders away."

It's some time before Cindy cries herself to sleep. Kathy realizes that until just then it was only a game to her, now it's so very real. Cindy sleeps in her arms; she doesn't know how long, but she hears the door open and the captain walks in.

"How is she?" he asks.

"She'll be okay," Kathy replies. "In a little while, she'll be okay." It sounds a lot like a prayer.

The captain says, "I'm sorry she saw that. It's hard for a grown-up, a baby shouldn't see such a thing."

"Yes, a baby shouldn't," she agrees.

"I'll be going, Kathy. Call me if you need me." The door closes. It's moments before she realizes it—he called her Kathy. She doesn't know it at the time, but it's one of the three times the captain will ever call her Kathy in the nine years she will spend on the *Rapier*.

* * *

Steve interrupts her; he's aghast. Kathy can feel Cindy tense up, and she knows what's coming, so she readies herself to stop her. Kathy calls up all her enhanced strength and reaction speed holding it in readiness. "They let her do that. They made a child do that. You'd think even pirates wouldn't do that to a child."

Cindy leaps, but Kathy's ready. She grabs her before she can get over the desk. "Cindy, stop it!" she yells.

Cindy's furious. It takes a couple of minutes, then she yells, "We weren't pirates! We were never pirates, none of us!"

Steve is so taken by surprise he nearly falls over. "Of course they were pirates. What else would you call them?"

Kathy says softly but firmly, "Privateers, we were privateers."

"Huh, what's the difference?"

"The difference is they were civilian spacers hired by a legitimate government to carry out raids on enemy shipping." Kathy brings up her holographic screen and opens a document. "Steve, do you know what a Letter of Marque and Reprisal is?"

"Uh, no."

"It's a letter issued by a government to private citizens, authorizing them to conduct raids on enemy commerce."

"What government authorized that?" he asks.

"The government of Delta 5 Gamma, more commonly known as Safe Port."

"The Chinese authorized all of this," he says incredulously.

"No, Steve, the legitimate government of Safe Port, the survivors of the Chinese attack." Kathy continues the story. "We got hurt on that raid…"

* * *

For days, Cindy won't leave her room. She refuses to talk to anyone but Kathy. Mostly she just sits, holds Oscar, and cries. The cook brings food for the two of them every day. He knocks on the door and waits for Kathy. Each time she answers, he asks, "How is she?"

"The same," Kathy replies.

He looks like he might cry. "Everyone is worried about her, about both of you, Miss Masters."

"Thank you, Cookie," she answers. "I'll let you know as soon as anything changes."

After a week, Mr. Gibb stops by. "How is she?" he asks.

"The same." Then Kathy asks, "Where are we headed?"

"Back to Safe Port."

That surprises her. "Why?" she asks.

He looks grim. "We lost five crewmen taking that merchantman. Apparently, they had Chinese troops on board. It was a very bad fight."

"Who was killed?" Kathy inquires.

"Jimmy Baker, Martin Lucas, Bob Levin, Mike McCurdy, and Jimmy Franks."

The last name jumps out in her mind. "Jimmy Franks, isn't he the young man from engineering?"

"Yes, miss," Mr. Gibb replies. Her heart sinks. Cindy had made friends with Jimmy during her engineering training. She would play games like Clue and Monopoly with him. Mr. Gibb continues, "We're taking them home, Miss Masters. Going to square up with their families and put them to rest on Safe Port."

"Yes, of course. How old was he?" she asks.

"Jimmy was seventeen," he replies.

That hits her hard. Kathy knew he was young, but she never thought he was that young. "Just a boy," she says.

"Yes, ma'am," Mr. Gibb replies. "But we've lost younger."

"Younger?" she asks.

"Yes, Miss Masters."

It never occurred to her that the ship would be crewed by such young people. "Why so young, Mr. Gibb?"

"Well, we're at war, Miss Masters."

"War?" she asks.

"Yes, ma'am, but you'll learn all about that when we reach Safe Port. Call me if you need me," Mr. Gibb says.

"Yes, of course." She sits on her bunk. *How do I tell Cindy?* Finally, she goes into her room. "Cindy."

"Yes, Kathy."

"I have some bad news."

She sits up; her eyes are red and puffy. "What?" she asks.

"Jimmy was killed taking the Chinese ship," she says. It just came out. Cindy is stunned. She wants to cry, but she has no tears left. Kathy sits and holds her. She shakes, shivers, but no tears. Oscar rubs up against Cindy, purring, trying to comfort her.

By time the *Rapier* approaches Safe Port, Cindy is going with Kathy to the crew's mess. All the crew try not to upset her, but it's easy to tell they're worried. The captain seems to not leave the bridge, so they don't see him in the mess. When the *Rapier* docks, the captain announces the shore party over the intercom; Kathy and Cindy aren't mentioned. When he finishes, Cindy is furious. She runs out the door, heading to the bridge. Kathy tries to keep up with her, but she's fast. She bursts onto the bridge.

"I'm going with you!" she shouts.

The captain is surprised at first, then he says, "I didn't think you'd want to go."

"I'm going!" she shouts.

The captain looks shocked for a moment, then he says, "Of course, princess."

She stomps off back to their quarters. Kathy looks at the captain. He won't look at her, but she can see he's hurting. However, Cindy needs her now. Kathy catches up to her in the passageway. She's steaming. "How could he leave us out of this?" she mumbles angrily. She stomps into her room. Kathy holds her until it's time to go. She shakes with fury and sorrow.

On the shuttle ride down, she says nothing; neither does the captain. Watching them Kathy can feel her heart breaking, and she's at a loss of what to say.

People greet the ship when it lands—hundreds of people, including the families of those killed. They all walk in a column to the churchyard. The priest is waiting there with five freshly dug graves. The coffins are carried from the skimmer and laid beside their final resting places. The priest performs the funeral rites, then they prepare to lower the coffins into the ground.

Cindy shouts, "I want to see him." Everyone stops.

"Cindy, please," Kathy says.

"I want to see him!" she shouts. She runs to Jimmy's coffin and starts pounding on it. "Open it, open it!" She keeps screaming. Jimmy's parents are about to collapse. Cindy keeps screaming, "Open it, open it!" The priest tries to pull her off, but she kicks him in the shin. She looks at Captain Black. "Open it!" she screams.

The captain walks up, bends over, and opens the coffin. Kathy holds Cindy as she looks inside. "Jimmy," she says softly. He was cleaned up well. It could have been an open coffin service, except for one thing. He was hit in the chest by a pulse rifle, and his shirt sinks into the hole.

His mother collapses, wailing.

Cindy reaches in and hugs him. "Jimmy," she says. "You're so cold." Then she cries. It's like an ocean being released. "Jimmy," she cries. She looks over at Jimmy's parents. His father is kneeling beside his mother; she's lying on the ground, weeping. Cindy says to them, "I'm going to kill them all." They look at her. Kathy holds her tighter.

"Cindy, don't say that." It's her voice and her words, but she doesn't remember saying it.

I'm going to kill them all!" she shouts. She looks at the captain. "I'm going to kill them all!" she yells louder.

Kathy looks at her face, and she knows the beautiful little girl she loves so much is forever changed, her innocence gone. Only six and no longer a child. It feels like an iron spike is being driven into Kathy's heart. Cindy looks at Kathy. "Mom, I'm going to kill them all."

The coffins are lowered; the graves, covered. Then the people all go to the town square. The Captain and the mayor step up on the speaker's platform as Mr. Gibb looks on. Kathy notices that the mayor keeps looking at her with a strange expression on his face. Captain Black starts to speak, "It's been eight years. I ask if the contract is completed, I ask the people if the contract is completed."

There's a lot of talk among the townsfolk, then the mayor steps up. "Before I call the vote, I state before all I don't believe it is completed yet. The Chinese are still here. We are still occupied. They still steal from us."

Captain Black says, "How many must we kill, Mr. Mayor. How many ships must we destroy?"

The mayor looks at Cindy before he answers, "All of them." He shouts to the people, "I move we vote the contract renewed, the letter of marque still active."

Captain Black asks, "How many of our own must we lose?"

"As many as it takes," replies the mayor.

The two men face off; the tension could be cut with a knife, but the townspeople all shout, "Continue the contract, blood for blood."

Captain Black's shoulders slump. "The contract is in force," he announces. Then he turns to the crowd. "Whose sons will go with me? I need five good souls that will be true before the mast."

Three men and two boys step forward. The captain looks at the boys, and so does Kathy. They are very young, maybe fourteen, certainly not older. "Are there any men that will step forward?" he asks. No others step out.

Kathy looks at him; she can feel herself saying, *Not these children.* "Truly," he says, "will no one take their place." No one moves. The captain looks at Kathy, then at Mr. Gibb. "Add them to the ship's rolls, Mr. Gibb."

The meeting is over. The townspeople go home, leaving the captain and all of the crew in the square. They go to the shuttle, lift off, and return to the *Rapier*.

CHAPTER 8

AN ACQUISITION

The *Rapier* moves on to its next destination. For the duration of the trip Cindy trains harder than ever, and she always is dressed like a buccaneer, hat and all. The only time she seems at peace is when she lies on her bunk, holding Oscar. Kathy tries, but she can't get her into a dress the whole trip. Kathy is worried she's losing the little girl part of Cindy and is at a loss for what to do.

A month later, the *Rapier* docks at Kyle's World. When the ship docks, the captain calls Kathy to the bridge.

"How is she?" he asks.

"Full of anger," she replies.

Sadness crosses the captain's face. "I'm so sorry, Miss Masters," he states.

"I know," she says.

Captain Black looks at Kathy. "We've got captives to sell. I'd like you and Cindy to accompany us to make the transaction."

* * *

Steve pauses the transcription bot. He looks at Kathy and Cindy. His expression is one of anger. Finally, he says, "I don't know which is more abhorrent, that he is selling people again or that he is making a young girl watch it. Kathy, what hold did this Svengali have on you?"

She touches the ring and says, "He had no hold on me, Steve. I did what I did because I chose to."

"That's not how it looks to me."

"Steve, once I became a member of the brotherhood, I could leave anytime I wanted to. I could take Cindy, cash out and go. They might not like it, but nobody would stop me, especially not the commodore. And yes, selling people like they were livestock is reprehensible, but you have no true knowledge of what life in the colonies is like. You most certainly don't know what life in the colonies the Chinese seized is like. What those people go through. You're making a judgment without knowledge of how these people live."

"And besides, if I hadn't gone to the auction, I would never have met my sister," Cindy says.

"What sister? We did a thorough check on you, and you're an only child," Steve replies.

"That's true," Cindy agrees, "but I'm a child of the brotherhood, and just like I got a hundred and seventy fathers-brothers, I could also gain a sister."

Steve thinks on that for a moment, then turns the transcription bot back on. Kathy continues.

* * *

"Why?" she asks. The thought of this turns her stomach.

"I'm hoping it will soften her heart seeing these poor wretches in this condition," he says.

"If you feel this way, why do you sell them?"

"Because they enslave us, and the letter directs me too, so I have to." Captain Black actually looks in distress over this, then he composes himself. "We leave in thirty minutes, Miss Masters. Please have our princess ready."

"Aye, Captain," she responds.

The party meets up near the shuttle bay. Mr. Gibb and two crewmen bring up the blindfolded captives. Three are men, one of which is a very distinguished-looking older man, and a young Chinese woman, perhaps fifteen or sixteen. "Miss Masters, I'd like to introduce Prince Chou Yen Yi and three of his grandchildren. He was on that freighter, which was quite a surprise. That's because he's a member of the imperial family and the architect of the Chinese invasion of several colonies during the Genetics War, and, of course, the man that directed the destruction of Safe Port." Kathy detects the emotion running rampant in the Captain. The casual observer wouldn't notice, but Kathy can feel it—it's taking all the restraint the Captain has to not kill this man. Kathy looks at Prince Yi with disgust.

Kathy looks over Prince Yi's grandchildren. The grandsons are tall like their grandfather. They're haughty, filled with their own selfimportance. Though frightened, they try to live up to what they believe their grandfather expects of them.

The young girl is a different story, she's terrified. Kathy estimates the girl is a few centimeters shorter than she is. Her long black hair hangs down to her waist. Though Kathy can't see her eyes the rest of her face is beautiful. Her nose is 'finely chiseled' and her lips are thin but provocative. Though she's part of the Yi family Kathy can't help feeling sympathy for the young Chinese girl. *She's just a child.*

Mr. Gibb pilots the shuttle to the planet's surface landing at the city of Helix. The party gets on two skimmers and rides into the city. They arrive at a large building with a fenced in courtyard, and they all go inside. A well-dressed man greets Captain Black.

"James, how are you, you old space dog?"

"Doing well, Sam. How about yourself?"

"Except for dodging Chinese, I'm doing well."

"That's good, Sam." Mr. Gibb brings forward the older Chinese gentleman. "I think you can get a good ransom on this one, Sam."

"Yes, I believe I can. Do you know who you have there?"

"Yes," the captain replies. "We also have his three grandchildren, Sam."

"Really," Sam says.

"I'd like them sold at auction to compensate my crew."

"That's dangerous, James."

"Life is dangerous, Sam." The captain glares at Prince Yi and continues "Besides Sam I want the prince to know what it's like to have those you love torn from you and enslaved. If I could I'd drop a massive rock on one of his grandchildren so he knows what that feels like too, but that wouldn't get my crew compensated." Captain Black's rage is so great he misses the momentary look of grief that his words cause to cross the older man's face.

"Okay, but I still think a ransom would be better. It'll take a day or two to set up the auction. Do you have a place to stay?"

"Not yet."

"Please stay with my wife and I. I think she'd enjoy the company."

"Thanks, Sam, we'd be delighted."

Sam has guards take the captives to cells, then leads the group to his estate. He obviously does well. His house is in the auction compound. It's luxurious and would be considered a Mediterranean villa on Earth. It has a large veranda with sweeping steps that lead up to a wide porch with huge wooden doors. Also on the grounds are patios, a garden, a gazebo, and a large lawn. Sam leads them into the entrance hall. This too is in the Mediterranean style. There is a vaulted ceiling and sweeping stairways that lead to the second floor.

Sam's wife is not what they expected. She's petite with blond hair and blue eyes. She says in a lilting musical voice, "Sam, you didn't tell me we were expecting guests."

"Viola, my love, this is Captain Black. I've told you about him."

"Oh yes, the great adventurer. I'm so pleased to finally meet you."

"It is an honor to be invited into your home, madam," the captain says as he bows. "This is my second in command, Mr. Gibb; our princess, Cindy; and her governess, Miss Masters."

"I'm so very pleased to meet all of you," she replies. "Sam, please show our guests to their rooms. I'll get refreshments started." She gives Sam a quick kiss on the cheek then disappears down the hall. Sam takes them upstairs and shows them to two large bedrooms that share a bathroom. The furnishings match the home's style and opulence.

They spend the next day relaxing. Good food, good conversation, and time to think—all except for Cindy. She spends most of her time practicing sword and pistol. And that's what Kathy thinks about most. *How do I get my little girl back?* is constantly on her mind. Kathy can tell that's what is foremost on the captain's mind too.

Sam and Viola have three children of their own, ages five through nine. They were expecting Cindy would be playing with them, but that's clearly not going to happen.

"James, what hatred burns so deep in one so young?" Sam asks.

"The hatred caused by the loss of a dear friend, and sadly the shame of causing another's death."

"Surely, one so young could not harm another!" Sam answers with surprise.

"Sam, my friend, because of my mistake, the little one killed a ship and got a close-up view of what she did. She saw men die in the cold of space because of her actions. And because of my hatred of the Chinese, I didn't prevent it. She burns inside because I failed her," the captain says sorrowfully. At first, Sam and Viola are without words. Viola actually starts to show anger at the captain, but Sam seems to feel his pain.

"My friend, we shall pray for you and her, pray for your healing."

The captain grips Sam's arm. "Thank you, brother."

That evening, Kathy and the captain walk through the garden. There's a gentle breeze that rustles the leaves.

"How do we get our little girl back?" Kathy asks.

"I do not know, Miss Masters. I truly do not know. I'm hoping the auction will have an impact that softens her heart." Kathy holds his arm while they walk among the flowers. As it grows late, the captain walks her to the room she shares with Cindy. He tips his hat to her, gives her a light kiss on the cheek, and says, "Sleep well, Miss Masters." Then he goes to the room he shares with Mr. Gibb. Kathy goes into her room. She spends a few moments, watching Cindy sleep. *She's so young. She needs to be a little girl. How do I help her through this?*

The auction comes together faster than he expected; bidders arrive the next day, so Sam gathers them together for the event,

"Come, my friends, it is time." He leads them from the house, down his private drive then they enter the courtyard of the compound. Mr. Gibb leaves to ready the skimmers to return to the shuttle while Kathy, the Captain and Cindy take seats in the bleachers of the bidding theatre. The bidders are already gathered there, though there is room for more people. The three young Chinese are brought to the courtyard as a crowd of onlookers gathers to watch them being sold. The auction begins.

First, they auction off the oldest grandson. He's obviously a healthy, strong man in his midtwenties. Though he's never done manual labor, he could do any kind of physical work. The auctioneer starts the bidding at $1,000. "Who will give a $1,000 for this fine specimen of a man? He'll work hard from sun up to sun down for many years." Soon people start to bid in earnest—$1,000, $1,050, $1,100, etc.

Cindy watches dispassionately at first. She remains distant. But Kathy can see her slowly becoming uncomfortable.

As the bidding increases, the young Chinese man grows more distressed. He tries to hide it, but his discomfort becomes more evident. The last bid is $2,200, and the man is taken away.

His younger brother and sister are weeping openly now. They hold to each other, crying out, "Let us go, we want to go home!" Both Kathy and Cindy remember being in the brig and crying out the same words, "I want to go home!"

The crowd is almost vicious in its actions at the auction. They jeer and cheer at the poor wretches being sold. "Serves you right, you Chinese beasts!" is shouted out often. Some people throw rotting produce at them.

Kathy looks at the captain. He appears to be totally devoid of feelings, but she knows him better now. She can see all the signs of his discomfort, and can feel his desire to put an end to this.

Cindy's uncaring demeanor is starting to crack. To those that don't know her, she's cold as ice. But Kathy can see the ice slowly breaking and sliding away.

The guards drag the younger brother to the auction block. His sister shrieks in fear, crying, "No, no, let us go. I want to go home!"

Kathy hears Cindy sniffle. The auctioneer shouts, "Who will give me a $1,000 for this fine specimen? He's young, he's strong, you'll get many years of hard labor out of him."

The man falls down on the auction block, weeping. He wails, "Let me go, I've done you no harm, let me go!" The bidding goes faster this time—$1,000, $1,100, $1,200, etc. The final bid is $1,800, and his new owners drag the young man away. He struggles as they do, and his new owners beat him with a baton to get control of him. Soon the poor wretch is bleeding from several lacerations and appears to have some broken bones. He also spits out a tooth.

Kathy feels sick inside. She looks around; the captain is visibly disturbed. Cindy has a tear in her eye.

When the girl is put on the block, the crowd gets real nuts. Woof whistles and catcalls ring out.

"Now, you'll get yours, bitch!" erupts from the observers.

"You're going to get what you deserve, you Chinese whore!"

The auctioneer starts the bidding at $500. "This beautiful young Chinese maiden will be a fine addition to your household. She can do all the housework. Or perhaps she can warm your bed, maybe both. Then again for you businessmen and businesswomen, she could be a new addition to your brothel."

Kathy looks about. She's sure she sees pimps, madams, and all sorts of deviants.

The girl is terrified. She falls down on the block, begging, pleading, "Let me go home! I want to go home!"

Cindy leans in. "Mom, we have to save her. We can't let those people have her."

Someone bids $1,500. The next guy bids $2,000. Suddenly Kathy shouts, "$20,000." Everyone stops. All eyes are on her. Cindy stares at Kathy with pride.

Captain Black whispers, "What are you doing?"

"I'm buying her."

"What?" the captain says.

"I'm buying her."

"How?" the captain asks.

"With my and Cindy's share," Kathy replies. "We are due a share aren't we?"

"Yes," the captain states.

"Then I'm buying her."

The auctioneer asks, "Are there any more bids?"

"She'll betray us," the captain says.

"Perhaps," Kathy states, "But I couldn't live with myself knowing what they'll do to her. Perhaps we can leave her someplace safe later. I don't care. I'm not going to let them hurt her."

The captain tips his hat to Kathy.

"Once, twice, three times," the auctioneer says. "Sold to the lady with Captain Black."

With the auction ended, the bidders and observers leave. They all look at the pirate queen that bought back what she was selling. Cindy glares at them. Apparently, she's developed a withering glare. They bow their heads and slink off. The captain calls Mr. Rawls, the ships purser, "Have Cindy's and Miss Masters's shares liquidated. If they don't come to $20,000 total, transfer the difference from my account. Wire it to the planetary account of Samson ben Guirion. Signal me when that's completed."

Sam comes up. "Well, this is a first for my little establishment," he says, grinning. He hugs Kathy. "Miss Masters, you are a wonder." He bows to her. "My wife will never believe this." Sam laughs out loud.

Captain Black picks up Cindy. "I'm proud of you," he says. "The hatred of the Chinese burns in all of us, my princess. But we must always remember we are all God's children and not do cruelty to others. I'm so proud of you."

She hugs the captain with all her might. "I will try, Father," she says to him.

The captain bows to Kathy. "You continue to amaze me, Miss Masters." Kathy blushes. The captain's comm beeps. He checks it. "Sam, our business is complete. Please thank your lovely wife for being such a great hostess to us. Be safe, Sam. I hope to see you again soon."

"Safe journeys, my friends," Sam says as they leave.

* * *

Steve asks, "So when did you meet this new sister, Cindy, and who was she?"

Kathy responds, "I thought that was obvious, Steve. We checked with her last night to be sure it was okay to publish this. Cindy's new sister is Lien Lan Yi, daughter of the house of Yi, princess of the imperial court and niece of His August Majesty Chou Zen Tse, emperor of the Chinese prefecture."

Steve's jaw actually drops.

* * *

They board the skimmers and head back to the ship. At first, the Chinese girl is still terrified. She shakes uncontrollably. But Cindy takes off her weapons belt, hands it to the captain, and slips beside the young girl and hugs her. "You'll never have to be afraid again," Cindy tells her. "I'll always protect you." Then she tells the girl, "I'm Cindy, and she is Kathy, and you are now our sister."

The Chinese girl hesitates a moment, then says, "I'm Lien Lan Yi of the house of Yi, and I am at your service."

Once back on the ship, the captain puts an additional bunk in Cindy's room for Lien. He provides her ship's uniforms and allows her to get additional women's clothing from the ship's stores.

Lien tends to hang on Kathy and Cindy. She's still terrified, but she knows she won't be hurt there as long as she's with them. The Chinese girl seems to be a loyal servant to Kathy and Cindy. She helps Kathy care for and teach Cindy. She knows history, math, and science in depth. She understands politics quite well, as one might expect of a member of the Chinese court.

Before long, she bonds with Kathy, Cindy, and Oscar. Lien becomes very fond of Oscar, and he showers her with his loving indifference. Often, Kathy finds Cindy and Lien playing with Oscar, now weighing in at five kilos, when it's past Cindy's bedtime.

Though the crew openly hate Chinese, they soon become neutral toward her, some even become friendly.

The *Rapier* moves on toward its next hunting ground.

CHAPTER 9

UPGRADES

Upon leaving Kyle's World, Captain Black heads toward Chinese space to continue raiding. By happenstance, he lays his course toward Safe Port. Soon the blue star can be seen from the observation dome.

Kathy's sleep is fitful. She tosses and turns all night. When she does sleep, her mind is filled with strange images, and she hears/feels, *Come*. She wakes in the morning covered in sweat. Cindy comes into her bunkroom. She too has not slept.

"Mommy, I think we are supposed to go see the gods."

Lien looks at her questioningly, "Gods?" she asks.

"Yes," Kathy responds, "the gods of the aquatic people of Safe Port."

Lien asks, "Are such things possible?"

Cindy hugs her. "Oh yes, sister, very possible, you'll see."

They go to the crew's mess together and sit near the captain. He too looks as if he hasn't slept. But before Kathy can say anything, a loud crash of pots and pans comes from the galley followed by Cookie yelling, "Cindy, get this damn cat out of my galley!" Then a loud screech and hiss from Oscar.

Oscar comes sprinting out of the galley and leaps up onto the table where Cindy is sitting. He rubs against her, then turns to face an enraged Cookie, who stumbles out of the galley armed with a rolling pin. "Where is he? Where is he?" Cookie shouts. Oscar hisses again, then growls. He's grown quite a bit. Oscar now weighs seven kilos and is over forty-four centimeters in length. He stands proudly before Cindy, ready to protect her from the ship's cook. "I'm gonna clobber that damn cat!" Cookie shouts.

"No you're not!" Cindy yells back. Lien is very distraught by the whole thing, but Kathy bursts out in laughter.

Captain Black tells Cookie, "Perhaps it would be best if you continue preparing breakfast. Mr. Jensen, please give Cookie all the assistance he needs."

"Aye, sir," they both reply. As they head to the galley, Oscar takes a victory lap around the table, then sprints out of the crew's mess down the passageway toward their quarters.

The captain looks at Cindy and says, "I think you need to teach Mr. Oscar some manners, princess. He seems to not respect Cookie's domain."

She chuckles. "Yep, that does seem to be the case."

Kathy asks the captain, "Did you have trouble sleeping too?"

"Yes," he replies. "Seems we are being asked to return to Safe Port."

"I think you're right," Kathy agrees.

After checking, it seems all those with implants are being called back—five in all when you add in Mr. Gibb and the doctor. So the *Rapier* makes best possible speed to Safe Port. After a week, the *Rapier* docks with the asteroid. The five of them, with the addition of Mr. Rawls and Lien, debark in the shuttle and head to the planet's surface.

For the first time, Lien sets eyes on Mr. Gibb. At first, she just thinks of him as another white devil. Then she notices his eyes, those deep-green eyes. For the rest of the shuttle ride, those eyes are all she can think of.

Mr. Rawls lands near the church. They unload the skimmer and secure the shuttle. Mr. Gibb drives them to the rocky cove. There, the sub awaits. Lien has never been in a sub before. She discovers she's very claustrophobic; they have to sedate her for that leg of the journey. Kathy sits with her, holding her hand for as long as they're on the sub. "It'll be okay, Lien," Kathy says gently. "It'll be okay."

Porge awaits them on the little island. "Yrbb lte." He admonishes them, then dives into the water. They follow him to the submerged mountain and the secret cave. They enter the cave and begin preparations. Cindy shows Mr. Rawls how to do the suit system checks under Mr. Gibb's supervision. Kathy tries to prepare Lien for the next stage of the journey. It's a tough sell, and she remains dubious.

"So was I," Kathy says gently. "But I made the dive and am just fine. You will be too."

"Okay," Lien replies, but it's clear she doesn't believe it.

The captain prepares the injections. Cindy walks over in her dive suit. She hands Kathy her underwater camera. "Mommy, it's time to get Lien ready."

Lien looks like she's near panic. Kathy tries to calm her, but it seems to only excite her more.

"Lien, sweetie, it's okay. Both Cindy and I have made this dive. They call for you. They will protect you."

"No, no, I can't do this, I can't." She's in a state of panic now.

"Sister, I made the dive and came back safe. You'll be fine, honest," Cindy says, trying to calm her.

"No, no, no, it's not possible, I can't do it!"

Kathy holds her hand and says, "Trust us, sweetie. We'll be with you all the way. Cindy will stay beside you, and I'll have your hand in mine."

"No, I can't. No, I can't!"

The captain solves the problem by giving her the injection before suiting her up. He adds a touch more in the shot, and she becomes very docile. Mr. Gibb and Kathy get Lien suited up. As he helps Kathy, Jimmy Gibb looks upon Lien. The thought strikes him, *She's beautiful.* But she's just sixteen and part of the hated Chinese royal family. He gets back to the task at hand. Then they help Mr. Rawls. Next, Mr. Gibb gets Doc Smith ready. Finally, the captain and Mr. Gibb get each other ready. Then helmets, fluid, cables, and they're ready to dive.

"Lbts gh," Porge says. He actually seems impatient. They all enter the water and turn on their lights. Kathy starts shooting pics. It seems to her there's even more variety of life than the last time.

Several varieties of fish flit about. Large aquatic mammals play in the warm water. The deeper they go, the stranger the denizens of this ocean world become.

The captain has Cindy monitor Lien. Mr. Gibb keeps an eye on Mr. Rawls as this is his first dive. Porge guides them to the bottom and then to the city. When Kathy sees the city, she starts to shoot a pic of it, then stops. As she thinks on whether she should, she hears/feels, *Yes.* She starts shooting.

It's even more impressive than she remembers. The gargantuan structures emanate light. The architecture is alien yet familiar. Massive obelisks rise from the ocean floor toward the surface of the sea. Wide boulevards are flanked by massive templelike structures. Porge brings them before the god on the dais.

Lien and Mr. Rawls are stunned into silence by the sight. For them, like it was for Kathy during her first time, it is mind-numbing. They move robotically for the duration of the visit. When they all wake, the checks of their upgrades are completed. That's when they are surprised by what the gods have for them next. They all hear/feel *New ship systems. All key areas. Propulsion, hyperspace, and maneuvering. Sensors, survey, and combat. Neutron armor 85 percent efficiency increase. Particle beam output 70 percent increase. Rail gun terminal energy increase 110 percent. Missile warhead energy release increase 40 percent. All needed modules ready for installation per ship's standard schematics.* Everyone is confused.

The captain says, "I don't understand."

Modules are being readied for transport to ship. Everyone is still confused. The god scans them all. *Modules install to ship systems. Enough for several ships. Will save your lives.* The last part resolves only in Kathy's and Cindy's minds, though they don't know it. *Will buy your freedom. Go now.*

They exit the throne room to the antechamber, where Porge waits for them. Then Porge leads them back. The captain has everyone adjust their suits for surfacing. They rise to the cavern entrance, then enter the lagoon. The seven of them rest for awhile and then board the sub. Cindy pilots the sub under Mr. Gibb's careful tutelage. This time, Porge stays with them all the way back to the cove.

When they get back, they find forty nanchiks stacking containers on the beach. Porge points to them and says, "Fr u." Then he swims out to sea. There's far too many of them for the shuttle. The captain calls the ship, "Mr. Hansen, have Mr. Hahn bring down shuttle 2 with a four-man work crew."

"Aye, Captain." It takes forty-five minutes for the second shuttle to arrive. In that time, the first shuttle is fully loaded. Everybody but the captain lift off for the *Rapier*. On the trip up, Cindy works with Lien, helping her get used to her new enhancements.

"These are totally cool, sister," Cindy tells Lien. "Now blink and at the same time think magnify."

Lien looks at the controls. She focuses in on the velocity readout. It takes up her whole field of view. She can actually see the circuitry behind it. "How . . . how is this possible?"

"The nanchik gods are the most amazing bioengineers, sister," Cindy replies. "We've been given great gifts, so we must use them as intended," she tells Lien.

Kathy watches, feeling a little better about Cindy. She has become close to Lien, and the hate in her doesn't burn as bright. Kathy can't help think, *Perhaps I'll get some of my little girl back.*

* * *

The nanchik gods start their commune.
Chosen.
Are they best choice?
Yes.
Son of the Stars?
Yes.
The debate starts. What is the best way to deal with mankind?

* * *

Upon docking, the crew off-loads the containers. By time the captain returns, shuttle 1 is completely unloaded. Chief Engineer Simms is going through a ship set of containers.

"Captain, this is amazing. If these work as described, no one will ever be able to catch us or outgun us short of navy ships. The sensors can detect a tick in the next quadrant. The neutron armor will be able to take a hit from a cruiser. This is incredible."

"Thank you, Mr. Simms. Let's get a set operational and test them out."

"Aye, Captain. Oh, Captain, I can't figure out how to open these cases to look over the components."

"Don't try, Mr. Simms. You can't, and if you did, you'd kill them."

"Kill them?"

"Yes, Mr. Simms, kill them. The components are alive." Mr. Simms is stunned.

It takes four days to install all the components and run basic system tests. The sensor package is the easiest to field test. The improvements are phenomenal. They are able to track Oscar-sized animals on the surface of Safe Port from where they are docked on the asteroid. The deep survey sensors allow them to pick up ships and space objects at one and a half times as far away as the unenhanced sensors. The tie into tactical and targeting indicates a significant improvement in weapons accuracy, but that has to be field-tested.

"Captain, I'd like to test maneuvering and weapons next, then hyperspace engines," Mr. Simms says.

"Agreed, Mr. Simms, set up your test protocols with Mr. Gibb."

"Aye, Captain."

An hour later, Mr. Gibb and Mr. Simms return with their test plan. Captain Black looks it over and approves it. "Mr. Gibb, have Miss Masters on tactical and Cindy on weapons for the duration of the test. Have Mr. Andjek stand by with Cindy. Also, have neutron armor at max power in case we bump into one of these rocks."

"Aye, Captain," Mr. Gibb replies.

After another hour, they're ready to start the test. Once all stations are manned, the ship moves into the asteroid belt. Kathy keeps close watch at tactical, feeding targeting information to Cindy and Mr. Andjek. Cindy vaporizes any errant asteroids that the sensors indicate could be a danger.

At first, Kathy doesn't notice them, but there's another set of controls on the tactical touch display. When she does notice them, she looks at them carefully, then calls out, "Captain, there are now weapons firing controls on the tactical display."

"What?" Mr. Gibb asks as he moves to the tactical station. "She's right, Captain. There's a set of firing controls for primary batteries, secondary batteries, and missiles."

"That's unexpected," Captain Black says. "Check all other displays that were affected by the upgrades. There may be more surprises." And there were. The helm now has an axillary reactor and power control. The weapons station has a limited alternate tactical system. Sensors are augmented by neutron armor activation and boost, plus a tertiary tactical display. All these receive basic testing. After an hour, Mr. Gibb and Mr. Simms report to Captain Black.

"Sir, she handles like a fighter among all this. None of the asteroids have come close. We slip around these rocks like eels," Mr. Simms says with a big grin.

"And the weapons, Mr. Gibb?"

"Cindy, how much power have you been using?" Mr. Gibb asks.

"Less than 30 percent, Mr. Gibb," she replies.

"Even on that last big rock?"

"Yes, sir," she says. The three men look at her with astonishment.

"Well, that's a surprise," Captain Black says. "I think short of actual combat we've tested that as much as we can. We still need to test the hyperspace generators. How much space do the remaining crates take up, Mr. Simms?"

"Too much. Some are stacked outside of storage."

"So we need to find someplace to cache them."

"Yes, sir."

"Then let's test the hyperspace generators Mr. Gibb, lay in course for our Alpha Six."

"Are you sure, Captain?"

"Aye, Mr. Gibb. It's the one place no one besides us has found."

"Aye, Captain."

"Captain, there's something else," Mr. Simms says.

"What's that, Mr. Simms?"

"We have small sets that would work for fighters or shuttles. I'd like to put a couple on the shuttles, sir."

"Okay, Mr. Simms, have them ready by time we arrive at our destination."

"Aye, sir."

The *Rapier* moves outside the asteroid belt. Course to Alpha Six is laid in, and the ship makes the translation to hyperspace. The instruments show the *Rapier* is traveling faster than it ever has before. This trip will only take a week, almost twice as fast as the last trip there.

When they arrive at Alpha Six, the whole crew is on pins and needles; everyone is on highest alert. This is because Alpha Six is deep in an American military zone and it is heavily patrolled.

It takes several hours to unload the spare sets and conceal them. American patrol ships passed close by twice as they worked. Soon all the ship sets are secured deep in a cavern. Vault doors are locked; boulders are moved into the opening. Camouflage materials cover the cavern entrance. The Captain keeps two ship and eleven fighter/shuttle sets onboard. Then the *Rapier* quietly slips back into Chinese space. The crew now knows they are on the fastest, most powerful ship of its type, perhaps the fastest in all the known galaxy. Full of confidence, they go on the hunt.

* * *

Steve sits with an astonished expression on his face. "You're telling me that you had biologically engineered system enhancements that were alive?"

"Being as they were biologically engineered, it only makes sense they'd be alive, Steve," Kathy answers.

"And they made your ship more powerful than any other ships of that type."

"Yes, indeed, more powerful, faster, better sensors, and better armor," she replies.

"And more powerful weapons," Cindy states.

"Do the Americans know about this?"

"Of course, Steve. We had to trade the extra ship sets for our freedom."

"Trade? No, the Americans rescued you."

"That's the story, but none of it is true." Kathy shakes her head; Cindy just burns with fury. "They told the world they rescued us from the infamous pirate. The truth is that after nearly a year of interrogation and medical experiments on us, we bought our freedom by telling them where we stashed the ship sets the gods gave us."

"Yeah," Cindy says with a grimace on her face. "How do you think the Americans are beating the Chinese? They have a special battle group equipped with what we gave them."

For the second time Steve seems shaken. "It's hard when things you've believed to be true are proven to be lies, isn't it?" Kathy says softly to him.

CHAPTER 10

HERE BE WHALES

The next three years seem to go by in a haze. Raids, deals made and ship life. Kathy documents it all in her journal, and captures everything with her camera in pics and vids. Still, time seems to just rush by.

In that time, the *Rapier* takes forty ships—mostly Chinese but about a dozen are American, French, and German. Four of the Chinese ships are auxiliaries, and they are particularly satisfying. The crew takes great delight in killing Chinese warships. It's more dangerous but, to the crew, it seems more like justice. Fortunately the captain is good at picking ships that aren't too powerful, and with the enhanced systems he always has an ace up his sleeve.

Cindy is more like herself now, but the child she was just isn't there anymore. Even Oscar and her closeness with Lien doesn't bring out the little girl she used to be. Kathy's little girl seems to be gone, except on birthdays.

The last two of her birthdays, the captain tried to do something special for her. When she turned seven, he took her to see the great floaters of Omega Delta Pi. For her eighth birthday, they went to Psi Beta 6 to see the moon bats. But this one he really outdoes himself.

A week before Cindy's ninth birthday, Captain Black has the *Rapier* go outside her usual patrol area. He keeps the destination to himself. When asked, he just smiles. But the *Rapier* stays in hyperspace most of the time and moves at flank speed the whole time.

The captain still trains Kathy and Cindy with the sword, and Kathy gets more training on ship functions. Kathy and Cindy study math, astrophysics, and astronavigation. Lien helps Kathy teach Cindy how to be a young girl, no small task, all things considered. She also teaches Cindy and Kathy Earth and galactic history, some from a Chinese perspective.

Another change is that Mr. Gibb and Captain Black start supervising Cindy and Kathy in teaching Lien how to use weapons. They were hesitant at first, but Cindy made a good case for it.

"What if we get boarded? We'll need everybody to stand and fight. And if I'm expected to defend the ship, she will be too. Besides, Captain, you can't expect her to watch over me if she can't fight," Cindy says, laughing. Then she cuddles the captain and says, "Besides, Daddy, it'll sharpen mine and Mommy's skills by teaching another."

"Princess, you can be a real pain sometimes," the captain replies.

"Thought that's why you love me," she giggles.

It seems Lien had some training growing up, so she's not totally ignorant on the subject. Her style is a good deal different than theirs with a sword, and she strikes fast as a viper.

The captain keeps his distance, yet whenever Kathy and Captain Black touch, the feeling is still strong. He tries to hide his reactions to her touch, but she knows him better now. To her he's an open book.

The ship moves into Russian space, carefully avoiding detection. The *Rapier* creeps deeper into the sector. It avoids five patrol ships on the way.

One day, Kathy bumps into the captain in the passageway.

"Are we going to raid Russian ships?" she asks.

"No, Miss Masters."

"Then why are we going there?"

"For Cindy's birthday surprise," he replies.

"What surprise?" she asks.

"You'll see," he says with a devilish grin.

The *Rapier* slips silently further into Russian space and approaches a large gaseous cloud. Tens of thousands of kilometers of a gas cluster—a colorful collection of hydrogen and other gases, perhaps one or more failed stars. It's here that the captain's birthday surprise waits for Cindy.

The big day arrives. The crew throws a great party for her, and she is much like the daughter Kathy adopted. For this little bit of time, she's a little girl again and, of course, their princess. The crew participates in games, and there's dancing. Each crew member has a short dance with her. Soon it's time for the cake and ice cream.

Lien tries to be joyful, but she knows she's a slave, and it's hard for her. Both Kathy and Cindy are acutely aware of this, so Cindy provides her own birthday surprise.

Just before the presents are opened, Cindy stands and says, "Brothers, my dear fathers, we have among us one that has been chosen by the nanchik gods to be worthy of gifts, yet here she is a slave. She was born of our enemies but to me she is my sister. To my mother, she is a dear friend, an older daughter. And many of you have awoken in Doc Smith's sickbay to find her caring for you. So I ask you all present, let us declare her free and sister to us all."

At first, silence. One could hear a pin drop. It's hard for them. Almost everyone here lost all they knew to the Chinese. And Lien Lan Yi is not just any Chinese. She is an imperial princess and grand-daughter to the author of the destruction of Safe Port. Everyone here knows all this. Mr. Hahn speaks first. "That's a lot to ask, princess. A lot, indeed." He looks like he's challenging all he believes inside.

Mr. Rawls says, "I was not born on Safe Port, so I know little of your pain. But Lien Lan Yi teaches our daughter. She tends our wounds, and to all of us, she has always shown a gentle hand. I vote yes to our daughter's request."

Mr. Hansen talks next, "I hate the Chinese and all they stand for. They took everything from me." He points to Lien. "But this woman has been so much to us. I stand with Mr. Rawls. Let her be free and let us compensate our princess, her mother, and Lien for time served."

Mr. Andjek steps up. "They took all from us, all. As far as I know, I'm the last of my family. There are no more. The hate of the Chinese burns deep in me. But I cannot hate her. She has made our daughter into such a fine young woman. Yes, she shall be free. I stand with Mr. Hansen and Mr. Rawls. Come, brothers, join us."

Mr. Gibb calls out, "What say you, brothers?"

All shout, "Aye!" Even Mr. Hahn.

Cindy hugs Lien tightly. "You are truly my sister now. You are sister to us all."

Lien cries tears of joy. She holds tightly to Cindy. Each man goes to her, hugs her, and calls her sister. Lastly, Kathy takes them both in her arms. She's so pleased with Cindy she feels she may burst. "I'm so proud of you, my little girl, so proud."

At the end of the party, the captain enters the mess; he picks up Cindy. "Time for your surprise," he says.

"What is it? What is it?" she asks. The little girl is back.

"You'll see," he says. "I heard what you did, princess. I'm very proud of you." Cindy glows with happiness, for anytime the captain praises her, nothing else matters.

He leads Kathy and Cindy to the observation dome. The ship skims through the cloudy gasses. Then they see them. *They are whale-like*, is the first thought Kathy has.

The girls are so enthralled by what they are seeing they barely hear the captain as he explains about these creatures to them. "They swim through the gases, gathering 'plankton', tiny animals, to eat converting the hydrogen and food to energy and oxygen. For their size, their flukes are twice as big as an equivalent Earth whale. Their width is nearly as long as the creature is. And the flippers are massive as well. But they need to be because they swim in gas and not water. Their bodies are wider than an equivalent Earth whale. This is needed for buoyancy. Their width is due to large gas bags they fill to keep them afloat on the 'surface' of the gas. To dive, they flush out the gas as they go 'under.' The deeper they go, the slimmer they get."

Like whales in Earth's oceans, they breach, dive deep through the gases, and play. If they notice the ship at all, it's to take advantage of its wake, playing and dancing about it. The pod "swims" by, and they are beautiful, almost beyond words. What adds to the wonder is the knowledge that in all of human space, very few people have seen what they are now witnessing. Cindy is totally enthralled. "Oh, Captain, thank you."

Kathy looks at her, and she sees the little girl she loves again. "Yes, Captain, thank you."

The captain surprises both of them by saying, "Do you want to touch them?"

Cindy is floored and so is Kathy. "Can we?"

Kathy says, "I don't know, sweetie…"

"Of course we can," the captain says. "Let's suit up, and I'll show you." Kathy looks a little frightened; Captain Black leans in and says, "Honestly, it's safe. They're very gentle." The three of them go to the airlock and suit up. The captain attaches very long tethers to all of them and opens the airlock. They drift out beside the ship.

It's not really vacuum here with all the gases. They can feel/hear the song of these space whales, the thrums and hums. The whistles and chirps. It's just like when the nanchik gods speak to them.

"Mommy, do you hear them?"

"Yes, sweetie, I do."

The three of them "swim" to the nearest one. It's a long grayish creature. Its eyes are as big as Cindy's face. They are gentle in appearance and blue. A great intelligence sits behind them. The whale's massive mouth opens to reveal its baleenlike teeth. It strains the gases for food and blows the gas out its blowhole.

"Back on Earth, sailors would shout out 'There she blows!' when a whale did that," the captain explains to Cindy. The captain sets Cindy atop it just behind the eyes, forward of the blowhole, then swims next to her holding Kathy's hand. The whale eyes them both but doesn't do anything. It's like it knows they are safe and will do it no harm.

Kathy hears the voice of the nanchik god in her mind, *Love them. They are children.*

Who are the children, them or us? Kathy thinks.

Yes, she hears/feels.

Kathy can see the captain's face through the face plate of his helmet. She sees joy there, one of the few times the captain appears at peace. To Kathy, this happens far too seldom; it makes her heart ache a little. And Cindy's face is full of light. She's filled with childlike wonder. Kathy feels all of it. The love washes over her. The warmth of it is amazing. She decides to fully give in to the feelings.

They swim with the great creature for what seems like hours. It dives but not too deep, like it knows they can't go far with it. When it breeches, it doesn't go high. The whale moves slowly so the captain and Kathy can keep pace with it. They swim alongside for the longest time. Too soon, it's time to return to the ship.

"Do we have to?" Cindy asks.

"Sorry, princess, but yes," the captain says. He picks her up off the whale. It looks her in the eye. Kathy sees an exchange of thought take place. Then she makes her way to the airlock. Before closing the hatch, the three of them take one more look at the whales. The captain puts his arm around Kathy and holds Cindy in his other arm. She waves at the whales. One seems to wave back, then they "swim" off, and the captain closes the hatch.

"Will we visit them again, Captain?" asks Cindy.

"Of course, princess. You'll see them again," replies Captain Black. Kathy notes some sadness in his voice and wonders why.

* * *

Steve stares at the photos. The one currently being displayed shows the whale head down in the gas cloud as it sings. Cindy sits on its head just before the blowhole. Commodore Black swims beside her, holding a tether. It's the tether connected to Kathy. She's off-view, taking the photo.

"This really happened?"

"Yes, we swam with the great space whales. We heard their song, some of which I recorded," Kathy answers.

"And we communicated with them, Steve," Cindy says.

"Cindy, no one's going to believe that, sweetie," Kathy tells her. The look on Steve's face confirms what she said. Kathy continues her tale.

"Next, we went to Reavers Cove for shore leave..."

CHAPTER 11

BLADES

The *Rapier* moves cautiously through Russian space toward the US and Chinese sectors. As it approaches the border, it's detected by a Russian frigate. For five nerve-wracking days, the two ships play cat and mouse—the *Rapier* slipping cautiously away, the frigate trying to get eyes on it, both ships moving closer to contested space and other military units.

In this area of space, the Chinese and the Americans regularly have violent encounters, and when the shooting starts, ships of other nations in the area run like hell as both sides automatically engage ships they can't identify. Over the last nine years, about a dozen Russian ships had been lost, so the captain of the Russian frigate becomes as cautious as he can be. It gives the *Rapier* its opening to scoot out of Russian space and into American. Once several hundred kilometers into American space, the crew relaxes, and for a few days, everyone lets off steam.

This area had been overrun by the Chinese, but the Americans decided to fight for it, and they took it back. It's a topic the crew discusses in depth, and the discussions all end with the same comments: why these people and not us, why fight for here and not Safe Port?

The *Rapier* eventually docks at Omega 4 Beta, more commonly called Reavers Cove. When the *Rapier* arrives, three pirate ships and another privateer are also docked there. One of the pirate ships is the *Raven*, captained by Black Jack Bartholomew.

The captain authorizes a shore leave rotation and strongly cautions the crew to avoid trouble with the other crews, reminding them that some of these people really are bad men. When it's Kathy's turn to go "ashore," the captain and Mr. Gibb are waiting. The captain says, "Come along, ladies, we have a special treat for you."

The five of them, Captain Black, Mr. Gibb, Kathy, Cindy, and Lien, head to the far edge of town, away from the docks. High on a cliff overlooking the sea is an old inn. It's a breathtaking setting. Here among some of the least trustworthy people in the galaxy is an island of tranquility with a lovely garden, a scenic overlook, and great food. For two days, no Chinese, no raids, no being hunted, just blissful peace.

Kathy and Cindy buy swimsuits and go down to the beach. Lien is too shy for a swimsuit; she sits under an umbrella on the beach, watching. The two of them splash around in the water, play in the surf, and swim a bit. When they come back to the shore, they see two men sitting on blankets, watching them. They're wearing shorts and Hawaiian shirts, sipping drinks.

It takes a moment, then Kathy realizes it's Captain Black and Mr. Gibb. They look totally out of their element, and for the first time since she's known them, they seem completely at ease. They wave Kathy and Cindy over, pour Kathy a drink, and give Cindy a soda. Kathy takes a sip; it's a strawberry margarita. Lien comes over and joins them. She has a Coke as well. Even Lien seems at peace. The five of them sit on the beach, take turns playing with Cindy in the surf, watch the waves wash in, muse as the clouds drift by, and watch the birds fly overhead. Well, the planet's equivalent of birds.

While the captain and Cindy are playing in the surf, Mr. Gibb starts talking to Kathy as Lien listens in.

"The captain and I used to be explorers—adventurers, if you will. Whenever we returned to Safe Port, we'd regale our families with tales of our adventures. Often my Aunt Jenny would be at these get-togethers."

"Is that where the captain met her?" Kathy asks.

"No, they grew up as neighbors. At that time the captain and uncle Marty treated her like a little sister, the captain was eight years older than Jenny. After they graduated from school the captain was doing field work for the magazine he and uncle Marty owned, and aunt

Jenny was often out on her own searching for subjects for her work, so they seldom saw each other. Then she was dating Uncle Marty, so the captain never approached her. She was six years older than my mother. I was eighteen then. I believe my mom was thirty-nine."

"So your aunt was forty-five then."

"Yes. Aunt Jenny was an adventurer in her own right. An artist, a painter, as I remember. Though Uncle Marty was in love with her, she was too much of a free spirit. For her, Marty was too uptight. Soon she stopped seeing him. But the captain, he fascinated her. All the adventures we had, all the exotic places, unknown animals. She just couldn't get enough of him."

"Oh," Kathy replies.

Mr. Gibb grins at her. "Yes, she was a lot like you. Anyway, soon they started dating, and within a year, they were married. That broke Uncle Marty's heart. But the captain and Aunt Jenny were so in love they were sure Uncle Marty would come to accept it."

"She was kind of old to have a baby, wasn't she?"

"That's what they thought. They even planned to adopt. But there was a surprise—some say a miracle—and Aunt Jenny got pregnant. It was a rough pregnancy because of her age, but with the captain's help, she made it through, and little Mary was born."

"How old was she when the Chinese came?" Kathy asks.

"Four," Mr. Gibb responds.

"Oh my god," Kathy says.

The captain and Cindy are returning, so Mr. Gibb changes the subject. The rest of the afternoon is spent frolicking on the beach.

Dinner is excellent. The inn's chef knows his business and could give Cookie competition.

After dinner, the five of them talk for hours, tell stories, talk about what they'd like to do when the contract is up, and express thoughts about the future. Even Lien participates. Later Lien, Cindy, and Mr. Gibb go to bed. The captain and Kathy stand out on the inn's veranda. The stars are spread brightly across the night sky. Starlight causes the breakers to sparkle as they crash onto the beach.

"Miss Masters, you light up the night better than the stars," Captain Black tells her. Kathy blushes. She's at a loss of what to say.

The inn's sound system plays an old song that can be heard in all the common areas. Captain Black takes her hand and leads her to the middle of the floor. He takes her in his arms and guides her across it. Captain Black is an excellent dancer. Kathy feels she's drifting above the floor, her feet barely touching it.

It gets late, and the Captain walks her to her cabin. He leans down and kisses her on the cheek, opens her door for her, bows, and says, "I had a lovely time, Miss Masters. Sweet dreams." Then he turns and heads to his cabin.

Cindy and Lien are sitting on the bed. They start giggling when she comes in. Kathy's face turns red as she enters the room, which just makes the other girls giggle harder.

"Get to sleep, young ladies," Kathy tells them. They lie down but giggle even harder. Kathy goes to sleep with a smile on her face.

* * *

As Captain Black prepares for bed thoughts of Kathy flood his mind. His affection for her is almost overpowering, he finds himself thinking, *I think I love her. But how can I be sure that it's not just how much she reminds me of Jenny. If things were different I think I could make a life with her. These thoughts are foolish, she needs a younger man, someone that will be with her for life, and I'm forty years older than her. That and the life I lead, what kind of future could I give her.*

* * *

The next day, they go back to the beach. Aquatic mammals dance on the waves. The sky is filled with birds. Cindy and Lien chase the mammals that come ashore. Kathy takes dozens of pics. The captain and Mr. Gibb watch over them as they play. The setting is idyllic, and the two days pass by far too fast. But now it's time to return to the *Rapier*. The five of them walk down the main street toward the shuttle field. As they do, they notice a crowd gathering.

Mr. Gibb says, "Captain, isn't that Jenkins, Samuels, and Marx?"

All of them look at the gathering crowd. Three crewmen from the *Rapier* are backing toward a store wall. At least eight from another ship are moving in on them. All have weapons drawn. The captain shouts, "What's going on here?" He moves rapidly toward them, his hand on his sword. "Back off now!" he shouts. As he gets closer, two other men move out of the crowd, heading behind him. Cindy takes off running toward them.

"Cindy!" Kathy shouts. Kathy and Mr. Gibb start running after her.

Lien shouts, "Stop, please!"

The men are poised to stab Captain Black in the back, but Cindy strikes first. Dropping to her knees she cuts the Achilles tendon of one of the men with her sword, then slashing up, she cuts across the other's butt before he can react. Then the fight starts in earnest. Captain Black takes down two attackers right off the bat. Each of the other crewmen fends off two attackers apiece.

Five more move out of the crowd.

Cindy rolls over and drives her sword up into one. The captain takes on another. Kathy and Mr. Gibb are facing three.

Lien rushes to the crew against the wall. Quick as an adder, she takes three. The rest of the crew take down the others but not before one of them runs Jenkins through.

Kathy's sword dances before her, the light flashes off it as it does its deadly jig. The ring of metal on metal fills the air. She knows she's there, that she is wielding the sword, but it seems she's watching it from afar. Suddenly it's over. Two men lie dying at Kathy's feet; blood drips from her sword. She doesn't even remember how it happened, but Mr. Gibb stands next to her, grinning. He looks over at Lien with admiration. He can't help feeling great affection toward her, she helped to save his mates.

Three men lie at Cindy's feet, all are severely wounded. "Move and I'll finish you," she growls.

The other attackers are all down, and so is Jenkins. Kathy recognizes him. He was one of the young boys that came aboard at Safe Port.

A man shouts from the crowd, "What the hell did you bushwhackers do here?" It's Black Jack Bartholomew, captain of the *Raven*.

Captain Black shouts, "Your men attacked us, you bastard".

"Then they were provoked." Bartholomew replies.

"Like hell they were."

The crowd grows larger, some from the various ships, most from the town. Captain Bartholomew starts to say something; hands are on weapons. Before anyone can do or say more, Cindy strides over to Captain Bartholomew and says, "You get your scurvy arse the hell out of my way, or I'll put you in the ground." Kathy feels the blood drain from her face. Captain Bartholomew stares down at this nine-year-old pipsqueak challenging him in the street. All eyes are on him; complete silence surrounds them.

"And who be you?" he asks.

"I'm Cindy of the privateer *Rapier*, and you're a slimy dog."

Captain Bartholomew's face burns with rage; he starts to pull his sword. Cindy goes en garde. The people hold their breath. He stops and looks around. All eyes are on him, and most of them are unfriendly. Kathy's heart beats wildly. Lien shakes with fear for Cindy. Cindy stands her ground; blood drips from her sword. Moments pass. Then Captain Bartholomew looks at Captain Black.

"You'll pay for this, Black," he scowls. "But for now, take your midget back to your garbage scow and get out of here."

The town militia shows up. "Both of you, get out of here," their captain shouts. Samuels and Marx help Jenkins up, and they all leave for the *Rapier*'s shuttle. Crewmen from the *Raven* are picking up their dead and wounded. Captain Bartholomew glares at them as they leave. Captain Black says in a low voice, "This isn't over yet."

The shuttle lifts off. On the way up, Captain Black contacts the ship. "Mr. Hansen, recall everyone ashore. Get the power revved up. Everyone to action stations."

Doc Smith meets the shuttle and takes charge of Jenkins; Lien goes with them. The captain rushes to the bridge along with Mr. Gibb, Cindy, and Kathy. "Everyone to stations!" he shouts. They all enter the bridge. "Full power, Engineering!" the captain shouts at the intercom.

Cindy jumps into the weapons seat. She starts powering up the main batteries. "Weapons going hot, Captain."

Kathy sits at tactical, brings up the holographic display, and marks the *Raven* as hostile. "Tactical ready, Captain."

Mr. Gibb watches both of them with an expression of pride.

"Helm?" Nobody is there yet, so Mr. Gibb takes the station. "Helm, aye, Captain."

"Head out on course 132. Give me maneuvering speed as soon as possible."

"Aye, Captain."

The crew is scrambling out of bed or out of shuttles and rushing to stations.

Kathy sees the display light up around the *Raven*; the readout dumps data onto the screen. "The *Raven* is powering up, Captain," she shouts. "Their weapons are coming online."

"Ahead one quarter, Mr. Gibb."

"Aye, Captain." The ship picks up speed.

"Bring that new drive online, Mr. Gibb."

"Aye, Captain."

"Weapons charged, Captain," Cindy sounds off.

"Strap in, everybody," the captain shouts. "Mr. Gibb, give me a vertical 360. Stand by weapons, Miss Cindy."

Both respond, "Aye, Captain." The ship rapidly rises in a vertical loop. Kathy watches tactical. The *Raven* is starting to move as the *Rapier* loops over it.

"Punch it, Mr. Gibb!" Captain Black shouts. The ship leaps forward as a particle beam rises from the *Raven* and just misses the *Rapier*.

"Target locked, Captain!" Cindy shouts.

"Fire."

Cindy hits the rail guns. Three bursts. The projectiles strike the *Raven*. The first three projectiles bounce off the neutron armor, draining its energy. The fourth and fifth crack the surface of the hull. The sixth punches through opening a two-meter-wide hole in the hull. "Let's leave, Mr. Gibb."

"Aye, Captain." He accelerates the ship, and the *Rapier* streaks away from Reavers Cove.

Later Doc Smith reports that Jenkins died of his wounds. As Kathy lies down in her bunk, it hits her. Jenkins was just fourteen when he came onboard, and he didn't live to see his eighteenth birthday. She weeps quietly until she drifts off to sleep.

CHAPTER 12

BROTHERS

It takes five weeks for the *Rapier* to return to Safe Port between moving covertly and avoiding Chinese patrols. When one Chinese patrol gets too close, the captain decides to take it. Kathy sits next to tactical with her camera. Mr. Andjek mans tactical while she captures the process of attacking the ship in pictures and vids.

"Captain, it's a Hong Kong–class patrol craft," Mr. Andjek says.

Mr. Gibb adds, "We can avoid it, but it's pretty close. Might pick us up if we try to slip away."

Captain Black ponders the tactical situation. "Let's nail the bastard. Time to weapons range, Mr. Andjek?"

"At current speed, ten minutes."

"Okay, let's do this. Helm, keep the asteroids between us as long as you can."

"Aye, Captain." The *Rapier* creeps in close enough for main and secondary batteries. Everyone is tense. Cindy is with Lien, studying hyperspace geometry, so Mr. Garrett is on weapons. Kathy starts a vid as the captain makes his move. "Helm, ahead flank. Weapons, target the reactor. I want a clean spread."

"Aye, Captain,"

Mr. Andjek sounds off. "He's spotted us." The *Rapier* leaps around the last asteroids and lines up its shot. The Chinese are turning rapidly to bring their weapons to bear.

"Fire."

Mr. Garrett punches the particle beam button twice. The bright beams lance across the intervening space. The Chinese never stood a chance. The beams converge on the patrol craft. They overwhelm the ship's neutron armor. Its structural integrity gives, and the ship collapses in on itself like a crushed tin can.

* * *

Steve sits back after watching the vid of the attack on the patrol craft. He shakes his head. Kathy says, "That's what it looks like when a ship dies, Steve."

"I never knew," he says. "There were people on that ship?"

Cindy answers, "On a ship of that class, about sixty."

He looks distressed. "And they all died."

"Yes, but they'd have done the same to us if they could have." Kathy states matter-of-factly.

"Steve, that's how life is out there. It's not what you think," Cindy says.

"Apparently, it isn't."

* * *

The comm officer speaks up. "They didn't get off a signal, Captain. We're undetected."

"Excellent," Captain Black says. "Let's get our boy home, people."

When the ship arrives, it's met by the townspeople. Captain Black goes to the mayor.

"Mr. Mayor, where is Jenkins family? I have their shares and wish to speak to them."

"He has no family, Captain Black. He's an orphan, no known relatives."

"So no one will be here for the boy?"

"That's correct."

Captain Black shakes his head. "Mr. Mayor, Miss Masters and I will stand as the boy's family."

"As you wish, Captain."

The funeral proceeds with John Gibb performing the service. The captain and Kathy accept the condolences of the townspeople. After the funeral, everyone gathers in the town square. The captain and the mayor move onto the platform. Captain Black looks over the crowd. He already can feel the futility of his next act. "I ask, is the contract completed?"

The mayor addresses the crowd. "The Chinese are still here. They still take from us. They still kidnap our children. They have not been driven off. I call the vote and vote the contract is not complete and still in force."

The townspeople speak among themselves and then shout out, "The contract is still in force, blood for blood."

At the end of the meeting, the captain calls for a replacement. "I need one good man that will be true before the mast." This time, a young woman steps forward. At first, the captain hesitates. "Are there no men to man my ship?"

The mayor replies, "They are needed for our new guerrilla unit. She is all there is, Captain."

The captain looks at Kathy, then Cindy. He looks back at the young woman and says, "Mr. Gibb, add her to the ship's rolls."

The meeting breaks up, and the townspeople go home. Captain Black seems angry; he follows the mayor and enters the mayor's house. Kathy follows him discreetly. The sound of shouting comes from inside. Kathy hears the captain shout, "When? Damn it. When will it be enough?"

The mayor shouts back, "As long as you're alive, it will never be enough."

"How many have to die, Marty?"

"Until you're dead, everyone, James, everyone." Kathy listens closer.

"Why Marty, why isn't it enough?"

"She chose you. Damn your soul, you James. She would have been safe with me. She'd still be alive, but she chose you, and you weren't even there when she died. She died alone, damn you, while you hid in a cave under the ocean."

"How was I to know, Marty? Don't you think I'd have been with her if I'd known? Somehow I'd have saved her. And damn you, Marty, she didn't die alone—our baby girl died with her. My wife and my daughter died that night. Not yours, mine."

"It doesn't matter. She's dead, and you're not. So I'll keep you out there for as long as you are breathing—even if everyone here dies before you, even if I do. Damn you to hell, James, she chose you."

The captain changes the subject. "Guerrillas, Marty, are you nuts? Have you lost your mind?"

"We need to kill more Chinese, and you're not killing enough of them."

"But guerrillas, they'll be slaughtered. And the Chinese will be all over the few of us that are left."

"Us? Where do you get off saying *us*? You're not and never will be one of us, James."

Mr. Gibb takes her arm. "Let's go, Kathy. It'll break his heart if he knows you've heard this." She walks with Mr. Gibb. He guides her over to Cindy and Lien, takes her hand, and the four of them walk back to the skimmer. Kathy waits there with the new member of the crew until the captain returns. She looks at his face. Rage, anger, and great pain exude from his calm demeanor. She wants to hug him, but she knows if she does, he'll know she heard everything, so she holds back. Kathy can feel the tears well up in her eyes. *I can't cry, I can't. If I do, he'll know I heard everything.*

They ride the skimmer to the shuttle, board it, and then it boosts and takes everyone back to the *Rapier*. Captain Black walks them to their quarters. The captain mumbles good night, then goes to his. Kathy watches as he walks away; his shoulders are slumped. For the first time since she met him, he looks old. The hatch closes behind him.

The next morning, Kathy and Cindy eat with Mr. Gibb. She tries not to ask but can't hold it in. "Why does the mayor hate the captain so?"

"Well, Miss Masters, I think the captain should tell you about that, if he chooses."

"Yes, yes, of course," she replies. Cindy and Lien listen to both of them, concern on their faces. "Could they ever be friends?" Kathy asks.

"I'm afraid not, though that would make my life a good deal better if they were."

"Your life?" Kathy says.

"Yes, miss. They are both my uncles. They are brothers. The mayor is my Uncle Marty, the one I was telling you about back on Reavers Cove." He looks sad for a moment, then says, "I need to get to my duties, ladies." He stands up. "Don't forget, Mr. Evans will be waiting for you three this morning, rifle training."

Mr. Gibb walks off. Kathy can feel all the emotions rise up inside her. *How can the universe be so cruel to this man?* Before she starts crying right there in the crew's mess, Cindy takes her hand. "Be strong, Mom. You have to be strong for him. He can't ever know that you know about this."

The *Rapier* continues raiding, mostly in Chinese space, though occasionally in American and French space.

For the next several days, the captain is edgy. He snaps at the bridge crew, something he hasn't done before. He even snaps at Mr. Gibb. When he starts to snap at Cindy, Kathy steps in and cuts him off with, "That's not necessary, Captain. I'll handle it."

The captain is about to say something, but Cindy kisses him on the cheek, and that seems to take the edge off him, at least for the moment.

A month after leaving Safe Port, the *Rapier* detects an American-armed sloop on patrol. At first, the captain is going to avoid it, but then he has a thought. "Mr. Gibb, do you think we can capture that ship?"

"We can if we get real close before they detect us. What do you have in mind, Captain?"

"Nothing really clear yet, but having a couple of ships could open possibilities. That's a good-quality sloop. Let's take it."

"Aye, sir. Action stations, silent running," Mr. Gibb commands. Kathy and Cindy take their stations on the bridge. Kathy pulls up the tactical holographic sphere.

"Target designated, Captain," she says.

Cindy charges the weapons with Mr. Andjek standing by. "Weapons ready, Captain."

"Mr. Garrett, set course to 133 plus 15," the captain orders.

"Aye, Captain." The *Rapier* rises toward the sloop, staying among the asteroids.

"On view screen and magnify," Captain Black orders. The sloop fills the screen in great detail. "Overlay ship floor plan." The view screen shows the bottom of the sloop along the long axis. Then it outlines the floor plan from the bottom up on the image of the ship.

The *Rapier* slides close to the asteroids it passes, using them to mask its presence from the sloop's sensors. "Cindy, I just want to knock out the armor and the engines. Hold the rail guns at full power in case they fight back, but the lowest power setting needed to do the damage we want with the particle beams," Captain Black tells her.

"Aye, Captain." Cindy sets the particle beams then has Mr. Andjek check them. He approves.

"Weapons power set and confirmed."

"Thank you," the captain replies.

"Fifteen kilometers," calls out Mr. Gibb.

"Flank speed helm, fire!" Just as the ship leaps forward and out of the asteroids, Cindy fires. The beams hit the sloop amidship. The massive lightning bolts that leap out of a discharging neutron armor streak out into the dark.

"Fire." The particle beams lance across the distance, striking the sloop in engineering. A small hole opens in the ship's hull. It's clear the engines are out because the ship continues to drift in the direction it was traveling.

Captain Black has the *Rapier* match vectors with the sloop. Then he calls over to it. "Commander US Navy sloop, this is Captain Black of the *Rapier*. There's no need for any more casualties. Surrender your ship, and our doctor will provide all assistance you may need, and we will land you on a safe planet with emergency beacons and rations for several days. What is your answer?"

"And why should I believe a pirate, Captain Black?" comes his reply.

"We are not pirates, and frankly, you have no other choice. We want your ship, but no one has to die today. Surrender, and you'll be treated well."

"I see your point. Very well then, I surrender to you the armed sloop *New York.*"

"Thank you, Commander. Please have your men deposit all small arms with your master at arms. Our chief will inventory them with him. Please have all your men stand down. We'll be boarding shortly."

"I'll gather my crew in the crew's mess. We have seven wounded, so your doctor will be of great assistance."

"I'll be sure he's on the first boarding party, Commander." The captain leaves the bridge to board the sloop. Mr. Gibb has the con. Everyone waits anxiously as the first boarding party enters the sloop. Soon the captain signals all is well and calls for the follow on teams to board his new acquisition. The wounded are moved to sickbay. Most of the sloop's crew are put in the *Rapier*'s brig. But it gets crowded fast; the rest are put in the sloop's brig. The ship is rigged for being towed, and the *Rapier* moves off to find a place to repair it.

It takes a couple of days to find a suitable place to leave the sloop's crew. In that time, there are many heated discussions between the *Rapier*'s crew and the sloop's. It becomes clear to the sloop's crew that the people of Safe Port don't appreciate being abandoned by the Americans.

"They used mass drivers on us, mass drivers!" said a *Rapier* crewman.

"No one uses mass drivers," responds the American sailor.

"They used mass drivers!" another *Rapier* crewman shouts. "There were over two million colonists, but now we are less than twenty thousand, twenty thousand."

"Why didn't you call for help?"

"We did call. We called and called, and the only thing that came was Chinese." And the argument goes on.

Once a suitable place is found—in this case, a small planet that has oxygen—the sloop's crew are marooned there. They are given two weeks of rations, tents, and field gear. They are also given some medicine and two emergency beacons, so they should be picked up soon. Though there is a great deal of animosity between the crews, the Americans have no doubt the *Rapier*'s crew consider themselves brother Americans that were abandoned in their time of need. Captain Black sees this as an added bonus. At least now they'll know why the *Rapier* raids them.

The *Rapier* makes a hyperspace jump as soon as it can, so the Americans can't trace them. Once the jump is completed, they locate a large moon where they can do basic repairs on the sloop. Under the watchful eyes of Mr. Simms, the sloop is repaired, enough to journey to Kyle's World. With a skeleton crew on board, the two ships move to their destination.

The crew renames the sloop the *Isis*. En route, Captain Black ponders who will captain his new ship. His first instinct is Mr. Gibb; his second choice is Mr. Rawls. The captain thinks long and hard about this and decides he isn't going to give the command to either of them. It's a gut decision. He feels he needs them for something yet to happen. So who will command the *Isis*? He looks over his bridge crew. Who here can do the job? Mr. Garrett the master gunner, he has the experience and knowledge, and he doesn't take unnecessary risks, something the captain is certain will be needed. Before arriving at Kyle's World, the captain calls Mr. Gibb to his quarters. "Jimmy, I'm giving command of the *Isis* to Mr. Garrett."

"Okay, Uncle James. I take it you want me to back you on this."

"Yes, Jimmy, but there's more. I think you are ready to command and should have a ship of your own. I just have a gut feeling that something more important is coming your way."

"Uncle James, you don't owe me an explanation. I trust you and your decisions. I'm always in your corner."

"Thank you, Jimmy. Now let's go get our new ship ready."

The ships arrive at Kyle's World. Soon work starts on the sloop. While the work goes on, the captain recruits additional crew from the brotherhood hall. The *Isis* takes a thirty-man crew. The captain moves twenty-men from the *Rapier* to the *Isis*. He then recruits thirty new men, placing ten of them on the *Isis* and the rest on the *Rapier*. Mr. Gibb presides over a quick election of captain Garrett and then repairs get underway.

The captain and Mr. Gibb are hard-pressed to get everything done, so they have little time to spend with Kathy and Cindy. The girls and Lien get some shore time, but even they're pressed into repair work and training new crew on their duties. Soon all is done, and the two ships head out to hunt.

By the end of the year, the *Rapier* has captured an auxiliary replenishment ship. It's slow and lightly armed. It could be crewed by as many as twenty men, but Captain Black only raises thirteen. As it's a replenishment ship, Captain Black decides to recruit a captain for it rather than to use one of the *Rapier's* veterans.

With these two additions, Captain Black is able to extend his operations. And though he doesn't accept the title, some of the crew call him Commodore.

Word gets around that Captain Bartholomew is gunning for Captain Black, but the captain doesn't seem to be concerned about it. He's keeping his focus on business.

CHAPTER 13

WOLF RIDERS

Like most things in life, the majority of the activities onboard the *Rapier* become mundane. Maintenance, training, supply runs, and other activities. Even the raids become commonplace.

The Chinese are getting smarter in their operations, and that means they become more dangerous. On too many occasions, there are narrow escapes and Chinese warships hunting them after a successful raid. A few times, the Chinese have even set ambushes. So for a while, different hunting grounds are needed.

Captain Black has the sloop upgraded with a ship set from the nanchik gods but decides not to put a set on the replenishment ship. The decision is based on having the sloop guard it. Later some would say that was a mistake.

The *Rapier* team sets out to raid deeper into Chinese space. They develop a routine where they'd move far into the Chinese sector and find a place for the replenishment ship to hide. Once it was securely hidden, the *Rapier* would go even further and raid the Chinese in unexpected locations. The sloop, the *Isis*, would hide near the replenishment ship. If an opportunity for it to strike appeared, Captain Garrett has to balance chances of success against the possibility of the replenishment ship being discovered. Overall, this system works well. Most of the time, Captain Garrett has to swallow his pride and let targets slip by.

Soon Cindy's twelfth birthday is approaching. Captain Black has been thinking on this for some time. About a month before the big day, he pulls the group out of deep Chinese space and heads for the South African sector. His destination is the Pi system.

The Pi system is the one system that mankind has discovered that's most like Earth's system, Sol. It has eleven planets, most being gas giants. An asteroid belt is in the fifth planet's orbit. Third from the systems star is Pi Beta 2. This planet is full of life. And there he plans to show Cindy the great dire wolves, creatures few have seen and most believe don't exist.

Sometime before Kathy and Cindy had been brought aboard the *Rapier*, the captain and Mr. Gibb had gone to find these creatures. They had heard about the wolves and wanted to prove they were real. They got to know them well, and so they know that visiting them for Cindy's birthday would be perfect.

As the *Rapier* approaches the planet, Mr. Gibb and Kathy stand on the bridge, watching the view screen.

"Kathy, remember the pictures I showed you on the *America?*" For a moment, he sounds like when she first met him.

"Yes," she replies.

"This is where I took many of them. This is where the wolves live."

"Oh," Kathy says.

"You're going to get tons of pics here."

"Will we see the wolves, Jim?" she asks.

"Oh yes, you know they hide and are hard to find. Most people don't believe they exist. But the captain and I know where to find them. It'll be a bit of a journey, but I promise it'll be worth it."

"Why do most people think the wolves don't exist?"

"Well, it's like the nanchik gods, Miss Masters. If you don't know where to look for them, you can't find them."

Kathy notes that Jim Gibb has gone back to using the formal title. On some level, it saddens her.

Captain Black brings the *Rapier* into port. As she approaches, the South Africans contact the *Rapier*. "*Rapier*, this is Pi Beta 2 control, what are your intentions?"

"Pi Beta 2 control, we ask to land for rest and refitting."

"Captain Black, your reputation precedes you. We would prefer you go elsewhere."

Mr. Rawls speaks up, "M'Butu, is that you?"

"Kuntu?" comes the reply.

"Yes, cousin, tis I. Would you deny me seeing my mother?"

"Of course not, cousin. Do you fly with these men?"

"Yes, M'Butu. These are good men. They will do no harm here."

"Okay, Kuntu, but their misdeeds will be on your head, cousin."

"Then my head will be unburdened, cousin."

"You are cleared to land, Captain Black."

The *Rapier* lands at the main spaceport in New Johannesburg, a great and bustling metropolis. Ships from all over the galaxy touch down here. The South Africans have not been involved in hostilities, so even ships from China, America, France, Germany, etc. call here. The South Africans are neutral, and they vigorously enforce their neutrality.

In case of trouble, the captain keeps the *Isis* and the replenishment ship, the *Fatman*, near the asteroid belt. He works out a shore leave rotation so they can get some down time. But the ships stay on alert.

Kathy stands on the dock, looking around. The scene looks much like Sydney or any other Earth city. This is how she imagined cities in the colonies looked, much like they are portrayed back on Earth. She knows that this is the exception, not the rule though, that most cities in the colonies are like Reavers Cove, Kyle's World, and Safe Port.

Mr. Gibb walks up to her. "The captain and I have a little adventure for you and Cindy. Let's get ready."

"What's that?" Kathy asks.

"As I was telling you earlier, we're going to see the wolves," he says with his devilish grin. They bump into Cindy as they enter the ship.

"Come, princess, we're going on an adventure," Mr. Gibb says.

Her eyes light up. "Where are we going?"

"You'll see," Mr. Gibb says with a grin. Mr. Gibb leads them to the equipment locker. He pulls out four rucksacks and four sets of field gear, sleeping bags, canteens, and cold-weather boots and parkas. "You ladies need to get some warm clothes, two sets, and four sets of socks and undies. Be sure to pack anything else you might need, but keep it light."

"Mr. Gibb, I'm not so sure of this," Kathy says.

He looks at her a moment. "I'm sure it's going to be okay, Miss Masters."

"Okay," she replies. Still it's obvious something is bothering her.

Mr. Gibb carries the equipment to the girls' quarters. Kathy and Cindy pack their personal clothing and other items. Lien watches, but when asked if she'd like to go with them, she declines. "No, Kathy, I'm not a camping type of girl."

Oscar watches lazily, he rolls over and adds his two cents' worth with a measured *meow*.

Cindy asks, "Should we bring our weapons?"

"I don't think we'll need them, but it's always better to be prepared, so yes," Mr. Gibb answers.

Soon they have all their gear packed and head to the shuttle. When they get to it, Captain Black is waiting. He has his personal stuff with him. Mr. Gibb hands him his rucksack, and the captain rapidly packs it. Next, they check each other's packs for balance, then the girls.

Kathy touches the captain's shoulder. "I'm not sure this is a good idea. I don't know why, but I feel something bad is going to happen."

The captain looks at her for a moment. He can see the deep concern in her eyes. "I'm sure everything will be okay, Miss Masters." Still he makes a mental note about her concern.

"You're probably right," she replies. Nonetheless, she's not convinced.

On the other hand, Cindy is very excited. "Camping, I've never been camping. This is going to be fun." She seems full of energy.

Mr. Gibb gets rations from Cookie and fills the canteens. He distributes them, and they all put them in their packs and field gear. Then Mr. Gibb stows all the gear in the shuttle.

"Let's go, Mr. Gibb," the captain says.

"Aye, Captain." Mr. Gibb gets into the pilots seat. Cindy jumps into the copilot's chair. Kathy and the captain sit behind them. Mr. Gibb pilots the shuttle northeast. He quickly gains altitude. Once at altitude, he lets Cindy take over. She's become quite a good pilot, but Mr. Gibb insists on limiting the amount of time she's at the controls. He knows he won't be able to for much longer, but sometimes, he wants her to stay a little girl.

The shuttle heads out over forests and hills. Kathy watches the terrain pass by below. Rivers meander through the countryside. Herds of animals move across the land, similar to creatures on Earth. Kathy doesn't recognize the differences from this altitude. Soon the land below becomes tundra. Patches of evergreens dot the landscape. Snow and ice, rolling hills, and herds of large animals with heavy fur coats.

Mr. Gibb takes over the shuttle controls. He banks and slowly circles until he picks his landing spot.

"We'll have to walk from here. No place to land further up." He lands the shuttle. Everyone gets up and moves to get their gear from storage. They all put on their field gear, then their rucksacks. Captain Black leads them out of the shuttle. They move single file down a ravine that winds to the north. After moving about seventy-five meters, they hear the howl of ship engines.

"Why would anyone be here besides us?" the captain asks.

They look up and see a different shuttle scream down toward their grounded one. It fires on the ship on the ground, blasting it to pieces. All of them take cover. They remain hidden, not moving and saying nothing, while the hostile shuttle searches for them from above. After several minutes, the shuttle flies away.

"Who was that?" Mr. Gibb asks.

"That is a damn good question," the captain states.

Cindy looks at the wreckage of the shuttle with fierce eyes. "Bartholomew" is all Cindy says. Kathy looks at her in shock. Mr. Gibb and the captain look at each other, then at Cindy. They nod agreement. "I guess your bad feeling was right on, Miss Masters," the captain says.

* * *

"How'd he know where to find you?" Steve asks.

"That was the sixty-four-thousand-dollar question, Steve," Kathy replies.

Cindy says, "We had two traitors among us."

"Traitors?"

"Yes, Steve, traitors. Bartholomew put up a bounty for us, and one of the new men on the *Fatman* decided to collect on it. Turns out he had a friend among the new men recruited for the *Rapier*," Kathy replies. "Of course, we didn't know that at the time. If we had, it would have saved all of us a lot of pain."

* * *

"We'd best get going," Captain Black says. "Mr. Gibb, take up the rear. We'll use the terrain to mask our movement. The equipment we've got will help conceal us from their sensors, so let's use it. Stay alert and keep your weapons ready."

They all reply, "Aye, Captain."

"Our destination is those hills," Captain Black tells them. He points toward wooded hills in the distance. "About fifteen kilometers, I believe."

"Yes, Captain," Mr. Gibb states.

"Miss Masters, do get as many photos as you like. There's plenty to shoot," Captain Black tells her.

They move cautiously along the ravine for as long as it goes. Then they move into the wood line. The trees are massive. Pi Beta 2 is about 93 percent of Earth's normal mass and gravity, so everything grows tall and lanky. The atmosphere is actually a little denser than Earth's, so the air pressure is a little over 15 psi. Scientists speculate that's because it has been hit by fewer asteroids than Earth. So there's plenty of oxygen, which energizes everyone.

The small party moves steadily for about four hours. The captain has them break for lunch and a short rest. They stay deep in the woods. Occasionally, the sound of a shuttle passing overhead can be heard. While resting, Kathy shoots lots of pics. The woods are alive with life. Insects, squirrel-like rodents, birdlike creatures flit about. All are larger than their Earth equivalents. Kathy thinks it must be the planet's spring as all the plants seem to be blooming.

"Let's move on," the captain says. Everyone checks their gear, puts on their rucksacks, and start moving toward the hills.

* * *

Mr. Rawls stands his watch on the bridge of the *Rapier*. The comm system alerts him to an incoming message. "*Rapier*," he responds, "what's your message?"

"Kuntu, I must notify you that a shuttle that landed at the coordinates of your captain's flight plan has been destroyed on the ground. We think it was fired on by a shuttle that has violated our air space."

"M'Butu, are you sure about this?"

"Yes, cousin, we are certain. I've had a ground crew check the wreckage. There are no bodies at the site. It does appear that some people have left the area on foot. But we lost the trail."

"That sounds like our captain," Mr. Rawls replies.

"We have fighters searching for the rogue craft, but so far, it has eluded us, cousin."

"Thank you, M'Butu. Please let me know when you find something."

"Of course, Kuntu. I hope your friends are all safe."

"Thank you, cousin."

Mr. Rawls calls together the ship's officers and briefs them on what he knows. He has them check all the ship for anything unusual, then he checks the captain's instructions for the watch. In it, the captain left emergency rendezvous information for just this kind of event.

* * *

Word of the destruction of the shuttle spreads throughout the ship quickly, and before long, Lien has heard of it. Like all rumors, it's exaggerated by time she hears. The thought that something could have happened to Kathy and Cindy has her beside herself with worry. To her surprise, she finds herself thinking about Mr. Gibb and his green eyes. As much as she tries, she can't get him out of her mind.

* * *

The little party is just a few kilometers from their destination. The wooded hills are quite close now, but it's getting dark. Captain Black decides to camp in a copse of trees on a little rise. Mr. Gibb sets about securing the location by putting out remote sensors and some trip wire devices. The captain helps Cindy and Kathy set up their air mattresses and sleeping bags. Though simple tasks, if it's something you've not done before, it can be frustrating, particularly the air mattresses. Once these tasks are done, Mr. Gibb starts dinner. It's not that difficult a task as the food is freeze-dried. Cookie often freeze-dries leftovers for field use, so the meals are quite good.

Though the four of them are thoroughly tired, the Captain and Kathy stay up a little after Cindy and Mr. Gibb turn in. They sit near the edge of the woods, looking at the planet's moon and stars. Neither says anything; they just sit together and take it all in. In the distance, some creatures howl. The sound is similar to the howls of wolves on Earth.

"That's them, Miss Masters," the captain tells her. "They sometimes travel at night, though they usually hunt in the day." Kathy snuggles with the captain but still says nothing. After a few more minutes, they too go to sleep.

Kathy sleeps fitfully. She dreams of strange creatures, being chased by unseen villains and dark ships. She feels pressure on her chest. Instinctively, she brushes at her chest with her hand, and she hits something. Her hand grasps it. It's thick and furry. She wakes holding the haft of a massive leg. Her eyes open to see a pair of great red eyes looking into hers. A wolflike snout, ten-centimeter fangs in powerful jaws. Ears lie back against its head. The creature's paws are huge, and unlike Earth canines, it has retractable claws in those massive paws. The creature stands as tall as a small to medium Earth horse, Kathy screams.

Cindy sits up. "Mom, what is it?" Then she realizes she's looking another of these creatures in the face. It stands bent down, staring at her.

The captain says, "Everybody, relax. They won't hurt you."

Kathy hears him but has some doubts. She looks around and sees Mr. Gibb. He stands with one of the great creatures scratching its neck. She also notices there must be twenty of them all around the camp. About half of them appear to be pups, each of which is nearly as big as she is.

"Mom, this is great," Cindy giddily says. She's already petting many of the pups.

The two mother wolves lie on the edge of the camp. The one nearest Kathy pulls her close to her. Several pups move to her and start to nurse, covering Kathy up. She's in a huge fluff ball of squirming puppies. She tries to move out of the dog pile but is knocked back down by excited puppy limbs. After a little while, she feels the captain's firm grip on her arm. Shortly, she emerges coughing up bits of fur. He moves her away from the great pile of suckling pups. She gives one last big cough and expels a wad of puppy locks.

Cindy rolls about with the other pile of pups. She's laughing as she wrestles with nursing wolf pups. They've completely accepted her as one of them. Mr. Gibb watches over her as she frolics with the young of the pack.

Kathy takes a long look at the wolves. They are lean and tall, with large paws and thick legs. The body shape is very similar to the wolves of Earth. Their underbellies are white, but the rest of their fur is grayish with blue tints and specks of brown. Their heads are canine in shape with massive teeth and fiery-red eyes. Their tails are long and whiplike.

The alpha male of the pack nuzzles the captain. The captain says to him, "Hello, old friend, you've grown so much since I last saw you." The alpha rubs up against him.

After several minutes, another wolf walks slowly into the camp. It's a male but smaller than the others. Its fur is all black. The other males bare their fangs; it appears they're going to run it off. Tension rises; it looks like a fight is about to start. Cindy goes to the black wolf; the others watch. She touches it on its snout. It bows its head. She scratches it on the neck; the others stop growling. The black wolf nuzzles Cindy. Then he bows down completely, and Cindy mounts him. He stands proudly with her on his back. All the pack watches this closely. They stare at the two of them. Then the alpha howls; the rest join in. The black wolf stands as tall as he can. It's clear the pack has finally accepted him.

Soon it's daylight. The captain and Mr. Gibb study the terrain.

"Let's get on the move, Mr. Gibb. Get the gear recovered and ready," the captain says.

"Aye, Captain." Cindy helps him recover the sensors and pack the rucksacks. He lashes them to two male wolves. "The gear's ready Captain."

"Miss Masters, keep your camera ready. There'll be lots of great shots on the way. Mount up everybody."

They all get onto their chosen wolf. The captain and the alpha lead out, and the rest of the pack follow. Soon, they're all running. Not too fast for the pups, but it's still a kilometer-eating pace. The wolves are well-practiced at moving concealed. They use the terrain and woods to keep hidden, yet they cover distance rapidly.

About midmorning, Kathy notices something in the sky. The captain halts the pack and studies the object. He relaxes. "That, Miss Masters, is a geosynchronous solar power station. It's not looking for us."

"Good," Kathy says.

They push on. The wolves seem tireless. They continue to move at a constant pace, traveling kilometer after kilometer with ease. Just after midday, the captain leads them into another wooded hilltop to rest. The females start to nurse the pups as the alpha takes two males with him to hunt. Mr. Gibb reconstitutes more of Cookie's freeze-dried meals. The four of them eat and then rest. Though riding their wolves is not as hard as trying to cover the distance themselves, it's still a very physical activity, and they feel it. While eating, Kathy spots something flying by. She uses her implants to look closer. It's sleek and armed with missiles.

"Captain, that's not a satellite," she says as she points to it.

"No, it isn't, Miss Masters," he replies. "That's a planetary fighter. It seems to be searching for something. I expect it's looking for the shuttle that attacked us."

"What makes you think that, Captain?" she asks.

"The South Africans prize their neutrality in all things, Miss Masters. They're convinced it's why all the troubles of this sector of the galaxy haven't affected them. They'll go to great lengths to capture or destroy anyone that endangers that."

They watch the fighter streak off to the east. There are a few more hours of sunlight, so the pack pushes on. They pass through the woods like wraiths. Few alive could detect their passing.

* * *

Mr. Rawls looks over the report his cousin sent him. M'Butu has sent over everything they have on the attack on the captain's shuttle. Though the government here is doing everything they can to find the attacking shuttle, there is little to go on. Who launched this attack and why? After reviewing everything, it becomes clear it must be Bartholomew. What next? The captain's rendezvous instructions are clear, heading to location xx:xx, will signal upon arrival, be prepared for immediate recovery. Mr. Rawls pulls out the code book and looks up xx:xx.

That makes sense, should take them four days on foot. It's thirty minutes by shuttle, if no problems occur. Perhaps I should coordinate fighter cover with my cousin.

* * *

In the afternoon a very large creature with two cubs moves by the pack. The wolves all stop and take cover in the wood line. The pups run to their Mother's, cowering underneath them. These creatures could be called bears, but they are bigger than Earth Kodiak's.

Mr. Gibb says, "Those are even harder to find than the wolves, I've never seen them until today."

Kathy takes several shots of these creatures as they lumber past the party. The wolves stay on alert incase the 'bears' come closer. The pack waits for several minutes once they've passed, then they continue onwards, avoiding the trail left by the 'bears'.

As it gets dark, they are still moving southeast, but once the "sun" sets, the wolves turn east. No amount of effort can get them back on course. Finally, they accept that they have to move further from their objective. They are dependent upon their mounts.

For two hours, the wolves push further east. Then they come into a massive ravine. There are over a hundred more wolves waiting. The large pack alpha acknowledges the arrival of the newcomers. They move in among the large throng of wolves. The captain rallies the small party on a rise within the ravine. They dismount and quickly make camp, then Mr. Gibb makes dinner. The small pack stakes out sleeping spots around them.

Nobody is sure about what's going on, so they keep quiet. Dozens of wolves come and go most of the night. The captain sits with the girls while Mr. Gibb watches all the activity. Eventually, they all slip into sleep.

Kathy sits up. She looks about; it's just before dawn. All the large pack wolves are awake. They sit quietly like they are waiting for something. Mr. Gibb touches her shoulder and says, "Ssssh!" He points toward a stream bed that wanders east. She looks where he's pointing. Shadowy figures move through the early-morning fog. She watches them move. They are tall, thin, long legs and arms. Their heads are egg-shaped, large ears and eyes.

She activates her implants. The creatures give off heat; the thermal imaging shows they have a warm body core. They must be mammalian in nature. She switches to night vision. The figures take on a slight greenish hue. They are bipedal and walk erect. The natives wear animal skins and carry stone-tipped spears. The readouts say they are over two meters tall. There are about two dozen of them. The alpha of the large pack meets them, they seem to be communicating.

The leader of these humanoid creatures looks toward Kathy and Mr. Gibb. He signals the others forward. They level their spears and move on line toward them.

"Captain, Cindy, we have company," Mr. Gibb says calmly.

They wake and look around. The small pack wakes with them. The wolves move between them and the newcomers. The approaching natives stop. The Captain stands and holds up his hands. He says in a calm voice, "We're no threat to you. We mean you no harm." The leader says something in a language no human has heard before. For the moment, it's a standoff.

* * *

Mr. Rawls looks over the wreckage of the shuttle. His cousin was correct; no one was killed here. Mr. Simms calls out, "They're here, Mr. Rawls." He points to several cases. "The modules are recoverable. We can install them in another shuttle."

"Good, Mr. Simms. Get them to the ship."

"Aye, sir."

Mr. Rawls looks at the few tracks they can find. Yes, all four of them had set out on foot but they've concealed their movement well, no way to follow them. The only choice is to watch the captain's designated rendezvous point, at least, that makes it simple. Mr. Rawls calls his cousin, "M'Butu, I will need some fighter support after all."

"I will see what I can do, Kuntu."

"Thank you, cousin."

* * *

The situation doesn't seem tense, but it's not good. The natives, distrustful of the captain, are ready for a fight.

"Well, Mr. Gibb, what do you suggest?"

"Honestly, not sure, Captain. I'm at a loss on how to communicate with them."

Suddenly, Cindy gets on the black wolf. She rides down the little hill before anyone can react. Kathy calls out, "Cindy, stop now!"

"It's okay, Mom, I can do this."

The natives stay ready to strike. They watch her approach with trepidation. But the large pack alpha moves forward to meet her. He stops just before the native warriors. Cindy moves up until she is face-to-face with the alpha. She dismounts from the black wolf, and nuzzles the large pack alpha. Kathy grips the captain's hand. He looks at her and sees the fear on her face. She says over and over, "It'll be okay, it'll be okay."

The alpha wolf rubs against Cindy. He acts much like a pet dog would. After a few moments, the leader of the native warriors moves up to them. He leans down until the three of them are all face-to-face. Kathy doesn't notice, but she stops breathing.

"Breathe, Miss Masters, breathe," the captain tells her.

"Captain, they're communing," Mr. Gibb states.

Cindy, the native leader, and the alpha seem locked together in thought. For several long moments, they do not move. Eventually, they break the spell and separate. The leader of the natives calls off his warriors. They move away toward the large pack. Cindy returns up the little hill. Kathy grabs her off the wolf and holds her. "Don't you ever do that again!"

"Mom, stop it. I'm fine," Cindy whines.

"Never again, do you hear me?"

"Yes, Mom, never again."

The captain looks cross at Cindy. He doesn't have to say anything; his look says it all.

Mr. Gibb asks "Well, what did you learn?"

Cindy tells them "They're afraid. They're almost extinct, the natives and the wolves. The colonists don't seem to realize it, but they're killing them off. They're here to meet with what's left of the wolves to decide if they'll war with the colonists. They know they can't win but many think it's better to go out fighting. The thing is, we're the first humans they've communicated with, now they're not sure what to think."

"It must be because they're so hard to find. This is the first time I've ever seen the natives," Mr. Gibb says.

"Could be," the Captain replies. "Unfortunately, we need to deal with our situation first. Get some sleep, everyone. We push on in a couple of hours." Captain Black moves off obviously deep in thought. Kathy senses that the thought of these creatures becoming extinct greatly troubles him.

The sun has risen when they wake. The captain gathers the equipment and packs it. Mr. Gibb gets breakfast ready for everyone. Cindy tends the black wolf, she starts calling him Midnight. The small pack starts its daily activities. Pups nurse; the males go on the hunt.

While all this is going on, Kathy walks down by the stream bed with her camera bag. She kneels down by the stream and starts to photograph the natives and the wolves. More of the natives arrive throughout the morning, including what seem to be children.

As she takes pics some of the children move next to the stream. They stare at her, trying to figure out what she's doing. To Kathy they look undernourished. She watches one of them chew on some leaves and twigs. *My God, they're starving!*

Kathy starts to tear up. *I've got to help them!* She remembers, there are some nut bars in her camera bag. Kathy developed the habit of carrying a couple dozen of these snacks in her bag when she was with the nomads in Australia.

She pulls out a bar and tears the wrapper off, putting the wrapper back in the camera bag pouch. Kathy holds out the bar and tries to coax one of the children over by softly saying, "Here, take this, it's good. Yummy." She rubs her belly repeating, "Yummy."

Cindy and the black wolf walk down to Kathy. "Mom, what are you doing?"

"They're starving honey, I'm trying to give them these nut bars."

"Here, let me try." Cindy takes the bar from Kathy. Her and the wolf cross the stream, walking up to one of the children. They look the child in the eyes as Cindy takes a bite of the bar. After a moment the child takes the bar from Cindy and starts to nibble on it.

Kathy slowly walks up to Cindy, trying to not startle the children. "Sweetie, how did you do that?"

"The implants Mom, they do more than we know. I think the natives have a telepathic connection to the wolves. My implant lets me patch into that. I bet you can do it too," Cindy tells her.

"How honey?"

"Stand next to Midnight and look into the eyes of one of the children."

Kathy takes out another nut bar from her camera bag and removes the wrapper. She leads the black wolf to a child, and bends down to look into the child's eyes. The wolf does the same. The child's eyes lock onto hers. Unfamiliar thoughts form in Kathy's mind. She takes a bite from the nut bar and thinks about the taste. After a few moments the child takes the snack from her and bites into it. Kathy can feel how much the little one likes the taste.

The two native children start sharing bits of their nut bars with the others. They point to Kathy and Cindy, and soon the girls are swamped by little ones with their hands out.

Kathy starts pulling the snacks out of her camera bag as Cindy takes the wrappers off and hands them out. There are so many children that Cindy starts breaking the bars in half so she has enough to go around. They are startled as the captain asks, "What are you ladies doing?"

"They're starving, we're giving the children these nut bars," Kathy responds.

He frowns at her saying, "That's not a good idea. Ladies, breakfast is ready."

The three of them, and the black wolf, cross the stream heading over to Mr. Gibb. As they do the captain keeps looking back at the natives.

Kathy asks, "What's wrong?"

"Miss Masters, you should never have given them our food."

"Why? We have plenty and the children were eating leaves and twigs!" she replies indignantly.

He says softly, "I know your heart is in the right place. But we know nothing about these people, leaves and twigs might be their natural diet. And our food could be poisonous to them. Mr. Gibb and I made that mistake once, and we killed a very rare creature. Hopefully, that won't happen here."

Kathy looks at the children. She shivers as the realization sets in that she might have poisoned them. Kathy sniffles as a tear runs down her cheek.

Cindy looks devastated. She tells the captain, "We didn't know daddy, they were so hungry, I'm sorry."

"I understand Princess, let's hope we did no harm."

As they eat the captain and Mr. Gibb keep looking over at the natives. They take extra time eating so they can watch the reaction of the children to the nut bars. After forty-five minutes they seem to be okay.

They finish breakfast and prepare to travel. Mr. Gibb secures the equipment to two large male wolves, and they mount up and strike out to the southwest. To their surprise, over twenty from the large pack, and an equal number of native warriors, follow behind them. They travel all day and into the night.

* * *

Mr. Rawls receives a signal from the ground. "Yes, Captain."

"Mr. Rawls, I take all is in readiness."

"Yes, sir, and we have fighter support from the South Africans."

"Excellent, Mr. Rawls. Be prepared for a hostile ground encounter."

"Aye, Captain."

* * *

As midday approaches, the ridge line destination is near. About a kilometer away from their destination, the captain brings them to a halt. He signals them to dismount. Then he studies the destination for several moments.

"It looks clear, Mr. Gibb, but let's approach it cautiously."

"Aye, Captain." They move forward stealthily. The captain and Mr. Gibb move side by side with about fifteen meters between them. The captain insists that Kathy and Cindy trail by at least ten meters. It's slow-going, nearly two hours to cover half the distance. The captain halts everybody and looks over their destination.

"It still looks clear," he says.

"A little caution, I think, Captain, all things considered," Mr. Gibb answers.

"Yes, a little caution."

They start moving again. The small wolf pack follows them about twenty meters back. They too feel the need for caution. Kathy no longer sees the native warriors and their wolves. *Did they leave?* she wonders.

Moving cautiously, they get within a hundred meters of their objective. It takes almost an hour, but only the most alert would have detected them. The captain looks intently for a couple of minutes. Then he gathers everyone together behind a couple of trees. "Someone is up there. I'm not sure who."

"Could it be our people?" Mr. Gibb asks.

"Let's check," the captain replies. He switches on his comm. "Mr. Rawls, do you have a team at our rendezvous point?"

"No, Captain, we're standing by for your call."

"Looks like we might have hostiles at our extraction point. Launch recovery now, expect a fight, Mr. Rawls."

"Aye, Captain."

"Well, Mr. Gibb?"

"We have to get closer, and obviously, we're in for a fight."

"Yes, girls, stay back."

Cindy snaps, "I don't think so, Captain. You need every weapon on line."

He looks cross at her, but Kathy can tell he knows she's right. "Okay, Cindy, you stay between Mr. Gibb and myself. Miss Masters, you stay on my left side. Fifteen meters apart. Keep to cover. Let's go."

The four of them move forward. Soon they're less than fifty meters from the ridge line. They all spot two men with plasma rifles. The men are looking to the east at an easier approach. They aim at the two men and fire. All make clean hits, and the two men go down. The ridge lights up with random fire. At least ten more gunmen are on the ridge, but it's obvious they're not sure where the shots came from that took down their friends. They fire again and hit three more shooters. They go down, but now the shooters know where they are. They bring seven plasma rifles to bear on them; all have to take cover.

"Looks like some of them are good shots, Captain," Mr. Gibb quips.

"Damn good," Cindy adds. She got clipped on the arm.

Kathy starts to move to her, but the captain yells at her, "Stay down, damn it!"

After a few moments, it's obvious that only four men are firing at them now. "They're going to try to flank us," Mr. Gibb shouts. One of them pops up near Kathy. He stands up and aims at her when a wolf jumps him. They tumble down together. The man screams in pain but somehow gets off a shot. The wolf howls, then both the man and the wolf go quiet.

Kathy makes her way to the wolf. He's still breathing, but it's clear he's dying. She holds its head as it tries to breathe.

"Shhhhh, I've got you. You're not alone," she says.

The wolf stops breathing, but she continues to hold it. She feels something grab her leg and looks down. The gunman's blood gurgles out of his neck wounds. She tries to move away as he plunges a knife into her leg, then he dies. Kathy screams and passes out for a few moments.

Two men pop up near Mr. Gibb. They both fire before he can react and hit him in the side. He gets off a shot, striking one of his assailants. Before the other gets off a second shot, three wolves hit him, and rip the man to shreds.

To everyone's surprise, a rain of stone spears showers the shooters on the ridge. Several native warriors rush forward as the men there are struck by the spears. They shout in pain, but at least three of the men fire on the natives. They hit five of the warriors; the rest run back to cover.

Kathy looks on the brave warriors lying dead on the ground. Her heart feels pain and anger at the loss. Kathy finds herself shouting, "No! No!" She looks up at the ridge yelling, "You bastards! You bastards!" She flips the power setting on her laser pistol to maximum, then aims at one of the ambushers. She gets off a shot that burns through the shooter. The laser beam strikes a tree behind her target as he slumps down, nearly setting it on fire. The low charge alarm sounds for the powerpack of her pistol.

The sound of shuttle engines screams overhead. They all look up and see the enemy shuttle lining up to strafe them. A fighter appears behind it and flames the shuttle; it breaks up and crashes to the ground.

Several plasma rifles fire on the other side of the ridge. The fire is intense for several moments, then stops. The silence is deafening, but moments later, Mr. Rawls calls out, "All secure, Captain." Then he stands on the ridge top and waves to them.

An older native warrior goes to Kathy; he sees her wounds and picks her up. The warrior carries her to Cindy. She's bleeding from a graze on her right arm.

"I'm okay, Mom. Please check on Mr. Gibb." Kathy and Cindy point toward Mr. Gibb; the old warrior nods. He gets Kathy to him just after the captain reaches him.

The captain shouts to Mr. Rawls, "Get the doc down here now!"

Doc Smith runs down the ridge to them. He looks Mr. Gibb over. There's a hole through his right side. Doc shouts, "Get me a stretcher down here now!" He starts bandaging Mr. Gibb's side. The captain holds him as Doc Smith works.

"I've got you Jimmy, I've got you," Captain Black says.

The old warrior sits Kathy beside them; she holds Mr. Gibb's hand. "We've got you," she says.

Doc Smith gets Mr. Gibb on the shuttle and lifts him straight to the *Rapier*. Cindy moves over to Kathy and treats her knife wound. She bandages it, then tells the Captain, "She'll be okay sir, as soon as we get her onboard the *Rapier*."

The Captain, Mr. Rawls, and his cousin look over the battle-ground. When they come to the dead native warriors and wolves, Mr. Rawls's cousin is stunned. "They really exist," he says in awe.

"Yes, but your people are killing them off," Captain Black tells him. "You've got to change things, or the natives and the wolves will soon be extinct."

"Then change we will, Captain. That I promise."

"Thank you," the captain replies. Captain Black takes M'Butu to the small pack alpha. He lets them get to know each other. While they commune with each other, the black wolf finds Cindy. He tries to care for her wound. Cindy hugs him as he does. "My good boy," she says as she holds him.

The shuttle returns. Mr. Rawls says goodbye to his cousin M'Butu, then they get on the shuttle and return to the *Rapier*. Once they arrive, they go straight to sickbay. When they walk in, Doc Smith is checking the monitors attached to Mr. Gibb. Lien is sitting beside him, gently washing his forehead. Though the doctor hears them enter, she seems to be fully focused on her charge. Doc Smith greets them. "He's sleeping, Captain. It was a bad one, but the nanites have him stable. I expect he'll be back on his feet in a week."

"Thank you, Doctor. Please keep me up to date on his condition."

"Of course, Captain." Then Doc Smith scoops up Cindy. "Let's take care of that scratch."

"Take care of my mom first," Cindy says. Doc Smith treats Kathy's leg and injects some nanites. They go straight to work on her wound. Kathy and the captain sit by Mr. Gibb's bed for a long while. Finally, the captain says, "I need to get our ship off the ground. Please stay with him."

"Of course," Kathy replies. The captain leaves sickbay. Shortly, the engines come to life, and the *Rapier* lifts off. As it heads out of the Pi system, the *Isis* and *Fatman* join up with her, and they head toward Chinese space.

* * *

Steve looks at the photos of the natives and the wolves. He whistles, "These are amazing. The South Africans don't allow them to be photographed or videoed. They won't let us send any researchers at all."

"I know," Kathy says. "I think I'm the only person that has pics of these creatures." Steve nods in agreement. Kathy continues…

CHAPTER 14

BLACK JACK
BARTHOLOMEW

A month later, the ship docks in Freeport. Kathy goes ashore with some of the crew leaving Cindy with Lien to study. That way Kathy can slip away to find a new dress for her. She is starting to fill out and mature and needs some ladies' health items as well. Kathy leaves the group to go to a drugstore. As she's shopping, she chats with the store clerk. Suddenly he stops talking. Kathy looks over to him, then something strikes her on the head.

When she wakes, she's in a ship's brig. A man moves out of the shadows, it's Captain Black Jack Bartholomew. "Welcome aboard the *Raven*, Miss Masters." He leers at her and instantly she knows what he's thinking.

* * *

Steve interrupts, "I didn't know you'd been captured by anyone except Commodore Black."

"Well, I was," Kathy replies.

Cindy jumps in, "My mom was taken by the worst scum in the galaxy. We looked everywhere for her."

Steve asks Kathy, "Did he hurt you?"

Cindy growls. "The bastard raped her!"

Kathy holds her hand. "Cindy, please, watch your language." Cindy seems as furious now as when she and Kathy were reunited. Kathy looks at Steve. "Steve, I was raped and tortured by that monster, but one thing good did come out of it."

"What was that?" he inquires.

"My son," Kathy replies, "My son…"

* * *

Captain Bartholomew walks up to Kathy. She tries to move away, but the chains hold fast. He slaps her across the face. "Not so brave now, are you?" She glares at him, then spits in his face. His eyes fill with rage. "We'll teach you. We'll teach you a lot!"

* * *

Captain Black falls to the deck. It hurts. It hurts so bad all he sees is red. The shout in his mind drives everything out of it. He hears/feels, *Find her!*

When he comes back to reality, Mr. Hansen is lifting him from the deck. Mr. Rawls sprawls on the deck of the bridge just a few steps away.

"Captain, are you okay?" asks Mr. Hansen.

"Where is she?" the captain mumbles.

"Where is who, Captain?"

"Where is Miss Masters?"

"I do not know, sir. She went ashore."

* * *

Red, all I can see is red, Mr. Gibb thinks. The voice inside fills his mind. *Find her!* When the pain leaves, he's lying on the deck in the main passageway. He gets to his feet and goes to the comm bulkhead. "Captain, she's in trouble."

"I know, Mr. Gibb. Come to the bridge now."

"Aye, Captain."

* * *

Lien screams as she rolls on the bed. Cindy grips the covers with steel fingers. My god, the pain. *Find her!*
"Mom!" Cindy cries out.

* * *

He cuts off her leather vest, then tears off her blouse and cuts off her bra. "Those are mighty fine," he says as he grabs and pulls her breasts. "Mighty fine." He slaps them hard, pinches her nipples, digging in with his fingernails, twisting them. He takes off his belt and whips Kathy with it across her breasts. The leather digs into her skin, leaving long welts across her chest. Then he whips her belly.

After several minutes, he stops and pulls off Kathy's boots and pants. Captain Bartholomew leers at her panties, then rips them off her. "Yes, mighty fine," he says. He whips Kathy's butt and her sex with his belt. The leather stings. The pain goes deep. She feels she's going to faint.

"No, not yet," he growls "You're going to suffer much more before you get to do that."

He unchains Kathy and drags her to the cot in the cell, throwing the mattress to the floor. Then he throws her face down onto the cot. The metal bands that hold up the mattress press into her skin. He chains her wrists to the bed frame so she is bent over the cot, and he whips her butt harder with the belt, striking her butt cheeks and her sex.

The edge of the belt nearly cuts into her skin, but Black Jack Bartholomew is an expert at cruelty. He wants her to hurt, but he doesn't want scars on her. That will reduce what he can get for her when he sells her. Then he pulls down his own pants and stabs his manhood into Kathy, actually tearing some of the delicate tissue.

As he viciously slams into her, Kathy screams. That just makes him hammer her more. "Not so proud now, are you, bitch? I'm going to fuck you whenever I want, and the crew is going to have you too!"

The pain is too much. Before he climaxes, Kathy passes out. Still, he mercilessly tears into her until his release. He stands and looks at Kathy, as blood drips from her. He sneers, pulls up his pants, and leaves. Kathy is still chained to the bed frame, the metal straps cutting into her.

* * *

They gather on the bridge of the *Rapier*. All are recovering from the massive mind blast. The captain asks, "Does anyone know where Miss Masters is?"

"No," they all reply.

"Mr. Hansen, contact our people that went ashore. Find her now!"

"Aye, Captain."

* * *

Several crew members go to the drugstore that Kathy had gone to. When they enter, they find the store owner dead on the floor. It's obvious some kind of struggle took place, but what? One of the crewmen goes into the store's office and plays back the security vid. It shows everything. Three men entered behind Kathy. One of them struck her on the head with a sap. Another shot the storekeeper. He calls the *Rapier*, "Captain, she's been kidnapped."

"Thank you, Mr. Flinx. Have everybody return to the ship." The captain has the bridge crew recall all the crew that went ashore. All return but one—one of the men recruited on Kyle's World, William Jennings.

Mr. Rawls states, "He had access to the bridge, Captain. If he was spying for someone, that could explain how they found you on Pi Beta 2."

"And who would he be spying for Mr. Rawls?"

"My guess would be Captain Bartholomew."

"That would be a good guess, Mr. Rawls. And that means there's at least one more spy among us. I want all three ships searched and all possible signal frequencies monitored. Use only our most-trusted people. Find the bastard fast."

"Aye, Captain," all present respond.

* * *

Cindy burns with rage. It scares Lien. Her little sister is fierce in her anger. Lien is weeping. She weeps because Kathy is lost and weeps harder because Cindy does not. At last, she goes to Captain Black. "Sir, we must find her soon."

"We're looking, Miss Yi. We're looking everywhere."

"Cindy does not weep."

The captain shakes his head. "I promise you we'll find her."

"Please, we must find her soon, or we will lose Cindy too."

"I know, Miss Yi, I know." The Captain walks away, leaving Lien standing alone.

After a moment, Mr. Gibb comes to her. He takes her hand and says, "We'll find her, I promise."

She looks into his deep-green eyes, saying, "Please," with desperation in her voice.

Mr. Gibb holds her hand a little longer, then he blushes and lets go. "I need to go help the captain," he mumbles and leaves her to join Captain Black at tactical.

* * *

Kathy's abuse is repeated over and over, perhaps for several days. She just doesn't know. All she knows for certain is the torture never seems to end.

Captain Bartholomew is a disciple, a disciple of torment. Though he whips Kathy mercilessly, he is certain to not leave any scars. He knows how valuable the merchandise is, and he's not going to let his cruelty reduce her value, but he is going as far as he can.

One time, he drags her out into the passageway after he's through with her. He chains Kathy to the passageway bulkhead and tells the crewmen passing through the passageway to do what they want with her as long as they don't leave scars.

Later, the only two female crewmen pass through the passageway. He puts them in Kathy's cell with her, tells them to use her however they want and when they're done they are to lock her cell. These women are even crueler than he is.

And so it goes for what seems an eternity. For the longest time, she's filled with hopelessness. She finds herself praying they'd just kill her, praying it will finally end.

After some time, a thought coalesces in her mind. *I'm alive! And where there's life there's hope!* The thought builds inside her like a small flame building to an inferno, an all-consuming conflagration. *I'm alive!*

After Captain Bartholomew's most recent visit, Kathy is lying across the cot when she notices the chains on her right wrist are loose. She moves carefully and eases her wrist out of the chains. She lies carefully so no one walking by will notice. With her freed right hand, she works her left hand free. As Kathy does, she sees one of the metal straps of the cot is loose. She's able to free it and carefully rubs the edge and tip of it on the deck of the ship, getting it sharp. Kathy is making what in the twentieth century would be called a shiv. No one notices. As a matter of fact, it's only when Captain Bartholomew is around that anyone notices Kathy at all. So she has hours, perhaps days, to get it nice and sharp, very nice and sharp.

* * *

It takes some days, but they intercept a signal being transmitted from the *Fatman*. The captain moves swiftly. He was prepared for this, and soon the spy is in chains. Mr. Gibb personally interrogates him and when he's finished, he goes to the captain. "He doesn't know where they're at, Captain. He's got no idea."

"Very good, Mr. Gibb. Push the SOB out the airlock, please."

"With pleasure, Captain, with pleasure." When Mr. Gibb leaves, the captain is deep in thought. Soon his thoughts turn prayerlike.

"Can you hear me? We can't find her, soon she'll be lost to us. Please don't let that happen, show us, please, show us where she's at." Several minutes go by. Captain Black stands still, unmoving like a statue, eyes closed. The bridge crew waits, they watch the man that has led them through so much and prepare for his commands. Absolute silence envelops the *Rapier*'s bridge. The captain moves, his eyes open. "Best possible speed to the Gamma Pi system, alert the *Isis* to accompany us. Have the *Fatman* move to Reavers Cove, we'll meet them there."

The bridge comes alive with activity. Orders are issued, and the course is laid in. The ships make the translation to hyperspace. Mr. Gibb returns to the bridge. The captain calls him and Mr. Rawls over. "I want two assault teams, all our best people. No quarter, gentlemen, until she's safe, no quarter."

To their surprise, Cindy cuts in, "Don't even think about leaving me out of this. I'm going, and that's that!"

"I wouldn't even think about it, princess."

* * *

Kathy waits. She waits when the cook feeds her and abuses her. She waits when one of the women abuses her then cleans her up. Kathy waits until Captain Bartholomew comes. She waits as he takes off his weapons, she waits as he unbuckles his belt, she waits as he starts to pull down his pants. In Kathy's mind, she hears, *Now!* then she strikes.

Surprised, he starts to speak, "Huh…" Before he can complete a word, Kathy drives the shiv into his left eye. He howls. "You bitch, you bitch!" Kathy missed the optic nerve canal to the brain, so he's still alive. He backs away, screaming. She thinks about stabbing him again, then she runs. "Get her!" he screams.

Kathy runs out into the passageway. At first, no one is there, but the crewmen are starting to react. She runs faster as both ends of the passageway are filling with Bartholomew's crew.

Kathy rushes through a hatch right into another crewman. She drives the shiv into his heart and locks the hatch. When she looks around, she sees she's in the armory. Kathy grabs a pulse rifle and two mags.

Bartholomew is pounding on the hatch. "I'll kill you, I'll kill you!" he shouts. Someone is cutting through the hatch with a torch. Kathy prepares to take on whoever comes through the hatch.

Suddenly, the ship heaves violently, and everyone is thrown to the deck. The ship heaves again, and then a loud blast echoes along the hull. Soon the sounds of battle echo throughout the ship. Bartholomew yells, "Cut open that damn hatch." The torch keeps cutting.

Kathy readies to fire, that's when she discovers she's got a bad weapon. "Shit!" she shouts. She grabs the keys from the dead armorer, fumbles as she opens the rifle rack, and grabs a pulse rifle. But before she can load it, he's in the compartment.

"I'll rip your lungs out!" he shouts. A crewman stands on either side of him, pointing their pistols at Kathy as Bartholomew starts to draw his sword. Kathy prepares to meet his attack. Suddenly, two shots ring out, and the men with him go down. As Bartholomew turns to face where the shots came from, Cindy rushes into the compartment, shouting, "Mom!" She charges right at him, and before he can finish drawing his sword, Cindy drives her sword through him. Kathy sees the tip of her blade come out of his back.

"Damn you!" he shouts as he hits her, and she flies across the compartment.

As Cindy slams against the bulkhead Kathy feels rage rise up inside her. It triggers her enhanced strength and reactions, she feels energized and furious. Kathy yells, "Don't touch..." as she swings the rifle like a baseball bat striking Captain Bartholomew in the head with the buttstock. He stumbles to the side. She swings again shouting "...my daughter..." striking him in the back of the head, Black Jack falls to his knees. Kathy screams "...you bastard!" as she slams the buttstock down on his head like a sledgehammer, he crumples to the deck. She kneels on the deck striking him again and again, before she knows it, she's caving in his skull. As she smashes in his head, Kathy sees Mr. Gibb and Captain Black staring at her. They are shocked.

Cindy looks up with tears in her eyes. "Mom, please."

Kathy stops. The captain steps up, and he puts his coat over her. "Come, Miss Masters, let's go home," he gently says.

Cindy takes her hand. "Mom, let's go." Kathy stands up. She, Cindy, and Mr. Gibb head back to the *Rapier* as Captain Black leads the rest of his crew to finish the battle, leaving Black Jack Bartholomew in a puddle of his own blood.

Soon the *Raven* is captured, and some of its crewmen are taken prisoner. When Captain Black finds out what they did to Kathy, he blasts the rest of Bartholomew's crew out of the airlock.

Mr. Gibb takes Kathy and Cindy to their quarters. Oscar runs up to Cindy and rubs up against her legs. He then looks Kathy over and says, *Meow*.

Lien waits for them impatiently. Mr. Gibb hands Kathy over to her. Lien tends her injuries, then takes Kathy into the shower. As Lien cleans her up, Kathy wants to break down, but she has no tears. She's sitting on the floor of the shower with Lien holding her. Kathy's trying to cry, but nothing comes out. Lien holds her close. "It's okay, Kathy, it's okay."

The Captain keeps insisting that Kathy see Doc Smith. He wants to be certain she's okay, especially now that he knows the extent of the abuse that was heaped upon her. After a week, Kathy finally gives in. Doc Smith gives her a thorough examination. When he's finished, he tells her that she's pregnant.

CHAPTER 15

COMMODORE BLACK

Captain Black decides to keep and refurbish the *Raven*. He now has two powerful raiders, an armed sloop, and a replenishment and repair ship. Safe Port has a fleet, and Captain Black is its admiral. Captain Black spends most of his time supervising the work being done on the *Raven*. Though they need a "dry dock" for most of the repairs, there is lots that can be done while the ships are in transit. During this time, Mr. Gibb is captain pro tem, a role he does well.

At first, Kathy thinks nothing of this; it seems like normal duties. But after awhile, she begins to notice things, things that start to bother her. What she notices first is the captain cancels sword training. Under current circumstances she might not have paid attention to it, except for all the years she's been on the *Rapier* the captain always spent at least one afternoon a week training her and Cindy. Now she finds her, Cindy, and Lien practicing on their own. The next thing she notices is, when he's around, the captain doesn't look at her. As a matter of fact, he barely acknowledges she's there. He still dotes on Cindy when he can, but he barely even speaks to her, and he never looks her in the eye. After that, it seems that if the captain is in the mess, he leaves shortly after she enters. He always excuses himself with the need to attend to a problem on the *Raven*, but this happens all the time.

Kathy starts to believe he doesn't want to be around her. Cindy and Lien tell her she's wrong, but she's convinced it's true. Add in the trauma of being kidnapped and raped, plus the hormone rush of being pregnant, Kathy finds herself on an emotional roller coaster.

The captain puts in at Reavers Cove to finish repairs and to load up the replenishment ship. The ships are in port for over two weeks; repairs and upgrades are done 24/7. He also makes sure Kathy sees an obstetrician.

During that time Doc Smith spends lots of time with Kathy and the obstetrician. By now, she's three weeks pregnant, and they are thorough in their exam.

Cindy is with Kathy the whole time. She's furious about what happened but is torn over whether Kathy should carry the baby to term. So Kathy tries to get her to be more accepting. "Cindy, sweetie, the baby didn't hurt me. We have to take care of it, after all, it's just a baby."

"I know, Mom," she says with a sigh. "But it's so wrong what he did to you."

Kathy hugs her. "I know, sweetie, but this is how things are."

Mr. Gibb spends as much time with Kathy as he can, and the whole crew seems to think they are the baby's dads. They go out of their way to care for Kathy. But the captain is scarce, and he seldom talks to her now. She doesn't understand, and it hurts—it hurts a lot. So Kathy decides to confront him.

After seeing the doctor, Kathy, Cindy, Doc Smith, and Mr. Gibb go to the tavern where the captain is recruiting crewmen for the *Raven* and to bring the *Rapier*'s crew up to strength. Nobody knows why Kathy wants to go there; all will be quite surprised.

When Kathy walks into the tavern, the captain is sitting at a table. A line of about ten men are being interviewed by him and Mr. Rawls. The rest of the tavern is filled with brotherhood members. Some are newly recruited crew for the *Rapier* and the *Raven*; the rest are brothers taking their ease. Kathy walks to the front of the line.

"Captain, I'm applying to be navigator of the *Raven*," she announces. Dead silence. Mr. Gibb and Mr. Rawls stare blankly at her. Cindy is aghast.

After a moment, the captain says, "Miss Masters, this is not the time or place for this discussion."

She snaps back, "Oh yes, it is! Apparently, my captain is no longer happy with me onboard his ship, so I'm looking for another berth. In accordance with the bylaws of the brotherhood, it is my right to ask for a transfer to another ship. Or is it because I'm a woman you'd deny me my rights of the brotherhood?"

"Miss Masters, this is not the time."

"This is the perfect time. What is it, Captain? Am I damaged goods now? Does the fact he touched me now make me repulsive to you?"

"Miss Masters, not now!" he growls.

"No, right now!" Kathy shouts.

"You're pregnant and shouldn't be getting so excited," he replies.

"Well, I am excited. I'm mad as hell! You won't talk to me, won't look at me. You just leave whenever I come into the room. Am I so repulsive now?" Fury fills her voice. But what he says back is not anything like what she was expecting.

"I leave because it hurts so damn much to see you. To know I couldn't protect you from that monster. To know again I failed a woman I care about. It hurts so damn much that I wasn't there when you needed me." He screams it. "You got hurt because I wasn't there." He sits down and slumps in his seat. "For the second time in my life, I wasn't there when someone I cared for really needed me." Everyone in the tavern is looking around uncomfortably, trying to ignore the captain's tortured expression, exchanging embarrassed looks. "I couldn't protect you," he says with a sob.

Kathy sits and takes his hand. "I'm here now, you saved me."

He looks at her, tears in his eyes. "But I didn't protect you."

"You couldn't have," she says. "No one could have, but you came for me."

He regains some composure. "Miss Masters, let's talk later. I would really love for you and Cindy to join me for dinner, but now I have to interview crew." He looks up at Mr. Gibb. "Mr. Gibb, please return the ladies to the ship for me."

"Of course, Captain. But first, there is brotherhood business that involves all present."

"And what would that be, Mr. Gibb?"

"Your status as captain is now in question." Everyone present stares at Mr. Gibb in silence. Kathy and Cindy look at Mr. Gibb with total surprise on their faces.

The Captain keeps his composure, just barely. "How so, Mr. Gibb?"

"Well, sir, you now command four ships, a squadron in anyone's navy. Now, in extreme circumstances, a captain commanding four ships is acceptable, but those circumstances have passed."

"Go on."

"So either the extra ships need to be released to go out on their own, something I'm opposed to, or you must give up your status as captain per brotherhood bylaws."

"And what would my new status be, Mr. Gibb?"

"Well, under brotherhood bylaws, your status would be commodore with all associated rights, shares, and privileges."

Now it's the captain's turn to be surprised and he is at a loss for words. Before the captain can recover, Mr. Gibb calls the question, "What say you, brothers?"

"All hail, Commodore Black" erupts from all present. For several minutes, Commodore Black remains speechless. At last, he says, "Mr. Gibb, please escort the ladies and the doctor back to the *Rapier*."

"Aye, Commodore," he replies. Mr. Gibb gently takes Kathy's arm. "Come, Miss Masters, you should rest."

The four of them, Mr. Gibb, Cindy, the doctor, and Kathy, return to the *Rapier*. By time they get there, the ship and the town are abuzz with what happened and the incident, and the story of the death of Captain Bartholomew, has an unexpected side effect. The scum don't go to the commodore's interviews, but those that want to fight the Chinese, they come out in droves. The commodore has more volunteers than he has room for, he even fills all the billets on the *Fatman*.

Many come to sail with the women that killed Captain Bartholomew. Soon some are calling Kathy and Cindy the Buccaneer Queens.

* * *

"Kathy, what was all that about?" Steve asks.

"What do you mean?" Kathy says.

"That whole status under the brotherhood thing?"

Cindy answers, "Steve, in the brotherhood, officers are elected."

"Elected?"

Kathy responds, "The brotherhood is a democracy in many ways, Steve. Captains, commodores, etc. are elected. Even a monster like Bartholomew had to be elected to the captaincy by his crew."

"No brother sails under a captain he does not agree to follow," Cindy adds.

"I thought the captains have absolute authority on their ships."

"True, Steve, but you don't become a captain without being elected by brothers in good standing. The bylaws are clear on that. And captains are not absolute monarchs. They can be challenged by their crew if the brothers feel aggrieved." Kathy continues, "In the case of a commodore, anyone on a ship that will serve under him can call the question. Of course, all the crew of the ships not present had to vote on it too, but by this point, it was more of a formality. They'd already accepted James Black as a commodore."

CHAPTER 16

CAPTAINS GIBB AND RAWLS

Toward evening time, Mr. Gibb knocks on the hatch to Kathy and Cindy's cabin. He sticks his head in. "The commodore's returned, and there's a meeting in the mess. It's a brotherhood meeting," he says. Kathy and Cindy go with him.

The commodore takes his seat. "What's this about, Mr. Gibb?"

"We respectfully ask that you keep your flag on the *Rapier*, Commodore."

"And who will captain her?" Commodore Black asks.

Mr. Rawls says, "I nominate Mr. Gibb to be captain of the *Rapier*." Mr. Gibb was definitely not expecting that, but before he can say a word, the crew shouts out, "Aye!" And it's now a done deal. Both Captain Gibb and Commodore Black are surprised by these events, though the commodore is quite pleased with the outcome. Before anyone can react to it, Mr. Rawls calls the brotherhood meeting adjourned, and it's decided. The crew give their congratulations to Commodore Black and Captain Gibb. Kathy and Cindy sit smiling at both men.

* * *

Kathy is quiet for several minutes. She rubs the wedding ring. Steve speaks up. "Did you and Captain, er, Commodore Black have dinner?"

"Huh? Um, yes, yes, we did."

Cindy pulls up a picture; it's of Kathy and Commodore Black dancing in the observation dome. She speaks up, "We had dinner, then they went and danced together for hours," she says with a giggle. Kathy blushes then starts back on telling her story.

* * *

Dinner is at seventeen bells. Cindy pesters Kathy all afternoon about what she is going to wear. Cindy keeps pushing her to dress sexy. Kathy finally settles on a form-fitting black dress with matching accessories, and she wears the earrings the commodore gave her.

Dinner is delightful. Good food, nice music, soft lighting, and Commodore Black is wearing his best suit. Several times during the meal, he touches Kathy's hand.

After the dinner, Cindy says she'd like to go watch the stars. The three of them head to the observation dome, but on the way, Cindy decides she's tired and leaves as Kathy and Commodore Black go into the dome. The commodore turns on the music, and he takes Kathy in his arms, and they dance. They don't know how long they dance. Nor do they notice Cindy taking some pics.

The commodore swirls Kathy around the floor of the dome, but after some time, he says, "It's late, Miss Masters, and you need your rest." He walks Kathy to her quarters, kisses her lightly on the cheek, bows, and says, "Good night."

Kathy goes into her cabin. Cindy and Lien are sitting on her bunk. "Well, Mom, tell us everything."

"We just danced, sweetie," Kathy replies. The three of them talk, laugh, and giggle like silly schoolgirls. After awhile, Lien goes to bed while Kathy and Cindy continue to talk. Finally, the two of them curl up together and fall asleep.

Kathy wakes still curled up with Cindy. This morning, she looks like a little angel. Kathy looks at her belly with sadness; she's already starting to show, she thinks. *How am I going to raise a baby on a privateer?* Then she smiles a moment, *at least the baby will have the best dads in the galaxy.*

Cindy opens her eyes and says, "Mom, I'm still sleepy."

"Me too," Kathy says. Cindy sees the sadness on her face and hugs her tight. "I love you, sweetie," Kathy says to her. Oscar gets on the bed and rubs against both of them. For a moment, he shows love without indifference. They get up and clean up. Lien is still sleeping, so they leave her in bed and head to the ship's mess.

Cookie has a special breakfast for Cindy as usual, but today he's made a special breakfast for Kathy as well. He smiles and says, "We've got to take good care of the little one."

Kathy dressed in a new dress, something that allows for her burgeoning baby belly, but it keeps coming loose. She tries to fix it but can't seem to. Captain Gibb sits with them. He notices she's having problems and helps her with her dress.

He's still trying to get used to being a captain. He says quietly to Kathy, "Frankly, it really creeps me out."

"Oh," she says.

"Yes," he replies. "I never expected to be responsible for so many people."

"It's different?" she inquires.

He whispers, "It's damn scary," then Captain Gibb says, "The Commodore is planet side," he shakes his head, saying, "That is weird too. Anyway, he'd like us to join him when we can."

"Yes, let's." Kathy rubs her belly. She's still finding the idea of being pregnant hard to accept.

"Uh, where's Lien?" Captain Gibb asks.

"She's still sleeping," Cindy replies.

"Oh." Kathy and Cindy both note the tinge of disappointment in his voice.

They go to Kathy's cabin, where she picks up a pack for Cindy's stuff, then leave the ship. Today Cindy seems more like a twelve-year-old girl and less like the battle-hardened trooper that she is. It's nice to see her that way.

The three of them go to the tavern where the commodore was signing in new crew. Cindy sticks close to Kathy and Captain Gibb. Kathy starts rubbing her belly again. Cindy looks up at her. "It'll be okay, Mom." She says, "If it's a boy, I think we should name him James." Then she hugs Kathy. Kathy smiles and hugs her back.

When they get to the tavern, all the crewmen are there. There are a bunch of new faces, and it's actually a little crowded. Kathy holds Cindy's hand tightly. When they walk in, the crewmen all make room for them. As Kathy and Cindy walk to the commodore's table, they hear some comments.

"Is that her?" some ask.

"Yes, it is."

"And the little girl."

"She stabbed Captain Bartholomew." Kathy looks about. It seems they are actually in awe of her and Cindy. Still, she walks with her head down, embarrassed. "And she killed him."

"Wow."

Captain Gibb guides the girls to the commodore's table. Commodore Black stands and takes Kathy's hand and helps her to her seat. Then he seats Cindy. Everyone watches. The two girls look at the commodore. He leans down and whispers, "I'm afraid it's gotten out that you finished off Captain Bartholomew. It's made you quite a hero around here, especially among the younger men."

"Oh," Kathy says as she holds her belly, and she looks down at her feet.

He whispers, "It'll be okay, Miss Masters." Then he stands up. "Last order of brotherhood business, I ask the brotherhood to remove Mr. Rawls as its speaker." The whole place breaks out in murmured conversation. Mr. Rawls actually looks shocked and surprised.

The supply chief asks, "Why would you ask that, Commodore? Officers normally have no voice in the selection of the brotherhood speaker for their ships." Kathy grabs a few peanuts.

Commodore Black replies, "He'll need to give up that post because I nominate him to be captain of the *Raven*." Rawls is stunned again. You could knock him over with a feather.

The whole assembly shouts, "Aye! Captain Rawls!"

Kathy starts chewing on peanuts like there is no tomorrow.

Commodore Black grins at her. "Not too many, Miss Masters. You don't want to gain too much."

Captain Rawls actually blushes at the approbation. Crew members come up and congratulate him. The assembly breaks up, and most of the crew return to the ships to make ready and finish repairs.

As the repairs continue, Captain Gibb comes across an extraordinary opportunity. He discovers there are some snub fighters available for purchase. Because of their size they are not as capable as a fleet fighter and have more limited range. But being smaller, they could be adapted to use by the *Rapier* and the *Raven*, and it may be possible to fit one to the *Isis*. So Captain Gibb asks the commodore for a meeting of captains.

They all gather in the *Rapier*'s crews mess. Kathy attends the meeting to photograph it for the record. Present are Commodore Black, Captain Gibb, Captain Rawls, Captain Garrett, Captain Giles of the *Fatman*, and Chief Engineer Simms.

"Captain Gibb has asked for this meeting, so I'll turn it over to him. Captain Gibb," states Commodore Black.

Captain Gibb begins, "Gentlemen, I've recently learned that there are seven snub fighters for sale here at Reavers Cove. If they are in good shape, I think they could add significantly to our capabilities if we can adapt them for use with our ships. So Mr. Simms, how hard would that be?"

"Well, that would be challenging, but it could be done," replies Mr. Simms.

"How difficult would it be, Mr. Simms?" inquires the commodore.

"Well, sir, we could attach one, perhaps two to the bellies of the *Rapier* and the *Raven*. We might have to remove a belly turret for two. Because of the location of the hyperspace generator on the *Isis*, it'll be harder to attach a fighter. Still it might be possible. And we could put one or two on the *Fatman*. That might actually be easier."

Captain Giles asks, "Does that mean the *Fatman* will be going into combat?"

"I'd prefer not," replies Commodore Black. "But if you have a fighter or two for protection, that could free up the *Isis* for more aggressive action." Captain Garrett grins at that.

"Very good, sir," responds Captain Giles.

Commodore Black thinks on the idea for several minutes. As he does, Kathy snaps what will become the most famous picture of him ever taken. In it, all four captains and Mr. Simms await his decision while he ponders the possibilities. The picture captures the respect that all present have for the commodore. Commodore Black looks up and says, "Okay, Captain Gibb and Mr. Simms, I want you to evaluate these fighters and their condition. Take their specs and match them to our ships. What is the most favorable configuration possible? Captain Rawls I want you, Captain Garrett, Captain Giles, and Mr. Hansen to work out tactical and operational options for our squadron with and without the fighters. We meet again in two days to go over your reports. Get it done, gentlemen."

With that, the meeting breaks up. For the next two days, the captains are very busy. Kathy and Cindy hardly see them. Even the commodore is stretched thin, but somehow he makes time for them. They even have an hour in the observation dome for cookies and cocoa.

When they meet again, the captains submit their reports to the commodore. He briefly looks them over. "What's the bottom line, Mr. Simms?"

"We can put two fighters on the *Rapier* and the *Raven*. To do so, we'll have to remove the bottom rear firing particle beam turrets. I've looked through the logs of both ships, and those weapons are seldom used. Also, the rail gun secondary batteries will still be in place and will be able to be fired even when the fighters are docked."

"And the *Isis*?"

"That one is a little harder. There are no turrets that need to be removed, but it may be necessary to cut a notch in the hyperspace generator foil. That means I'll have to reinforce the foil frame."

"What about the *Fatman*?"

"Piece of cake. I can put two fighters on the bottom with minimal modifications."

"How long will all of this take?"

"Three weeks, if no problems. Up to five, if there are issues."

"Thank you, Mr. Simms. Captain Gibb what about these fighters?"

"There are actually eleven fighters. All need some work for them to be operational. Five just need some minor repairs, nothing terribly difficult. Two need extensive repairs, but nothing beyond our abilities. The rest should be disassembled for replacement parts."

"Thank you, Captain Gibb. Captain Rawls?"

"Tactically and operationally, having the fighters increases our capabilities significantly, one could say exponentially. With just the ships, we have a threefold increase in our abilities. Most of the raiding will be performed by the *Rapier* and the *Raven*, and the *Isis* will need to continue to operate as it has to date. With the fighters, we can take on larger ships and small convoys. The *Isis* can be used at least half the time in raids, while two fighters protect the *Fatman*. We can bring up to five fighters into the mix and, if needed, the four armed shuttles. That is a significant edge."

Kathy watches the commodore looking for a sign of his decision. She looks around the room. All eyes are on him. "Captain Rawls, you were purser. Can we cover the cost of this?"

"It'll be tight, but yes, sir, I believe we have enough and shouldn't have to ask the crew to give up their earned shares."

Commodore Black considers all he's been told, eventually arriving at a decision. "Let's do it. I'll read your reports tonight and may have more questions, but this seems to be a move we should make. I want regular updates on progress. Captain Rawls, I want you to focus on simulations to train everybody on how to work all these elements in battle. Captain Gibb, please oversee the upgrade of the *Raven* as well as the *Rapier*. That's all for now, gentlemen." Everyone but the commodore and Kathy leave the mess. "Well, Miss Masters, what do you think?"

"I think if you do this, you'll have more capability."

"Yes, go on."

"With more capability, you'll launch more devastating raids, especially against the Chinese."

"True."

"And that means the Chinese will do more to destroy you."

"I'm afraid that is true, very true."

"So why are you doing it?"

He looks her in the eyes, takes her hand, and says, "To do as much damage as I can before my luck runs out."

His words cut into her like a knife. *Before my luck runs out.* She holds his hand for a few more moments, then runs out of the mess. When she gets to her quarters, she runs in past Cindy and Lien and runs to her bunk, throwing herself on it. *Before my luck runs out* echoes in her mind. An ocean of tears flood out of her. *Before my luck runs out.* She feels Cindy put her arms around her.

"Mom, what's wrong?"

"Nothing, sweetie, it's just being pregnant." Lien looks into her eyes. Understanding passes between them.

"It'll be okay, Kathy."

"Yes, of course it will." The ocean continues to flow.

CHAPTER 17

BABY JAMES

It takes four weeks to finish repairs, modify the ships to accept the fighters, and repair the fighters themselves. Another week is spent training with the fighters and the flotilla. Of course, Cindy insists on being trained on them as well. Turns out she has a knack for fighter tactics. Still, she needs weeks more training before she can be considered qualified. As luck would have it, the commodore is able to recruit eight qualified former fighter pilots from among the brothers. Though not familiar with this particular model fighter between them, they are able to adapt to the differences.

By time they finally put out, Kathy is now two months pregnant. After her last visit to the obstetrician, she goes to the commodore with a big smile on her face dragging Cindy and Lien with her. The doctor ran the latest in fetal tests, and she can't wait to tell the commodore what the doctor told her. The commodore sits in his chair as she bursts onto the bridge and runs up and hugs him.

"It's a boy!" she shouts as she kisses him on the cheek. The commodore turns red in the face. Captain Gibb stifles a chuckle.

"Umm, that's great, Miss Masters," the commodore says. He holds her for several minutes. Cindy and Lien giggle, then take Kathy by the arm.

"Come, Mom, the commodore is busy now."

As they leave, he says to them, "Let's have dessert in the observation dome to celebrate."

"Yes, that would be lovely," Kathy replies.

The little flotilla sets out to raid Chinese trade routes. By that evening, they've completed their first jump.

That evening, Kathy, Cindy, and Lien wait in their cabin. It's been an hour since dinner, and they wait for the commodore to let them know dessert is ready. There's a knock on the door. Cindy answers it. It's Captain Gibb.

"Are you ladies ready?"

"Yes," Cindy says with a chuckle. Kathy and Lien get up, and the four of them go to the observation dome. When they get there, the commodore has prepared a surprise for them. There is a table with six chairs. A white tablecloth covers it. There are candles, and in the center sits a large chocolate cake and a gallon of Neapolitan ice cream. The commodore sits at the table, and Cookie stands behind him in a suit, wearing a big grin. On the cake, Cookie wrote using icing, "Welcome, Baby James!" Kathy starts crying.

"Mom what's wrong?" Cindy asks.

"Nothing, sweetie. Everything is perfect."

The commodore stands and pulls out the chair next to his. "Miss Masters, if you'd honor me by sitting next to me?"

Kathy slips into the chair, and the commodore slides her seat forward. Cookie seats Cindy, and Captain Gibb seats Lien, then they sit next to them. Once all are seated, the commodore stands and announces, "In honor of our soon-to-arrive new mate, Cookie has prepared these delicious cakes. I ask all the crews to join us in celebration." Then he takes Kathy's hand, and they cut the cake together. Throughout the flotilla, cakes are cut, slices served, and all the brothers join in the celebration.

They sit in the observation dome for two hours, eating cake and ice cream, telling stories and jokes, and just sharing each other's company. Kathy notices that Captain Gibb is paying special attention to Lien. He looks at her with longing eyes. And she notices too; Lien blushes at his attention.

Cookie and Cindy clear the table then leave. Crewmen remove the tables and chairs. Captain Gibb puts on some music. The commodore takes Kathy's hand, and they start to move rhythmically across the deck. Lien starts to leave, but Captain Gibb touches her on the shoulder. She turns to him. "May I have this dance?" he asks her. She moves into his arms, and they join the commodore and Kathy moving rapturously about the observation dome. Cindy returns stealthily and snaps a couple of pics. Then she melts away to their cabin. It's getting late, so the commodore and Captain Gibb walk the ladies to their cabin.

"It's been a lovely evening," the commodore says to Kathy. He gently kisses her on the cheek, bows, then opens the door for her.

Captain Gibb sputters, "I had a... but mean it was, uh I..." Lien leans in and kisses him on the cheek, then she and Kathy go into their quarters. Cindy sits with Oscar on her lap. She giggles at them as they enter. Kathy and Lien both blush. "Wedding bells soon, I bet," Cindy chides them.

They take their time moving into Chinese space. There are a couple of reasons for this. First is getting the pilots used to the modifications to the fighters. The enhancements from the nanchik gods make the little snub fighters perform like nothing the fighter pilots have ever flown before.

The second reason is the Chinese have significantly improved their border security. After over a decade of pirate and privateer raids, they are making a concerted effort to end them. The Chinese have instituted a small convoy system. This is a recent development, and none of the brotherhood captains know of it. From now on, merchant ships move in groups of at least three, and often, there are one or more military escorts, depending on the importance of the convoy. Then there are the Q ships. These are auxiliaries, sloop, or corvette-sized ships disguised as merchant ships. They wait until a raider is close then expose their weaponry. Often, a raider is outgunned and doesn't know it until it's too late.

After finding a suitable location, Commodore Black leads his flotilla into Chinese space and heads in the general direction of Safe Port.

Kathy is over four months now, and it's harder for her to perform her duties. Captain Gibb restricts her duties to just photography and keeping her journal. This is just as well because she can't fit into tactical anymore, and the pressure on her bladder has her running to the head often. However, Cindy still stands a watch at weapons. She's on the bridge when tactical picks up "bogies."

Mr. Hahn calls out, "Captain, I've got three Beijing-class freighters and what appears to be a Nanking-class destroyer escort at bearing 23 plus 66. There's something else, sir. It looks like a brotherhood ship is near them, and it's getting pounded." Commodore Black starts to say something but stops himself.

Captain Gibb says, "Put it on the view screen and give me maximum magnification." Kathy looks at the screen. The destroyer escort is between the merchantmen and the raider. Normally, the merchantmen would have run by now, but instead, they stay close to their escort. The raider is a corvette-class similar to the *Rapier*. It is clearly outgunned by the destroyer escort but for now seems to be holding its own.

"They won't last for long, Commodore," Captain Gibb says.

"If we take the time to sneak in, the raider will be destroyed before we get there," the commodore replies. "Captain Gibb, give me tight tactical comm to all ships please."

"Aye, sir."

The commodore issues his battle plan. "*Fatman*, stay here and launch your fighters for protection. All other fighters, launch and move with us. We're going to jump right into this. Speed is our advantage. *Raven* and *Rapier*, concentrate on the warship. *Isis* and fighters, disable the merchant ships. Everyone, be on alert for other warships. Let's do this."

As soon as the fighters are launched, they go to flank speed and jump into the fight. They were fairly close when they detected the battle, so it only takes a couple of minutes to get to weapons range. Before the Chinese can react, they fire and disable the hyperspace generators on their targets. The *Isis* and the fighters quickly disable the merchantmen. They drift helplessly in space.

The destroyer escort is another story. It has already done significant damage to the other raider, so it tries to bring all of its firepower to bear on the *Rapier* and the *Raven*. Had they not been modified by the nanchik gods, they would have been severely damaged. Still, the Chinese warship manages to land some good hits.

The *Rapier* and the *Raven* focus all of their main and secondary batteries on the destroyer escort. Cindy paints the warship with particle beams, which, coupled with the *Raven*'s, quickly overcome the ship's neutron armor. She then pumps four salvos from the rail guns into the warship amidship. The first four projectiles pound the ship's hull, cracking it. The next four punch through the hull opening a three-meter hole. The *Raven*'s rail guns strike near the impulse engines, damaging the warships ability to maneuver.

But this is a warship and it's designed to take punishment. The Chinese captain rolls his ship away from the attackers to protect its injuries and to bring his bottom batteries to bear. He fires. The *Rapier* heaves from the hit. Kathy is thrown to the deck.

Cindy fires particle beams, followed by rail guns. She rips a five-meter gash in the bottom of the Chinese ship. The *Raven* strikes home as well. Its rail guns tear into the ship's impulse engines. An actual section of the plasma tube breaks off and drifts away. Both ships fire rail guns a second time, followed by a full spread of missiles. Also, the *Isis* and the wounded raider fire on the warship.

It's more than it can take. The ship's frame gives in several locations, causing the crushed-can effect. Then sections of the ship bend and snap; it breaks up into three pieces.

As the tension eases, the commodore looks over to where Kathy was seated and sees her sprawled on the deck. He rushes to her. "Miss Masters, are you all right?"

She looks up at him; confusion covers her face. "Did I fall?" she asks.

He picks her up and heads to sickbay. On the way, he commands, "Captain Gibb, take over."

The Commodore charges down the main passageway, holding Kathy in his arms. He rushes into sickbay. "Doc, she fell. I think she hit her head."

Doc Smith points to a bed. "Put her there." He finishes examining a crewman that was injured in the battle. "Crabeye, take over," doc orders then he goes to examine Kathy.

* * *

The *Rapier* receives a transmission from the damaged raider. "Whoever you are, this is Captain French of the *Banshee*, thank you."

"Captain French, this is Captain Gibb of the *Rapier*. You're welcome. However, I doubt we have time for conversation at the moment. Are your hyperspace engines operational?"

"Yes, but just barely, we'll need help to jump."

"Understood, we'll have the *Isis* tow you. We'll also tow two of the freighters to loot once we're out of here."

"And the third freighter?"

In response, Cindy fires four salvos from the rail guns into the last merchantman. It breaks apart. "Can I go check on my mom now, Captain?"

"Yes, of course, princess. Mr. Hahn, take weapons, please." Then he says to Captain French, "Your crew gets the larger load of the remaining merchantmen, seems to me you've earned it."

"Thank you, Captain. Let's get out of here."

"Yes, let's." They quickly get the *Fatman* back among them. The fighters are recovered. Towlines are secured, and the ships coordinate their hyperspace jump. As the jump prep continues, Mr. Hansen at tactical shouts, "Multiple jump points opening. I'm reading three Lanchow-class destroyers."

Captain Gibb shouts, "All ships jump." The little flotilla translates into hyperspace.

* * *

Cindy enters sickbay. She looks around and sees the commodore and Doc Smith with Kathy. Doc Smith has Kathy on oxygen and has started an IV. He's checking various monitors that he has hooked up to her. Cindy walks over. "Is she going to be okay, Doc?"

"If she drinks more water and quits banging her head on the deck, she should be."

Cindy sits beside the commodore; she puts her hand on his arm. "You're needed on the bridge, Dad. I'll stay with her, I'll get you if anything changes."

"Thank you, princess." The commodore stands, kisses Kathy on the forehead, then heads back to the bridge.

The ships stop at a small planetoid the commodore knows of. There they make repairs on the *Banshee* as best they can. They also clean out the Chinese merchantmen. As soon as the *Banshee* can, she departs for Reavers Cove. The commodore's flotilla returns on course toward Safe Port.

Doc Smith keeps Kathy in sickbay for two days. Then he gives her grief for not drinking enough water. She goes to her cabin and gets in bed. Lien stays with her while Cindy stands her watches.

Three months go by. There are raids, trades, and pregnancy. It's like the little flotilla is directly involved as Kathy prepares to give birth. Everyone is a dad to her baby; they all try to be there for her. Several times, the commodore has intimate dinners with Kathy, often dancing in the observation dome. Some gentle intimate touches, even a couple of gentle kisses.

It seems on many raids there are far too many narrow escapes. So the commodore and the captains analyze all aspects of their operations. It's during this time they discover something different the Chinese are doing. They have a new signal system that contacts ships in hyperspace. The Chinese are keeping destroyer detachments in hyperspace, and when they get a call from a convoy, they jump straight to that location. It takes a little experimentation, but they come up with a way to jam the signal. After a few trial runs, they have the system working.

By this time, Kathy is due; it's time for the baby. Kathy goes into labor early in the day. Cindy and Lien rush her to sickbay. The commodore and captains find a good place to hide the ships, then the commodore and Captain Gibb go to sickbay.

Kathy cries out in pain. Even in this age, they still haven't found a way to ease labor pains. As she braces for the next wave of pain, she hears/feels, *Life, new life*. A calm feeling washes over her. Her pain eases and becomes bearable.

The commodore is in the delivery room with Kathy. He holds her hand and tells her to breathe. Cindy, Lien, and Captain Gibb wait outside. The delivery goes late into the night. Every crew member that's not on watch is waiting to hear the news.

At three bells, little James Connor Masters-Black takes his first breath and lets the universe know he's arrived. Word is flashed throughout the little flotilla along with pics and vids. The commodore even allows two drinks per crewman. Drinks for those on duty are held until their watch ends.

Doc puts little James in her arms. The commodore looks at them both. He's grinning like a fool. To this point, Kathy has been torn. The whole pregnancy she'd been sad, at times angry. Many times she thought about an abortion. But now with this little baby boy in her arms, so tiny and helpless, this life that came from her, she has no doubt she'll love him for all of time.

Commodore Black holds Kathy's hand, and with her, he marvels at this little man. Cindy and Lien come in and snuggle with Kathy, and the commodore, she smiles and says, "Our family."

Kathy hears/feels, *Family*. It's euphoric.

Kathy spends a day in sickbay with little James, then Doc Smith releases her to her quarters. For the following weeks, Lien spends most of her time helping Kathy with the baby. When not on watch, Cindy helps as well. Even Oscar accepts the new invader to his world, showering baby James with his loving indifference. When their duties allow the commodore and Captain Gibb spend time with the new mate. Soon they're taking them to the observation dome, where Cookie has cocoa and cookies ready.

Captain Gibb spends more time with Lien. They grow closer with each passing day.

After two weeks, Kathy starts going to the crew's mess again. The first few days she can hardly eat as the crew are constantly swamping her to have time with the baby. It's weird, she thinks. *These fierce raiders are goo in little James's hands. It seems the old adage is true—a baby reduces perfectly normal adults into babbling idiots.* The thought makes her grin.

The euphoria lasts for three weeks.

Two Chinese merchantmen and an armed sloop are picked up by the *Raven*'s sensors. They are just a hundred kilometers away. The commodore decides to take them. Though it is not the best location, they leave the *Fatman*, the *Isis*, and their fighters among some random asteroids and start to stalk their targets. It takes thirty minutes to move in close. Once the commodore is satisfied with their position, he gives his orders. "Now, gentlemen, flank speed."

The *Rapier* and the *Raven* leap forward like cheetahs running down their kill, closing the distance to their targets rapidly.

"They've seen us," Mr. Hahn shouts. On the view screen, they can see the two merchantmen turn away. The sloop turns toward them to protect its charges. Both ships fire on the sloop. Particle beams paint the forward section. They overwhelm the sloop's neutron armor. Enough energy remains in the beams that they literally smash in the sloop's nose, destroying the bridge, its weapons, and comm stations. Three salvos from each ship's secondary batteries finish the sloop, reducing it to debris. They rush past the wreckage after the merchantmen. And that's when everything goes to hell.

The two merchantmen turn broadside to the raiders and drop their sides. The weapons within swing around to aim at the *Rapier* and the *Raven*.

Everyone hears Captain Rawls shout, "Q ships!" Then Captain Gibb and Captain Rawls simultaneously command, "Weapons, power to neutron armor. Fire all missiles!" At the same time, Mr. Hahn yells, "Multiple jump points opening!"

Captain Garrett calls out, "Chinese destroyers!" The *Isis* and the three fighters with it charge toward the Chinese warships.

Two Lanchow-class destroyers and a Hankow-class frigate come out of jump points, forming near the *Fatman* and *Isis*. One of the Chinese destroyers opened its jump point too close to the asteroids. Three large asteroids are caught in the gravity wave created by the jump point and are drawn into it. They crash into the side of the destroyer, disabling it. The frigate turns toward the *Fatman*; the remaining destroyer rushes toward the *Isis* and the fighters.

All missile batteries on the *Rapier* and the *Raven* unleash their deadly cargo as the Q ships particle beams hit the raiders. The additional power from the primary and secondary batteries keeps the particle beams from penetrating the armor.

Commodore Black orders, "All ships emergency jump to point bravo!" a predesignated rendezvous location.

Captain Garrett takes a calculated risk. He fires his main and secondary batteries at the Chinese frigate, hoping to give the *Fatman* a chance to jump. He strikes true and does damage to the frigate, but he fired a moment too late. The frigate has unloaded all it has on the *Fatman*. Captain Garrett watches in horror as his charge breaks up into hundreds of pieces.

The destroyer fires on the fighters and the *Isis*. Particle beams strike two of the fighters, vaporizing them. The third fighter is clipped by a rail gun projectile. It spins wildly out of control. The *Isis* takes a particle beam hit, but its neutron armor holds. Captain Garrett turns toward the damaged fighter and translates to hyperspace. He drags the damaged fighter into the jump point with him, saving it.

As the *Rapier* and *Raven* start to jump, they repower and fire their forward primary and secondary batteries at the Q ships. But before they can see the results, they make the translation into hyperspace.

* * *

Kathy looks over at Lien; she's lying on the deck. Kathy holds little James against her chest. "What the hell just happened?"

"I don't know," replies Lien.

Kathy examines little James to be sure he isn't hurt. As she does, she listens to the sound of the engines. *We're in hyperspace. Why'd they jump early? There was no boarding party. What's going on?* Kathy gets up and helps Lien to her feet. Then she says, "Let's go."

"Where are we going?" Lien asks.

"To the bridge. Something's wrong." They go out the door and head to the *Rapier*'s bridge.

* * *

Commodore Black transmits to all ships, "I want damage reports ASAP."

Mr. Hahn asks, "Where's the *Fatman*?"

Captain Garrett reports, "It's gone. The Chinese got it."

"What?" Commodore Black asks, surprised.

Captain Garrett replies, "Sir it was destroyed with all hands. Also, we lost two fighters and their pilots. The third fighter is severely damaged. I don't think we can repair it."

Commodore Black slumps into his chair. Captain Gibb watches him; he can see the shock on his face.

After a few minutes, damage reports start coming in from the *Isis* and the *Raven*. Then the *Rapier's* crew start reporting.

Kathy and Lien walk onto the bridge in time to hear Cindy report, "Forward batteries received 30 percent damage, mostly to targeting systems. We can have that repaired in a couple of hours."

Commodore Black tells all the captains, "Advise me when all repairs are completed."

Captain Gibb moves over to the commodore as Kathy and Lien get closer. "It could have been worse, sir."

"Worse?" the commodore says. "We lost twenty good brothers. The ship, the supplies, the repair parts, some of the loot from raids, and most of all, twenty true brothers before the mast, all gone." The commodore takes it hard, he holds himself responsible. "Twenty men."

Captain Gibb says, "Sir, we've lost men before," but it sounds hollow. Lien goes to him and takes his hand. They move to the view screen so she can talk to him in private.

Kathy takes the commodore's hand. "Come, James. Let Captain Gibb do his job." She walks him to the observation dome and sits him on the recliner. She sits beside him, holding little James, and lays her head on his shoulders. "It's not your fault," she says softly. "You couldn't have known they'd be found." She holds him most of the night.

CHAPTER 18

BURNED TO THE GROUND

The loss of the *Fatman* hits the little flotilla hard. Though everyone here is an experienced raider and has lost mates in battle before, none of them has lost an entire ship and crew. It's staggering, especially for Commodore Black. Though Kathy tries to comfort him, it's clear to her she's having little impact. For two days, he says little and spends his time either in his quarters or with her in the observation dome. He doesn't eat, and it seems from his appearance he hasn't slept.

On the third day, as repairs on the ships progress, he holds a meeting with his captains on the *Raven* and doesn't bring Kathy to record it. Once all are seated, Commodore Black opens the meeting.

"Gentlemen, we are privateers, under contract. We know the hazards of our profession and the probable outcome. But we have some among us that in my view are too precious to risk in this endeavor."

Captain Rawls speaks up first. "Who do you refer to, Commodore?"

"Miss Masters, little James, Princess Yi, and of course, our daughter, Cindy. I believe we have taken far too many risks with them onboard, and we need to take them someplace safe, someplace where they can find transport back to Earth. Some place nearby."

Captain Gibb speaks next. "In this sector of space, *safe* is a relative term and open to much interpretation. Someplace nearby limits things even more as we're in Chinese-occupied territory. And getting them to Earth past Chinese security is no small feat either."

Captain Garrett says, "I've heard some grumbling among my crew, some concern over little James. I believe morale would be a good deal better if the men felt they were in a safe place. Some of these men are fathers, and they don't like seeing children in danger."

"Neither do I, Captain Garrett. Neither do I," replies the commodore.

"You'll have to fight like hell to get them off our ships, sir," Captain Gibb points out.

"I know," the commodore says softly.

To Captain Gibb, the commodore seems filled with doubt, something he's never seen in him before. It makes him feel very uncomfortable. He looks around the table, the other captains don't seem to notice this, perhaps it's because they don't know the commodore as well as he does. That's good; they all need to believe in him now more than ever. Doubt would kill that; doubt would kill them all.

Captain Gibb says, "It's not ideal, but there's always Safe Port. It's nearby, for the last couple of years, they've left them pretty much alone, and recently, the Chinese have allowed some commercial shipping between there and Earth."

Captain Rawls adds, "All things considered, it may be the best option."

"Perhaps you gentlemen are right. Safe Port it is then. Captain Rawls, have your comm officer contact them and advise them of our intentions. Please keep this among yourselves, gentlemen, until I've informed the ladies."

Captain Garrett brings up something unexpected. "One thing, Commodore, I tried to contact my mother last week to wish her a happy sixtieth birthday and never got a response. Has anyone been in contact with them recently?"

The commodore looks blankly at Captain Garrett for a moment. "Why haven't you brought this to my attention before now?"

"Sorry, sir, but you know how spotty communications with Safe Port can be. Then with all that has happened in the last week, it slipped my mind."

"Has anyone heard from Safe Port recently?" The captains all shake their heads. "Okay, we proceed as planned. Captain Gibb, I want possible alternates for the ladies. I need it ASAP. Captain Rawls, please proceed as directed. Captain Garrett, I want a tactical analysis of our last encounter with the Chinese, I need to know how this happened. Once we have it worked out. I want everything we've learned ready to send to as many brotherhood sites as possible. We'll use drones, no transmissions. Let's get it done, gentlemen."

The commodore and Captain Gibb pilot their shuttle back to the *Rapier*. At first, they're contemplative, then Captain Gibb asks, "What are you worried about, Uncle James?"

"Lots of things, Jimmy. Could you be more specific?"

"Safe Port."

"I'm worried that that damn fool brother of mine used his guerrilla units and the Chinese came after them."

"Oh."

"I'm also worried about Kathy and little James, Jimmy. What if I screw up again and get them killed? I don't think I could live with that."

"Don't worry about that, Uncle James, you won't."

Captain Gibb guides the shuttle into the shuttle bay. He touches down and turns off the engines. Then the two of them head to the *Rapier's* bridge.

After dinner, the commodore asks Kathy, Cindy, and Lien to join him in the observation dome. When they arrive, Captain Gibb is already there.

"Please be seated, ladies," the commodore says.

"What's this about?" asks Kathy.

"What this is about is your safety, ladies. The captains and I have discussed this in detail. Many of the crew are very concerned about you. They feel as we do that it's time to find a way to get you back to Earth."

The girls are floored by that statement. Kathy holds little James close to her. She feels anger well up inside and actually worries it might wake the baby. She's so mad she trembles. Before she can say anything, Cindy bursts out, "No, no way. I'm not leaving, and you can't make me."

Kathy agrees, "We're members of the brotherhood in good standing. Our berths are here, and here we will stay."

Cindy turns to Kathy. "No, Mom, you and Lien have to go. It's too dangerous for little James. You two have to take him to safety."

Kathy is taken aback by her words. So are Captain Gibb and the commodore. "Cindy you can't stay without us."

"Yes, I can. It's not that I don't need you, because I do. But little James is just a baby, and he needs you more. And I'll have all my dads, and they'll take care of me. You need to go, Mom. It's what needs to happen."

Kathy's not sure if she should be proud of Cindy for being so grown up or mad as hell that she's trying to get rid of her. She looks over to Lien for support. The young Chinese princess is staring at Captain Gibb, her eyes holding back an ocean of tears. Captain Gibb looks at Lien, obviously fighting back his emotions. For several moments, all of them are quiet. Little James coos in his sleep.

Commodore Black breaks the silence. "We are bound for Safe Port. There we'll leave you in the care of Pastor Gibb. He'll help you get the needed papers and safe passage to Earth. We are setting up accounts, so you'll have plenty of money, you'll want for nothing."

Lien finally speaks. She's looking straight at Captain Gibb as she says, "We'll want for nothing except our home and all we love." Then she stands and leaves. Kathy gets up and follows her. She can feel the heat of her anger build inside like an inferno. *How could they do this? After all they've been through together, how could they just discard them?* Both of them sit in their cabin with the lights turned low. The fire of their anger keeps them up.

After an hour, Cindy returns. She hugs Lien, then hugs Kathy and kisses her on the cheek. "Good night, Mom," is all she says, then Cindy goes into her bunk room and goes to bed. Eventually, Lien and Kathy go to bed too. Both silently weep and rage at the injustice of it all.

* * *

Steve cuts in, "So they were trying to get you to Earth?"

"Yes, they were afraid for little James and me," Kathy replies.

"But not Cindy?"

"The Commodore wanted me to leave too, but I refused." Cindy points to an intricate tattoo on her inner arm. It's a field of stars with a gold lightning bolt across the field. "I'm a master gunner," she states "and it's hard to get rid of one of those."

"Cindy, how old were you then?"

"It was about two months before my thirteenth birthday," Cindy replies.

"Let me get this straight. You weren't even thirteen, and you were a master gunner. You regularly fired on ships in raids."

"Yes, that's right."

"Sounds to me like you needed to get out of there as much as the others, Cindy. From what you've told me, you never had a childhood."

Cindy thinks a moment then says, "I had a great childhood. I saw and did things kids only dream about. And I had great dads, four hundred of them."

Steve waves his hand. "Okay, we'll argue that later. So what happened, why didn't they get you to Earth?"

"Well, we hadn't been to Safe Port for awhile, so we didn't know…"

* * *

It's been nearly two weeks; the big blue star is close enough now to see the equatorial disk, and still none of the ships have been able to contact Safe Port. The commodore and Captain Gibb are extremely worried. This close, they should be able to get something. As they know nothing, they continue with preparations for leaving

Kathy, little James, and Lien with John Gibb. In a way, it helps ease the tension; doing something always does. But the lack of contact adds a different tension to the mix. A little over half the crewmen of these ships come from Safe Port, and now they don't know if their people are okay.

Kathy hasn't spoken to the commodore the whole time. She's still furious over this. When she thinks about what's right for little James, she can see the commodore's point. But when she thinks about how she feels, the thought of leaving them, being forced to leave her home, it just makes her want to rage more.

Lien spends as much time as she can with Captain Gibb. When he can get away, they are inseparable. At this point, it's obvious to everyone what their feelings are for each other. It's so obvious they no longer try to hide it. And as Safe Port gets closer, their feelings turn into a flame of passion. The kind of passion that cannot easily be contained. When they are three days out from Safe Port, that fire bursts out. Kathy has gotten used to talking with Cindy and Lien every night before bed, but this night, Lien doesn't return to their quarters.

At first, Kathy isn't worried; she just thinks her and Captain Gibb are still talking or dancing. But as the night wears on, and there's no word from Lien, Kathy gets concerned. Has something happened to her? Did a crewman with too much hate toward the Chinese waylay her? When it turns one bell, Kathy is fraught with angst. Sometime after two bells, Lien comes into the cabin.

"Where have you been?" Kathy snaps.

Lien looks at her. "Um..." Kathy looks closely at her, which makes Lien blush.

"Oh! I see." Kathy gets up and walks over to her. Lien looks down at her feet. Kathy takes her into her arms and says, "Oh, sweetie, I'm so happy for you. Was he gentle with you?"

"He was perfect, Kathy. Everything was perfect."

"I'm so happy for both of you, sweetie. Tell me everything."

Lien blushes again, but the two of them sit and talk until it's time for breakfast. Cindy wanders in from her bunk as they talk. Rubbing her eyes, she says, "Hey, it's breakfast time." Then she looks at Lien and realizes what she and Kathy are talking about. "Oh my god!" she squeals, then runs over and hugs Lien.

They almost miss breakfast, and Cookie scolds the three of them. Captain Gibb sits with the commodore. All through breakfast, he looks at Lien and she at him. At first, the commodore doesn't realize what's going on, but then the light comes on, and he smiles his approval.

After breakfast, everyone but Kathy and the commodore attend to their duties. The commodore has a second cup of cocoa. He looks better to Kathy, like he's been able to sleep, and he ate breakfast. It's been a while since she's seen him eat. Kathy stands up with little James in her arms and moves into the chair next to the commodore's.

"Are you still going to make us leave, especially now, now that Lien and Captain Gibb have, ummm, become closer?"

"Yes."

"Why are you sending us away?"

"Because it's too dangerous, Miss Masters, especially for little James."

"I don't understand. It's no more dangerous now than it was when you brought me onto the *Rapier*."

"But it is more dangerous now, Miss Masters, and this discussion is over." The commodore stands and takes his cup with him, leaving Kathy sitting with little James.

The little flotilla approaches the docking asteroids. Everyone is at stations except Kathy. Instead, she sits near Captain Gibb with James in a bassinet next to her as she records everything. The commodore and Captain Gibb study the view screen. "Commodore, the usual docking asteroids are gone."

"Yes, what happened to them? Any contact with Safe Port yet?"

"No, sir."

"Okay, let's go to our secondary docks and get down there and see what's going on."

"Aye, sir."

The ships slip through the asteroids to a backup location to dock. The *Rapier* and the *Raven* "loose" dock to the asteroid. The commodore transmits to all ships, "Captain Rawls, you have command of the flotilla until I return. Captain Garrett, I want continuous close patrols. If any Chinese ships are detected or appear, your orders are to get the ships to safety."

"And what about you, sir?" Captain Rawls asks.

"We'll figure that out once the ships are safe."

"Aye, sir."

"Captain Gibb, let's go."

"Aye, sir. Mr. Hansen, you have the con. Jenkins, Fritz, and Murphy you'll accompany the commodore and myself."

"Hey, what about me?" Kathy says.

"Miss Masters, you'll stay on the ship," replies Commodore Black.

"Like hell I will. Lien can watch James. I'm going with you."

Before the commodore or Captain Gibb can respond, Cindy cuts in, "I'm going too!" Commodore Black starts to say something then stops. Finally, he responds with, "Okay, ladies, let's go."

They all head to the shuttle. Cindy gets into the pilot's seat, Captain Gibb sits in the copilot's seat. Once everyone is strapped in, Cindy guides the shuttle out of the *Rapier* and heads for Safe Port. She deftly slips around all the asteroids and then heads toward the planet. On the way, Kathy glares at Commodore Black. Like Cindy, she has developed a withering gaze, the commodore can't help being uncomfortable.

Cindy takes the shuttle into the atmosphere and heads to the settlement. Once there, Cindy takes a pass over it. Not a building is standing.

"What happened?" she asks.

"I don't know," replies Captain Gibb.

Cindy lands near the edge of the town. They all get out of the shuttle. The commodore leads the party through the ruins of the town. All that remains of the buildings is burned beams and boards. Not one building stands. Near the east edge of the village are the burned-out hulks of two Chinese armored personnel carriers. Looking around, they find just over a dozen desiccated corpses, some colonists and some Chinese. The only way to tell the difference is the tattered remains of clothing and equipment.

"Where are all the people?" Cindy asks.

"That's a good question," replies Captain Gibb.

Kathy looks at Commodore Black. She sees his eyes burn with rage. She walks over and takes his hand in hers. She wants to say something, but there are no words for this.

Captain Gibb breaks the silence by saying, "I think we need to check the caves. If anyone survived, that's where they'll be."

"Yes," is all the commodore says.

The little party returns to the shuttle. Captain Gibb takes the pilot's seat this time. The shuttle lifts off and heads toward the coast. It passes over the old church ruins, but instead of heading to the cove with the sub, he turns the shuttle southwest toward some nearby hills. Captain Gibb lands at the base of a tall hill. They all get out of the shuttle and start walking toward a trail that climbs the hill. As they walk up the trail, someone calls out, "Halt! Who are you people?"

The commodore responds, "I'm Commodore James Ulysses Black, commander of the Safe Port raider flotilla."

A man steps out from behind a tree along the trail. He's dressed in military clothing, is wearing battle gear and armor, and he holds a pulse rifle. Mr. Fritz calls out, "Mike? Mike Murray?"

"Chuck, is that you?"

"Yeah, Mike, where is everybody?"

"Up the trail in the caves. Go on, folks." Then he melds back into the woods. They walk on up the trail until they reach a cave entrance. There are two guards at the entrance. They wave them into the cave. For a moment it reminds Kathy of when she was brought in by the nomads as a young girl in the 'dead lands' of Australia.

Kathy looks around the inside of the cave. There are hundreds of people inside the cavern. Smoke from cooking fires fills the air. Cots are strewn about; many are occupied by injured and wounded. Some people managed to bring various personal treasures with them. Luggage, coolers, clothes, and other odds and ends are stacked all over the cavern. She turns to the commodore; he's holding Cindy's hand, standing ramrod straight; to the unfamiliar eye, he looks like a statue. But Kathy can see him clearly. He's furious; he vibrates with anger. All that had been rebuilt was gone, more people dead. And for what? He stops a woman that is walking by. "Is the mayor alive?"

"Yes, sir."

"Where can I find him?"

She points toward an antechamber. "He's over there, sir."

Commodore Black strides off in the direction she pointed. Cindy tries to keep up. Kathy follows with Captain Gibb and the rest of the landing party. When people see the commodore's face, they scramble out of the way. He gathers speed.

As she catches up with the commodore, she notices about half a dozen nanchiks moving about, helping the people. *We must be close to the sea.*

The commodore is moving as quick as he can toward the antechamber. Cindy is nearly running to keep up with him. Kathy and Captain Gibb are running. For a moment, the commodore comes to a stop when he's confronted by black curtains. Someone put them up to separate the antechamber from the main cavern. Commodore Black yanks them open, nearly ripping them off the bar they're attached to. Within are the mayor, a couple of other men that he's talking to, and a nanchik.

"What the hell did you do, Marty? What happened?"

"Where do you get off yelling at me, James? What makes you think I owe you an explanation about anything!"

Kathy arrives at the antechamber in time to watch the anger of both men ratchet up to a higher level.

"Jesus, Marty, it's all burned down. Nothing's left, and there are bodies all over the place. Everything we built is gone."

"You didn't build anything, damn you, James. I did." He waves his arm around. "They did. You were off playing pirate while *we* were rebuilding. You didn't do a damn thing as usual."

Kathy and Captain Gibb are frightened this will come to blows. Both men are standing facing each other, trembling with rage. Everyone that can hear them is looking at the antagonists. "How many did you get killed, you egotistical bastard? How many of our people are dead because you refuse to listen to me?"

"Screw you, James. Get the hell out of here. Nobody here needs you anyway. They're not your people, they're my people. You don't belong here, you never have!"

Commodore Black yells, "Damn you!" and he charges at the mayor. Captain Gibb tries to stop him, but he's too fast. The mayor charges at him; they're nearly on each other when the nanchik grabs them both. Its tentacles wrap around them, holding them apart.

"Cmdur Blk stbp, bth yu stbp!" it says calmly. The nanchik lifts them off the ground as they struggle. It's no use; they struggle with all their might, but the nanchik is far stronger than both men.

"Porge, put me down!" the commodore yells.

"Wbn yu stbp!"

Kathy takes the commodore's hand. "James, please stop," she begs. "These people need our help, and you two fighting isn't helping them." He looks at her, and she can tell he feels ashamed at his anger getting out of control.

Cindy is crying, their little battle-hardened warrior is in tears. "Dad, please, you have to stop."

He stops struggling, and Porge sets him on his feet but doesn't release him yet. The commodore forces himself to become calm.

"Captain Gibb, contact the ships. Have the shuttles bring down everything we can spare."

"Keep your crap, James. We don't need it."

"Shut up, Marty," the commodore says. "Just shut up."

Porge releases him, and the commodore moves away. Kathy follows him. "It'll be okay. We'll help them, and they'll be okay."

He says nothing. Commodore Black finds a place to sit. He steams but is under control now. Kathy sits next to him and holds his hand. She says nothing as well, just keeps him company as he works through his anger. As she sits there, she hears the mayor say something but isn't clear what. What she does hear clearly is Cindy's response. "Shut up, Mr. Mayor, or I'll run you through myself!"

Captain Gibb moves Cindy away from the mayor. They come over and sit with Kathy and the commodore. "Captain Rawls has the ships pulling all they can. The shuttles will be arriving soon, sir."

One of the men that was talking to the mayor comes over. He sits down. "Thank you, James. Anything you can spare will make a huge difference."

The commodore looks at him and asks, "What happened, Charlie? How'd all this happen?"

"The guerrillas, they started to do some damage, so the Chinese came after them. That led them to us."

"How long ago?"

"It's been two months now."

"Two months. Why didn't anybody call us?"

"All our communications gear was destroyed, almost everything was destroyed."

The commodore just shakes his head. "How many of us are left?"

"So far, just under three thousand."

The commodore is shocked. "That's all?"

"So far. A lot of people headed to the hills when they heard the Chinese were coming. We're hoping they made it. But still most were killed. We're less than half of what was left."

"Less than half, my god. That's all?"

"As far as we can tell, yes."

Commodore Black sits with his head in his hands. Captain Gibb looks devastated. For a few moments, both men seem defeated.

The shuttles start arriving. Captain Rawls wisely uses men from Safe Port to man them, giving them a chance to check on their loved ones as they bring aid. Sadly, too many of them find their few remaining family members are dead or missing, so many of them return to the ships filled with loss.

It takes several trips to bring the aid. The crews have been generous indeed. Not just what was in stores is brought down, but every crewman gives from their own possessions, anything they feel they can spare.

As the shuttles are unloaded, Captain Gibb goes looking for his brother. After looking for a couple of hours, he talks with one of the survivors of the guerrilla battalion. They talk for several minutes, then he comes back to the commodore. Kathy can see his pain clearly on his face.

"Commodore, Pastor John Gibb was killed in action, defending the town so the people could escape. It's clear now we can't leave the ladies and little James here. We must find another way to get them to Earth." He sits.

The commodore pulls him into his arms. "I'm so sorry, Jimmy. I really loved your brother, and I will miss him greatly."

Kathy and Cindy move in and hold both men. They make sure none of the crew can see Captain Gibb weep.

The last shuttle run is completed, the crewmen unload them and carry it all into the caverns. Everyone says goodbye to the survivors and gets into the shuttles. They lift and return to the ships then the ships move away from Safe Port, not sure of where they'll head next.

Commodore Black has Captain Gibb go rest once the ships are moving. Lien goes to him in his quarters. At first, she can see the conflict on his face. He is looking at a princess of the hated Chinese and, at the same time, the love of his life. The conflict almost explodes out of him. Lien considers leaving, then she reaches out and takes his hand. He weeps openly in front of her, then pulls her close. They close the door to his cabin.

CHAPTER 19

THE DEATH ADDER

Commodore Black and Captain Gibb sit at the commodore's table. They had breakfast early, and now they are talking, making plans. Captain Gibb sips his coffee; the commodore sips his cocoa. The girls haven't come to breakfast yet, so they feel free to discuss options to get them to Earth.

"Not a whole lot of options open to us, sir. We won't go to Muhammad's World. Safe Port is closed to this now, and Rachel's World is in as bad of shape as Safe Port. I hate to say it, but unless we leave Chinese space, we only have one option, Blackbeard."

"That's not much of an option, Captain."

"Agreed, I'd rather leave Chinese space than go there, but they have direct shipping to Earth, and we still have friends at that location. If we keep the girls' identities concealed, they can get out of the colony fairly fast. So it comes down to Blackbeard or risk detection, leaving Chinese space."

"Just once, I'd like a good option, just once."

"Me too," Captain Gibb agrees.

At that moment, Kathy, little James, Lien, and Cindy enter the mess and go to the table the crew holds for them. They all sit and say good morning to the commodore and captain. Cookie whips up their breakfast and has a steward serve them. Captain Gibb finishes his coffee, stands, and walks over to Lien. He leans down and kisses her cheek, then leaves for the bridge to stand his watch.

Commodore Black takes a second cup of cocoa and sips it slowly. Kathy is no longer angry with the commodore, but she hasn't given in on staying either. She's made it clear she has no intention of leaving, and this has strained the relationship between her and the commodore. As she finishes her breakfast, the commodore stands to leave. He walks over and gives Cindy a hug, then kisses Kathy on the forehead. Then he leaves for the bridge to hold his morning video-conference with the captains. Cindy goes to stand her watch. Kathy will care for little James this morning and then stand an afternoon watch at tactical, so Lien has the morning to herself. She finishes her breakfast then heads to engineering.

* * *

Lien was raised a Chinese princess. She learned all about the things a virtuous Chinese lady of royal birth was required to learn. But she was also much more adventurous than the other daughters of her house or the other princesses of the imperial families. That's why her grandfather schooled her on imperial politics. As she grew, her grandfather recognized she needed outlets for her adventurous nature. So he hired the best of kung fu instructors to teach her that ancient art. By time she was eight, he had an instructor teach her the Chinese art of the sword. At ten, she added the bow and arrow to her repertoire.

Had she not learned the other things required of her, her grand-father would have put an end to these "pastimes," but she excelled at all subjects, so he encouraged her "hobbies," thus by time she was sixteen, she was quite expert in all these arts. Once Commodore Black allowed her to be trained by the crew, she added knife and other sword skills, small arms and explosives training, and of course, ship operations knowledge to her hobbies. But even these things didn't satisfy her curiosity.

As the crew came to accept her, Lien found some of them had backgrounds she didn't expect. A few had been scouts and intelligence officers for the Americans before becoming members of the brotherhood. From them, she learned the covert arts, infiltration, secret communications, codes and information analysis. Lien was learning how to be a spy and assassin. None of this was done out of maliciousness or anger; she learned these things because of her insatiable curiosity.

It would turn out later that Lien's skills would be so very useful, but for now, it was the love of learning that drove her.

In engineering, she meets Junior Engineer Michaels. In a former life, he was a covert operative of the Americans; now he happily keeps the *Rapier*'s power systems working smoothly. But his pastime is teaching Lien and sharpening her skills. This morning, as so many in the past, they spar, keeping each other's skills sharp.

"You are remarkably fast," Mr. Michaels tells her.

"It is the quality of the teacher that makes the student shine," she replies.

By eleven bells, they've finished their sparring. Lien thanks him for his time, then goes back to her quarters. She showers and cleans up, looking like a true Chinese princess. She and Kathy eat lunch, then Kathy goes to the bridge. Lien takes little James back to their quarters to care for him. Her time with little James is her favorite onboard the *Rapier*. She has truly taken to this little man, and watching him grow gives her great joy.

* * *

Commodore Black closes the videoconference with "Then it's settled, gentlemen. We make course for Gamma 6 Delta, use our contacts to get the ladies Earth-bound, then move to the Erandi sector to conduct further raids."

All the captains signify agreement with "Aye."

"Very good, gentlemen. Let's make it happen."

Captain Gibb gives instructions to the helmsman to set course to Blackbeard. Soon news of the course spreads throughout the little flotilla. Most of the crew are not happy with the destination, all of them know the kind of ships that put in there. If you are looking for real pirates, this is where you go.

The week long journey increases the tension between Kathy and the commodore. As the ships move closer, the two of them have more arguments. "Damn it, Commodore, I'm not leaving. This is my home, and I'm not leaving Cindy here by herself!"

"Miss Masters, we have to get little James to safety. It's just too dangerous. You and Lien have to take care of him. I'd prefer another choice, but there isn't one. For the sake of little James, you must leave."

"No, I'm not going!"

This is too often the discussion they have, and they grow louder as their destination gets closer. At this point, most of the crew avoid the observation dome where this verbal sparring normally takes place. Even Cindy is avoiding them.

Kathy finds she's going to bed angry again. *How can that man be so stubborn? Why can't he see we belong here?* she thinks as she looks at little James. *And sending Lien away, that'll break Captain Gibb's heart. How can he be so cruel?*

* * *

Mr. Michaels fakes to the right then sweeps Lien's left side. She reacts perfectly, leaping above his leg sweep, she kicks at his head. He blocks, but her foot still catches part of his forehead. He falls backward, rolls and then jumps to his feet, ready to strike.

Lien pushes her attack. Fists, arms, legs, and feet fly at lightning speed toward each of them. Mr. Michaels is more than a head taller than her and weighs twenty kilos more. He's ten years older with eight years of real experience. Still, she pushes him hard. He's never seen anyone faster than her.

Lien fakes to her right, exposing her abdomen. Mr. Michaels strikes not knowing she just trapped him. She rolls to the left, sweeping his legs. As he loses his balance, she moves in, wrapping her legs around his waist, driving him down to the deck. They strike the pads on the deck hard. She drives the air out of him by squeezing her legs.

He strikes the mat with his open hand, indicating that he's giving in. Lien releases him and gets to her feet. Mr. Michaels stands and faces her. They bow then relax.

"You are incredibly fast Lien, incredibly. Very well done."

"Thank you, Mr. Michaels."

"Looks like this is our last training session. I think I'm going to miss them."

"Yes, I will too."

"I know leaving the captain will be hard for you, but this war cannot go on forever. I'm sure you two will be reunited soon."

"Yes, I'm sure we will." But the look on her face shows doubt. He takes her hand for a moment.

"I know he'll come for you as soon as he can, Lien."

She trembles a bit then smiles. "Yes, I know he will."

"We probably should get back to our duties. It has been an honor, Lien Lan Yi, a true honor."

"The honor has been mine, Mr. Michaels."

They leave the training room and head back to their quarters to clean up. Lien feels a pang of loss. She has truly loved training with Mr. Michaels, and now it is over. She knows the commodore is right, but she really resents his decision.

* * *

The *Rapier* moves into Blackbeard while the *Raven* and *Isis* orbit near its primary moon. Gamma 6 Delta was nicknamed Blackbeard by the first pirate crew to stop there. The captain of that ship was a fan of the old Caribbean pirates, and Blackbeard was his favorite. The name caught on with the colonists and stuck.

As the *Rapier* moves into port, it counts seven pirate ships and no privateers. Yes, they are members of the brotherhood, but their adherence to all the bylaws is open to interpretation. Also, if Black Jack Bartholomew had any friends, this is where you'd find them.

Captain Gibb has the girls dress like men. It'll be hard to disguise little James, but Blackbeard is a loud rambunctious place, and concealing the baby may be easier than they think. The girls are fully armed, including swords.

The commodore, Captain Gibb, and six crewmen accompany the girls into town. Kathy, Cindy, and Lien are kept to the middle of the group as they walk the streets of Queen Anne, the colony's Capitol.

The docks for commercial shipping are kept separate from the pirate ships. A ridge runs through the center of the town, dividing the spaceport in two. On the east side is the pirate zone; on the west are all the respectable people. Businesses that occupy the area in between cater to both.

The commodore leads the shore party through the crowd westwards. Some people in the crowd recognize Commodore Black; none of them give him friendly looks.

Lien feels very uncomfortable. Not only is she dressed in an unfamiliar manner, but the hostile looks make her feel like she did on the auction block.

They move quickly to the market square. The commodore leads them to a large general store. They enter the store, and the commodore asks for the owner. An elderly man comes to the counter and looks at him for a moment.

"James?"

"Hello, Francis, how've you been?"

"My god, man, what are you doing here?"

"It's good to see you too, Francis."

"Jesus, man, have you lost your mind coming here?"

"Francis, I really think any issues here are slightly exaggerated. No one will risk losing their lives for the sake of a dead pirate."

The man looks at Captain Gibb. "Jimmy, can you talk some sense into this man?"

"Frank, you should know by now how hard that is."

"Francis, I need a favor."

"As long as it gets you off this planet fast, sure."

The commodore brings the girls up.

"Francis, I need you to keep them safe and get them on the first ship bound for Earth, and no one must know." The commodore makes a hand motion that covers all the girls, including Cindy.

"Commodore, I'm not going!" Cindy shouts.

"Yes, you are. I need you to help Lien protect your mom and baby brother. By time they get off-planet, we'll be gone. You'll be here alone, so yes, princess, you're going."

Cindy is steaming, but she holds her tongue.

"James, that's not going to be easy, not easy at all."

"I know, Francis, but I have to get them to safety."

"I'll try, James. That's the most I can promise."

"That'll have to do, Francis. Thank you."

Kathy feels the anger build in her again, but she also feels deep loss. *This is really happening, he's really sending me away. And Lien, he's making her leave Captain Gibb, and it's tearing them both apart. Why is he being so cruel?*

He turns to face her. "Miss Masters, I know you hate this, we all do, but it's too dangerous for you and the baby. It has to be this way." He kisses her on the cheek.

Captain Gibb takes Lien in his arms and kisses her hard. "When this is all over, I'll find you, I swear."

"I know, my love, and I'll be waiting."

No one notices the man that has been listening to them slip out of the store.

The commodore leads Captain Gibb and the crewmen out of the store. Kathy watches them leave. She feels her heart sink. But it's Cindy that breaks out into tears. It's like she has lost her whole world. Kathy holds her close as she cries a river of hurt and betrayal out. Little James wiggles between them. Lien tries to hide her tears, but she can't. She clings to Kathy and Cindy, and they all let it go. After several minutes, they are all cried out.

Once he's sure they're done, Francis tells them, "Let's go. We need to get you on a ship fast. Word spreads quickly around here." Francis leads them out the back of the store and down an alley. They move about two blocks then head to a street.

After another block, Lien says, "We're being followed." They all look around.

"I don't see anyone," Kathy replies.

Lien says to Francis, "You should go. You have to live here."

"I told the commodore I'd take care of you."

"You will, we're going down this block to the first alley. Have the commodore meet us there."

"But he's leaving."

"He'll come when you tell him we're in trouble, but you have to hurry. Make it look like you're abandoning us. Go now." Francis nods and then runs away toward his store. Lien takes Kathy's hand and says, "Come sister."

The girls walk swiftly down the street like they are trying to get to the spaceport. They weave in and out of the crowd on the street. Kathy looks back and sees four men following them. As they do, they talk to others, and soon, a group of at least ten is coming up behind them.

"This way," Lien says as she leads them down a blind alley. They reach the end of the alley and turn to face the entrance. About fifteen men and a couple of women block the opening of the alley. Cindy stands in front of Kathy as she draws her sword. Lien stands at Cindy's right, her head covered by a hood. Kathy holds James in her left arm and draws her pistol with her right hand. She looks about for any opening; the only ones she can see are barred.

"So you're Black's bitches. We're going to give you a real welcome to Blackbeard. We're going to show you what happens when you kill one of ours," says the man in front. He and two men start to move forward with swords drawn. The rest wait a moment then follow slowly.

Cindy goes en garde. Kathy cocks her pistol. Lien stands passively with her hand on her sword's hilt. A woman from the crowd calls to the men, "Don't hurt the baby, I want it."

"Okay, Maive, I'll get you the baby," the man in front says.

When they are twelve meters from Kathy, Lien moves about a meter in front of Cindy and takes off her hood. She announces,

"I am Lien Lan Yi, daughter of the house of Yi and princess of the imperial court. Get back, and you will be spared."

Everyone stops for a moment. Then the man in front calls out, "Oh, my princess, of course we will. Who wants the Chinese whore to be left alone?"

The crowd chides, "Why, we do. We'd never hurt you, princess."

Many of the men in the crowd draw swords. "Get them, Danny. Cut them up." The three men in front charge. Cindy is ready to match them; Kathy aims her pistol.

Lien moves; the speed of her strike is beyond anything Kathy and Cindy have seen. She meets the men halfway; her sword flashes in the light like it's on fire. Metal on metal rings out, then the three men fall to the ground. No one sees her blade strike home, but now she stands en garde, and the three men lie on the ground with their bellies laid open.

The crowd stands silent. They all look at Lien. Some grow visibly angry, and five of them rush forward. Lien waits until they're just a few meters away, then she strikes. It's like a brawl mixed with a ballet. The attackers wildly hack with their swords while Lien gracefully slashes and kicks, dances and strikes. In moments, these men join their friends in death on the ground. Lien moves back one step closer to Kathy, then goes en garde again.

The crowd looks at Lien in awe. They have seen nothing like this ever. At first, they are quiet in their shock. Then they start to mumble, "Have you ever seen that before?"

"No one can match her with the sword."

Of course this isn't the end; seven men sheath their swords and draw their pistols. The rest of the crowd eggs them on, "Shoot the bitches!"

Maive shouts, "Don't hit the baby."

Cindy pulls her pistol, as does Lien, but they know they are outgunned. Kathy sweeps the area with her gaze. There's almost nothing that can be considered cover but a few steel barrels.

"Mom stay behind me," Cindy whispers to Kathy.

All Kathy can think is, *They're going to shoot my little girl and steal my baby.* She feels battle rage rise up in her. *The hell they are,*

I'll kill them first. For a moment it's as if all the girls have the same thought, and altogether they agree. Kathy grabs Cindy and dives behind some of the heavy steel barrels. Lien dodges right and toward the crowd. The rapid movement momentarily stuns them, giving the girls three precious seconds before anyone reacts. As they start to react, Lien is upon them. She kicks the head of the man in front of her. As he rolls back, Lien stands on his chest and drives her sword into the chest of the man behind him. Then she shoots the man to his left. Kathy aims around a trash can and fires. She misses on the first shot but clips a guy on the second. Cindy takes out a man with a plasma rifle. Before anything else happens, a man's deep voice cuts in, "Everybody, freeze!"

Kathy looks up and a snub fighter hovers above the crowd. The crowd look around and then lay down their weapons and raise their hands. "Move back from the alley." They move back, revealing Lien standing over the man she kicked. "Now disperse and go home." It takes a while for the crowd to leave, but after ten minutes, they're all gone.

Commodore Black and Captain Gibb walk into the alley. The captain goes to Lien and takes her hand. The commodore walks over to Kathy. They look at each other for a brief time, saying nothing. Then the commodore holds out his hand to her and says, "Let's go home, Miss Masters."

"Is it my home?" Kathy asks.

"Yes, always."

Kathy stands and takes his hand. Cindy gets up and walks up to them. "Is it my home too, Dad?" she asks with biting sarcasm. Cindy glares at him, showing her feelings of betrayal clearly on her face.

Her words sting the commodore deeply, but he replies, "Yes, princess, of course it's your home."

Kathy adjusts little James to a more comfortable position, then she takes Cindy's hand. "Come, sweetie, let's go home," she tells her. They walk out of the alley. Both sides of the street are held by two dozen men from the *Rapier*. Mr. Michaels is among them. He nods approval to Lien.

Both shuttles sit in the street as two fighters fly overhead. They board the shuttles and lift for the *Rapier*. It's a quiet ride as both Kathy and Cindy are furious with the commodore. *At least Lien and Captain Gibb have time to be with each other* Kathy thinks. As they sit together, Mr. Michaels moves to them.

"We heard about and saw what you did, Lien. Like I said, you're amazingly fast. Back on Earth, there used to exist a venomous snake that was faster than any other creature. When it struck, it took 0.12 of a second to hit its prey and inject its venom. They named it the death adder. I think that's your name now, Lien. From now on, your brotherhood name is The Death Adder."

Lien blushes; Captain Gibb chuckles. Mr. Michaels nods, then goes back to his seat.

The shuttles dock, and everyone gets out. Captain Gibb and the commodore go to the bridge. The crewmen return to their duties, and Kathy, Cindy, Lien, and little James go to their cabin.

The *Rapier* moves out of Blackbeard on highest alert. Captain Gibb has the armor fully charged, all weapons at the ready, and both fighters escort it as it moves. The *Raven* and *Isis* are on alert as well and move toward the *Rapier*.

"Tactical, what's the status of the possible hostiles?" asks Captain Gibb.

"The ships are powered up, but their weapons and armor are not charged, Captain."

"Keep an eye on them, Mr. Hansen." Commodore Black watches all the displays. It seems they are going to get out of here in one piece. Soon they link up with the *Raven* and *Isis*. Captain Gibb has the *Rapier* recover the fighters, and then the little flotilla makes the translation into hyperspace. The tension ebbs and the ships go to normal routine. Cindy walks onto the bridge.

"Captain, shall I stand my watch?"

"Yes, princess, you have weapons until eighteen bells."

She replies with "Aye, Captain."

As Cindy moves to the weapons station, she gives Commodore Black a withering glare.

Later that evening, Commodore Black sits in the observation dome, sipping cocoa when Kathy walks in. She sits across from him, and for several minutes, there's a strained silence. At last, Kathy says, "Is this really our home?"

"Yes, Miss Masters, but I need a promise from you, one that includes Cindy, Lien, and little James."

"And what promise is that?"

"When it's time, you all have to leave without a fight."

"That's asking a lot."

"Yes, yes, it is."

"How will we know it's time?" Kathy asks.

Commodore Black finishes his cocoa then stands. He leans over and kisses Kathy gently on the lips, then he says, "It will be obvious, Miss Masters, there will be no doubt." He tips his hat to her, then leaves the observation dome. Kathy ponders his words. *There will be no doubt.*

CHAPTER 20

THE WHALE

The only good thing about having gone to Blackbeard is it's near Pi Delta Epsilon and the whales. The commodore takes the *Rapier* to see them again for Cindy's birthday.

It's a week until Cindy's thirteenth birthday, and she's still not talking to the commodore. Kathy can see it's wearing on both of them, but Cindy is being stubborn. They're both miserable, but she will not give. Kathy decides she must do something to end this. When Cindy goes on watch, Kathy approaches Lien and says, "We have to do something about Cindy and the commodore. This can't go on."

"Agreed, but what should we do?"

"I wish I knew," Kathy says with a sigh. They put their heads together and discuss various ideas for ending the conflict. Most are quickly discarded, but they have eight hours and continue on as they play with and care for little James. It takes some hours, but they come up with a plan. It's dangerous, but it seems the only way.

* * *

That night, Kathy talks with the commodore. "Can we have sword practice in the morning? I want to sharpen my edge."

"Of course, but I don't think you need me anymore. You, Cindy, and Lien are quite skilled now."

"Well, sir, I think it would be helpful to have your eye critique me."

"Okay, Miss Masters. I'd be delighted."

* * *

Lien sits on Captain Gibb's bunk. He is putting away his laundry as she watches. The scars on his back and arms remind her of the life they both live. The thought disturbs her, so she takes this moment to include him in the solution she and Kathy came up with. "Captain, we have an aggrieved crewman."

He turns to face her, his green eyes flash with concern. "Who?" he asks.

"Miss Cindy, she feels the commodore has wronged her greatly."

He shakes his head. "I was worried that might be the case."

"I think this is a challenge situation," Lien says bluntly. She studies the expression that crosses his face. That certainly upset him.

"Is it truly that bad?"

"Yes, I believe it is."

"Damn!"

"I think it needs to be settled tomorrow morning. The sooner, the better. As captain, you must be present, so should Mr. Hansen."

"Yes, of course, the speaker of the brotherhood must be there. I'll speak to him at breakfast." Captain Gibb looks very grim. Lien understands why, if not carefully handled, this could end badly. She stands and walks over to him.

"It'll all work out, my love," she tells him. "Kathy and I will be there with you. We'll be sure it doesn't get out of control. All of us together can make this right."

He grins at her. "Yes, of course, my princess. Together we can make it right." They kiss for a long time, then Captain Gibb picks her up and carries her back to his bunk.

* * *

Kathy, Cindy, and Lien bring little James to breakfast. The commodore has already finished and left the mess. As they're finishing, Kathy says, "Let's go get some practice in. We don't have a watch until this afternoon."

Cindy says nothing; she just shrugs.

"I can show you some different moves, some ancient Chinese things," says Lien to her.

"Sure, why not," Cindy grumbles.

They finish and go to the training room. Kathy carries little James and his bag with her. Once in the training room, Kathy sets little James in his carrier on the floor, then she joins Cindy and Lien in warm-up exercises.

They warm up for about fifteen minutes, then the commodore enters. Cindy looks at him as he enters, turning red with anger. The commodore stops just inside the room. She glares at him, then starts to move toward the door. Just then, Captain Gibb and Mr. Hansen enter; Captain Gibb locks the door.

Mr. Hansen points to Cindy and commands, "Move to the center line." Cindy looks at him questioningly. He repeats, "Move to the center line, crewman." Cindy looks at the lines painted on the deck and walks slowly to the center line then turns to face Mr. Hansen. Mr. Hansen then says to Commodore Black, "Move to the end line, Commodore, and face the aggrieved crewman."

"What?" the commodore replies incredulously.

Mr. Hansen says again, "Move to the end line, Commodore, and face the aggrieved crewman." Commodore Black walks slowly to the line and faces Cindy. Kathy picks up Cindy's weapons belt from the floor and draws her rapier. She walks to Cindy and hands her her weapon. She then kisses Cindy and walks back over to Lien and little James. Mr. Hansen directs Commodore Black, "Draw your weapon, sir." Commodore Black draws his saber.

Mr. Hansen asks, "Do the witnesses agree that all attempts to resolve the issue between the aggrieved crewman and the officer have failed?"

Kathy, Captain Gibb, and Lien answer, "Aye." Little James just coos.

"Then," Mr. Hansen continues, "according to bylaw 37, I direct the aggrieved and the officer to face each other until the issue is answered." They both look at Mr. Hansen and then around the room. All the faces are blank except for Kathy's. She can't hide the look of concern.

Mr. Hansen commands, "Per bylaw 37, begin."

For a few seconds, Cindy and the commodore face off. Then Cindy goes en garde. From a perfect stance, she shouts, "Ahhhh!" and pushes off, driving forward. The commodore goes en garde and moves to the left away from the others. Cindy strikes, and the commodore parries.

Strike and parry, slash and parry. Again and again. Cindy is fast, very fast. Occasionally, she gets through the commodore's guard and leaves a small cut, but his greater experience and heavier weapon ensure he's in no danger. Still, Cindy keeps going at him. Finally, her anger bursts out.

"You left us!" Her rapier flashes out, leaving a cut on his arm. "You left us!" At first, the commodore says nothing. This time, she screams it, "YOU LEFT US!"

"I had to, princess. I had to."

"They nearly killed us. They nearly took little James!"

"I know, I'm sorry."

Cindy's blade just misses his ear and cuts off a piece of his hat. "My mom was almost killed because you left us!" She thrusts hard toward his belly. The commodore's blade sweeps hers aside just as its tip cuts through his coat. Kathy gasps.

"I was trying to get you to safety."

"YOU LEFT US!" She charges. Over the years, Cindy has become an excellent swordswoman, skilled and swift. But she's angry, furious really, and dueling filled with anger makes her careless. She strikes recklessly. Commodore Black parries her thrust and disarms her. Cindy's rapier clangs on the deck; the sound of metal against metal rings out. She jumps at him slapping and punching. The commodore drops his saber and wraps his arms around her, picking her up. Cindy pounds her fists against his chest like a little girl as he carries her across the room, pinning her against the bulkhead. "Daddy, you left us. We were all alone."

"I know, princess, I know, I'm sorry."

"You took away our home, our family. We were all alone." Cindy's crying like a young girl now, tears rolling down her cheeks.

"I know, princess, I'm sorry. I was on the way back before Francis called. I couldn't leave you. You're my princess. Until God calls me home, I'll never leave you again."

Cindy stops and looks at him. "Really, Daddy?"

"Yes, princess, really." She goes limp in his arms and lays her head on his chest. "Where are we going, Daddy?"

"We're going to see the whales, princess,"

Mr. Hansen announces. "The issue is answered. Per bylaw 37, these proceedings are closed." Captain Gibb unlocks the door, and Mr. Hansen discreetly leaves. Kathy, Lien, and Captain Gibb walk over to Cindy and the commodore. There's nothing to say, so they just embrace each other.

* * *

Steve stares at Cindy for several minutes. "You had a sword fight with Commodore Black?"

"Yes, we fought, but he was never in any danger. I would never hurt him."

Steve coughs his disbelief.

Kathy just grins, "Now, Cindy."

Cindy giggles. "And my dad would never have hurt me."

Steve looks blankly at Cindy then says, "Kathy, please continue."

"That was three days before Cindy's thirteenth birthday…"

* * *

The little flotilla moves closer to the Pi Delta Epsilon gas cloud.

Commodore Black approaches Mr. Simms, chief engineer for the little flotilla, with a challenging project. "Mr. Simms, can you make a spacesuit for an infant in two days?"

"Excuse me, Commodore?"

"I'd like Miss Masters to be able to take little James with her when we greet the whales. Mr. Simms, can you do this?"

He thinks on it a moment, then answers, "I can try, sir. It's an interesting idea, and I'm sure it's been done before, so I'll try."

"Thank you, Mr. Simms." The commodore leaves engineering.

* * *

The night before the big day, Kathy, the commodore, Captain Gibb, Lien, and Cindy are in the observation dome. Oscar lays on Cindy's lap. Cookie has just brought cocoa, coffee, tea, and cookies. Cindy tries to grill him about her birthday cake. "Is it chocolate? Or maybe a marble cake?"

"Could be."

"Oh, come on. What about frosting? Is it vanilla, chocolate, or strawberry?"

"It could be." Cindy displays frustration on her face. Cookie just chuckles and heads back to the galley. "Then again it could be banana."

She groans, "Arghh!"

Oscar just says, *Meow*. The others can't help but laugh.

"It's not funny, damn it," she grumbles. That just makes the others laugh harder. She gets quiet and stares at the stars, pouting.

* * *

As she walks into the head Cindy asks Kathy, "I'm thirteen now. Can I wear lipstick?" Cindy stands in front of the mirror, looking at herself, while Lien showers. Kathy watches her look herself over. She frowns and says, "My thighs are fat, and my boobs are too small." Lien almost chokes from laughter. "Mom, will I ever be as pretty as you?"

Kathy walks in and hugs her. "Cindy, you're beautiful, truly." They walk into Kathy's bunk room. Kathy pulls a gift out from under her bunk and hands it to Cindy. "Open it." Cindy unwraps it and opens the box. It's a complete makeup kit.

"Oh, Mom, thank you!"

"Now get dressed, let's not be late for breakfast."

"Okay."

Lien stands in the doorway to the head wrapped in a towel. "She's growing up too fast."

"I know," Kathy replies.

Later in the day, Kathy and Lien help Cindy get ready for her party. They teach her how to use the makeup, correct a couple of small mistakes, and then fix her hair. To their surprise, Cindy wears a dress. It fits her figure well and isn't too short, about midthigh. Kathy looks at her and can't help notice how grown up she looks. She feels a little pang of loss in her heart.

* * *

The crew holds Cindy's birthday party. It's kind of difficult for them because Cindy is no longer their little girl, she's thirteen and turning into a woman. The old games are no longer appealing to her. Now it's darts, knife, and hatchet throwing and wrestling. But for the crew, there's still music, dancing, presents, and cake and ice cream. The presents have changed as well. No toys, dolls, or games. Now it's jewelry, clothes, shoes, and boots. The crew members feel uncomfortable, not really sure what to buy when it comes to clothes.

Another change is Cindy gets her first crush.

A newer member of the crew, Michael Compton, a sixteen-year-old from Safe Port has caught her eye. They compete in all the games as she tries to prove she's better at everything than him. Kathy gets particularly concerned when their wrestling match goes too long. After five minutes, she and Lien move in and break it up. This leads to several older members of the crew pulling the young man aside and making sure he understands the limits they are setting on him. It also causes Kathy to decide it's time to have a long uncomfortable talk with Cindy about boys and girls.

Young Mr. Compton walks up to them. "I want to apologize for not being more of a gentleman with your daughter."

Kathy replies, "Apology accepted. Please remember she's just thirteen."

"Yes, ma'am. Cindy, will you dance with me?"

"Yes, Mike, I'd like that."

Kathy and Lien watch them dance. They are together almost every song. It's clear neither has learned to dance but they do what teenagers for hundreds of years have done, they hold each other close and sway rhythmically. They sneak kisses every so often even though they are closely watched by the crew. Again, Kathy thinks it's going to be an uncomfortable talk.

After cake and ice cream, Commodore Black and Captain Gibb leave the bridge to join the party. Captain Gibb gives her his gift, a dress he asked Lien to pick out. It's in the Chinese style, made from real silk and cut surprisingly well to her figure. Cindy goes into Cookie's office and changes into it, then comes out and models it. Kathy is wowed by how grown up she looks. Young Mr. Compton notices too, which gets him another talking to by the senior crewmen.

Then Commodore Black brings her his gift. "I had this made for you last year, but it wasn't ready in time." Cindy opens the long box to reveal a new custom-made rapier. The blade has words engraved in Latin; the handle and hand guard are jewel-encrusted. There are several cut emeralds. Cindy carefully handles it as she tests the balance.

She looks at the inscription and asks "What does it say?"

"Cynthia, princess of the *Rapier*," he answers.

She hugs the commodore. "I love it!"

He holds her tight for several moments, then says, "I'm glad princess."

After the hug, he walks over to Kathy. "I've something for you and little James, Miss Masters."

"What?" Kathy asks with a giggle.

First, the commodore gives her a small box. She takes it and quickly unwraps the box. Inside, she finds a diamond necklace. "I had it made to match the earrings. I was going to give it to you sooner, but it didn't arrive until three days ago when the *Isis* returned from the supply run. Do you like it?"

"Oh yes, it's gorgeous."

The commodore hands her a larger box. She unwraps it. Within she finds a very small spacesuit. Kathy looks up at the commodore and says, "Uh?"

He grins and says, "James will need that to go to the whales with us."

Kathy is unpleasantly surprised by that.

"It's okay, Miss Masters, the suit clips to yours, and it can feed off your oxygen. You'll hear him on comm circuit 2. He'll be perfectly safe because he'll be with his mother the whole time."

Kathy replies, "Okay," but she's obviously not convinced.

* * *

The ships slip into the gas cloud, moving toward its center, traveling at slow ahead. They carefully keep formation so they don't get separated or injure the great beasts they seek. Kathy, Commodore Black, Cindy, and little James are in the airlock. The commodore checks everybody's suit, then hooks up the tethers. Once he's checked little James, he uses the buckles Mr. Simms installed on his suit to connect him to Kathy. Then he connects an air hose from little James to Kathy. Once all is checked, he puts on little James's helmet and charges the oxygen. Kathy checks the comm and can hear the baby clearly. Commodore Black checks everyone once more; all is in readiness. Over the comm, they hear Captain Gibb say, "We've found a pod."

The commodore opens the airlock. They all stare out the hatch. Soon they can see the shapes of the whales in the mist. After several moments, they come clearly into view. Again, Kathy is struck by their beauty, their gracefulness, and their peace.

They follow the commodore out of the hatch and slowly swim toward the pod. At first, the whales don't notice them, but as they approach, the whales turn toward them.

"Captain Gibb, the pod is stopping. Bring the flotilla to a relative stop, please," the commodore says into his comm.

"Aye, sir."

The ships stop moving relative to the whales.

The pod is a family, a large male, three females, and five young varying from infant to young adult. The male leads them to the commodore, Kathy, Cindy, and little James. He stays in front of the pod to defend them if needed. Soon he and the commodore are face-to-face. The commodore touches him on his snout. They stay like that for a minute. Then the commodore leads them over the male's head until they're just before his blowhole. Commodore Black sets Cindy before the blowhole, then he sets Kathy and little James just behind it.

The great beast eyes them carefully. The rest of the pod forms a circle around them, all of them facing the male, Kathy, and the others. Their grayish skin glistens in the mix of gases and starlight.

Kathy looks around at their faces. She thinks to herself, *Are they smiling? Can whales smile?* She puts her arms around little James. He wiggles against her. The sound of his happy cooing comes through the comm.

The peace of these creatures washes over her like before. The whales all go nose down and start to sing. The song fills the gas cloud, with the male leading and the pod following. The song is answered by distant pods, and soon, it seems the gas cloud is alive with singing. As she listens to the chorus, she hears/feels, *James, they sing to James.* The idea shakes her a little. *They sing to my son? Why?* She hears/feels, *Son of the Stars.* The song goes on, each pod adding its own variation to the chorus.

Commodore Black points in the direction the great beasts face. "Good God, look!" Kathy looks the direction he's pointing. A massive shadowy figure can be seen moving toward them in the mist. Though it cannot be clearly seen it's obvious whatever it is it's larger than the beasts they swim with.

"Commodore, can you see this?" Captain Gibb asks over the comm.

"Yes, it's nearly here." The creature swims next to the *Rapier*. It's over twice as long as the ship.

The creature is a whale but not the same as the ones they've seen before. Like a gray whale is different than a blue whale on Earth, this creature is different than the pod they are communing with. Proportionally this whale is leaner than the one Kathy sits on. It has two sets of flippers along its body. The massive whale's flukes have long trailing tips. In the light, it's hard to tell if the great creature is black or navy blue.

It swims around the ships, then approaches the pod. They open the circle for it to enter. The male rights itself, so it looks the newcomer in the eye. The commodore reaches out to touch it; the massive creature moves up to his hand. Kathy thinks the commodore looks like a speck next to this creature. It seems to Kathy the new whale is looking directly at her, or is it looking at little James? She hears/feels, *The great one comes to the Son of the Stars.*

The thoughts are too much for Kathy. She thinks back at the great mind, *No, he's just a baby, my baby. You can't put all this upon him.*

Not his time yet, not yet is the thought that comes back.

After several more minutes, the massive beast swims back into the mist. It dawns on Kathy she's been shooting pics since she saw its shadow. Inside, she smiles that she's still a photographer, still loves to capture these images. She hears/feels, *Still true, still you.*

"Let's go," the commodore says. They swim back to the *Rapier*. Once inside, they look back at the pod. They are nose down singing their song. The ships slowly pull away and move out of the cloud.

* * *

Steve looks at the pics of the massive floater. "This is amazing. And you hadn't seen this before?"

"No one had ever seen this creature before," Kathy replies.

Cindy says, "He came to see my little brother."

"Why?" Steve asks.

"We don't know," Kathy answers, trying to hide the concern in her voice. She continues her tale.

* * *

The ships move to Chinese space. They pass through the border and cruise toward newer hunting grounds.

It's been over eight years since that fateful day on the SS *America* and so much has happened. Kathy has grown so close to Commodore Black and Captain Gibb, she can't imagine life without them, but it's the unspoken truth of this life that someday the odds will catch up with all of them. It's inevitable.

CHAPTER 21

MICHAEL COMPTON

Steve asks Cindy "So what ever became of Michael Compton?"

Cindy chokes up, a single tear runs down her cheek. Steve is surprised by her reaction. All this time she seemed so tough, so hard, the thought that something could make her show any emotion other than anger throws him off balance for a moment.

Kathy puts her arm around Cindy and pulls her close. They embrace for several minutes then Kathy whispers to her "It's okay sweetie, I've got this."

"No mom, this part is my story, I'll be alright."

Kathy takes her arm from around Cindy and holds her hand instead. Cindy wipes the moisture from her eyes. She sniffles and sits still a moment. Then she starts to speak in a low emotion filled voice. "Mikey was the most beautiful boy, I mean man, I ever met. He was strong and tall, the most musical voice and I truly loved him ..."

* * *

Kathy and Lien are amazed at the change in Cindy, she is acting like a girl, it has both of them pleasantly surprised. Cindy is constantly asking them about style and makeup. It seems that each day she's asking them to do her hair in styles she sees in fashion magazines and vids. Most out of character is that when she's not on watch,

Cindy is wearing a dress. Kathy thinks back on all the times over the years that she tried to get Cindy into a dress and failed but now it seems that's all she'll wear.

Whenever they are not on watch Cindy and Michael are inseparable. Cindy even brings Michael to training with her. They also accompany the Commodore, Kathy, Captain Gibb and Lien to the observation dome to dance.

Young Mr. Compton has never learned to dance, so he goes to the commodore and asks him to teach him. After a month, Michael has become quite good, he literally sweeps Cindy off her feet; and she loves it. "Mom, it's like his touch makes me melt," she confides to Kathy. They both giggle.

It also seems the two young love birds find every nook and cranny of the *Rapier* to cuddle in. On numerous occasions Kathy answers a knock on her cabin hatch only to discover Cindy, Michael and a senior crewman with a cross expression on his face. The two teenagers have sheepish grins from being scolded for their amorous activities. For some time, Kathy and the commodore are concerned about these activities until Cindy confides to Kathy and Lien about them.

The three of them sit on Kathy's bunk talking when Cindy blurts out, "Mom, how do you know when you're ready to make love?"

Kathy's mouth goes dry. She looks at Lien and sees concern on her face, and so does Cindy. "No. No way we haven't done that. We've thought about it, but I know I'm not ready. And he insists we wait until I'm older. But how do you know when you're ready?"

Kathy relaxes. "It's hard to explain sweetie." Lien nods agreement. Kathy continues, "You just know when it's time, when it's right."

Lien speaks up, "Cindy, I just knew when it was right for the Captain and me."

Cindy shakes her head. "Why does it have to be so complicated?"

Kathy and Lien laugh. "Sweetie, women have been asking that question since God put Eve in the Garden of Eden."

"He's so handsome, so strong, so smart. I just can't find anything wrong or bad about him," Cindy says with a sigh.

Kathy and Lien hug her tight. "We're so happy for you sweetie."

It's during this time that Cindy learns Michael's birthday is in a month. For some reason this really excites her. She finds herself thinking *I've got to get him the perfect gift.* She secretly asks everyone she can about what to get him but all their answers just don't seem right. Then two weeks before Michael's birthday she comes across an odd note in the history of the old North American republic, which seems to be the perfect gift.

Filled with excitement, she rushes down to engineering before her watch starts to talk to Mr. Simms. She explains what she wants, and Mr. Simms takes her to Mr. Connelly the ship's master machinistmate. Cindy excitedly explains what she needs him to make, and Mr. Connelly agrees to make them. He tells her it will take him a couple of days to make the gift.

Two days later, Mr. Simms calls her at the end of her watch. As soon as Cindy is relieved, she rushes to engineering where Mr. Connelly is waiting for her. He hands her two charm bracelets made from Martian silver. Each has a half heart hanging from it that when you put them together makes a complete heart. On the front, when they're together, is inscribed *Cindy and Michael.* On the back it says, *In love forever.* "I hope this is what you wanted princess."

"Oh yes Mr. Connelly, they're perfect." She kisses him on the cheek, then rushes back to her cabin to wrap them. When Kathy walks in Cindy shows them to her, "Mom, look, aren't they beautiful?"

"Yes they are," Kathy replies.

* * *

Three days before Michael's birthday, the little flotilla comes across a small convoy skirting along the Chinese-Russian border. It appears to be headed for the French sector. The commodore's ships are hiding in a gas cloud, and it seems they haven't been detected.

"They appear to be French. We could let them go Commodore," Captain Gibb says.

"Yes we could, but those two big merchantmen are very tempting," replies Commodore Black.

"Those two frigates could be a problem."

"If we hit them hard with the *Rapier* and the *Raven* and then leave the *Isis* and the fighters to drive them off as we move on to cut off those big freighters, it could be fairly profitable."

"The French usually don't put up much of a fight," Captain Gibb adds.

"That's why we let them recover their damaged ships," the Commodore states. Then he says "Let's take them."

The Commodore gets on the ship-to-ship comms and issues his orders as Captain Gibb orders the *Rapier's* crew to action stations. Lien watches little James while Kathy mans tactical and Cindy takes the weapons station.

* * *

Crewmen move rapidly to their action stations as two boarding parties gather at the boarding tubes. Mustering among the team for boarding tube number two is Michael Compton and another new crewman, fifteen-year-old Billy Campbell.

Chief James briefs his thirteen man boarding team. "Captain Gibb will be with team one, and I'll lead this team. The usual drill boys: clear the tube fast and clear the compartment we enter. Once it's cleared setup a barricade with containers. Once that's done, we leave a security team behind and move to join up with team one. Mr. Kelley, you'll have the security team. That'll be young Mr. Compton and young Mr. Campbell."

"Any special instructions Chief?" Mr. Kelley asks.

"No, just the usual. Hold the end of the tube. If any enemy crew show up call for help. Now, let's get to the armory and get our weapons and comms," says the chief.

Chief James leads his men to the armory. Michael and Billy feel anxiousness and a little fear. This is their first boarding party, and the first time they've ever been in a fight. Michael thinks on how he feels, and the butterflies in his stomach. *Can I do this? Why am I so scared?*

* * *

Still in the gas cloud, Commodore Black deploys his ships. He has the *Rapier* and the *Raven* line up side-by-side with about half a kilometer between them. The *Isis* is about a half kilometer behind them so the ships form a 'V'. The fighters form up around the *Isis*.

The commodore waits until the convoy is close to the gas cloud, then has his ships move foreword towards them. They approach carefully, keeping the debris drifting in the cloud between them and their prey to confuse the escorts sensors.

* * *

The boarding teams check their weapons and comms, then take on extra ammo and first aid gear. Michael notices that some of them get sonic grenades including Mr. Kelley. *Damn, are we going to need those?*

They move back to their boarding tubes and sharpen knives and swords. Michael looks around at all the grim faces and thinks *Shit we're really going to do this!*

* * *

The convoy moves closer to the gas cloud, when they are a mere forty kilometers away, the commodore's ships burst out of the gas and debris. He signals his captains "Fire when ready gentlemen."

Cindy locks her weapons onto the nearest frigate as Kathy calls out targeting information. As the ships pickup speed, Kathy calls out, "Thirty kilometers to target."

"Fire," commands Captain Gibb.

Cindy punches the particle beam fire button twice. She watches the beams lance out across the intervening space striking the turning frigate. The ship is struck just behind the bridge. Cindy sees the lightning leap from the ship as the beams drain the neutron armor. The target is now just twenty kilometers away, and readying its weapons. Cindy fires again. The beams rip a gash along the side of the frigate. As the *Rapier* passes the frigate, she fires four salvos from the railguns. The solid projectiles hammer the frigates hull, punching two holes in its flank.

The *Raven's* target is damaged just as badly, and both frigates start to limp away as the corvettes rush past them like a pack of wolves, cutting off the two large freighters from the rest of the convoy. The *Isis* and the fighters position themselves between the rest of the convoy, and the corvettes and their targets. Soon the distance between the escorts and the other merchant ships and the Commodore's flotilla and its prey is over fifty kilometers.

The frigates keep themselves between the remaining cargo ships and the raiders but make no attempt to aid the doomed freighters. The *Isis* and the fighters stay just out of weapons range keeping the frigates at bay.

Cindy rapidly disables the engines of the freighter before her. Captain Gibb orders "Come along side her, prepare to board. Mr. Andjek you have the con." Then he heads for boarding tube one.

* * *

Michael waits with his team trying to control the fear inside him. He looks around. The veterans of the Rapier appear calm, almost bored as they wait. But Billy looks as scared as he feels.

He hears over the intercom "Fire grapples," the ship shakes as the grappling cables shoot out grabbing onto the freighter. Then he hears "Extend boarding tubes." The tube before him starts to move as it extends out against the other ship. Next the sound of Captain Gibb's voice rings out from the intercom "Now Mr. Andjek," then he hears the breaching charges detonate, the explosion shakes both ships. "Boarders away," commands Mr. Andjek.

They all rise, Chief James draws his saber and his pistol "Let's go lads," he commands as he charges down the tube. They rush down the tube behind the chief shouting "Hurrah!!" Michael thinks *Shit, this is really happening!*

* * *

Kathy watches the commodore pace back and forth on the bridge of the *Rapier*. He looks lost and she knows he's thinking *I should be leading them*. But he's a commodore now and his place is here, the crew would not allow him to lead the fight, that's Captain Gibb's job.

Kathy looks over at Cindy, it's clear she is worried about Michael. Kathy finds herself praying, *He'll be okay, he'll be okay*. She continues to watch Cindy as she pleads, *Dear God, he has to be okay*.

* * *

The boarding team rushes out of boarding tube two into a side cargo compartment. None of the freighters crewmen are present so Chief James has them move some heavy containers in front of the breach hole. He nods to Mr. Kelley then leads the rest of the team to the freighter's main passageway.

Mr. Kelley gets the boys behind the barricade. "All we have to do is wait here lads, just relax and everything will be fine." They settle down to keep watch over the breach hole.

Michael listens to the comm monitoring the fight. Suddenly, he hears voices coming from the passageway. They're speaking a language he's not heard before. Both him and Billy stand up to see who's there. Mr. Kelley jumps up shouting "Get down you idiots." As Mr. Kelley shoves them both down shots ring out. Michael feels fire burn through his thigh as a slug passes through it, he calls out in pain. A burst from a pulse rifle strikes Mr. Kelley in the chest killing him instantly. He falls to the deck between the boys.

Billy panics and jumps up shooting wildly. Amazingly he hits one of the Frenchmen. However, he's hit in the chest by a slug thrower, and slumps down gasping for air.

Michael calls out over the comm, "Help, help ..."

* * *

Cindy, Kathy and the commodore all turn to the comm as they hear Michael call out with panic in his voice. "Help, help, Mr. Kelley is dead, Billy has been shot, so have I, we need help now."

Cindy starts to jump up but Commodore Black points to her and says, "Stand at your station princess."

They next hear Captain Gibb respond, "Calm down son, where are you and how many enemy are there?"

"Sir it's Michael, I mean crewman Compton. I'm at breach tube two. I don't know how many bad guys are here."

"Okay son, keep under cover and hold tight, I'm on my way."

Commodore Black thinks less than a second. He looks at Cindy as he says, "Mr. Andjek, Mr. Hansen you're with me," then he rushes down the main passageway.

Mr. Andjek shouts, "You have the con Mr. Covington," as he runs after the commodore.

Cindy jumps up but Kathy shouts, "Sit down right now young lady. Man those weapons and stand fast!" Cindy looks torn, she so desperately wants to run to Michael, but her mother has made it clear, she is to stay where she's at. After a few seconds of indecision, Cindy sits down, but her eyes never leave the comm screen.

Kathy can see the tears forming in Cindy's eyes, and she can feel them welling up in hers. *He's going to be okay, he's going to be okay*, she keeps saying to herself.

* * *

Captain Gibb orders, "Mr. Hahn you have the boarding party, Chief James, Mr. Campion you're with me." Then he dashes down the main passageway.

* * *

Michael stares at Billy trying to think of what to do. He tries to move to Billy, but is forced back by a fusillade of small arms fire. He watches as the boy struggles to breathe. After several moments Billy calls out, "Mommy, Mommy." He raises his arm like he's reaching out to someone. "I'm coming Mommy." A moment later Billy says, "I can't play anymore, I have to go home now." Then his arm drops to his side and the last of the air in his lungs rushes out. He stares at Michael with lifeless eyes as if to say, *Why didn't you help me.*

Michael can hear the enemy planning just a short distance away. He doesn't understand what they're saying, but he's sure they plan to rush him. For a moment he thinks, *If they get into the ship they'll hurt Cindy.* Michael pulls a grenade off Mr. Kelley's belt, then checks his pulse rifle. He twists the safety cap starting the grenades timer. Using his pulse rifle as a crutch he pushes up with his good leg and throws the grenade toward the voices. It flies over the containers they're hiding behind landing among them.

As he drops down he brings his rifle up to the ready. Just then, a Frenchman that was closer to him pops up and fires. Reflexively he fires back hitting the Frenchman in the chest. As the man he shot drops down Michael feels the bullet his opponent fired rip through his belly. The searing pain sets every nerve in his body on fire. He cries out, "Ahhh!!!" and falls to the deck.

* * *

Michael's cry of pain rings out from the comm followed by the sound of the grenades detonation. Cindy jumps up and starts to run toward the main passageway. Kathy tackles her taking her down to the deck. "No baby, no you can't go. You have to stay here." She holds her tight as Cindy struggles to get away. Mr. Covington helps Kathy hold her down.

Cindy shouts through her tears, "Let me go! I have to go to him! Let me go!"

Kathy grips her tighter as Mr. Covington helps hold her down. "No baby, I'm not letting you go. You're my baby and you have to stay here!"

* * *

Both the Commodore and Captain Gibb hear Michael's cry of pain over their comms, and run faster towards the boarding tube.

* * *

Michael lies on the deck. He can feel his strength bleed away, he wants to go to sleep, he's shaking. *I'm going into shock, no, I've got to stay awake.* Michael focuses on the cries of the man he shot. "Mon Dieu, mon Dieu!" the man weakly cries out in pain. Michael listens as the man's cries get weaker and weaker. After a few moments the man stops speaking. Michael can hear his labored breathing, the gurgling of blood in his throat. Finally the man makes no sound at all. Overwhelmed with remorse Michael thinks, *I killed him, I killed that man.*

Michael fights to stay awake, *If I go to sleep they'll hurt Cindy, no I must stay awake.* He can't feel his legs anymore. *No I must stay awake.* He reaches deep down inside himself, *I will stay awake, no one is going to hurt her!*

He hears boots pounding against the deck. Michael tries to ready his rifle, but he feels so weak. His hands shake as he fumbles with his weapon. Suddenly he hears Commodore Black call out, "Mr. Compton, where are you?"

"Heeerree siiirr," he calls out. *I taste blood in my mouth.*

Commodore Black bursts out of the boarding tube into the compartment. He quickly looks around, but there are no active enemies. As Mr. Andjek and Mr. Hansen rapidly secure the area the Commodore kneels down beside Michael, and lays his weapons on the deck. He lifts michael gently switching off his comm as he does. The boy shakes violently in his arms. "Hold on son, I've got you," he says. The Commodore then calls into his comm, "Get the doc down here now!"

Captain Gibb and his team enter the compartment. While Chief James and Mr. Campion help secure the area the captain moves over to the commodore and Michael.

"Did theyyyyy gett byy mee siirr?"

"No son, you kept them off the ship. You did good. Now just stay with me, doc Smith will be here shortly."

"Sooo Ciindyy's saafee?"

"Yes son, you kept her safe. Now save your strength, just stay with me."

"Gooooddd," the boy says then the air drains out of his lungs. It makes bubbles in the blood on his lips as he goes limp in the commodore's arms.

"No, no, no, no!" Commodore Black cries out. He starts giving the boy mouth-to-mouth to try to restart his breathing. The commodore is frantic in his efforts to revive Michael. The harder he works the more of the boy's blood gets onto him.

After a minute Captain Gibb kneels down placing his hand on the commodore's shoulder. "He's gone uncle James, he's gone."

He looks into the boy's now lifeless eyes, staring blankly at the overhead, and slowly closes them. Commodore Black gently lays Michael on the deck then wipes the blood off his hands. He picks up his weapons sheathing his saber and holstering his slug thrower. As he slowly stands up Captain Gibb rises with him.

"I'll tell her uncle James," Captain Gibb gently says to him.

"No Jimmy, that's my responsibility," the commodore replies. He turns to walk down the tube back to the *Rapier*. As he does Doc Smith runs into the compartment. "You can go back to sickbay doc, there's nothing you can do here," Commodore Black tells him. Doc Smith looks at the crewmen lying on the deck then nods, and walks back to the *Rapier* with the commodore.

Captain Gibb softly says, "Mr. Andjek, Mr. Hansen go with him, I think he'll need you." They follow the commodore onto the *Rapier* heading for the bridge.

Commodore Black walks onto the bridge. He sees Kathy, Cindy and Mr. Covington on the deck. They look up at him, there's blood on his trousers, coat, hands, chin and right cheek. It's clear he wants to say something, but seems to be having trouble. The commodore tries to speak a couple of times, and doesn't get anything out. Finally he says, "Mr. Andjek please take the weapons station, Mr. Hansen if you would take tactical. Princess, Miss Masters, you're relieved."

Cindy starts to cry, a waterfall of tears floods out of her. Kathy starts crying too. Cindy jumps up and runs towards the main passageway. The commodore stops her. "You don't want to see him like this princess." She looks up at him, her expression breaks his heart. He lets her go, and she runs down the passageway, with Kathy following close behind her.

They burst into their cabin, and Cindy throws herself onto Kathy's bunk letting loose all her grief. Kathy sits next to her weeping. Lien comes in holding little James. "What's wrong?" she asks.

Kathy looks up at her. "Michael, he's ..." but she can't finish saying it. Lien gasps, then joins them weeping on the bunk. Oscar hops up with them, he lets out a mournful wail vocalizing their grief.

* * *

It takes less than an hour to loot the two freighters. The medical staff helps the wounded from the two of them as best they can. Once all is done the little flotilla moves off leaving the wounded freighters to be recovered by their convoy.

As they move off the ships tally their loses, three from the *Rapier* and four from the *Raven*. Most of those lost come from Safe Port so the commodore has his ships head there. They're taking those they lost home to lay them to rest.

On the way Cindy contacts Safe Port and gives instructions to the colonies stonecutter, then she spends the rest of the trip in her quarters. Kathy stays with her trying to be a rock for her to pour out her grief on. Lien and Cookie makes sure they eat, but the rest of the crew leave them alone for now.

The day before they arrive at Safe Port Kathy goes to the observation dome. She finds Commodore Black sitting watching the stars sipping cocoa. Kathy sits down beside him. He pours her a cup and they sit sipping in silence for several minutes. Eventually the commodore speaks up. "I'm tired Miss Masters. Tired of burying children. Tired of running. Tired of this damn war. I'm so tired." He drops his cup onto the deck.

She sets her cup on the table and pulls him to her until he lies his head on her lap. She holds him until he drifts off to sleep, then watches over him all night.

The next morning they arrive at Safe Port. They shuttle the ones they've lost and their close friends down to the settlement, following a routine they all know to well. The people meet them at the landing field, and all move solemnly to the graveyard. The coffins are laid next to their final resting places. The mayor and the priest take their places.

Commodore Black asks for the families of those they lost. "I must tell them how their loved ones died," he says softly.

The mayor tells him, "All those you lost have no surviving relatives."

"Then Miss Masters and I will stand for the families," the commodore states.

Cindy speaks out, "Dad, I'll stand for Michael, I'll stand as his wife."

Kathy and the commodore look at her. Kathy's not sure what to say, but Commodore Black says gently, "Of course princess."

Cindy walks over to Michael's coffin and opens it. She takes something out of her purse, and fastens it around his arm. Then she closes the coffin, and walks over to where the family would stand. Kathy notices Cindy is wearing a black dress and shoes, also she wears the silver charm bracelet with her half of the charm on her left wrist. Cindy puts a black veil over her head, and the service starts.

When the service ends the people start to move over to what now serves as the town square. Before Kathy joins them she looks closely at the headstone Cindy had made. Above the name an angel holding a sword hovers protectively. She reads the inscription on the stone. Michael Andrew Compton. Born August 23, 2368. K.I.A. August 20, 2385. Forever the true love of Cindy, Princess of the Rapier. She gulps back her tears, then Kathy walks slowly over to her grieving family.

Commodore Black stands next to the mayor. He starts to speak then stops, looking over the few survivors of the colony he knows there's no point in asking about the end of the contract. When the commodore finally speaks all he asks in a faltering voice is, "Whose sons will go with me. I need seven good men that will be true before the mast."

Two men that are obviously in their sixties step forward. Next two women, probably in their thirties. One has lost an eye, the other is missing her left arm. Then three boys step out, probably ages thirteen through fifteen. Both Kathy's and the commodore's hearts sink. *This is it? This is all there is?* they both think.

They move to the shuttles, and lift to the ships. The three boys and one of the women are assigned to the *Raven*, the others are assigned to the *Rapier*.

* * *

Steve looks closely at Cindy. She has moved onto Kathy's lap as she weeps into her shoulder. The girls hold tightly to each other. He watches them cry as if the events they related to him just happened. Their grief is so powerful it's hard to believe this happened nearly four years ago.

Steve notices something on Cindy's left wrist. It's a silver charm bracelet with half a heart dangling from it. *My God, she's still wearing it!*

Kathy says to no one in particular, "My baby hasn't worn a dress since the funeral."

"I'm so sorry Cindy," Steve says. It sounds lame to him, but he doesn't know what else to say.

Kathy starts to talk. "When we left Safe Port we went deep into Chinese space, very deep. The Commodore set our course in the general direction of Xerxes Major, the Chinese Imperial Capitol."

CHAPTER 22

THE LAST DEAL

Another year of raids, mostly on Chinese shipping, but some American, British, French, and German. In one raid, they capture a senior Chinese intelligence officer, his wife, and two aides. This is gold and leads to several long question-and-answer sessions.

For Cindy's fourteenth birthday, they go to Sigma 5 Omega and see the dragons. These reptile-like creatures actually look the way dragons have always been portrayed on Earth. They are as long as paleontologists think the stegosaurus was, with a wing span that's much longer. The main difference between them and the mythical dragon is they don't breathe fire. These creatures are quite dangerous, so they had to observe them from a distance. The only time they got close to any of them was when they helped an injured yearling, and even that was hazardous. Nonetheless, Cindy had a wonderful time.

Seeing how close Lien and Captain Gibb are and how well Commodore Black does as a dad to Cindy and little James, Kathy starts to think they might have a future after all; she thinks about the possibilities.

A week after Cindy's fourteenth birthday, all chances of romance and any chance of a "normal" life suddenly become no possibility at all.

While making minor repairs at a small asteroid port, the three raiders are surprised by the sudden appearance of an American light cruiser, destroyer, and frigate. Everyone is shocked, American warships deep in Chinese space. Quickly Commodore Black considers his options. There appears to be no place to run; it's either fight or surrender. But the little flotillas ships have been modified with nanchik tech. He's certain he can get at least one, possibly two ships out, but at what cost? He looks over at Kathy then Cindy. *Can I really risk them?* All eyes are on him. To Kathy, he seems so terribly tired. Both sides are prepared to go at each other with all they have. It all rests on Commodore Black's shoulders.

Commodore Black calls up the American commander; his image forms on the comm screen. "Order your ships to surrender!" the young American captain demands.

"Now let's be serious," the commodore says. "This could get very messy, and we're both in unfriendly space. So I think I'll make a proposal. I'll turn over some key Chinese personages and files showing Chinese undermining of *America*, things that are acts of war, things that will make your career, Captain."

"And what do you want in return?" the American captain asks, suspicion in his voice.

"Safe passage to Earth for some of my captives, the non-Chinese. A full pardon for my crews. They go home with their weapons and possessions and are never bothered or charged with piracy, a reduced sentence for all of my officers, no more than two years in a minimum security prison, and when they are released, they go home with all their weapons and possessions and are never bothered."

"Is that all, Mr. Black, nothing for yourself?"

"That's all."

"Truly, you know you'll be hanged."

"Yes, I know, and considering what has happened over the last twenty years, someone should be hanged. Lots of people should be hanged. But as to our situation, I'm the only one responsible for the actions of my men. Just me."

"And you'll be held to that standard."

Kathy hears his words, and her heart crashes. *No, he can't let them hang him.*

"So you know I mean it, prepare to receive a very special file. Keep it secure." The commodore selects a file from the computer and sends it to the American. "When your spies have authenticated it, we'll talk more, Captain," the commodore says.

Both sides keep weapons at the ready, and the wait begins, a wait that at the end of it, if the Americans accept his terms, sees Commodore Black being hanged in some American high-security prison. Kathy fights to hold back her tears; she's on watch and needs to be ready. Besides, she can't let him see her cry.

That evening, Commodore Black sits in the observation dome, sipping cocoa. He looks at the stars and feels lighthearted. *If I can get them safe, then it's all worth it. They'll finally have a life, a future. If I can save them all surely that's worth the price.*

Kathy enters the observation dome. She walks over and sits beside him. They sit quietly for a long time. After a while Kathy takes his hand in hers. The commodore pours Kathy a cup of cocoa. They sip in silence, looking at the stars. Kathy wants to ask him so much. *Why are you surrendering? What about little James? What about Cindy? What about me? How are we supposed to go on without you?* But she knows the answer to all those questions. She knows why he's doing what he's doing. There's nothing to be said, so she sips her cocoa and holds his hand. She looks at her cup; it's almost empty. As she swirls it, he says, "I'm so very tired. I just want to rest now."

It feels like icy fingers are squeezing her heart, but she can't let him see it, not now. So she sets her cup down and holds him tight for a long time. Eventually, he falls asleep in her arms.

For one full cycle, twenty-four hours, the two flotillas face each other. Communication is cordial but strained. The Americans send the file to Earth for analysis, and politicians at all levels argue the merits of the deal offered by Commodore Black. The clock ticks.

* * *

What the Americans don't know is they have a traitor in their intelligence service. The traitor doesn't know the details of what Commodore Black has given the Americans, but he knows it's bad for his masters. He transmits the location of the two flotillas to the Chinese. The Chinese intelligence service reviews the message. Alarm strikes the hearts of all that see it. Quickly they take it to the emperor. Orders are issued, and a special tasks force is organized. They head at best speed to the location of the standoff.

* * *

Breakfast is a somber affair. Crewmen eat quickly, then head back to their stations. Captain Gibb rushes through his, then kisses Lien, and goes to the bridge. Cindy's face is grim, set; she is ready to fight to the end. Kathy holds little James on her lap. She looks around the table. It's like being at a wake.

Kathy reports to tactical. Everyone on the bridge is tense. Captain Gibb and the commodore talk quietly by the view screen. The tactical alarm sounds. Kathy checks the readout, "Captain, multiple jump points opening at 130 plus 15." She's surprised at how calm her voice is. "I'm reading a Hankow-class frigate, two Lanchow-class destroyers, a Nanking-class light cruiser, and a Yalu-class cruiser."

The Chinese task force storms out of its jump points. Commodore Black calls the American captain. "You bastard! What treachery is this?"

"Mr. Black, we know nothing of this. For all we know, they plan on attacking us," says the American captain.

"Bullshit! You sold us out, you bastard!" Commodore Black is furious. "And it's commodore, you son of a bitch!"

Captain Gibb pulls Commodore Black aside. "Commodore, he's as surprised as we are. You can see it on his face." Commodore Black goes back to the comm screen. He is still furious, but he makes himself study the American captain. Slowly he accepts what Captain Gibb is saying; the American is surprised.

The Chinese deploy but stand back. The two cruisers move side by side facing them; the two destroyers line up to their left and the frigate on their right. They hold back, unsure if they'll have to fight the Americans and the pirates.

"Mr. Black, the Chinese have asked us what our intentions are."

"What are your intentions?" Commodore Black asks.

"The Chinese allowed us transit rights on the basis that our orders were to capture or destroy your command. We will not engage the Chinese if they do not fire upon us."

"No surprise there. You won't even come to the aid of one of your own colonies when the Chinese attack. Please hold off on replying to the Chinese for a few minutes."

"Why should I?"

"Because, Captain, I would like to propose a new deal and need a few moments to do so. Besides, I think we both don't mind if they stew on doubt for a bit."

Perhaps it's some level of respect, or perhaps it's a courtesy to a doomed man, but the American captain now uses the commodore's title. "What do you propose, Commodore Black?"

"We give you everything if you'll get the people we send over to Earth, and make sure they get no jail time."

"I can't guarantee you that."

"Yes, you can, especially with what we're giving you. Also, set up your systems to record the battle. You're going to see and get telemetry on all the tech we're providing you. All my ships and fighters are equipped with it. What you're getting will give America a half-century advantage in propulsion, armor, sensors, weapons, and even ground combat over everyone else. Surely, that's worth keeping a woman, a teenage girl, a toddler, a doctor, and a cook out of prison. Oh yes, and we're sending over a Chinese princess that needs asylum. Plus, the four Chinese hostages, you're getting more than America deserves. Oops, and the young girl's cat."

"I'll do everything I can, Commodore," the American captain replies. "Everything," he repeats.

"Thank you," The commodore says.

Commodore Black walks up to Kathy. He leans down and kisses her on the lips then hands her his wedding ring. "Perhaps you'll be able to return this to me someday." He kisses her again and says, "Kathy, I've loved you since I first set eyes on you, and I will, forever. But now it's time, Miss Masters. Remember your promise."

The commodore stands and faces Captain Gibb. "Mr. Gibb, please escort these women off my ship and take them to the Americans."

"If it's all the same to you, Commodore, I'll stand my watch on my ship." Captain Gibb then calls the two youngest crew members, Mike Thompson and Thom Jansen. "Take them to the shuttle and get them to the Americans, then watch over them."

They have to drag Cindy to the shuttle; Kathy has to help them. The Chinese hostages, Lien, Oscar (protesting being on a leash), and little James, are there already. So are Doc Smith and Cookie.

Captain Gibb says over the intercom, "You have to go, Cookie. Someone has to make Miss Cindy her pancakes."

Lien asks, "Kathy, what's going on?"

"A Chinese battle group is here. We have to leave. We're going to the Americans. They're going to take us to Earth." Kathy starts weeping; so does Lien.

Cindy tries to struggle, but these young men, just fifteen and sixteen, are eighteen centimeters taller than her and fifteen kilos heavier. Plus, Kathy is helping, but she has to use all her enhanced strength. They drag Cindy into the shuttle while the others pile in. As they prep for launch, the ship's computers download all the data to the shuttle's memory. When that's done, they launch toward the Americans.

The commodore maneuvers cautiously at first, keeping between the Chinese and the shuttle. The Chinese cruisers deploy their six fighters; the destroyers deploy their four. The *Rapier* and *Raven* each deploy their remaining shuttles and their four fighters.

Kathy's shuttle docks with the American cruiser. Some naval ratings are standing by when they arrive. They arrest everyone, and take them all to the ship's captain.

The opposing commanders are testing each other, wondering who will flinch first. Then the Chinese fighters start their attack run. Commodore Black turns the flotilla into them, and so it begins.

The commodore's flotilla sends all its telemetry to the Americans. Every second of the fight is recorded and analyzed. Every move, every weapon being fired, every hit registered or received. The special improvements to the maneuvering engines of the commodore's flotilla are quite a surprise to the Chinese and the Americans. It almost makes the fight an even match, almost.

Kathy, Cindy, and the rest are on the bridge of the American cruiser under guard. They watch the battle from there.

The bridge crew of the American cruiser are amazed at what they see on the view screen and on their sensors. Commodore Black also links the Americans into his tactical comm network, so all their communications are monitored by them.

Kathy looks at the Americans' comm screen. She sees Commodore Black and all the captains displayed on it. "Captain Garrett, first work with our fighters and shuttles to destroy those fighters, then take whatever is left and disable or destroy the frigate. Captain Rawls focus on the nearest destroyer. Captain Gibb, we need to keep the cruisers busy."

"Aye, sir," they all reply.

The *Rapier* and the *Raven* are equivalent to corvette-class ships. They should be no match to the Chinese destroyers and not a threat to the cruisers at all. The sloop, the shuttles, and the snub fighters should be easily handled by the Chinese fighters. So at first, the Chinese are a little reckless.

Because of their speed and maneuverability, less than 10 percent of the Chinese weapons fire even gets close. Constantly, the bridge crewmen of the American cruiser are shouting, "Captain, did you see that?"

"How did they turn like that?"

"He outran that missile. How did he do that?"

The few times the Chinese do score hits, the sensor operator is asking, "How'd he survive that? That ship doesn't have the power to take a hit like that!"

After four minutes, all ten Chinese fighters are destroyed. Commodore Black has lost two shuttles and a fighter, but all the remaining fighters and the *Isis* have taken hits. They drive hard at the Chinese frigate.

The *Rapier* and *Raven* score more hits that are more accurate on the Chinese than ships of their class should be able to. And those hits do much more damage than they should. This too is accompanied with choruses of "How'd they do that?"

All of this has Kathy, Lien, and Cindy hoping beyond hope. After all, it's Commodore Black; he's always won before. Of course, he'll win now. In her heart, she knows he can't win, but so far, the battle is going his way.

In the end, it's the number of big guns the Chinese have that make the difference. Once they make significant hits, the commodore's ships just can't take that kind of pounding.

First, the commodore loses the *Raven*.

Captain Rawls decides to take advantage of the damage done by the *Rapier* to the light cruiser. The *Rapier* managed to knock out its main batteries. The *Raven* has been firing on the destroyer next to it, and Captain Rawls sees an opening to put it out of action.

The *Raven* rushes in close to its prey. Captain Rawls puts all his available power into main and secondary batteries. Also, he has a full complement of missiles. The *Raven* dodges a salvo from its target, flares, and unloads on the destroyer. It hits dead center on its nose with particle beams and rail guns. Further, it unloads all its missiles. The particle beams completely drain the destroyer's neutron armor. The *Raven* gets off ten rail gun salvos. The projectiles pound at the ship's bridge, breaking through on salvo six.

Eight more rail gun projectiles smash the hole larger and pound into the bridge and comm compartment of the Chinese destroyer. Then the missiles arrive. Twenty ship to ship missiles strike the nose of the destroyer. Most rip open the ship's hull, making the whole nose break up. But about a third enter the ship through the opening. Missiles tear open bulkheads, and enough explode inside where they set the flammable materials in the destroyer on fire. The high concentration of oxygen in the air cause the fires to burn intensely. Soon the ship is in flames.

* * *

Steve interrupts, "The ship caught fire?"

"Yes, Steve," Kathy replies.

"How can a ship catch fire in space?"

Cindy answers, "The oxygen, once something catches fire the higher levels of oxygen makes it burn fiercely and that ignites everything. It burns as long as there is any oxygen to consume." Kathy pulls up a pic of the burning destroyer.

Steve examines it. "I would never have believed it." Kathy continues...

* * *

Both Chinese cruisers target the *Raven* with all their weapons, though the light cruiser only has its secondary batteries left. To unload all its weapons on the destroyer, the *Raven* had come to a complete stop, so the Chinese cruiser barrage hits it cleanly. The concentration of fire drains the neutron armor of the *Raven*, allowing damage to the hull. Rail gun projectiles from both the Chinese light cruiser and cruiser rain down on it. Enough of them punch through the hull, that they shatter the frame and bulkheads. The *Raven* starts to breakup.

At first, Kathy feels shock; the *Raven* is gone. She holds little James closer, then looks around. Lien and Cindy are on the verge of weeping. Doc Smith and Cookie fight back their own tears. Mike and Thom shake with fury.

The sloop succumbs to the Chinese next.

The surviving shuttle is too damaged to fight, so it slips away, looking for some shelter until the fight ends. The *Isis* and remaining fighters assault the Chinese frigate as the *Raven* engages the destroyer. They score several hits on the frigate, which takes out its propulsion. It coasts, unable to turn; the fighters make a second pass. The frigate paints one fighter with its particle beam. A second flies into a barrage of rail gun slugs. They're both vaporized. The third fighter hits the frigate with its four ship-to-ship missiles, then breaks toward the cruiser.

At that moment, the *Raven* is destroyed, and the cruiser can change target.

The *Isis* fires on the frigate, punching a hole near its engineering section. The cruiser paints the sloop with its particle beams. It overwhelms the sloop's neutron armor. The *Isis* collapses in on itself.

With one destroyer and the frigate crippled and the light cruiser heavily damaged, the remaining Chinese ships focus on the *Rapier*. Though it seems a one-sided fight, it's not an easy one. The *Rapier* scores several particle beam and rail gun hits on the Chinese flagship. Captain Gibb pulls in all the ships available power except neutron armor and supercharges the *Rapier*'s particle beams. He unleashes its deadly power on the cruiser's bridge; the damage is significant. The *Rapier* fires its rail guns and empties its missile batteries. The projectiles and missiles slam into the cruisers bow, smashing its sensor arrays and forward particle beam turret.

The Chinese bring all weapons to bear, and the *Rapier* is raked by fire again and again. Its impulse engine is hit, and the starboard hyperjump foil snaps off. Kathy and Cindy listen to the last voice transmission from their home of nine years.

Commodore Black says to Captain Gibb, "I'm sorry I brought you to this, Jimmy."

Captain Gibb replies, "Uncle James, there's no place I'd rather be than at your side."

Commodore Black looks into the comm. "Kathy, I…" Then the *Rapier* takes another hit and goes silent.

Kathy looks over to the view screen. The *Rapier* shudders from the continuous hits. Sections start to buckle and then crush, the crushed-can effect. She heaves to the side then breaks into five sections; some of them shatter into smaller pieces.

As the *Rapier* breaks up a last particle beam lances across the void towards the Chinese flagship. A final act of defiance?

Captain Gibb must have scrounged every last watt of power from the ship for the beam because it burns right through the Chinese warship's neutron armor, striking it on the bow, just under the bridge, punching a five meter hole through the cruiser's armored hull. It opens into the warships CIC, causing a catastrophic decompression in that compartment. Over a dozen Chinese sailors are ejected through the opening into the cold vacuum of space.

The Chinese pay a high price for their victory, but in the end the *Rapier*, *Raven*, and the *Isis* are destroyed.

As the ships break up, some of the crewmen get to escape pods. The Chinese target and destroy each of them. The remaining fighter rakes the Chinese flagship one last time, but it is hit by a barrage of rail gun projectiles and disintegrates. The wounded shuttle attempts to hide among the asteroids, but the remaining operational destroyer finds and eliminates it.

The Chinese commander signals the American cruiser captain. The comm screen shows the havoc wreaked upon the Chinese flagships bridge.

"Captain, your mission here is over. You are to leave Chinese space immediately."

The American captain replies, "Admiral, can we be of assistance to you?"

"No! Leave now, or we will take you under fire!" The communication is ended. The Americans turn about and leave Chinese space. As they do, they record the Chinese being very thorough about eliminating the pirate scourge.

* * *

Steve asks, "You mean none of them were rescued."

"The Chinese were very thorough. No, none were rescued," Kathy replies.

Steve says, "Oh."

Kathy continues her tale.

* * *

Kathy collapses, falling to the deck. She holds little James close to her chest and lets her grief pour out. She hears this sound, a terrible wailing, like a banshee screaming. Her mind focuses in on the sound. "Noooooooooooo!" someone or something wails. Slowly she comes to the realization the sound is coming from her.

Kathy forces herself to stop her outcry and look around. Cindy and Lien hold each other now, openly weeping. Doc Smith holds Kathy while Cookie embraces Cindy and Lien. Thom and Mike join them on the deck. The American captain waits a respectful time then has them taken to the ship's brig. To Kathy, it's ironic; it was from its brig her life on the *Rapier* began and it's in the American cruiser's brig it ends.

It's an eleven-week journey back to Earth. The first week, all of them are kept in the brig. It's during that time that a young American sailor comes to Kathy and Cindy. He has a magazine in his hand.

"Miss Masters, could you sign this for me?" Kathy takes it only to discover it's a digest of adventure stories about the colonies, pirate stories. And on the cover is an artist's depiction of her and Cindy fighting Captain Black Jack Bartholomew. She flips to the story and reads for about five minutes.

"I'll sign it, but this is all wrong. It didn't happen this way."

The sailor looks disappointed.

"Let me see, Mom." Cindy takes it and starts to read the story.

"It didn't happen that way?" he asks.

"No, it didn't. Do you want to know how it really happened?"

"Yes, please."

Kathy and Cindy sign the magazine and hand it back to the sailor. Then Kathy starts to tell him the real story, with Cindy and Lien adding to the tale.

It becomes a habit for the young sailor to visit and ask about their time on the *Rapier*. He starts bringing friends to hear their tales.

After the second week, they're allowed to have meals in the crew's mess. Meals become story time, complete with pics and vids, except for anything related to the nanchik gods. The stories start to spread throughout the ships of the little battle group. The captain of the American cruiser decides to allow story time to be transmitted to the other ships and records the transmissions. Before long the crew of all the ships join into listening to and talking, debating, and even arguing about the stories told by the Buccaneer Queens and The Death Adder.

By the time they reach Earth, all the American sailors know the tale of the nine years they spent on the *Rapier*.

Once the battle group reaches Earth, the prisoners are turned over to the North American Intelligence Service. Sailors line up to watch the survivors of Commodore Black's flotilla be taken away. Many sailors, including officers, salute them as they leave the cruiser.

* * *

"After that, Steve we had to endure at the research facility. Eventually, between pressure brought by Lien and negotiating our release for the location of the extra nanchik sets, we were finally freed, and that brings us to today." Kathy finishes the story.

He sits in silence for a moment, then says, "The story will be out tomorrow morning. It'll come out in installments over the next eight weeks. I'm not sure how people will react, not for certain, but I think they're going to love the story."

"I hope so, Steve. We really need this," Kathy replies.

CHAPTER 23

GOING HOME

Steve was right; within days, all copies of the magazine had sold out. By the end of three months, the movie people show up; they want the rights to do a movie based on the article in Galactic Geographic. Hollywood and Bollywood start a bidding war, with Bollywood getting the upper hand. Lawyers, producers, actors, it's surreal.

The money is unbelievable; Kathy never imagined being rich, but now she is. She, Cindy, and Lien now have access to all they need. Also, the government finally allows Kathy access to the inheritance, as long as she's off-planet, and they won't let her off-planet. Still, Kathy just feels empty. Movie openings, news interviews, all of it, and she just wants it to go away.

But Cindy seems to have picked up like she is energized by all of it. She becomes the little group's front man, and the crowds eat it up. Brash, rash, and rambunctious, she keeps the fans enthusiastic and coming back for more. After the movie openings, there are the meet-and-greets and dinner parties. Cindy dominates these, with Lien supporting her. She seems to be everywhere talking to everyone.

Sometimes Kathy gets worried because Cindy will disappear during these events for long periods of time, but she always turns up. Kathy, on the other hand, tries to not be noticed at all. She'd disappear into the shadows completely, totally unnoticed, if not for little James. People are always looking for him, wanting to get their picture taken with the pirate baby, so Kathy puts on her best face and tries to be sociable.

What the article and movie brought out about China's invasion, especially the occupation of Safe Port, has all the colonial regions joining the war against the Chinese. Each week another colony gets involved. And now that the Earths governments have knowledge of the nanchik gods and their biotech the Americans are under a lot of pressure. Everyone now knows why they've been pushing the fighting the direction they have, and they all want a piece of that pie. It causes a good deal of infighting among the allies. Still, with the capabilities the Chinese have, it will take years for the Americans to get to Safe Port.

To their surprise, the Chinese can no longer access Safe Port. Apparently, the nanchik gods have decided to close off the planet. Now there's an impenetrable shield around that world; only certain ships seem to be able to land there.

Because of the public demand, the government brings all the people that were on the shuttle back together. It's been nearly three years since Kathy has seen the men. Doc Smith, Cookie, Mike, and Thom are released and brought to Australia to be with Kathy, Cindy, little James, and Lien.

Kathy learns that Lien was much more involved in the movement that helped get Kathy, Cindy, and little James released than she knew. She even risked losing her asylum by working with a Chinese businessman to fund it. Together they pushed the Americans hard and it payed off. All of them thought they'd never be freed, then suddenly they were. No more medical probes, no more questions, just the government spies that follow them around all of the time.

What isn't known by the public is that part of the release agreement included Kathy giving the Americans the location of Alpha 6. The Americans couldn't get there fast enough. Once they had, they found a treasure trove of nanchik tech for both ships and fighters. Twenty American warships and their fighters are now equipped with it; they lead the American drive into Chinese occupied space.

Since the release of the story Kathy, and to a lesser extent Cindy, have been having alien thoughts appear in their minds again. At first it was just a feeling, and then random images, dark and cold, uncomfortable visions. They tell no one about them, but when Kathy started hearing/feeling *Seek* she tells Cindy. "Mom, me too!" Cindy says to her, "Are the gods trying to talk to us? What does it mean?"

"I don't know sweetie," Kathy replies. But from then on they always tell each other whenever it happens.

The fans can't get enough of seeing them together, especially little James. The crowds love to see him in a pirate outfit. Almost five years old, and he wins over the moviegoers at every opening. And of course, Oscar. There are so few cats in the world that almost no one has seen one, and nobody has seen a cat like him. Now seventeen kilos and over a meter long from tip of tail to tip of nose, Oscar is the largest cat on record. Of course, he happily shares his loving indifference with anyone that will scratch his chin.

After another movie opening the group is at Kathy's hotel room. Cindy is taking off her boots when she says, "Mom, I want to go home."

"We can't go home, sweetie."

"Yes, we can, Mom."

"How? The ships were destroyed."

"We can start our own home. We just have to get off-world. We have more than enough money, and if we don't go now, they'll never keep us together. As soon as interest in the movie wanes, they'll split us up again."

Kathy thinks on it; she knows Cindy is right. The others listen closely. "Okay, what's your plan?"

"Just follow my lead, Mom. You'll know when."

From that point on, Kathy pays closer attention to what Cindy is up to, who she's talking to, and where she's going. The first thing she notices is the number of men paying attention to her.

She's seventeen now and beautiful, so it doesn't surprise Kathy that men are attracted to her. Sadly most of them are fakes and players, men looking to add her to their list of conquests. Kathy has been inundated with the same types, as has Lien. But they are drawn to Cindy in droves. The amazing part is how well she handles them. Cindy seems to have a natural ability to play them off against each other and keep them coming back for more. Some of this she learned from Kathy and Lien, but she has so much more skill at this than they do. The best part is that all of these "gentleman" think they are playing her.

Often Lien acts as Cindy's wingman working the players as a team, keeping them off-balance. This way, they don't realize they're not going to bed, either of them, but think just one more move and they'll fall to their skill at seduction.

Soon Kathy sees that a few of these men are different. They act like the others, but it's just a show, that behind the fawning there's something else, something familiar. She can't put her finger on it, but the few that stick out seem to be more to her liking. Sometimes Cindy will talk to one of them privately for several minutes then the others would engulf them. That's when Lien would leave with the man Cindy was talking to. After several minutes, she'd return without him. This happens four times in the week after Cindy's declaration. Kathy is sure something's going on, but she's not sure what. As each of these incidents happen in a different city and involve different men, it's hard to make a connection.

At least twice that week, Lien disappears for several hours, and Kathy has no idea where she went. The last time this occurs, when she returns, Lien is very quiet and sullen. Kathy tries to find out what's bothering her, but she won't talk about it; all she does is stare at a picture of her and her grandfather.

On the forty-five minute shuttle flight from Tokyo to Bombay Kathy decides to take a nap. She drifts into a deep slumber, and soon her head fills with dream like images. First the wreckage of the Rapier manifests. She feels herself weep as her mind peruses the shattered sections of her former home. Then darkness, the sound of dripping water, and next soft, pain-filled moaning. She thinks *That sounds like Captain Gibb*. Finally more darkness, and tortured cries. *James!* she mumbles in her sleep. She hears/feels *They call to me, find them!* Then Kathy is shocked into consciousness by Lien's terrified scream "Jimmy! Jimmy!"

Kathy and Cindy move to Lien, then they embrace each other tightly in silence for several moments. Eventually Cindy breaks the quiet by saying, "My God, they're alive!"

Their chance to get away comes a week later. For the opening in Bombay, India, the government gives them their weapons to go with their outfits to please the crowds, though, they make sure they don't have power packs or magazines for their sidearms. They've just finished the premiere; everyone is backstage after a late-show appearance.

Cindy takes Kathy's hand. "Let's go, Mom." They all head to the fire escape, then out the door and down the ladder to the ground. Thom is last out and jams it before their "tail" can react.

At street level, everyone hops into two waiting vans, and off they go. Kathy wonders how Cindy managed to arrange all of this. She recognizes the driver of the van she's in as a man she'd seen talking to Cindy in Tokyo. He nods to Kathy and says, "I'm Greg Wilson, a brother in good standing and rated as an able spaceman first class. It's an honor to meet you, Miss Masters."

Lien tells Kathy. "He's very modest. Before he became a brother, he was an American Special Forces soldier. That's why we picked him for this part."

"Special Forces?" Kathy says.

"Yes, we'll need his skills before this is over," Lien answers.

Cindy sits in the back of the van, talking to another man. They use a flashlight to look over a map. He looks familiar to Kathy too. Oscar crawls out of a box onto Cindy's lap and complains to her about how he's been treated with a mighty *Meeeeooow.*

Greg hands Lien a box. She opens it; inside are power packs and magazines for their sidearms. Lien hands them out quickly. For the first time in years, Kathy has a functional weapon in her possession. For a short time, it seems odd; she has a sword and loaded pistols on her. Then the old training takes over; her confidence comes to fore. She holds little James on her lap as he looks at her pistols. "Mommy, are those your guns?"

"Yes, sweetie, and Mommy is never giving them up again." She hears police sirens in the distance. "They're looking for us," she says to no one in particular.

"Yes," replies Lien.

* * *

In the Bombay police command center, the computers are going crazy. It's obvious they've been hacked. The techs are doing everything they can, but for awhile the computers are inaccessible. The street cameras are out, phones ring constantly, robots shut down, and control systems for drones go haywire.

In the midst of all this chaos, three men in suits walk into the police chief's command center, brushing off his guards. They walk up to the chief and flash their IDs. The man in charge is older. He stands 175 centimeters. Though obviously in his sixties, the man is athletic with broad shoulders. He is from the planet's federal government, the Planetary Law Enforcement Agency. The other two are Americans, tall and athletic and obviously spooks. Their IDs are from the North American Intelligence Service.

Crap, I hate spies!

The older man says, "We're taking over, Chief. These men will set up the satellite feed for the command center. Concentrate your mobile units along spaceport way. Focus on private spaceports."

The police chief thinks, *Shit, now I have to take orders from these assholes.* Then he commands, "Recall all foot units. Have the mobile units start checking all the spaceports."

* * *

The vans take preselected side streets for most of the way. This limits exposure to areas that are heavily patrolled, but it adds two hours to the drive. Further, they have to drive the main thoroughfare for the last five kilometers. They drive to a small private spaceport, turn off the van's lights, and stop short of the gate. Everyone sits quiet, observes, and listens. Shortly, Greg says, "There's a roadblock, two cars, four men. There may be two more along the tree line."

Kathy strains her eyes then activates her implants. "Yes, Greg, there are five men with plasma rifles by the cars and three men with some kind of heavy weapon twenty meters northeast of the cars on the far edge of the road. There's no one else." Greg looks at her with surprise. He's heard rumor of the implants, but until now, he didn't believe them.

Cindy gives the group orders, "We split up into four groups. Greg, you take Mike, Thom, and Mr. Haines, and be ready to hit the heavy weapon team. You'll have ten minutes to get into position. I'll take everyone else except for Lien and Mom. We move as close to the roadblock as we can. Lien in ten minutes pull the other van up to the road to the spaceport entrance. When they get ready to check her, we hit them. Mom, you and little James stay here and keep quiet."

Kathy starts to say something, but Cindy cuts her off, "No, Mom, you have to take care of little James."

Kathy is a bit cross with Cindy, especially as she's right. "Cindy, ten minutes isn't enough time, and I can hit those transformers across the road, which will give you an edge by knocking out the power here, shutting down the lights."

She looks at Kathy for a few seconds. "Okay, Mom, Oscar will watch little James when Lien drives the bait and you take out the transformer, but then you get right back here. Twenty minutes, and we take our targets."

"Oscar watches little James?"

"He's much more than just a cat, Mom," Cindy replies with a grin. "Lien, hand out the comms." Lien gives everyone subvocal comm devices. They all do a weapons and comm check.

Kathy rubs the commodore's wedding ring. *God, I wish he was here.*

"Let's go," Cindy says. They move out to their respective targets. Kathy's target is closest, so she gets near it and waits. After some time, she checks her chronometer; five minutes left. As she waits, a cop walks up near the transformer. He leans his plasma rifle against the transformer pole and lights a cigarette. *Shit!* With two minutes left, Kathy calls Cindy, "Got a stray cop that's not leaving."

"Okay, Mom, stun him and destroy the transformer."

Lien starts the second van and drives toward the entrance. As she does she hears/feels *Kathy, in trouble!* As soon as she's sure the cops at the roadblock are moving towards her Lien stops the van, hops out, and runs to Kathy while Cindy and her team move on the policemen.

Kathy moves swiftly and gives the cop an elbow to the head. The blow would have knocked out most people, but this guy is a Sikh warrior. He falls to the ground and nearly passes out, then he lies there, stunned for a moment. Kathy fires her laser at the transformer. It bursts into flames spitting sparks.

That's when she feels the needle. Kathy's enhanced reactions take over. She moves instinctively, knocking the injector away from her and the cop. Very little of the sedative is injected, but the cop doesn't know this.

"Just relax. It'll make it easier," he says to her. She does feel the effects of the drug, but it's not enough to put her down. It just makes her dizzy. The cop grabs Kathy, trying to cuff her, when Lien walks up behind him and puts her pistol against his neck. "Freeze." He lets Kathy go, then holds still. She searches the cop, removing his weapons and comm device. Then Lien says, "Help her get to the van." The cop steadies Kathy and helps her walk to the van little James is in.

By time they get there, the other groups are gathering. Each has successfully captured their targets and subdued them. All the cops are disarmed, cuffed, and searched. All comms and backup weapons have been secured.

Cindy runs over to Kathy. "Mom, are you okay?"

Kathy tries to say just a little sedative, but it comes out, "Mbfl spedtufv."

Doc Smith administers an antidote; Kathy steadies but is still woozy for a couple of minutes.

They cuff and gag the cop, leaving him with the others, then get in the vans and head to the spaceport's main entrance. At the gate, an old guard stops them. He checks their papers and manifests, then waves them in and points toward the freighter loading terminal.

"Where to?" Greg asks.

"Launch pad 27," Cindy replies. They drive to the launch pad. Sitting on it is an old freighter, a tramp system hauler named *Jolly Dodger*. The group gets out of the vans and walk to the freighter, except the former SAS brothers. They drive the vans away.

Kathy asks, "Why aren't they coming with us?"

"They're creating diversions for us," Greg replies.

The ship's captain meets them on the loading dock. "This way please," she says. She leads them to a concealed compartment. "In here, just in case we get a customs inspector." They all move into it and strap into the acceleration couches. It's tight, but they manage to get everyone inside. A few minutes later, the freighter boosts to orbit. It gets into the customs queue, goes through inspection, then heads to the moon.

Kathy thinks, *We still have a long way to go, but at least we've started.*

* * *

It takes several hours before the police command center gets the news about the police officers being subdued and cuffed. The chief reviews the reports then takes them to the old man that's now in charge. He looks them over, nods, then dismisses the chief. Once the chief is out of earshot, he places a call. "They've left the planet." He listens to the response. "Are you sure you want to do that? They're very popular." He listens again. "Yes, sir, I'll see to it right away." He looks over at the Americans. They nod to him and leave. The old man thinks for a moment; *This is going to get messy. I don't like messy.*

* * *

They move swiftly from the secret compartment down the passageway to the airlock. According to traffic control, the freighter stopped to assist a yacht having power plant trouble. Moving quickly through the airlocks into the yacht, the owner ushers them into the crew cabin. Kathy recognizes the owner; he's one of the men that has been chasing Cindy, a player. She doesn't like this at all. The two ships quickly separate and move back on their registered courses—the freighter toward the moon, the yacht heading to "The High Road to Mars".

"The High Road to Mars" is an annual yacht race. When they arrive at the starting line, there are another nineteen participants. Their host pulls in among the other yachts. They scramble from one yacht to another until even they're confused.

The race begins, and the yachts streak off to Mars. It's a three-day race with very competitive participants.

They are on the *Amanda*, owned by another player that has eyes on Cindy, Martin Haines, a movie mogul. And he has three days with Cindy as his captive audience. Oscar takes an immediate dislike of the man. Martin is wearing sandals, so Oscar goes up and bites him on the toe.

"Shit!" he yells. He tries to kick Oscar, but he's too fast for him.

Cindy scoops Oscar up and says, "Martin, if you hurt my cat, I'll break your legs."

He looks at her like he doesn't believe her, but leaves Oscar alone.

The *Amanda*'s captain is a retired brother and raider, Ron Pulaski. He's in his late forties, still athletic and known in the brotherhood as a master pilot and navigator.

The first day is all about racing, but on day 2, Martin is constantly trying to get Cindy alone in his cabin. His constant conniving gets on everybody's nerves. It finally comes down to Cindy setting him straight. He grabs her bottom, and she flips him over her shoulder and pins him to the deck. Cindy puts her dagger to his throat and says, "Martin, I wouldn't have sex with you if you were the last man in the galaxy. Try again and I'll castrate you."

Kathy grabs him by his manhood. "Touch her again, and I'll cut it off."

"Ron, get the crew. Get them off my boat. Toss them out of the airlock."

"No, Mr. Haines, these are brotherhood legends. You can fire all of us, but no one here will lift a finger to help you!" Martin Haines shouts in frustration.

* * *

The old freighter starts its final leg toward the moon. There's a small segment of space that's part of the approach but isn't covered by sensors. As the freighter disappears on the traffic control sensors, a shadow moves in front of it. Two quick blasts from a particle beam, and the old freighter breaks up. The shadow moves off.

* * *

The *Amanda* is just six hours from the finish of the race. Eleven of the yachts are within "sight" of each other. Thanks to Ron Pulaski's expert piloting, the *Amanda* is in the lead. Kathy and little James are on the bridge, watching Ron race the *Amanda*. A news blurb comes across the comm. The day before, the system hauler *Jolly Dodger* was lost with all hands; cause of the disaster is unknown.

Kathy says, "That's the ship."

"What ship?" Ron asks.

"That's the freighter we were on to get off Earth." Ron ponders that, then he makes calls to all the yacht captains. His expression turns grim.

"What's wrong?" Kathy asks.

"I can't raise three of the racers. They should be in comm range, but I'm only getting static when I call them."

"What's wrong?" Cindy inquires as she walks onto the bridge. Ron tells her about the freighter being lost and not being able to talk with three of the racers. "What kind of sensors and weapons do you have on this boat?" Cindy asks.

"Standard yacht sensors and a pitiful rail gun," Ron replies.

"Not much help there," she says.

"Nope, not much."

Three hours out from the finish line near Deimos, thirteen yachts move as a group. The *Amanda* is currently in third place. Ron decided that being in the lead was an unnecessary hazard. He carefully lost position to two competitors. The *Amanda* is now in a more defensible position.

There are eight retired brothers captaining yachts in the race. Ron has signaled all of them about his suspicions that they may be attacked. He hasn't told anyone why. But the brothers don't need to be told why. Experienced privateers and pirates know it's always possible and will take the warning to heart.

An hour later, Kathy lays little James down for his nap. Oscar jumps up on the bunk and curls up with him in a protective manner. Kathy smiles and says, "Watch over our boy." Oscar meows then lies down to sleep. She goes back to the bridge and stands watch with Ron and Greg. Cindy and Lien sit on the deck playing cards.

A particle beam lances through the dark, striking the lead yacht. The power of the beam pulverizes its target, leaving debris rushing forward the direction it was traveling.

"Shit!" Ron shouts.

"Where did that come from?"

"I don't know," Cindy says.

"Stealth, it's a stealth ship," states Lien.

"How do we make it visible?" Cindy asks.

"Electrical power or magnetic fields can disrupt the stealth generator," replies Lien.

"We've got extra power cells, if that helps," Ron says.

"How big are they?" Kathy asks.

"About the same size as a rail gun projectile," answers Ron.

Cindy orders, "Ron, make us hard to hit and tell the others to be ready to shoot. Lien, come with me." They rush off the bridge to the engine room.

All the yachts do their best to evade being hit. They try to call for help, but find their long range comms are jammed.

Kathy asks, "Where's the weapons controls?"

Ron points to a panel left of the helm. She goes to it and examines them. Simple controls and weapons locks. "Are the sensors on?"

"Yes," Ron replies. He flips a switch. "They're live-feeding to the weapon controls now."

"Got it," she replies. It's a very rudimentary tactical display. Kathy can ID all the other yachts. Also, she's getting some weird signals that appear to be power output, but she can't pinpoint its location.

Lien and Cindy take four power cells each. Cindy also grabs a roll of circuit tape. It's used to repair electrical circuits in a hurry by closing broken circuit connections. They rush off to the rail gun turret.

Another yacht is vaporized; it was near the edge of the cluster of yachts.

"Damn!" growls Ron.

Kathy estimates the probable location of the stealth scout from the flash of the particle beam. "Ron, have everyone orient their weapons to 56 minus 22." Ron calls the other captains and relays Kathy's instructions.

Cindy wraps the power cells with the circuit tape, then hands them to Lien. Lien starts to load them into the ammo hopper at the front. She asks Cindy, "Why the tape?"

"It'll hold charge from the rail guns and overload the power cells. They should discharge seconds after being fired with more energy."

"Smart. How'd you figure that out?"

"You taught me that when you tutored me in advanced energy physics."

Lien laughs. "Glad you listened to something I said." She finishes loading the ammo hopper. "Let's go," she says to Cindy. They rush back to the bridge.

"It's ready, Mom!" Cindy shouts.

"Tell them to be ready to fire, Ron!" Kathy shouts. "Have them aim where I shoot." Ron swiftly relays her instructions.

The particle beam cuts through the darkness and destroys another yacht. Kathy punches the rail gun fire button four times. The eight power cells streak toward where the beam came from glowing brightly. The overcharged cells become unstable, vibrating as they fly toward their target. They start to burst, releasing the stored energy.

The first three burst too soon, revealing nothing. When the fourth bursts, sparks splash onto something. The fifth and sixth shower little lightning bolts onto something dark and solid. All the ships that are armed fire at that point. The remaining power cells smash into the side of the stealth scout, engulfing it with electric charge.

For the stealth tech to work, the scout can't power its neutron armor. Rail gun projectiles from nine ships, including the *Amanda*, smash into the scout's hull, punching holes through its skin. It becomes visible as it starts to break up.

Out of the twenty yachts that started the race, thirteen cross the finish line. According to the news, the others were destroyed by a rogue meteor cloud. The *Amanda* finishes second.

* * *

There's nothing more to be accomplished by staying in Bombay, so the men in suits take their leave of the police chief. They drive to the shuttle port and book a flight to New York. The older man receives a call as he boards the shuttle. "Yes, I understand. We're boarding now and should be there in twenty minutes. Yes, right away." He looks at his companions. "The mission was a failure. The prototype was destroyed."

"How is that possible?"

"We don't know; it's still being investigated. What we do know is they're on Mars and we've lost track of them. You Americans have really jacked this up."

They take their seats. No one says anything during the flight from Bombay to New York. Upon landing, they're rushed into waiting limos and drive off toward the government sector of the city. As he settles into the seat of the limo, the old man thinks, *Messy, damn messy.*

* * *

The brothers from the yachts all gather around them. Though men who've made their own names, they stand in awe of the

Buccaneer Queens and The Death Adder. For Kathy, it's all embarrassing and uncomfortable. She holds little James close to her as each brother comes by to meet her, Cindy, and Lien. They all fuss over them, and now the legend of the Buccaneer Queens and The Death Adder grows with the addition of the battle of the yachts. The brothers hug and thank them for saving their lives, then help sneak them out of the spaceport.

They get into ground transports and head out to a desolate spot known for smugglers. It's out past the old air processor, built for the first attempt to terraform a planet. Greg travels with them; the others stay behind with the yacht's crews.

About a kilometer from their destination, they are stopped by a black limo and three black Mars rovers. Five Chinese men stand before them; four are young men and heavily armed. The one that is obviously in charge is a much older gentleman. To Kathy, he seems familiar.

Lien gets out of their transport. She looks at Cindy and Kathy. "I'm so sorry, but I must leave you now." Kathy and Cindy get out and stand by her. Lien's eyes fill with tears. Cindy asks, "What do you mean you have to leave us?"

"I must go with my grandfather now; it's the price I must pay for you to get free."

"No, sister. You must come with us."

"I cannot. You must go on without me." They hug each other and start to cry.

Lien goes to Kathy. "I will miss you so." She hugs her hard, then she picks up little James. "I will miss you most, little man."

Kathy holds Lien, not wanting to let go. "You have to come with us. We need you. You have to help us find the commodore and Captain Gibb. They need you."

"No, Kathy, you have to find them. You have to save them. I must go with my grandfather. He will make sure the Chinese don't stop you getting to Reavers Cove. It is the price for your freedom."

"It's too high a price," Kathy mumbles.

"No, Mom, it's what has to be," Lien whispers.

Oscar meows loudly at her, and she scratches his neck. "You'd better take care of them for me furball."

The older Chinese man says, "Come, granddaughter, we must go now."

Lien walks to him and takes his hand. They walk to the limo, and he helps Lien get in. He stops for a moment, then turns to Kathy and Cindy. "Thank you for caring for my granddaughter, and for keeping her safe." Then he gets into the limo, and they drive away. Kathy and Cindy stand watching them drive off; there's nothing to be said, so they get back into the transport and drive to their destination, a large crater smugglers often use.

Sitting in the crater is a sleek corvette. It's smaller than the *Rapier* was, but to Kathy, it's just as beautiful—it's freedom. They board the smuggler and are met by its captain.

"It's an honor, ladies. Welcome aboard the *Zephyr*." Once aboard, the ship they are assigned quarters. As soon as everyone is settled, the smuggler boosts to orbit, then heads for the asteroid belt.

EPILOGUE

After eleven weeks of dodging the Feds, the Americans, and a number of their allies, the group reaches Reavers Cove. The weeks of changing ships, close calls, and covert border crossings have them worn and tired.

They stand on the docks, looking at the ships berthed in the spaceport. Kathy, little James, Cindy, Doc Smith, Cookie, Mike, Thom, and Greg gaze over the collection of raiders being tended in the port. Kathy smiles proudly at Cindy. She made all of this happen, planned everything, and set it into motion. She and Lien made all the coordination and got everything in place, and no one suspected. It was her greatest caper yet.

"Well, Mom, now we need to buy a ship," Cindy says.

"And recruit a crew," Kathy adds.

"Let's head to the brotherhood hall. They may have a line on a space-worthy ship," Cindy says. The group moves down the street toward the center of town.

* * *

The old man looks at the comm screen on his desk. His contact reports they've arrived at Reavers Cove. *So everyone involved couldn't stop them*, he thinks. He ponders it for a minute then grins in admiration, *impressive*. With the federation government, the Americans and their allies, and the Chinese after them, they still made it to the one place in the galaxy no one can reach them. *Impressive, indeed.*

He places a call. "They are at Reavers Cove." He listens to the response. "Yes, of course, they're going to get a ship. They've got more than enough money for that." He listens again. "No, they moved all the off world money before anyone could get to it." Once the other man finishes talking, he responds, "Yes, sir, I'll get right on it." *Why does everything have to be so messy?*

* * *

It takes three more weeks, but Cindy buys a space-worthy heavy-armed sloop and, through the help of the brotherhood, raises a crew of sixty. Next, there's four weeks of repairs, updates, and outfitting.

The sloop *Razor* has dual lower hyperspace generator pylons, an improved impulse engine with vortex maneuvering jets, forward and rear facing particle beam, and rail gun jack turrets. Port and starboard pop-out missile pods and a snub fighter half bay completes the ship's offensive capabilities. Cindy adds a used snub fighter to the mix—two, actually. One she readies for use the other is cannibalized for spare parts.

The biggest surprise is Kathy managed to keep hidden a ship and fighter set of nanchik tech. She and Cindy recover them on a shakedown cruise and quickly get the modules installed. With the modifications from the nanchik tech, the heavy sloop *Razor* is the fastest and most powerful ship of its class in the galaxy.

The new crew all came to fly with the legends—the women that killed Captain Black Jack Bartholomew, the Buccaneer Queens. Kathy feels uncomfortable with all the adulation, but it helps get quality recruits for the crew, so she plays the part.

* * *

Even though most of them have left Safe Port, the gods of the nanchiks commune regularly. The thoughts pass among them instantaneously.

They are there.

Soon they will be here.

Yes, the Son of the Stars is among them.
He is in pain. They must find him.
They are children.

Among them, the debate continues. What is to be done about mankind? Will they ever change?

* * *

The ship is ready to go. Doc Smith has sickbay ready. Little James is with Doc, Cookie is in his galley, Thom stands watch in engineering, Greg has the second watch on the helm so he's sleeping, and Mike is at weapons. Kathy sits at the helm; all await the arrival of the captain.

She strides through the hatch in sixteenth-century buccaneer garb, complete with resplendent hat. A rapier on her left hip, a laser pistol on her right, slung low gunfighter style, and a slug thrower on her belt by the buckle, holstered for a left handed draw. Captain Cynthia Elaine Masters-Black stands before her seat on the bridge. "All stations report," she commands.

They all sound off in turn, "Engineering ready, Captain."

"Sickbay standing by, Captain."

"Weapons ready, Captain."

Kathy reports last. "All stations manned and ready, Captain."

"Move to the launch ring, Miss Masters," Cindy orders.

Kathy rubs the commodore's wedding ring, then starts the thrusters, and maneuvers to the edge of the launch ring. A new addition to the spaceport at Reavers Cove, the launch ring conceals the signature of ships going into hyperspace. Cindy says, "Helm lay in a course for Safe Port."

"Aye, Captain," Kathy responds.

Then Cindy addresses the ship. "We're going to search for Commodore Black and Captain Gibb. I don't believe they're gone. I think the Chinese have them, and we're going to free them. But first, we go to Safe Port to see the nanchik gods. They will have gifts for all of you. Best speed to Safe Port, Miss Masters."

Kathy pulls the ship out into the hyperspace launch line and punches full speed, making the translation into hyperspace. She looks proudly at Cindy as she sits in the captain's seat with Oscar on her lap. She so very much belongs there.

Kathy starts to feel different, free. Somehow she feels the commodore's presence. To Kathy, it's as if he's standing beside her, instructing her on steering the ship. It seems she can hear him say, "Steady as she goes, Miss Masters. Steady as she goes." And now she feels she is home.

ABOUT THE AUTHOR

I was raised in Los Angeles, California in the 1950's and 1960's. I graduated from Eagle Rock High School in June 1970 and entered the US Army in December after graduation. Having served in the Army for nine and a half years, Army Reserve for four years, and Rhode Island Army National Guard for eight years, I retired from the military in 1993. During that time, I served as a battlefield medic, LRRP, surgical tech, scout section leader, LRS assistant team leader, team leader and training/ops NCO in a LRSD. I graduated from Colorado Technical University with a bachelor's degree in computer science in 1999. Afterward, I worked as a systems and applications test engineer, test lead, and test manager from 1998 to 2009.

I've had a number of poems published in various publications.

My wife and I have four children, three grandchildren, and three great-grand-children. We currently reside in the San Luis Valley of Colorado.

I've recently released my first novel, Rapier, a Sci Fi adventure. The story is set in the late twenty-fourth century shortly after the Genetics War. Currently, I'm working on Razor, the sequel to Rapier, and The Young Kathy Masters Chronicles, a prequel to the series that takes place in Australia.

CPSIA information can be obtained
at www.ICGtesting.com
Printed in the USA
LVHW042224100120
643318LV00001B/152/P

9 781684 095742